Our Lady of Roswell

A Novel

Brian Allan Skinner

Nighthawk Press

TAOS. NEW MEXICO

Nighthawk Press
P. O. Box 1222
Taos, New Mexico 87571
www.nighthawkpress.com

Publisher's Note: This is a work of fiction. Names, characters, places, and incidents are a product of the author's imagination. Locales and public names are sometimes used for atmospheric purposes. Any resemblance to actual people, living or dead, or to businesses, companies, events, institutions, or locales is completely coincidental.

Book Design © 2020 Brian Allan Skinner
Cover Illustration © 2020 Brian Allan Skinner

Our Lady of Roswell/ Brian Allan Skinner. -- 1st ed.
ISBN 978-1-7334483-4-5

Library of Congress Control Number: 2020949614

Dedication

— To the memory of my parents, George and Elaine

CONTENTS

Acknowledgments

I thank executive director Jan Smith of SOMOS, Society of the Muse of the Southwest, and publisher Rebecca Lenzini of Nighthawk Press for their advice and encouragement.

This manuscript was brought to completion with the help of Dianne Vona and Sandra Richardson, the latter especially for her excellent critique. Thanks to Anthony Fountain for his many insightful suggestions.

The genesis of this story goes back to my introduction to the work of Carl Jung in my early twenties. He proposed an interior world going on in our heads almost entirely behind our backs. Elements of that hidden world, artefacts of the collective unconscious, are shared by individuals and cultures throughout history in every place on Earth.

A second theory propounded by Jung influencing this book is the idea that modern UFOs and aliens are the flaming chariots and angels of former times. There is truly nothing new under the Sun.

I remind the reader this is a work of fiction, adhering neither to religious dogma nor historical fact, but taking liberties with both. It is not my intention to insult or offend anyone in so doing.

Dr. Richard Feynman appears as a fictional character. While some of his dialogue contains his actual quotations (marked by italics), most of it is completely made-up. The details of his life are sometimes true but often fictionalized to suite the narrative of the story.

I had no plan or outline when I set out just over a year ago to tell the story of "Our Lady of Roswell." I merely awoke with the title in my head—no other details and no idea what it was about.

I learned to listen to my characters. They presented me with the story they wanted me to tell—a sort of unauthorized autobiography, one might say. We argued. Sometimes—rarely—I got my way. But I always trusted them to tell me the truth.

Brian Allan Skinner

CHAPTER ONE

SIDEREUS NUNTIUS
The Starry Messenger

My Tio Nicolás is grumpy tonight because he couldn't tune in the president's fireside chat on the radio.

"Reception comes and goes around here like it was carried on the wind," my uncle complains.

"Maybe it is, Tio," I say.

He blows air through his teeth as his way of dismissing the idea, a gesture that's gotten louder and less tuneful in recent years as he loses more teeth.

"Nonsense, Antonio. If radio was borne on the wind, you'd only get reception in one direction. But radio fans out in all directions, like ripples on a pond. Better stay in school."

His remark is his polite way of calling me brainless. I wonder what he'll say when I turn eighteen in two years and graduate high school. My uncle only finished grade school.

Tio plugs his rattletrap refrigerator back in and takes out two Dos Equis. The refrigerator is unplugged on broadcast nights because its cycling on and off interferes with reception. It's a rare occasion he lets me drink beer.

"I was hoping for some good news about the war tonight," he tells me, taking a long swallow of his beer. He doesn't talk much when he's crabby.

My father, Tio's younger brother, was killed at Pearl Harbor two-and-a-half years ago. Papa was not even on a ship when it happened. He'd been assigned to the infirmary as an orderly. The base hospital was strafed and he was killed trying to get the patients to safety. I don't think I could be that brave.

I miss my father so much. It makes me sad when I remember his helping me build a house for the bluebirds in our back yard. They come back every year, but my papa does not.

Mama went off a mental cliff the day the Western Union man showed up at the door and handed her the telegram. She's in a ward at the state hospital that does not allow outside visitors. That's why I live with my Tio Nicolás.

My uncle asks me to fetch him another beer. I only pretend to sip mine so I'll have one to give my buddy later. After Tio falls asleep, I'll be able to sneak out.

I laugh every time I pass his creation on the shelf beside the kitchen window. His sister, my Tia Ana, makes plaster knickknacks she sells in town at the farmer's market. She paints and varnishes them, but I think they're grotesque. My uncle got her to cast a plaster mold of the cute skunk she makes and decorates with paper flowers. Tio Nicolás had other ideas.

With his pocketknife, a file, and some sandpaper, he rearranged the skunk's face. He asked to borrow my tempera paints. I hadn't used them since grammar school. They had dried up, but Tio got them liquid again by adding water and stirring them with a spoon handle.

"Good as new," he declared, borrowing one of my brushes, too.

My uncle produced a plaster statue of a skunk with the face of *der Führer*. My aunt was annoyed he'd taken liberties with her sculpture—but she laughed anyhow.

I pry the cap off his third bottle of Dos Equis. I figure I might have a shot at sneaking away tonight. If he has another, he'll fall asleep and I'll be home free.

"Please bring me one more, *mi sobrino*," he asks about a half-hour later. It's almost eight o'clock. It will be getting dark soon.

I open a beer for him and place the last unopened bottle on the kitchen windowsill to retrieve later from the back yard. Tio never remembers how many he drank. I'll be OK so long as I remember to bring the empty bottles back home. The carton of beer has six bottles.

I'd like to alert my friend that I'll be coming over. He's got a telephone—or at least his Grandpa Otto has one. But my uncle doesn't want a phone in the house.

"If you can talk on the telephone, somebody can listen on the telephone," he had said. "I never trusted Hoover—neither the president nor the G-man. Their eyes are shifty—like one of those black cat clocks."

Tonight's soapbox subject is government trampling on our liberties. He has polished the topic to gleaming. I listen as hard as I can in order to stay awake, but his lecture puts me to sleep.

My uncle's snoring at last awakens me. I leave the truck key on its hook in the kitchen so he doesn't think I've gone someplace. It's rarely locked anyhow. I tiptoe out, carrying my full bottle of beer. I pound the cap back on with my fist so it does not spill all over the inside of my uncle's truck.

After retrieving the other bottle of beer from the sill in back, I open the truck door. It is a good thing I greased the hinges. I stash the bottles behind the seat, stuffing an old blanket around them so they don't roll around and break.

My father's heavy navy binoculars hang around my neck, safe in their leather case. I set them carefully on the floor.

Putting it in neutral, I inch the truck forward until it's hidden and muffled behind the red willow bushes. I climb in and push the starter of the old Ford pickup, a 1934 that my uncle sanded by hand and painted turquoise with a brush. I'd be a little embarrassed to be seen driving it in daylight. Tio does not know I know how to drive. I'm not quite sure I know how myself.

I've gotten a couple of dents and creases in Tio's truck, but he keeps the can of turquoise paint in the barn. No one is the wiser once I brush over the damage. He's never said anything to me about it. I didn't have to lie, so I didn't have to mention it in confession. Still, it bothers me a little to deceive him.

The moon has not yet risen. The only light is starlight. It will be a waning quarter-moon tonight. My best friend, Six, named after his great-grandpa Sixtus, has taught me the patterns and rhythm of the moon.

He is up in his room. I switch off the headlamps so his Grandpa Otto doesn't see me. My amigo and I are going to look at Mars tonight with my papa's field glasses.

I toss a pebble at Six's window and lean the ladder from the side of the house against the back porch roof. He tosses two bedrolls out his window and turns off the light.

Six climbs out onto the tin roof and clambers down the ladder. He turns to me and, wrapping his arms around me, kisses my cheek. I kiss his in return. It's been two days since we last stood in each other's company.

"I missed you, amigo," he tells me.

We stand holding each other for a minute, looking into one another's eyes. We've been best friends since first grade—ten years ago now. It's still pretty new to me, what we call being "cozy" with one another. I really like it, though.

We take up our bedrolls and toss them into the back of my uncle's old pickup. Tio keeps a bucket and shovel in the bed of the truck—from his days as a volunteer firefighter. I prop our gear against them to keep them from rattling around. We push the truck to the end of his grandpa's driveway before hopping in. I push the starter and turn on the lights.

My friend and I turn to each other and smile. Six has a fair complexion, blue eyes, and light brown hair. I'm practically his opposite: brown-skinned, brown-eyed, and black-haired.

My ancestors arrived here from Mexico about a hundred-fifty years ago. Six's family came from Norway around the same time, led by a prospecting great-great-grandfather. His *gran bisabuelo* found hardly any gold, but he loved the scenery and the weather and the people so much, he got married and never went back East.

Six was raised by his grandparents. I think that's why he's so old-fashioned and fits right in with my Mexican family. I call my buddy *mi dulce gringo* sometimes. It makes him laugh.

Roswell falls away, one street lamp at a time, in the rearview mirror. Taking the back roads is the safest bet, so no one sees my uncle's truck tooling around without him behind the wheel. The ruts and potholes have gotten deeper. I'm afraid Tio's transmission will fall out or an axle will break.

After the last bump, the Philco radio squawks and crackles. My uncle had it put in at some expense, but he tinkered with it and it hasn't worked right in a couple of years.

"The liberation forces now streaming across the Channel, and up the beaches and through the fields and the forests of France..." the president says, before the next pothole knocks the wind out of him.

Six and I laugh.

"...still many people in the United States who have not bought War Bonds, or who have not bought as many as they can afford..." the president pipes in before the radio falls silent once more. We do not hear another peep out of him for the rest of the short way to our favorite place atop the embankment overlooking Bottomless Lake.

I stop the truck at the crest of the dirt road and pull off to the side. No one ever comes this way—it's too far from the water. I leave the parking lights on. Six and I climb out.

In the fan of the headlights, we gather dead sagebrush by the side of the road, pulling the dry roots out of the dry soil.

Though it is the middle of June, it is going to be a cool night. I left my jacket on the peg by the front door so my uncle does not get suspicious thinking I've gone somewhere. I have a heavy flannel shirt on. Six wears a gray gym sweatshirt. There is the blanket behind the front seat. If that's not enough, my amigo and I will have to get cozy to keep warm. I hope so.

We build our campfire in the road near the back of the truck, but not close enough to blister the paint. Once our little fire is blazing, I switch off the headlights and fetch the threadbare blanket and two bottles of beer from the cab. My Tio keeps an opener, what he calls a "church key," in the glove box. I hang my father's binoculars around my neck.

I let down the tailgate and Six and I climb up into the bed. There's more dried sagebrush and a couple of broken fence posts we gathered lying beside the truck so we can keep feeding the fire. We unroll our bedrolls and sit down on them, leaning our backs against the cab. We rest our shoulders against one another and I pull the blanket over our legs. We clink our warm bottles of Dos Equis.

The sparks from our fire fly up into the air, seeming to add new stars to the constellations. I take my papa's binoculars from their case and pass them to Six.

"You take the first squint, Antonio. They're yours, " he says, handing them back to me. "That's Mars over there."

He points out a reddish star about a third of the way above the horizon. He turns sideways so I can steady the heavy binoculars by resting one forearm on his shoulder. Mars looks bigger through the lenses, but it's just as fuzzy. Maybe I don't have them focused properly. I hand them over to Six. He sets them in his lap and looks up.

The firelight glistens in his eyes. His hand creeps beneath the blanket and rests on my thigh. His touch gets me a little bit aroused. He turns and smiles, his teeth reflecting the fire's glint.

"There," he says, pointing up with his other hand, but I do not see anything. "A meteor," he exclaims. "There. Another one."

I think he's trying to distract me from his getting frisky with me under the blanket. I scoot closer, leaning my head against his shoulder, and look up at the sky. His ear and cheek are cold.

The deep indigo heavens fill with meteor streaks like a Fourth of July fireworks finale. There is nothing to block our view of the wide sky above Bottomless Lake, and no lights or houses to wash out the darkness.

"What meteor shower are they?" I ask Six. "That's quite a show."

"There aren't any meteor showers this time of year. June is the quietest month."

If my amigo doesn't have the answer, nobody does. He's read every astronomy book in our school library.

"Maybe they didn't get the message," I joke.

"Guess not," Six says, pushing his hand between my thighs. "To keep warm," he says, grinning.

"Sure," I reply.

I think of grabbing the crotch of his dungarees. I'm feeling frisky tonight, too, but I don't ever want to go farther than he wants me to go. He's my best friend. I don't want to hurt him or make him feel bad.

Six and I have never *done it*—gone all the way. We're still virgins, trying to figure out what we like. I wouldn't mind another heavy make-out session like the last time we were out here, though. I'd like to fool around with my friend a little bit—to keep warm on a chilly night.

It's hard to tear our eyes from the dazzling display of meteors. Six has his mouth open.

"I think some of 'em might be reaching the ground, Antonio. We'll have to come back in daylight and look for the meteorites," he says.

I watch the brilliant streaks reflected in his eyes.

"Wow," he cries. "That one reached the ground. I'm sure of it. Did you hear it, amigo?"

"Yeah, I think so," I reply. "Are we in any danger of being struck out here?"

"Sure," he says. "But the odds are pretty slim: even rarer than getting hit by lightning."

Turning towards Six, I kiss his cheek. I feel so comfortable when I'm with him—and safe. I think if a meteor headed straight for us, he'd throw himself in its path to protect me. I hope I would do the same for him, but I don't know if I'm that courageous.

A blinding flash lands just behind us, in front of the truck—close, close enough to feel the deafening shock.

Six and I scramble to our feet, our bedrolls sliding beneath us, nearly sending us onto our rear ends. We lean on the roof of the truck to see where the meteor struck.

The fireball landed no more than twenty yards away. It has set clumps of sagebrush on fire. A small crater has been blasted into the road.

"Oh, no," Six exclaims. "It's a woman. She's been hit. She's on fire."

Before I can get any words out, my friend jumps over the side of the pickup. He grabs the bucket and shovel and takes off down the dirt road towards the burning woman.

Six stumbles in a pothole and tumbles over the edge of the embankment above Bottomless Lake. I hear his descent in a small avalanche of clattering stones and his echoing cry as he slides down the steep incline.

I open the cab and switch on the lights. Taking the flashlight from the glove box, I stand cautiously at the edge of the drop-off. I see Six scramble out of the shallow water and struggle to climb up the steep embankment of loose stones and dirt.

Then I turn the flashlight beam on the glowing woman in the road. She stands—she hovers—above the crater, her feet not touching the ground. She seems solid, yet I can see through her. The gleaming rays surrounding her on all sides are like neither a fire nor an electric light. It is not a continuous radiance. It wavers like the coals in a campfire when the breeze blows over them. She shimmers, shining from within.

Her face is extraordinarily beautiful in a simple way, her smile both innocent and mirthful. The glimmering light emanating from her on all sides blurs her image at times. She wears a pink tunic robe and a deep blue mantle emblazoned with golden stars. She looks a little like the Virgin on Juan Diego's cloak—Our Lady of Guadalupe.

"Oh, my God. Dear Jesus," I mutter.

At last I realize who the woman is. I make the sign of the cross and fall to my knees. I hit a stone.

"H-H-Holy Mother," I stammer.

It is hard to speak, I am so nervous. I feel light-headed. It is hard to focus on her for long. The changing light makes me dizzy.

"Antonio Sanchez?" she asks, her radiance rising and falling with her voice.

"*Si, Santa Madre.*"

Her smile lights up the air around her.

"I am worried about my friend," I tell her.

"I know you are, Antonio. You are a good friend. Sixtus is safe. Do not be concerned. Please, get to your feet."

"No disrespect, Holy Mother," I say, looking down at the ground, scratching the dirt with the toe of my boot. "I think you could find someone far more worthy of your visit. I am a sinner. And I like boys, Holy Mother."

The Virgin smiles. Her mantle glimmers, changing from one hue to the next across the entire rainbow of pale colors.

"Jehovah, God the Father, can be hard-headed at times, Antonio. He is a stickler for the Law, the Letter of the Law, crossing the last *I* and dotting all the *T*s."

She smiles and I laugh at her joke. I don't recall reading that the Blessed Virgin was renowned for her sense of humor. It puts me at ease—at least a little bit.

"Our Savior is more like me than He is like His Father. His understanding of the world is not so literal, His Nature more forgiving. He has only one rule, the Golden Rule: in a word, *Be kind.*

"You are a kind person, Antonio, and innocent of the world. It is your telling me you are not worthy that convinces me of your worthiness. I have found the right person."

An arc of bright stars appears over the Virgin's head. I'd have to ask Six which ones they are, but they seem too evenly-spaced to be real stars.

"You have a poetic mind, Antonio."

I smile. "Thank you, Holy Mother. May my friend not also gaze upon you?"

"This time I wanted to appear only to you, Antonio. You are the Catholic. I feel a certain loyalty. You understand."

"Yes, Holy Mother."

"I have a mission for you, Antonio. That is why I am here. Sixtus may help you—if he believes you, that is. Next time you shall both see me so he will have no doubts."

"*Si, Santa Madre.*"

The Virgin holds a white envelope. Her shining robes flow like water around her. She extends her hand, holding the glowing envelope out to me. The cloud of light flows outward with her arm.

I reach for the note. My arm tingles. I feel the hairs stand up.

The golden ink shimmers on the white paper. It's impossible to make anything out. Then the paper becomes more solid and opaque in my hand. I feel its rough texture, like a homemade paper. The name on the envelope is no one I know or have heard of.

"Is this about the end of the war, Holy Mother?"

"Yes, in a way it is, my child. But it has more to do with preventing the war after this one."

"Another war? Oh, dear God. What's to become of us? I am afraid for us, *Santa Madre*."

"I fear for humanity, too, Antonio. That is why I have come: in answer to many prayers."

"Where will I find this Dr. FANE-man?" I ask the Holy Virgin.

"I believe he pronounces it FINE-man, dear. He works in a secret United States government facility outside of Los Alamos. Do you know where that is?"

"It's almost at the other end of New Mexico. How will we get there? Six and I have summer jobs. When will we find time to go?"

The Blessed Mother frowns. Her light dims. Everything she is thinking is written on her radiant face.

"Forgive me, Holy Mother," I say, embarrassed by my unwillingness. "I shall do whatever you ask of me. So will Six."

I shift from foot to foot in the dirt. It is hard to look at the Blessed Virgin directly.

"You and your companion will be able to drive to the laboratory unobserved until you reach the security gate."

"Begging your pardon, Holy Mother. How will we know where it is if it's a secret government compound?"

She smiles.

"You have been scratching the map in the dirt with your boot, Antonio."

I look down at the markings I'd absently scratched on the ground, unaware I'd been doing anything but nervously fidgeting.

"You must copy the map down before you leave this place, Antonio. I shall appear to you next on the eve of your arrival in Manhattan."

"Manhattan?" I exclaim. "That's in New York. We'd need a miracle to get there."

"No, my child. It is not in New York. Something at Los Alamos is called *Manhattan*."

She grows fainter and wispier and ascends so slowly and noiselessly I'm not sure it's happening. Maybe I am sinking into the ground.

"*Santa Madre*, please bless me before you go."

"Oh, *mi hijo*. You are already so blessed."

"Bless my friend," I say to her.

She nods and smiles.

Just as the Holy Mother fades and disappears, Six clambers over the edge of the embankment. He enters the arc of light from the headlamps. Another meteorite slams into the ground some ways off.

Six still carries the red bucket and shovel. He rushes to me, dropping everything. The last little bit of water splashes from the metal pail. He wraps his arms around me.

"Oh, Antonio," he says, stuttering and shivering. "Are you all right?"

He hiccups like a misfiring engine, a sign he is scared or upset. I think it's kind of cute, but I would never embarrass him by telling him that. He's wet and cold. He shakes like an unbalanced flywheel.

"I'm OK," I tell him. "I was worried about *you*. We've got to get you out of your wet clothes."

I turn on the truck engine and dim the lights to save the battery. I switch on the heater.

Six sits on the tailgate, trying to remove his wet cowboy boots. He holds on as I tug them off. Then he unbuttons his Levi's overalls and I help him pull them down his legs. They are not only wet but also muddy from his scrambling up the embankment. I yank his socks off, too.

"How'd you put the fire out?" he asks. "What about the burning woman? Is she all right? Where is she?"

"The woman was not on fire," I tell him. "She was merely glowing."

His boxer shorts and the bottom of his T-shirt and sweatshirt are stained brown from the muddy water. He smells like a frog pond.

"Glowing?" he asks, stripping out of his undershirt and sweatshirt

Removing my flannel shirt, I take off my T-shirt and hand it to him. He pulls it on, then strips out of his muddy shorts.

I tug off my own boots and socks, and strip out of my waist overalls.

"Here," I say, passing my Levi's to him. "You're lucky we wear the same size. Put my socks on, too. Then you get inside the truck."

I pull my boots back on. Six gets in the truck without an argument.

After stuffing his muddy clothes into the fire bucket, I open the door of the cab. I put our bedrolls in his lap, draping the old blanket over his shoulders. The heater pumps out more noise than warmth. Six shivers.

After shoveling dirt over the embers of our fire, I climb into the cab, getting behind the wheel. Before I start the engine, I take a stubby pencil and an old gas receipt from the glove box. The dashboard is gritty. I draw the map I'd unconsciously traced on the ground. I put the drawing in my shirt pocket.

"What do you mean the woman was glowing, Antonio?"

"I meant that she wasn't on fire, Six. She shined, illuminated from within."

"What? Did one of those meteorites clock you on the noggin or something?"

"No, Six. It was the Mother of Jesus. She gave me this," I tell him, handing him the envelope from my other pocket.

"Dr. Richard FANE-man," he says. "Who the hell is he?"

"The Blessed Virgin, the Mother of Christ, told me he pronounces it FINE-man."

"I know who the Blessed Virgin is, Antonio. My family are Protestants, not heathens. We just don't make the big deal of her that Catholics do."

I start the engine and turn the pickup around, driving back down the steep road the way we'd come.

"I hope we don't get stopped," Six says, laughing at my state in just boots and undershorts and my flannel shirt.

"Me, too. Neither of us has a license. Are you getting warm?" I ask, turning to him.

"Yeah. But what about you? You don't have any pants on."

Six tosses the blanket from his shoulders into my lap, covering my legs. It still holds some of his heat. I hadn't realized how cold I am.

I haven't had a moment to think about the Blessed Virgin's visitation. I have not even asked myself whether I believe it happened. But the note from the Queen of Heaven is still in Six's hand. I guess the Holy Mother *did* appear to me. I *hadn't* imagined it.

"So where do we find this Dr. Feynman?"Six asks.

"I drew the map on the back of the gas receipt."

"I saw that. But where is it?"

"Somewhere near Los Alamos. That's all I know. We'll talk about it later, Six. I just want to get us home safe and sound."

"OK," he says, and touches my shoulder.

He waits until I stop at the intersection with the highway to hand the letter from the Blessed Virgin back to me.

"She has very fine handwriting," he remarks. "Very... *celestial*."

It's his way of telling me he does not altogether disbelieve my account of the night's adventure. I smile, and stash the letter back in my shirt pocket. I'm sure my amigo has as many questions as I do, but I don't have any more answers right now than he does.

We pull onto Main Street in Roswell. We do not pass a single car or truck. The streets are deserted, as though there's been an evacuation. I shiver.

The clock at the corner of the bank says 4:15, only an hour to sunrise. I'm not worried, though. I'll get Six home before his grandma and grandpa wake up. And I'll get myself to bed a couple of hours before Tio Nicolás stirs himself.

I switch off the headlights and coast into Six's yard. His house is dark.

"I'll have to be at work in less than four hours," I grouse.

"If you want, I'll take the morning for you, Antonio."

"Thanks, buddy. I can do it. I'll sure be dragging my butt, though."

We work full-time at Mila-Grow Nursery & Greenhouse now that school's out. The name's a pun on the Spanish word for *miracle*. It's hard and dirty work, but I like it: putting things in the ground and watching them blossom and grow, bearing fruit and flowers and homes for the birds. I know Six finds the job satisfying, too. He thinks we should open our own little operation some day, or maybe buy Mila-Grow from the owner when he retires.

We get out of the truck, tossing the bedrolls and blanket into the back. I hear a pack of coyotes howling at the now risen moon. We lean the ladder against Six's porch. He wears my socks and T-shirt and Levi's, carrying his wet cowboy boots in his hands.

"Good night, amigo," he tells me. "Thanks for loaning me your dry stuff."

My buddy kisses my cheek and ascends the ladder. He waves from the porch roof before climbing through his window. His light flashes on for half a minute and then winks out. I stash the ladder in its customary spot on the ground at the side of his house.

The back of my uncle's pickup is a mess. There's all of Six's muddy gear and the damp bedrolls and blanket. I'm happy *mi dulce gringo* was OK. That's all that counts. The rest of it is just stuff that can be washed and mended.

I push the truck down the gravel driveway and hop in. I do not turn on the engine or the headlights. Leaning back in the seat, I close my eyes for a minute.

As though it were tattooed on the inside of my eyelids, I see the glowing apparition of the Blessed Virgin, like the after-image of a camera flash.

Did this really happen? I ask myself again. *Did Holy Mother appear to me or am I cracking up? Why would she come to me? I'm certainly not worthy of the honor.*

I open my eyes. The sky is brighter. I see the first smudges of dawn at the edge of the field across the road from Six's house. As I am about to push the starter, another meteor flash streaks across the sky. It is the first I have seen since we left Bottomless Lake.

But it is no meteor. I watch the path it traces across the deep blue heavens. It stops all at once, high in the sky, suspended. I have no idea what it is or what it means.

I start the pickup and watch the starry messenger on the way home. The light neither fades nor stirs from its position. By the time I reach my yard, the moon outshines it. I sit for a moment, watching the star blend slowly into the growing brilliance of the sky.

I have to wash my uncle's truck before he gets up. I'm too worked up to be able to sleep anyhow. I pull a pair of my waist overalls from the wash line and hang up the bedrolls. Though I'm not likely to awaken my uncle before his alarm goes off, I do my best to be quiet.

I toss Six's muddy overalls and underwear and sweatshirt into the wash-tub beneath the hand pump in the back yard. The pump makes noise no matter how much grease we put on it. I wrap the blanket around it to muffle the squeaks.

Rinsing out my buddy's clothes as best I can, I hang them over the wash line and pin them.

I fill Tio's fire bucket several times and splash water into the back of the pickup. I dry the bucket and shovel with my flannel shirt so they do not rust. It is still chilly out.

I take a last look around to make sure I haven't overlooked anything that might tip my uncle off that I'd borrowed his truck without asking.

Creeping into the house, I return the two empty beer bottles to the carton. I climb the stairs up to my room, knowing where to step on each stair so it does not creak.

I set my papa's binoculars atop my chest of drawers and lie down on the bed in my clothes. I have to get up in two hours when my co-worker, Tomás, picks me up, blaring his horn in the back yard at exactly 7:45.

As soon as I shut my eyes, the night's events swirl around inside my head, flashing and changing, like a movie getting all tangled up in the projector.

I am comforted a bit when I remember the Virgin's promise that upon her next visit Six would also see her. Six and I have shared everything since we were little boys. It is important to me that my best friend see the Virgin, too.

It helped that my amigo didn't tell me I was off my rocker as he sometimes does. He certainly saw the Blessed Mother as well, even if for only an instant. After all, he had run off with the bucket to put out the woman he thought was on fire.

I drift off to sleep so slowly I don't remember when it happened. I am dreaming.

Six and I lie in the bed of my uncle's pickup looking up at the star-filled heavens. Lacing his fingers between mine, he holds my hand.

"There," he says, pointing up with his other hand.

But I do not see anything.

"A meteor," he exclaims. "There. Another one."

I see it's not a meteor. It is the Mother of Jesus, descending on a cloud, glowing to beat the band. In her hand is a message, a starry message she is counting on me and Six to deliver.

In my dream I pray to her Son for the strength and courage Six and I will need to carry out her charge. I promise the Holy Mother that I will do my best to complete the task she has given us. She smiles, holding the palms of her hands out to me as though in welcome.

Morning comes quickly.

CHAPTER TWO

ORA PRO NOBIS PECCATORIBUS
Pray for Us Sinners

Six and I have no chance all week to talk about the Blessed Virgin's visit. I start work at Mila-Grow Greenhouse early in the morning. Six begins at noon and works until eight o'clock. The boss doesn't usually assign us to the same projects, either, so our time doesn't overlap much.

My amigo gives me a new composition notebook and urges me to write down everything I remember about the Virgin's appearance and what she said to me.

I fill a page or so each night before turning in. The exercise eases my mind. I see on paper my account of what happened. It becomes real for me in black-and-white.

Last night I drew the Holy Mother's likeness. It's one of my best sketches. I wish I'd used drawing paper instead of the notebook page with blue lines across it.

* 2 *

After work on Saturday, I ask our co-worker Tomás to drop me and Six at Nuestra Madre de Dolores (Our Mother of Sorrows) Church. I want to go to confession and to tell Father Consuelo about the Holy Mother's appearance. Six waits outside as he usually does, by the churchyard.

I draw the heavy curtain of the confessional booth. The velvety material, like everything in the hundred-year-old church, smells like incense and lemon oil. The screen of the confessional slides open. My heart pounds.

"Bless me, Father, for I have sinned," I recite, making the sign of the cross. "It has been two weeks since my last confession."

I see the shadow of his hand bless me through the screen as he mumbles in Latin.

"I borrowed my uncle's truck again—twice—without asking his permission."

"Three *Our Father*s and three *Hail, Mary*s," he says. "Wait. I recognize your voice. Are you the young fellow who has confessed to fooling around with his friend?"

"Yes, Father Consuelo," I say. "But he is *mi mejor amigo*—my best friend."

"That makes no difference. You are playing with fire, young man—hellfire. You and your friend are going to go too far one of these times. You won't be able to stop yourselves. Then you'll have committed a mortal sin, endangering your eternal souls, the same as if you'd taken a knife and stabbed someone to death."

I see his shadow lean forward. His chair creaks.

"Please, Father Consuelo. I mean no disrespect. I'm very confused. I do not understand how loving someone is the same as killing someone."

"You are not required to understand, young man. It is the Law of God. That is all you need to understand. Your penance will now be three rosaries. Is there anything else?"

"Yes, Father," I say, looking down at my folded hands in the dim light. They tremble.

He sighs.

"Was anyone waiting behind you?"

"No, Father."

"All right. What is it?"

"The Blessed Virgin Mary appeared to me and my friend."

His shadow rocks back and forth. He stifles a laugh.

"And why would the Mother of God appear to a couple of no-accounts? The world is filled with thousands of people far worthier of a visitation from heaven."

"The Blessed Mother gave me a letter," I tell Father Consuelo.

He chuckles to himself

"Show me this letter," he demands.

I take the envelope from the Holy Mother from my work jacket and pass it through the little slot at the bottom of the confessional screen. I'm not sure I should have given it to him, but it's too late. I hear him rustle the envelope.

"It feels like ordinary paper to me: nothing particularly heavenly about it," the priest says. "I'll have to examine it in better light. If there's anything to your claim—which I doubt—I'll have to present the letter to the bishop. He is the one who must look into all such questionable reports. It is out of my hands now."

"But... Father Consuelo. *Santa Madre* told me we must deliver her letter to a doctor in Los Alamos."

"I am not surprised the devil has appeared to you under a deceptive guise. You and your friend have opened yourselves up to his wiles, young man. You must pray for the strength to resist all carnal thoughts and desires as though the life of your souls depended on it. Your penance remains three rosaries."

I say the *Act of Contrition*. Father Consuelo recites the absolution. He raises his hand and the shadow of his blessing passes across my face.

I leave the confessional. My knees are wobbly. I hold aside the curtain for the white-haired woman in a mantilla now waiting behind me.

The blood pounds in my ears like a flood through a gorge. I kneel down in the nearest pew. I need to talk to God in private.

Dear God, I don't know what to do. Please help me. I do not want to disappoint the Holy Mother—Your Mother. Help me get her letter back. Please, dear God. Show me what to do.

I recite The Lord's Prayer and then leave the pew, still a little shaky.

After the dim light of Nuestra Madre de Dolores Church, the early evening sun is blinding. Six rushes up to me. I see concern in his expression.

"What's the matter, amigo? You don't look so hot. What happened?"

He puts his hand on my shoulder and leads me to one of the low stucco walls surrounding the churchyard. We lean against the rough plaster.

"Father Consuelo kept the Virgin's letter, Six. We will fail in our mission for her."

My lips tremble. I am ready to cry.

"How'd he get hold of the letter?"

"I handed it to him," I reply. "I feel like *él tonto*. What are we gonna do?"

"Let's pray to the Blessed Virgin for starters. Come on. We'll pray on the way home—for the safe return of her letter to Dr. Feynman."

My amigo, *mi dulce gringo*, has a knack for making my heart feel lighter. I want to kiss him right there in the plaza—but I hold back. Father Consuelo's words of warning about carnal thoughts are on my mind.

We walk slowly beside one another. I'm not used to praying while I'm walking. I have to watch where I'm going. I apologize to the Blessed Virgin for being such a fool to let her letter out of my hands. Then I ask God to forgive me in case getting "cozy" with *mi mejor amigo* is somehow wrong in *His* eyes.

Six and I reach my road and turn into the dusty lane.

"I need to tell my aunt about the Holy Mother's appearance, Six. I've wanted to talk to Tia Ana all week. Maybe she could ask Father Consuelo for the letter back. Please, come with me, amigo."

My Tio Nicolás and his sister, Tia Ana, live at opposite ends of the short dirt road, Calle Alegre (Lighthearted Lane). Both their adobe *casitas* are small and slightly rundown, but my uncle's house has a second floor. That's where my room is.

I unlatch Tia's gate. She sits beneath her covered front porch, the *portál*. She has lit an old kerosene railroad lantern. As though she'd been expecting us, there is a bottle of tequila and three short glasses on the little porch table. We sit in two of the other wicker chairs. I look at my aunt, then at Six.

"I was hoping you boys would stop by after work. Not a word," she says. "I think you are old enough for a small glass."

She pours just enough tequila to wet the bottoms of two of the glasses. The third glass she fills to a quarter. We toast to our health and take a sip. Six chokes. I try not to laugh but don't quite succeed.

"No doubt you can fool your Tio Nicolás from time to time, am I right?"

Six and I glance at each other and laugh.

"My brother is not very observant. But I noticed you've been uneasy all week, Antonio, fidgety like there was something on your mind. Now that we have a chance to talk, I hope you'll tell me what's troubling you, *mi sobrino*."

I am not too surprised my aunt suspects something. She has always been able to read me as though I'd sent her a handwritten note.

"I know you are devoted to the Blessed Virgin, Tia—more than anyone I know. There is something I must tell you: something very special."

"I love *Santa Madre* as I did my own mother, Antonio. She has a special place in my heart and in my home."

She nods toward the terra cotta likeness of Our Lady of Guadalupe in her garden, standing among the lengthening shadows of her roses. The clay statue looks so heavy and dense, so earthbound—not at all like the floating, shimmering, light-filled Virgin Mary I beheld at the lake.

My aunt sets down her glass and looks at me. She searches my face. I don't know if I can tell her. My mouth is dry, but the tequila does not help.

"The Holy Mother appeared to me and Six, Tia."

She makes the sign of the cross. Looking into my eyes, she bursts into tears. Then she leans forward and kisses both my cheeks. She takes my hands. Hers are trembling.

"Oh, *mis hijos*. When did this happen, Antonio? Where did *Nuestra Señora* come to you?"

"We were at the lake, Tia," I tell her. "It was just last Tuesday, after midnight. Tio doesn't know we borrowed his truck."

"Did *Santa Madre* explain what she wants of you?"

Six and I look back and forth at each other.

"You do not doubt we saw her, Tia?" I ask.

"No, child. Why would I? You are an honest young man and so is your friend. I knew when I first laid eyes on you, *mi amado sobrino*—not ten minutes after you entered this world—that there was something special about you, a gift from heaven. Of course I believe the Virgin visited you and Sixtus. I am so proud that she appeared to you boys."

My aunt splashes another film of tequila into my glass and Six's. She has not yet finished hers and swallows it all in one gulp. She coughs.

"What did *Nuestra Señora* tell you, Antonio? May you speak of it to me? Please. Don't keep me wondering."

"We do not know much, Tia. The Holy Mother gave me a letter that we are to deliver to a doctor in Los Alamos. I did not open it."

"You didn't peek?"

"No, Tia. That wouldn't have been right."

"No, of course not. A doctor in Los Alamos, you say? Perhaps it is a cure for cancer."

"I do not know. I'm not sure he's a medical doctor. I get the idea he's an egghead doctor."

"Perhaps, before you go, *mi sobrino*, you might touch me with the letter."

"I do not have it, Tia. Father Consuelo took it from me. He said the bishop must investigate all such appearances and told me the Holy Mother was probably a trick of the devil."

"Father Consuelo does not know everything, Antonio. Perhaps he knows very little," she says, making the sign of the cross on her lips with her thumb.

I realize, through her devotion to the Blessed Virgin, that my aunt probably knows more about *Nuestra Señora* than Father Consuelo and Bishop Abelardo put together.

"Father Consuelo also told me it is a mortal sin for me and Six to love each other."

"Perhaps he doesn't know much at all," she remarks. "He has his superiors and they have theirs, all they way up to God. Speak to God and pray to the Holy Mother. You will know in your heart what is right. Everything will be well, Antonio."

"I don't understand, though, why the Holy Mother would come to me and Antonio, Tia," Six says. "We are sinners."

I am glad he calls her *Tia*. I look over at Six, then down at the porch boards.

"I do not know anyone who is not a sinner, Six. *Nadie*. You and Antonio are good boys, always kind. Your uncle tells me how good you both are to him. You are blessed in your friendship and God's love shines through you. That is why *Santa Madre* came to you."

"Thank you, Tia. Thank you for believing us and for taking our side," I tell her.

"Of course," she says. "*Eres mi sobrino*. You are my nephew. I love you."

She is about to pour another coating of tequila into our glasses. Six and I hold our hands over them.

"Maybe my brother will let you drive me to church tomorrow, Antonio, now that you have turned sixteen. It is getting hard to walk all that way."

"Of course, Tia. But he's a stickler about getting my driver's license first. Maybe in a couple of weeks.

"Six and I will come by to walk you to mass tomorrow morning. My amigo is going to stay over tonight."

She smiles and nods her head.

"We have to go, Tia," I tell her. "We are tired from working all week. I have to cook supper for Tio, too—for all of us."

"You must take the goat stew I made, Antonio. Nicolás knows I will be sending it along. I have already set aside a bowl for myself. Please. Go get the big soup pot on the stove. All you have to do is heat it up."

I go into her kitchen and take the heavy cast iron pot. It has a lid and a wire handle for carrying. It has made many trips back and forth, up and down Calle Alegre.

"You should ask my brother about our Tio Oscar, Antonio. It is time. He will tell you the story of our favorite uncle."

Six and I bend to kiss my aunt good night. We go down the steps.

"I will pray to *Nuestra Señora* that her letter be returned to you, Antonio. I will light a new candle."

"Thank you, Tia. God bless you."

We go out the gate into the road. The last streaks of sunset are turning to smudges of gray. Six and I take turns carrying the heavy kettle.

My uncle sits at the kitchen table, reading his *National Geographic* magazine and nursing a beer. Six and I hang our dirty work jackets on the hooks by the front door.

"There you are," he says, grinning. "Good to see you boys. Good to see supper, too."

Six puts the cast iron pot on the stove. He stirs the coals and adds a small log. He turns to my uncle.

"May I spend the night, Tio?" he asks.

"Of course, my boy. It has been a while. I thought maybe you two were having *una disputa*."

"No, Tio," Six says, smiling. "Just busy with school—and now work."

My friend stirs the goat stew while I set the table. I get the bread and butter from the larder and cut two thick slices for each of us.

When the stew is hot, Six fills our bowls and brings them to the table.

"Do you boys care for a beer?" my uncle asks. "That way you won't have to try to sneak one from under my nose."

I'm surprised he knows about my taking one of his Dos Equis every once in a while to share with Six. He never said a word until now. I thought I was so clever and covered my tracks. I feel embarrassed.

"Yes. Thank you, Tio," I say.

I take an extra bottle of beer from the ice box and set two glasses on the table. My uncle always drinks his beer from the bottle.

We bow our heads and Six says grace.

After we get a few spoonfuls of my aunt's goat stew in us, our supper conversation begins.

"Tia Ana asked whether I might borrow the truck to take her to mass to-morrow," I tell my uncle. "She says her arthritis is much worse."

My uncle's spoon pauses halfway to his mouth. He looks over his glasses at me.

"When did you get your license?" he asks.

"I didn't, Tio. But I'll have time in a couple of weeks."

"Then what do you think I'm going to say?"

"That I have to wait."

He smiles.

"You're not so good at reading my mind, *mi sobrino*. I was going to give you permission to drive the truck—for my sister's sake."

Six grins at me on the sly. He gets up and refills our bowls with the last of the spicy goat stew. He slathers his bread edge to edge with butter. My uncle and I break our bread in pieces to sop up the gravy.

"May we also borrow your truck after church, Tio?" Six asks. "We'd like to go look for meteorites."

I like that my amigo calls him *Tio*, too. And I'm glad *he* asked to borrow the truck after mass. My uncle finds it much harder to say *No* to Six. He takes his time mopping his bowl with his bread, letting us dangle on the edge of his answer.

"Did you see something? my uncle asks.

"Yes," I reply. "At Bottomless Lake."

"I see," he says. "I wonder how you boys got out there. I hope you didn't have to touch up the truck with paint. That can of paint is almost empty."

My buddy and I look back and forth at one another, then at my uncle.

"I think you'd have to get up so early to pull one over on me, Antonio, that you'd get no sleep the night before."

We all burst into laughter. Again I feel sheepish. I thought I was being so careful, so clever.

"Meteorites can be worth a lot of money," my uncle remarks. "Do you pass any filling stations on the way to Bottomless Lake?"

"Two," Six replies.

"Then maybe you might stop at just one of them to put in a little gasoline. What do you think?"

"Certainly, Tio," I reply.

"Good," is all he says.

I clear the kitchen table, pumping water into the sink. Six pours the last of our beer into our glasses. It tasted good with my aunt's spicy goat stew. There are no leftovers.

Six fetches another bottle for my uncle. He opens it and brings it to him. I rinse the supper dishes.

"Tia Ana said we should ask you about Tio Oscar," Six says, sitting down next to him.

My uncle seems surprised. He takes a swallow of beer and clears his throat.

"Yes," Tio replies. "It is past time to have this discussion. Come sit with us, Antonio. You may bring another beer for yourself and Six."

I bring his last bottle of Dos Equis to the table and sit down next to my uncle on the other side. I get the idea this is going to be a big deal.

"Do you like girls?" my uncle asks, addressing neither of us in particular.

"Yes, of course we do, Tio," Six says. "But we like each other more."

My uncle takes another sip of his beer. I smile at my amigo.

"Our Tio Oscar had a friend named Fernando. My sister and I—and your father, Antonio—never saw one of them without the other. They were best friends. They did everything together."

Six and I glance at each other.

"Fernando inherited a little farm and they added on to the *casita*. They were never rich. Tio Fernando liked to hide things in their woods for me and your father to find. Your papa was better at spotting them than I was. I remember a small blue robin's egg of polished stone.

"When Tio Fernando died, Tio Oscar joined him three days later. They were inseparable—like you two."

"So what should we do, Tio?" I ask. "Father Consuelo thinks it is a great sin for me and Six to love one another."

"Well, you know what I think of Consuelo. *Él es un tonto.*"

I try not to, but I laugh.

"There was only one bedroom in our Tio Oscar's small house, Antonio, and only one bed in the room. It was nobody's business.

"Not everyone in the family was comfortable with their arrangement, of course. If someone didn't like it, they stayed away, that's all. Tio Oscar liked to say, *We don't have time to worry about who doesn't like us. We're too busy loving everyone who* does *love us.*"

"But what will people think, Tio?" I ask.

I pour a little more beer into my glass and Six's.

"Tio Oscar and Tio Fernando went to church every Sunday, like you two. They were well-loved in the parish. The ladies, concerned that a couple of helpless bachelors were not eating properly, loaded them up with food every chance they got. Fernando and Oscar didn't have to cook for themselves much. It was a pretty good racket."

My uncle chuckles. Six and I swallow the last of our beer.

"Some bachelors live together, particularly when they work the same job, Antonio. It's certainly cheaper than living alone. It's not so uncommon for a pair unmarried women to keep house, either, especially schoolteachers.

"People will think what they want. But it's none of your business what other people think, *mi sobrino.*"

"Thank you, Tio," I say. "I feel so much better after talking to you and Tia Ana."

"Of course," he replies. "We love you."

Six and I smile.

My uncle retires to his rocker in the parlor with his magazine and his bottle of beer. But he has left his eyeglasses on the kitchen table. I take them to him.

"Thank you, Antonio."

"I'm going to take a bath, Tio. Do you need to use the bathroom first?"

"I'm all right for now. There's always the back yard if I can't hold it. It's been dry lately," he says, laughing softly.

I touch his shoulder and return to the kitchen.

Six and I finish washing and drying the dishes, and scrubbing Tia's stew pot. We use the pot and a big kettle to boil water for the bath. It is after dark. There's no time to heat water for two separate baths. We've never taken a bath together except in the creek or the old horse trough.

My heart races at the thought of seeing Six naked. The idea gets me excited.

While the water boils, Six pours three buckets of cold water from the pump into the bathtub. I go upstairs to fetch him a pair of my shorts and a clean undershirt so he doesn't have to put his sweaty work clothes back on. The idea of his wearing my clothes gives me a thrill.

My uncle's bathroom is the former pantry, long and narrow. With no space for a door to swing either in or out, there's an ugly flowered curtain across the doorway for privacy.

Six and I carry the hot water from the stove and pour it into the tub. I strip to my boxer shorts, throwing my dirty stuff into the wicker laundry basket in the corner.

Six unbuttons his denim work shirt and strips out of his undershirt. My heart pounds. I want to touch his chest. I don't know why I don't except that I'm afraid where it might lead.

He sits down on the old stool to tug off his boots and socks. As he unbuttons his Levi's and steps out of them, my amigo looks over at me. Then he pulls down his shorts.

The more I want to look away, the harder I stare. His little guy perks up, too.

He pulls me toward him, folding his arms around me. I do the same. We kiss.

As I press against Six's stomach, I feel his erect penis next to mine. It is hard not to rub against him. It feels so amazing and I love him so much. I shut my eyes but see him still in my mind, smiling at me.

Our chests heave with panting. I know that if we do not separate, we will take that last step over the brink. Six must sense it, too.

We let go of one another and step into the tub. The water is only barely warm. I'm still excited at seeing my amigo naked. I can't hide it.

Six sits down. I do the same. We sit cross-legged facing each other, our arousal diminishing as we immerse ourselves in the lukewarm water.

We get down to the business of getting clean. Taking the old chipped enamel pot, I scoop water over his head. He takes the cake of lye soap and lathers up. Then I pour more water over him. He does the same for me.

We pass the washcloth and soap and rinsing pot back and forth. Standing up, we scrub and rinse each other's back.

Six and I climb out and pull the stopper, saving one last pot of water to rinse away the scum. I take the towel and dry his back and chest. He takes the towel and ruffles his hair with it, then ministers to me. Despite his strong and muscular arms, his touch is gentle.

We pull on our clean shorts and undershirts, and hang the towel and wash-cloth over the edge of the old claw-foot porcelain tub. I pull aside the curtain to the bathroom.

My uncle rests, snoring gently, in his rocking chair. His eyeglasses sit atop the magazine in his lap. I set them on the table. Then I light the kerosene lamp in his bedroom, right next to the parlor, so he'll be able to find his way to bed when he awakens.

Six and I tiptoe upstairs in our bare feet to my room. I pray to stop thinking about it, but getting cozy with my best friend is all I have on my mind.

We climb into bed in our undershorts but take off our undershirts. We turn to each other and kiss, and wish each other good-night.

It gives me such a thrill to lie so close to my amigo that I feel his heat.

Though I am exhausted, the day's events swirl inside my head, keeping me awake. Six falls asleep at once. Nothing ever spoils his appetite or his night's sleep.

I wish I could be more like him.

* 3 *

When I open my eyes, Six sits at the edge of the bed. He looks at me and smiles, putting his hand on my naked chest. It makes me feel so good to be loved and to be in love.

"Good morning, buddy," he says. "Can you loan me a clean pair of overalls? I don't want to put my dirty ones back on to go to church. And a pair of socks, while you're at it."

"Sure. What's mine is yours, Six," I tell him. "In my dresser, bottom drawer. You can toss me a clean pair of overalls, too. Socks are in the top drawer."

I sit up and swing my legs over the side of my narrow bed.

"Your last pair," he says, handing my newest pair of Levi's to me, my

Sunday pair.

I pull them on and tug on my white dress shirt over my undershirt. I loan Six a clean workshirt.

I have only one necktie. It's navy blue. It was my father's.

Six watches me in the mirror as I fumble with tying it. He grabs hold of my tie and pulls me toward him, kissing me.

"I guess neckties are good for something after all," he remarks, grinning.

I've never seen Six wear a tie, not even a Western tie like his grandpa wears. We make the bed and go downstairs.

My uncle sits at the kitchen table with his cup of coffee. He does not make any for me on Sundays because I take Communion and only water is permitted beforehand. Six refrains out of sympathy for me.

My amigo and I sit down long enough to tug on our cowboys boots.

"You boys be careful," my uncle says, sliding the truck keys across the table to me.

"Of course we will, Tio. Thank you for the use of your pickup."

"It is for the convenience of my sister. You are just the chauffeur," he says, smiling.

We head to the front door and reach for our denim work jackets.

"Maybe if we shake them out they'll look a little better," I tell Six.

We go outside to the *portál* in front. We hang our jackets over the railing and give them a thrashing with the broom. It raises a bit of dust. Six takes my jacket by mistake.

"That's mine," I tell him. "I got a hole in my sleeve on the barbed-wire, remember?"

"Yeah, I remember," he says. "Then we must've switched jackets by mistake at work yesterday."

Six passes the jacket to me and I slip it on. He puts on the other one.

"Wait a minute," I exclaim, reaching into my jacket pocket.

My hand trembles. My heart is in my throat. The letter from the Blessed Virgin Mary is still there. I show the envelope to Six.

"Yahoo!" he shouts, flinging his arms up. "That didn't take the Holy Mother long at all to answer our prayers. I knew she'd come through, but that's awfully quick."

We laugh and dance around each other like two kids. We hook our arms together and swing each other in circles, stomping the porch boards like at a barn dance. My uncle comes out to see what the commotion is about.

"I thought you two were finally starting to grow up. It looks to me like you're going back the other way."

He shakes his head and closes the door.

"What envelope did you have in *your* pocket?" I ask Six. "What letter did I hand to Father Consuelo?"

He laughs.

"Must've been my grandma's grocery list. Gramps always forgets it, so she gives her lists to me. She doesn't waste paper, and writes on the back of old mail."

It makes me smile. I put the Holy Mother's envelope back and pat my jacket pocket.

"We'd better get a move on," I suggest. "We don't want to be late."

Six and I cross the yard, still chuckling. I unlock the door handles and we climb into my uncle's truck. I put the key in my jacket pocket and push the starter.

"I bet your Tio is watching from behind the curtains," Six says.

We turn to each other and smile. I'm happy again knowing I haven't disappointed the Holy Mother. I say a silent prayer of thanksgiving. We've been given another chance to deliver her letter.

My aunt waits for us in her front yard, expecting we will walk with her to church. She seems surprised to see her brother's truck with me behind the wheel. She makes the sign of the cross.

"*Mi sobrino*," she says. "How wonderful of your Tio to loan us his truck. I will have to bake him some cherry *empanadas*, his favorite."

I take the Blessed Virgin's letter from my pocket and show it to her. She crosses herself again and bursts into tears, clasping her hands together and shaking them. She's beside herself with joy.

"Oh, Antonio. It is a miracle. The Holy Virgin heard your prayers. You are blessed by God, *mi sobrino*. I am so proud of you boys. I knew you were special. You two will be saints some day. Mark what I say."

I struggle not to laugh at her prediction. I do not want to hurt her feelings.

"May I touch the letter, child?"

I nod. *How could I deny her?*

My aunt rests the fingertips of her right hand on the envelope. She sucks in her breath and closes her eyes. Despite its going to work with me every day, the white paper is still dazzling.

She opens her eyes. Withdrawing her hand, she makes the sign of the cross and smiles.

"Thank you, Antonio. God bless you, *mi hijo*. My heart is bursting with happiness. I touched something *Nuestra Señora* once held in her hand. Now I have been blessed, too."

I decide we are not going to tell my aunt about the mixup of jackets and envelopes. She is happy to believe in a miracle. I do not want to disappoint her.

We help her get up into the truck. It is not easy for her, even with me pulling and Six pushing. She is out of breath.

As the pickup jostles along, Tia holds onto Six's hand. It is only a five-minute drive to Nuestra Madre de Dolores. It is even harder to get my aunt down out of the truck.

There is time for me to make my confession again before mass. I want to explain to Father Consuelo about the mixup of letters.

Six helps my aunt to the last pew where we usually sit. I enter the confessional.

"Bless me, Father, for I have sinned. It has been one day since my last confession."

"You again," he says. "I suppose you think it funny to deceive an old priest. A shopping list from the Blessed Virgin, indeed. I can no longer be your confessor, young man. You'll have to confess your sins, which are doubtless many, to Father Miguel. God bless you."

The screen slides closed.

I am not surprised Father Consuelo thinks I was pulling a prank on him. I leave the confessional in time to see him enter the sacristy to put on his vestments for mass.

Six and my aunt slide further into the pew. I sit next to Tia as she fingers the beads of her rosary.

The sacristy bell rings and the congregation stands.

My aunt nudges me several times as I fail to stand or sit or kneel with everyone else. I feel I am sleepwalking through mass. I am somewhere else, thinking how bad I must really be that I've been told to confess my sins to another priest.

I remember nothing until Communion when my aunt stands and touches my arm. Taking her hand, I help her up to the communion rail.

After the final blessing and dismissal, Six scoots around me and takes Tia's other arm as we help her out of church and down the steps. The bright sun brings me to myself. We help my aunt up into the truck.

"Please let me out at your Tio's house, Antonio. We are going to catch up with each other," she says. "Before you go out to the lake, you boys must come have breakfast. You have not eaten. I will make you some *huevos*."

"That's all right, Tia," Six tells her. "We want to get going. We won't waste away missing one meal."

We help her down from the truck and up to the *portál* in front.

"I shall light another candle to *Nuestra Señora*, Antonio, in thanksgiving. Oh, to think it is my nephew who has been chosen. God has surely blessed you, *mis hijos*."

Six and I kiss her cheeks and get back in the truck. My uncle watches me from the porch as I back up and turn around and pull out without hitting anything.

Six turns to me, knitting his eyebrows.

"What's the matter, Antonio? What happened? You came out of that confessional white as a ghost—almost as white as me."

I know he is trying to get me to laugh.

"Thank you for not saying anything in front of my Tia, Six. She worries."

"Ah... So that's where you get it from," he says.

"Father Consuelo thinks I tricked him on purpose," I tell him

"Well, if you didn't do it, then it must've been the Holy Mother who tricked him. She's got a great sense of humor, just like you said."

He chuckles.

I realize that, like my aunt, Six thinks the return of the Virgin's letter was a miracle that had nothing to do with our jacket mixup. He has a deeper faith than I do. I feel bad all over again.

I pull the truck over and stop. Despite gripping the steering wheel with all my might, my tears flow like an *acequia* in the spring melt.

When they have run their course, my buddy turns to me and puts his hand on my arm.

"Cheer up," Six tells me. "Jesus loves you. The Virgin loves you. And I love you."

"You always make me feel better, Six," I tell him. "God bless you, amigo."

"He *has* blessed me, Antonio. He brought *you* to me—or was it *me* to you?" he asks, grinning his dimpled smile.

I pull the truck onto the last stretch of dirt road to Bottomless Lake. It is even scarier driving here in daylight. At night, I hadn't realized how steep the precipice was and how easy it would have been to roll my uncle's truck over.

I'm not concerned we'll miss the spot where the Blessed Virgin appeared. The crater where she stood was in the middle of the road. We won't be able to drive any further unless we plow through the scrub.

Up ahead I see the remains of our campfire, smothered with sand. I stop the truck and turn off the motor. Six and I climb out and lean against the front hood. The crater appears unchanged from when we last saw stood here earlier in the week.

Six fetches my uncle's shovel and red metal fire bucket from the back of the pickup. I get my canteen from up front.

We strip out of our denim jackets and take off our Sunday shirts and clean undershirts. Then we put our jackets back on, leaving them unbuttoned. It has gotten very warm. The blazing sun is at nearly its highest point of the year.

Six scoots down into the sandy pit. He's already gotten the overalls I loaned him dirty.

He thrusts the point of the shovel into the ground every few inches, turning it this way and that. Well off the crater's center, the shovel blade makes a clunk. Six digs into the dry soil just a few inches and comes up with what looks like a thick shard of blackened pottery.

He hands the meteorite up to me, cautioning me that it is both heavier and sharper than I might think. He's right on both counts.

Six struggles to climb out of the crumbly crater. I give him my hand.

He slips off his sweaty kerchief and folds it into a triangle. I set the iron stone in its center. He ties the three corners together.

"This one is special," he says. "It's the first meteorite we found, Antonio—the one from where the Blessed Virgin stood."

"You're right," I tell him. "It will be a memento of her first visit to us. We'll look for other meteorites we can sell."

He places the wrapped stone in the glove box. I hang the strap of the canteen over my shoulder and we set off. Six puts the shovel handle on his shoulder and takes up the metal bucket. It is nearly noon. Our shadows hide beneath our feet.

We fan out, weaving back and forth among the scrubby sagebrush, keeping Tio's truck always in sight. Each time we meet up, Six takes a swig of warm water from the canteen.

Most meteorites, he tells me, do not crash beneath the ground but lie on the surface, hiding in plain sight, indistinguishable from ordinary stones. I find only ordinary stones.

Six discovers one small meteorite fragment before the truck gets vanishingly small in the distance. Our water is getting low. We head back.

I put the shovel on my shoulder. Six carries the fire bucket. The single meteorite specimen rattles around in the bottom, reminding us how empty it is. The way they came crashing down the other night, I thought we'd find more meteorites than we'd be able to carry.

Our shadows grow longer. At last we reach the truck.

Our overalls and work jackets are coated with dust. Dirty sweat streaks down my buddy's face. I'm sure mine looks no better. I take off my cowboy hat and wipe my forehead with my already sodden kerchief.

"What do you say we go for a swim, amigo?" he suggests.

"I dunno," I reply. "We should be getting back. I don't want them to worry."

"Why should they worry? You can't get any marks against your license. You haven't got a license yet. And any marks you get on the truck you've got paint to cover over."

I laugh and punch his shoulder. He leans towards me and gives me a kiss. I smell his sweaty smell, like when we're at work. Truth be told, I like it.

Six puts the red bucket in the back of the pickup. I set the shovel against it and we climb into the cab. I back up and turn around, almost missing the narrow side road that leads down to the lowest part of the embankment overlooking Bottomless Lake.

After parking the truck at the edge of the dirt road, we take off our sweaty work jackets. We shake them out and hang them over the open doors.

We follow the path down a gentler slope through grass and red willow bushes to the water. Despite its being a brilliant blue Sunday, there is no one there. We have the place to ourselves.

We walk along the shore to an alcove not visible from the road. It is our favorite spot, sunny and secluded. We sit on one of the rounded boulders that tumbled down from above and tug off our boots. We hang our socks over their shafts. Then we strip off our Levi's and lay them over the rock.

Keeping our boxer shorts on in case someone chances to come by, we step to the water's edge.

The hot sun hasn't done much to warm the crystal blue water. Some of the old ones in my family say Bottomless Lake connects far below ground with the water-filled limestone caves down in Mexico called *cenotes*.

Six steps deeper into the water and kicks up waves. After our sweaty hike to collect meteorites, the water feels freezing cold. He splashes me. The only way to pay my amigo back is to wade in deeper and splash him. He uses his hands and forearms to scoop water at me. My shorts are soaked. They've become transparent.

I charge my friend and tackle him into deeper water. It is breathtakingly cold. He squirms away and, coming up behind me, pulls me into deeper water still. We nearly lose our shorts trying to wriggle free of one another. I try to yank his down on purpose. My heart thumps.

Suddenly, there is nothing beneath me but water. We are swimming.

Six takes off for the opposite shore of the tiny cove. It's a race and he got a head start.

After two laps across the cove and back, we lie on our backs in the shallow water along the sandy shore. The water here feels warm.

I rest my hand on his naked thigh. His skin is red from the ice-cold water. Our boxer shorts do nothing to conceal our growing excitement.

We turn to each other. I watch his ice-blue eyes watching me and see myself in them. He smiles.

My amigo rolls over on me and, holding my wrists, pins me down. I push against him with my knees, breaking his hold. We wrestle in the wet sand, grappling for the upper hand, taking turns pinning one another and breaking free, splashing in and out of the water.

Six squirms beneath me, his muscles hard and straining. I feel his hard-on next to mine through our soaking wet shorts.

My heart pounds, my breath grows quicker. My whole body trembles with excitement—not just my pecker. The sensation is twice as intense wherever our skin touches.

I roll away from him, afraid one more wrestling hold will push me over the edge of my desire for him and I won't be able to stop.

We sit up, wrapping our arms around our legs, our chins on our knees. Six is breathing hard, too. It is the closest we've ever come to *doing it*.

I feel regret that I put on the brakes before we got to the end of the road.

Maybe next time, I think. *But one of these times, neither of us will be able to stop.*

We look at each other. He smiles weakly. I see disappointment in his eyes.

"I'm sorry, Six," I tell him. "I just couldn't do it. It's not you. It's me. I'm not ready."

He puts his arm around my shoulder.

"I love you," he says. "I will wait as long as it takes."

I put my palm on his cheek and smile at him.

"Come on. Let's get dressed," he says. "I'm starving."

"You're always hungry," I remark. "Your legs must be hollow."

We strip out of our wet shorts and dry ourselves off with our undershirts, flipping the sand out of them before pulling them on.

Six puts his socks on first; I step into my overalls first, then tug on my socks. I'm not sure they're the same pair of Levi's I took off. It doesn't matter. I like wearing his stuff. We pull on our boots.

We hike back up the sandy trail to Tio's pickup. Taking our jackets from the doors, we fold them and put them in the cab. We wring out our boxer shorts and hang them over the back of the seat. We put on our still clean Sunday shirts.

I decide to let Six drive back to his house. He is a careful driver: maybe even better than I am.

His grandma invites me in, but I want to get home. I do not want my family to wonder what's keeping me.

I hope my aunt does not say anything to her brother about the Holy Mother's visit. He would not believe her and they would get into an argument. Their feud would last until they forgot what it had been about. I don't want that to happen because I love them both.

* 4 *

"Bless me, Father, for I have sinned," I say, blessing myself. "It has been a week since my last confession."

Remembering Father Consuelo's reaction, I don't know whether I can go through with it. I don't know if can say it. *Please, dear Jesus, help me.*

"Yes?" Father Miguel says. "Go on."

My heart is in my throat. All the air has escaped the confessional. My hands shake.

"I... I... I came very close to having sexual congress outside the bonds of Holy Matrimony, Father. I'm not sure I'm a virgin any longer."

Now that the words have flown my lips, I feel lighter—but just as scared.

"I see, young man. But I'm not sure that *almost* counts. Did you perhaps take precaution against an unwanted pregnancy?"

"No, Father. Using rubbers is a sin, isn't it?"

"Some sins are more grievous than others, son. Bringing an illegitimate child into a hungry world is worse. Is your girlfriend also Catholic?"

"No, Father Miguel. I nearly had sex with my best friend. He's Protestant. We were sort of wrestling."

"You'd better watch out, young man. One of these times it will no longer be something you *almost* did. You'll have committed a mortal sin. It doesn't matter if it's with a boy or a girl.

"Your penance is two *Our Father*s and two *Hail, Mary*s."

"Is that all, Father?" I ask.

He chuckles.

"No penitent in thirty-nine years has ever asked me that. Until now. Is there something else you're not telling me, young man?"

I am afraid to confess to the Virgin's appearance again. It didn't turn out so good last time. But I cannot lie in confession. *Jesus help me.*

"The Blessed Virgin appeared to us, Father Miguel. Two weeks ago."

I hear soft footsteps in the church. Father does not say anything. I wonder if he's filling his lungs for a good belly laugh like Father Consuelo did. I hear the blood in my ears.

"You must speak to Father Consuelo. He is the pastor here, young man. He will report it to Bishop Abelardo and seek advice."

"Father Consuelo did not believe me."

"Oh. I see. Well, I cannot contradict my superior. You must have a talk with Brother Asinus then. He has a very special devotion to the Holy Mother. He will advise you."

"Yes, Father. Thank you. Where do I find Brother Asinus?"

"He maintains the chapel to the Holy Mother at Nubes de Tormenta (Storm Clouds) Pueblo. I will send him a note so he knows you're coming."

"Thank you, Father Miguel."

I recite the *Act of Contrition* and he blesses me. I leave the confessional grateful for God's mercy. I feel light enough to float.

Six sits in the pew, waiting for me. He smiles. I kneel beside him to say my penance. It takes me no time to recite two *Our Father*s and two *Hail, Mary*s. I stand up and my amigo looks over at me.

"Is that it?" he asks, getting up. "I figured you'd be praying until tomorrow morning."

"Father Miguel is not so strict," I reply.

We leave the church and head home.

"Did you mention the Holy Mother's appearance to him?"

"Yes, I told him, Six. I don't know that he believed me, but Father Miguel was trying to help. He told me to talk to a lay brother on the pueblo who is devoted to the Blessed Virgin."

"Then maybe it's time to go get our driver's licences, amigo, so your uncle and my grandpa will allow us behind the wheel in daylight."

He punches my shoulder and chuckles.

Six has the knack for making me feel better.

* 5 *

Two weeks later, after we've both gotten our licences, Six drives his grandpa's 1942 Chevy pickup to the Indian pueblo a ways outside of Roswell, close to the army base. The Nubes de Tormenta Pueblo has been occupied for hundreds of years.

"Are you sure it's all right for us to be on the pueblo?" Six asks me.

"Yes, so long as we're visiting someone or going to the chapel."

"Chapel. Church. Friar. Monk. You Catholics have a lot of fine distinctions," Six tells me.

"A church usually has a resident priest. A chapel usually does not. Monks live in cloisters, away from the world. Friars live in the world. Yet both are brothers."

"So we're visiting a friar in a chapel who is someone's brother?" he asks.

His joking around makes me feel calmer.

"You got it, amigo," I reply.

Six pulls into the shade beneath a grove of towering cottonwoods. We get out. The chapel to the Holy Mother at Nubes de Tormenta is in serious need of *enjarre*—re-plastering.

Brother Asinus comes out and stands on the top step of three. The friar wears his black cape over his white habit. The hems are dusty. The crown of his head is shaved, his black hair encircling it like a fuzzy wreath. He is short and squat. His quick smile tells me he's friendly.

"*Art thou he that should come, or do we look for another?*" he asks, quoting from the Bible.

He takes my hand in both of his. His smile is as wide as his face. It puts me at ease. Brother Asinus shakes Six's hand, too.

"I'm Antonio Sanchez," I tell him. "And this is my best friend, Sixtus Thorson. Father Miguel sent us."

"Of course," he says. "Welcome. I have read your letter of introduction, as it were," he remarks, taking the note from Father Miguel out of the pocket of his habit.

"You can call me *Six*," my amigo tells the brother.

We go inside the chapel. There are several rows of two-seat wooden benches with backs on each side of the narrow aisle. The windows are ordinary double-hung sashes of frosted glass. The altar is painted wood, white and gold. Two candles burn upon it. A carved and painted plaque of Our Lady of Guadalupe hangs on the narrow wall to the left of the altar.

It feels like a holy place: old and dim and quiet. Everything smells of sweet incense.

Brother Asinus kneels in the first row. Six and I follow suite on the opposite side. There are no kneelers, only the pounded dirt floor painted with a cement of clay and ox blood.

The friar takes the rosary from his belt and, fingering the beads, recites the prayers to which my amigo and I respond with the second half of each prayer. We say the entire rosary.

Brother Asinus stands and brings a short chair from the sanctuary. We sit back down in the pew. He sits opposite us and leans forward.

"Did you know that the first rosary was presented by *Santa Madre* to the founder of our religious order, Saint Dominic?"

"No, I didn't," Six replies.

"That was over seven hundred years ago, young man. It remains a special part of our devotion to the Blessed Mother to this day. You must recite the rosary every day. You will always know what to do," he tells my friend.

"My family is Lutheran, Brother Asinus," Six says, "but we also pray the rosary."

"I didn't know that," the friar says, smiling. "I learned something. Thank you.

"Did you know that this would be the first time the Blessed Mother has appeared to a Protestant, Six? You saw her, too, did you not?"

"Just for half a minute. I thought she was on fire. I fell in the lake going to fetch water."

The friar laughs. It is deep and full and makes me want to laugh with him.

"Father Miguel provided no details in his letter. Why had you gone out to the lake that night? What can you tell me of our Holy Mother's visitation?"

"We borrowed my uncle's truck," I tell the brother. "We were going to use my papa's binoculars to look at Mars."

"So you know how to distinguish among celestial objects, Antonio?"

"No, Brother Asinus. That's Six's hobby. I like drawing and carving. But we both saw a glowing woman descend out of the sky. She spoke to me and told me she was the Holy Mother."

The smile falls from the friar's face.

"How did you know the apparition was not a manifestation of the Great Deceiver, the Prince of Lies?" he asks me.

I answer the friar with the first thing that pops into my head.

"How did I know she wasn't the devil? The same way I know right from wrong, good from evil. My conscience tells me, Brother Asinus. I felt only love in her presence."

His smile returns.

"And why do you think the Holy Mother appeared to you and your friend?"

"I don't know, *mi Hermano*. We wondered the same thing. But the Holy

Virgin told me my saying I wasn't worthy convinced her of my worthiness."

The friar chuckles.

"Do you know why she appeared to you? Did she tell you?"

"She gave us this letter we are to deliver to a doctor in Los Alamos," I tell him, taking the envelope from my jacket pocket.

Brother Asinus makes the sign of the cross and bows his head, but he does not touch the envelope. He smiles. I put the letter back inside my new jacket, the one I wear on Sundays.

"For what my opinion may be worth, Antonio, Six, I have no difficulty believing the Mother of Christ came to you. I shall pray for guidance and strength.

"You must keep a record of *Santa Madre*'s appearances, *mis hijos*, before you forget. You must write down everything you saw and anything she told you. Each detail is important."

"Six gave me a new notebook to write down my recollections, Brother Asinus."

"Good. God bless you, Six," the friar says. "And you must keep and hold sacred anything the Holy Mother presents to you and Antonio."

"There is a stone from the crater where the Virgin stood, Brother Asinus," Six blurts out excitedly. "A meteorite. There was a whole shower of them that night."

"A similar astronomical display preceded an appearance by the Blessed Virgin outside a small town in Bavaria in the year 1663," the friar reports.

"We brought the meteorite with us, Brother Asinus. It's in the truck. Want me to fetch it?"Six asks.

"Yes. Please," the friar says.

Six leaves the chapel. The hinges of the front door squeak.

"How do you and your friend get along with your own mothers, Antonio—if I may ask?"

"We're both sort of motherless, Brother Asinus," I tell him. "My mother is in the state mental hospital and Six's mother abandoned him as a baby. His grandma and grandpa raised him."

"Perhaps that helps explain the Holy Mother's appearance to you boys in particular," the friar says. "How long have you and Six known each other?"

"For most of our lives: since we were little boys. My amigo and I are in love, Brother Asinus. Six is my best friend and I love him more than anybody."

"Your affection for each other is quite touching, Antonio. But I cannot advise you on matters best discussed under the seal of confession. You must do as both your heart and your conscience tell you, young man. They need not contradict each other.

"But you must focus on your mission for *Nuestra Señora*. Nothing else is important right now. I shall pray to Our Lord to help guide you through the thickets and pitfalls of the world."

Six returns with the meteorite wrapped in his blue bandana. He hands it to the friar who, not expecting its great weight for its small size, nearly drops it. He unwraps the iron stone and cups it in his hands. He shuts his eyes.

A smile appears on his lips and he breathes a deep sigh.

"Thank you," Brother Asinus says, looking up. "We must preserve anything pertaining to the Holy Mother's appearance, such as this meteorite. There is a crypt beneath the altar."

"A crypt?" I ask.

"It does not sound as impressive to say it was the former friar's root cellar," the brother confesses, chuckling. "Anything we put there will be safe. I am the only one who knows of it—and now both of you. I promise to help you boys all I can."

Brother Asinus sets the iron meteorite, wrapped again in Six's bandana, on the altar cloth. He genuflects before the altar and blows out the candles. He leads us out of the chapel.

"I'm afraid I still have many questions about the Holy Virgin's appearance. Will you both come speak with me again and tell me more of the story?"

"Yes, Brother Asinus," Six and I say.

"Maybe we could come again in a coupla weeks if my uncle or Six's grandpa lets us borrow his truck," I tell him. "I'll remember to bring my notebook next time."

"I shall keep an ear out for you. If I am not here, I am praying in the woods. God bless you, *mis hijos*. Godspeed."

"Thank you, Brother Asinus," I tell him. "Thank you for believing us. Thank you for helping us."

"It is all in the service of God and His Holy Mother," he replies. "Do not forget how blessed and special you both are to have received a visit from heaven. I shall pray for you."

The friar shakes our hands, bowing to us. We do the same. Then he steps into the road.

"I must visit an old grandmother who is leaving on her journey to God," Brother Asinus says. "She asked to see me."

Six and I watch the friar for a minute. He walks down the dusty road towards the center of the pueblo.

"He strikes me as a very holy man," Six says. "I'm not sure how I know it. I just feel it."

"I felt it, too," I admit. "God has brought us another ally."

My amigo and I turn to each other and smile. We climb up into his grandpa's spotless tan pickup and go home.

CHAPTER THREE

VOX CLAMANTIS IN DESERTO
A Voice Crying in the Wilderness

Friday was our last day of full-time work at Mila-Grow tree nursery before school starts—our junior year. The summer has flown by the way I wish the school year would.

My amigo and I put on muscles over the summer. It was heavy and sweaty work, but it carried us over the threshold from boyhood to manhood a shovelful at a time.

Six is even more handsome than before. When we sit together out of sight, I love putting my hand on his hard thigh. When we lie on the ground, he rests his head and hand on my chest as though I were his pillow. It makes me feel pretty important that a fellow of his caliber pays attention to me. He's my compass: I always know where I am when he's with me.

My buddy and I found time only once to go speak further with Brother Asinus about *Nuestra Madre*'s appearance. He gave us a question to ask the Holy Mother upon her next visit.

We got our New Mexico driver's licenses at the end June, though it will be another four months before we'll be allowed to drive between midnight and dawn.

It is Labor Day, 1944, the fourth of September already. Six and I will have the entire week to travel up to Los Alamos and back on our mission for the Blessed Virgin Mary. We can't sit still, we're so excited. I confess I'm scared at the same time—scared we won't succeed in delivering her letter.

I wish we could leave tonight instead of having to wait until tomorrow morning. We have not been back to Bottomless Lake since early summer, the day we found two meteorites and nearly lost our virginity wrestling in the water. We look forward to getting cozy with each other—and that adds to our delicious impatience.

I had a little extra money in my pocket even after I gave most of my paycheck to Tio Nicolás towards my room and board. I thought it would be nice to buy my uncle a bottle of Presidente, his favorite Mexican brandy. I'm not sure it was bribery exactly, but it worked. He's letting us borrow his pickup for our adventure to Los Alamos. I didn't breathe a word of what our trip is really about to him. Six kept his trap shut, too.

It's my uncle's custom to throw a big Tex-Mex barbecue on Labor Day, the last outdoor party of the summer. He has invited all the family and neighbors he can think of. The crowd is nearly too big for his back yard except that some people leave as others arrive.

My uncle has again invited Six's Grandpa Otto and his Grandma Matilda. His grandma is best friends with my uncle's sister. Tia Ana lives at the other end of our short road, Calle Alegre.

The crowd of our first and second cousins has grown from previous years. I cannot remember all their names. It's easy to tell most of Six's family from mine. His people are mostly fair-skinned and light-haired, many with blue eyes like his. My family, like me, are brown-skinned and brown eyed, with black hair that glistens like a crow's wing. But there are some young ones in both our families who are a mix of both Anglo and Mexican. They are beautiful kids.

I see Six from across the yard. My stomach does a somersault. I weave my way towards him. He holds a plate heaped with barbecued brisket and my aunt's tomato and onion salad. An ear of roasted corn, slathered in butter, rests precariously at the edge of his plate.

"You packing a lunch for tomorrow, too?" I ask him. "Remind me to check the tire pressure before we set off in the morning."

"Very funny," he replies, smacking his lips and licking his fingers.

My anxiousness about our mission and our trip has squelched my taste for food. Nothing ever seems to damage Six's appetite.

I put a small slice of his Grandma Matilda's lingonberry torte on my plate. I can probably get that down. She notices and comes over, smiling.

"Don't forget the whipped cream, Antonio," she tells me, slapping an enormous blob of it onto the fruit torte, hiding it completely.

"Thank you, Grandma," Six tells her on my behalf.

She goes back to the conversation she was having with my Tio Nicolás. I look down with dismay at the mound of heavy cream. I don't care for rich deserts.

Six blocks his grandma's view of me.

"There," he says, using his fork to deftly fling the gob of whipped cream out among the sagebrush.

We know where it landed by following where my uncle's barn cat goes among the scrubby plants, his tail raised high.

"Boy, I wish we could leave tonight, Antonio. I feel like a trap about to spring. I want to be with you. Alone."

"Me, too, amigo," I tell him. "But we'll have the whole week together. And you'll be sleeping up in my room tonight."

He smiles and winks.

"Come with me, Six. My Tia Ana is finally alone. She wants to talk to me before we leave in the morning."

My aunt sees us approach and holds out her hands for us to take hold of.

"Tia," I say, kissing her cheek.

Six kisses the other.

"Oh, my," she says. "Two handsome young men paying attention to me in a single evening. God bless you both. Did you boys get enough to eat?"

"Yes, Tia," Six tells her. "A little bit more than enough."

She smiles.

"Come. You boys can walk me home. There will be just enough daylight to see where I am going."

My aunt waves to the remaining guests and takes her leave. She grabs hold of each of our elbows. We have to walk sideways through the gate into the dusty road.

An autumn chill accompanies the lengthening shadows of the cottonwoods. My aunt shivers.

"My shawl," she says. "I forgot it."

"Where?" Six asks. "I'll fetch it."

"I left it on the rocker under the *portál*, dear."

My aunt unhooks from his arm and he runs back to the house. I am happy my family likes him so much. He and I are so lucky.

Six catches up to us and wraps Tia's knit shawl around her shoulders.

"Thank you, Six," she tells him, touching his arm.

She walks between me and my amigo. Her gait is a bit unsteady. We stop now and again so she can gather her shawl about her shoulders.

We reach her yard and walk my aunt to her front door.

"God bless you on your journey, *mis hijos*. Have you told your uncle why you are going all the way to Los Alamos?"

"No, Tia," I say. "He has no use for the Church. He would not believe us. It would only invite him to deliver a long sermon. But I would receive no grace for listening to it."

My aunt chuckles.

"You are a good boy, Antonio—a fine young man, I should say. The kindness in your heart shines in your eyes. I am happy that another loving soul has found you," she adds, turning to Six. "You two are like brothers raised by different families."

"Thank you, Tia," I tell her. "We should be going home. We have a long drive ahead of us and we want to start out early. What did you want to ask me?"

She presses her rosary into my hand and looks into my eyes.

"Perhaps you can ask *Santa Madre* to bless it for me."

I nod to my aunt and put her rosary in the pocket of my new overalls. Six and I bend to kiss her. We descend the porch steps and enter the lane.

It is dark. The moon is not yet risen and the stars are hidden by the overhanging arches of the old cottonwoods. We grab hold of each other's hand and walk slowly. I am so happy when I am with him. I am never afraid with my amigo beside me.

My uncle's gate squeals as we enter the front yard. The glowing windows light our way to the porch.

All the guests have left but Six's grandma and grandpa. They both wear white aprons. They're busy making a racket at the kitchen sink while my uncle sits at the kitchen table drying and sorting the silverware. Six's grandma and grandpa hear us come in and wipe their hands on their aprons.

"There you are," Six's grandpa says. "We've packed you boys a good bit of the leftovers for your camping trip. Your uncle has even plugged in his refrigerator in honor of the occasion."

Tio Nicolás laughs.

"Don't you boys forget it in the morning," Grandma Matilda cautions. "Keep the food as cool as you can and out of the sun."

"Yes, Grandma," Six tells her.

"I think Six and I had better turn in," I announce. "We want to be on our way by dawn."

"God be with you boys," Grandma Matilda says. "I will pray for your safe travels."

"Thank you, Grandma," we tell her.

She kisses us both. Tio Nicolás and Grandpa Otto shake our hands and chuck us on the shoulders.

Six and I will miss our families. It is our first long trip away from home. But it is also an adventure we've been looking forward to all summer. We take the mission for the Blessed Virgin with great seriousness. It is the whole reason for our trip, though Tia Ana and Brother Asinus, our two allies, are the only ones who know that.

My amigo and I climb the stairs to my room. We haven't slept together since the start of summer. Our sexual desires have gotten stronger since then. It's getting so hard to hold back.

At the landing, Six takes my hand and I open my bedroom door. My heart pounds. I switch on my bedside lamp. I open the window a little and shut the door.

Six removes his new denim workshirt and I take off my flannel shirt. We sit down at the edge of my bed. We pull off our boots and hang our socks over them. Six tugs off his T-shirt.

I put my hand on his chest. I feel the thumping of his heart, and ruffle his little patch of fur. Six grins, showing his dimples.

We continue undressing. As soon as *mi dulce gringo* pulls off his Levi's, I yank them from his hand.

"Those are mine," I tell him. "I only loaned them to you so you wouldn't have to put your dirty ones back on for church."

"OK. And where are my overalls then, the ones I got all muddy at Bottomless Lake?" Six asks, jabbing me.

"I washed 'em, so now *they're* mine, too," I say, poking him beneath his ribs, his most ticklish spot.

He tries to pull the pair of overalls away from me. I tackle him backwards onto the bed, both of us in just our boxer shorts. I straddle his chest and use my knees to pin his arms. Six uses his legs to push up and squirm away from beneath me. I try to re-pin him. We both wind up on the floor, tangled in the blanket.

I'm sure my uncle must have heard the crash from downstairs. We scramble back into bed and hastily cover ourselves with the sheet and blanket. I switch off the lamp just as an arc of light from the hallway shines into the room.

"Everything all right in there?" my Tio Nicolás asks, not opening the door any farther.

"Yes, Tio. Six dropped his watch."

He chuckles.

"Sounded like a couple of watches to me. You boys be careful tomorrow. Don't drive when you're tired. I love you both."

The shaft of light narrows and the door closes softly.

We nudge closer, falling into the center of the sagging mattress. It's a small bed and it's not used to two bodies. Six rests his hand on my thigh and I reach over, touching his. I feel his warmth. It is a nice feeling, being cozy with my best friend.

I want to climb on top of Six, like a boy and girl do, and rub against him until I have a wet dream while I'm awake. But we're trying not have sex if we can help it. It's sure not easy.

I've been having wet dreams every few nights. I am always with Six. We are in bed or lying in the meadow or beside the creek, naked or clothed, wet or dry, but always holding onto each other with all our might. I dream we rub against each other until we come. I always awaken with a wet spot in my shorts.

It is only a matter of time before Six and I make love in the waking world. We have come to the edge of the cliff a few times. I wonder what it will feel like to finally jump off—and fly.

The last-quarter moon has risen, shining enough light through my window to make out my friend's face. I turn to him. He turns to me.

Six and I kiss. Like kindling a fire, it gets me a little bit excited. But I don't want to start anything. We might not be able to stop.

I turn on my side. Six does the same, spooning up against me. He puts an arm around me and rests his hand on my chest. It feels as though he is protecting me—as best friends do. I love him more than anybody.

* 2 *

Unable to fall asleep or get comfortable for long, we stay up most of the night, talking excitedly about our mission for the Blessed Virgin Mary and how unlikely our being chosen was. Our worries kept us awake, too, in sweaty tossing and turning. I'm not sure when I finally drifted off to sleep.

I awaken with the smell of coffee coming from downstairs, even through the closed door of my bedroom. It is way past dawn. I am still sleepy.

Six and I have exchanged positions. I untangle myself and sit up. I nudge him.

"We overslept, Six. Tio's already made coffee."

He turns to me and opens his eyes. His first expression upon awakening is a smile.

"You can't oversleep on vacation," he tells me. "And you can't be late."

I wish I could be as unconcerned as my friend. I'm afraid we will not find the right guy to deliver the Virgin's letter to. I think of the many things that could go wrong, from a broken fan-belt to running out of gas or getting lost. I'm worried that we'll be unable to fulfill the assignment the Holy Mother has entrusted to us.

"I'm here to help you, Antonio. We'll get the job done," he says, pulling on his socks. "Don't fret so much."

It's as though he listened in on what I was thinking.

We sort through the jumble of clothes flung over the chair.

"Do you know which are mine?" I ask him, holding up both pairs of overalls. It doesn't help that we wear the same size.

"Those are yours, so that means they're mine," he says, taking a pair from me.

It makes me laugh. I feel less anxious. My amigo works good medicine on me. I admit it gives me a thrill to put on something that he has worn against his skin. I'm guessing he feels the same.

We pack our newest denim overalls and jackets in our knapsacks and finish getting dressed. Six and I tiptoe down the stairs even though there's no need to since my uncle is already up. We set our new sleeping bags and knapsacks by the front door.

"Ah, the early birds," my uncle says. "There's a fresh pot of worms on the stove for you."

We smile at him.

"The fire must have been too high, Tio," Six tells him. "They're all melted," he says, pouring coffee in each of our cups.

I like that he calls him *Tio*, too.

"Six's grandpa left his Coca-Cola ice chest for you boys," my uncle says. "I gave you all the ice I've got. Make sure you take care of it. It's brand new."

"Of course we will, Tio," I tell him. "We're not boys any more."

He looks down at us over his glasses, but he does not say a word.

"I'm going make you two a couple of burritos. It's important to set off on the right foot."

"I couldn't eat a thing, Tio," Six says. "I'm still full from last night."

"I'm too nervous to eat," I tell him.

"Well, you go pack your gear and the cooler chest. Maybe you'll be hungry by the time you finish your coffee."

Six and I take up our sleeping bags and knapsacks packed with our clothes. We set them in the back of my uncle's hand-painted pickup. His shovel and red fire bucket are permanent fixtures in the back of the truck. We push our gear against them so they don't rattle. We put his grandpa's ice chest on the floor of the cab between us so it will be out of the sun.

I give my amigo a playful punch on the shoulder. I'm excited to be going to Los Alamos at long last. I didn't think today would ever get here—just like when I was a boy waiting for Christmas. That's when my papa taught me to count the remaining days in English and Spanish.

We go back into the house. The aromas of my uncle's cooking fill the kitchen. Six and I look at one another and sit down at the table. He's made us each a burrito with eggs, spicy sausage, and cheddar cheese from the old woman with the goats. I bless myself and say grace. Six lowers his eyes.

"Thank you, Tio," I say, looking up from the steaming plate of food.

"Mm-hmm," Six says, salsa dripping to his chin.

My burrito disappears before I remember tasting it.

"Is there any more coffee, Tio?" I ask.

"No, I'm sorry, Antonio. I poured the last of the coffee into my new Thermos flask—which I am loaning you. You boys will have the best outfitted camping expedition since Teddy Roosevelt."

We get up and hug my uncle. He kisses us both on the cheek.

"I expect you won't be able to help being teenage boys. I haven't forgotten what that's like. But I expect you to be grown-ups when you're behind the wheel."

"Yes, Tio," we say in unison.

We descend the porch steps and cross the yard to the pickup. I am still not used to my uncle's watching me drive his truck. It makes me nervous. There are sunglasses hooked on the visor. I put them on and adjust the rearview mirror.

I see my uncle waving to us. He and the house get smaller until they vanish when I turn the corner from our street onto the county road.

"You can breathe now if you like," Six tells me. "He can't see us."

Mi dulce gringo turns to me and smiles. I laugh and punch him on the shoulder.

"Both hands on the wheel," he admonishes.

It is a day of perfect clouds, drawn by God's finger on a blank sky of blue slate. Even with the sun behind us, it is getting warm. We roll down our windows. The wind roaring in our cars makes it hard for me and Six to talk without shouting.

Once we turn off East 2nd Street in town, we enter County Road 409 east of the Pecos River. After that, there are only rutted gravel and dirt roads leading to Bottomless Lake. We roll up the windows again to keep from choking on the dust.

We do not pass a single car or truck. It's the Tuesday after Labor Day weekend. I guess everyone's back at work.

We take the road that runs along the high southern embankment overlooking the lake. The truck springs are being put to the test.

"I think it's not much further where I fell overboard," Six says, pointing.

"I'm looking for where the meteor struck," I tell him. "We won't be able to drive any further than that anyhow."

We reach the shallow crater and get out of the truck.

"Holy mackerel," Six says. "Are those all meteorites? How'd they all wind up in one spot?"

The meteorites and fragments are neatly arranged into a cone-shaped mound like an anthill. The stack is over two feet high. The crater was empty the last time we came out here.

"Do you think the Blessed Mother piled them here in one place for us?" Six asks.

"I doubt it," I tell him. "Why would she do that?"

"I dunno," Six says. "It looks like one of those big junkyard magnets scooped 'em all up and just dropped 'em here.

"That doesn't seem likely, either," I tell him. "It's sure a puzzle."

We return to the truck. Our gear and the bed of the pickup are coated in dust. Six retrieves my uncle's fire bucket and we go back to the stack of meteorites.

My friend and I are inclined to fill the bucket up, but we'd never be able to carry it. Even half-full, the wire handle presses into our hands.

We stash the heavy bucket in the back of the pickup. Everything is gritty. Monsoon season didn't bring us much rain this past summer.

Each taking a handle, we carry his grandpa's Coca-Cola ice chest from the cab over to the shady side of the truck, facing Bottomless Lake.

The water in my canteen is warm. I drop a couple of ice cubes into an enamel camping mug and we share the cold water. Six sits down on the lid of the cooler chest. I park myself on the running board and turn to him.

"What d'you figure those meteorites might be worth, Six?" I ask.

"From ads I've seen in *Astronomy Magazine*, it could easily come to a thousand dollars."

"Holy cow," I exclaim. "But we'd have to make a lot of trips to get them all. They're awfully heavy. I don't want to ruin the springs on my Tio's truck."

"I don't mean the whole pile, Antonio. I'm talking about just what we collected in the bucket."

He gives me a playful punch in the gut.

"A thousand dollars?" I ask. "*No manches.* You're kidding me."

"Pretty sure. They're not weathered. Collectors pay big bucks for what they call *pristine specimens*, especially if we can connect them to a particular meteor storm."

"That's unbelievable," I say.

"We can check with the guy who runs the shop for rock hounds in So-corro on our way home at the end of the week," Six suggests. "But we don't want to tell him how many there are. That'd water down their value."

"Yeah, I get it," I reply.

"Wanna have some lunch?" Six asks.

"Nah," I tell him. "Go ahead if you're hungry. I'm still too excited—and scared. My stomach is doing flip-flops between one and the other."

Six gets up from the ice chest and gets himself a roast chicken sandwich. He closes the lid and sits down.

"Sure you're scared," he says. "So am I. This is the most important thing either of us has ever done. But I'm sure we'll get there and deliver the letter to the right guy."

"I don't know. I think I dreamed it all sometimes," I tell him, "that it didn't really happen. And then when I believe it's true, I'm afraid I am going to fail the Blessed Mother.

"It's up to us, amigo, to get the Holy Mother's letter to Dr. Feynman. That's a lot of responsibility. If we fail, there might be another war. What if we get lost? What if Tio's truck breaks down and we run out of gas? Or water?"

"I'm pretty sure we'd figure something out, Antonio. Holy Mother wasn't going to trust a couple of dimwits to deliver her message," he says, chomping down on his sandwich.

The aroma gets to me. I guess I was hungry after all. My watch says it's one-thirty.

"Can I have a coupla bites?" I ask.

He hands me his sandwich. I take a mouthful and pass it back. He finishes it in two more bites. We take a couple of healthy swallows from our canteens.

"Time for a siesta," Six declares. "I didn't get any more sleep than you did last night, you know. I'm still bushed."

He takes our old denim work jackets from the front seat. Rolling them up as pillows, we lie down beneath the truck in the shade, covering our eyes with our cowboy hats.

There's not much else to do during the heat of the afternoon. A siesta might make up for some of last night's lost sleep. And it'll help us stay awake tonight for the Blessed Virgin's visit. I hope I can stop worrying and thinking about things long enough to doze off—even if for just a little while.

Six takes hold of my hand and laces his fingers between mine. He doesn't say anything, but the gesture comforts me. I know I'm not in this by myself. God bless my friend.

* * *

When I awaken, Six is already stirring, getting our gear ready before nightfall. He's built a teepee-shaped campfire near the rear of the truck like last time, but he has not yet lit it. I hadn't heard a thing. I feel better: I'm not so logy and dragged out.

The sky is gold and rose and orange, layered like the rocks of the canyon walls. I scoot out from beneath the pickup and dust myself off, choking on the cloud I raise up. I go over to Six and sit next to him on the tailgate.

""It's late," I say, glancing at my watch. "When did I doze off?"

"I dunno. I was asleep."

I give him a playful chuck on the chin. He repays it with a kiss.

"What's for supper, Six?" I ask.

"We'd better finish off the other two sandwiches. The leftover barbecue from your uncle's party and the stuff in tins will keep until we get to 'em."

"Then the fire's not for cooking?"

"Nope. It's gonna be cold tonight, Antonio. It's to stay warm."

"That's not gonna be enough wood to last the night," I tell him.

"I know. But we picked this area pretty clean of deadfall last time. It's all I could find. We'll just have to keep each other warm."

"OK. I think I can do that," I say, grinning.

I place my hand on Six's thigh. The outline of his growing arousal shows in his overalls. I take my hand away.

"Oh, Six," I say. "What are we gonna do? We know what comes next, but we're both too chicken. We hike all the way to the river, but we're afraid to jump in."

My eyes fill with tears. He turns to me and dries my cheeks with his fingers.

"Maybe we just need a push," he tells me. "We love each other, *cuate*. That's what's most important. We'll figure the rest of it out."

We jump down from the tailgate. We each grab a handle of the Coca-Cola ice chest and hoist it up onto the truck bed. Climbing up, we sit on our new sleeping bags, our backs leaning against the cab, the ice cooler between us. I unlatch the handle and remove the lid.

I hand Six one of the two remaining barbecue beef sandwiches and a hard-boiled egg, taking the same for myself. The ice has all melted. I find four bottles of Dos Equis at the bottom. The ice chest has a built-in bottle opener on the side. They thought of everything.

Taking out one of the beers, I snap the cap off and hand it to my buddy.

"What's this?" he asks, grinning. "You sly dog. No wonder it was so heavy."

"No, it wasn't me, Six. I didn't find the beer till now. I guess my uncle wanted to surprise us. He's been awfully nice to me lately."

He takes a sip and passes the bottle back to me. I take a bite of my sandwich and wash it down with a little beer. Six has already made most of his sandwich disappear. I wish I could take everything as easy as he does.

I finish my sandwich and hard-boiled egg and take a last swallow of beer. I feel content, happy, especially sitting next to my amigo. I hand him the bottle which he finishes off.

"God bless Tio Nicolás," he says, raising the empty bottle.

"God bless us all," I reply.

He leans over and kisses my cheek.

"What if it really is wrong to love each other, Six?" I ask. "What do we do then?"

"How can love be wrong, amigo?" he asks, chuckling. "What'd be left for the devil to do if love was wrong? You worry too much."

He pats my thigh and scoots down to the tailgate. Now that the wind has died, Six lights our little fire. The moon has risen.

I unsnap our sleeping bags, unrolling one in the bed of the truck for us to lie together on and the other to cover ourselves with. They are much better than our old oiled-canvas bedrolls. Our knapsacks of clothes will be our pillows.

I drag Grandpa Otto's ice chest to the tailgate and unscrew the drain plug, letting out the water from the melted ice. Six scoops the wet sand into a mound beside the fire with the shovel in case the wind comes up again and we need to put the fire out. He hops up onto the tailgate.

We get ourselves arranged and comfortable between the sleeping bags, holding hands but not wanting to get frisky with each other. The Holy Mother could show up at any minute.

There's not much heat coming from the fire, but it's glow is cheering. I hope it is a bright enough beacon for the Blessed Virgin to find us again. I watch the sparks fly up, seeming to merge with the few stars that can be seen in the light of the quarter-moon.

"Look at that," Six says, taking his hand from beneath the sleeping bag and pointing.

He has let cold air in. He wriggles his hand beneath the covers again. I rest my hand on top of his. We nudge closer.

"Another meteor?" I ask.

"I don't think so. I never saw one behave like that," he remarks, "zigzagging like a horsefly."

"Maybe it's the Virgin. She's here, amigo. Get up," I shout. "She's here."

Jumping up from beneath the sleeping bag, we hop down from the truck and lean against the tailgate. We look up.

I see the bright meteor streak halfway across the sky, pause stock-still for a few seconds, and then dart off at a sharp angle to its original course before disappearing behind a cluster of clouds. Six and I look at each other. He raises his eyebrows.

I am disappointed and sad that it is not the Blessed Virgin. Waiting is so hard.

Six puts his arm across my shoulders and draws me closer. I put my arm around his waist, watching the fading firelight gleam in his eyes.

The moon hides behind a veil of wispy clouds like a mantilla. There's still a little warmth from the fire, but there's not much more wood we can add to it. We both shiver.

"Come on, amigo," he tells me. "Let's get warm."

We climb back into the truck bed and snuggle between our sleeping bags. We rest our heads on our knapsacks. Six takes my hand and weaves his fingers among mine. It's not so cold now.

My eyelids grow heavy. I watch the sky, trying to stay awake. Six snores gently. The fire has burned out.

I'm afraid I'll doze off and miss the Blessed Virgin when she finally appears. I think of getting some of the coffee left in my uncle's Thermos bottle, but it's lying on the front seat. My crawling out of the sleeping bag would disturb my amigo.

I touch my aunt's rosary in the pocket of my Levi's. I take it out and recite the prayers to myself—to keep my mind occupied, to keep from falling asleep. Fingering the beads, I soon lose count and forget where I am. I start over.

Twice my legs jerk me awake, as though I were trying to catch myself from a fall. Six mumbles in his sleep.

The stars turn so slowly they seem hardly to be moving at all. I drift off to sleep, dozing in and out among the constellations, trying to keep track of them.

* * *

It is utterly black when I awaken except for a splash of stars, the Milky Way. There is no sign of the Holy Mother.

Six and I lie on our sides, spooned together. I put my arm around my friend and nudge closer. He emits a throaty noise halfway between purring and growling. I smile.

It is too dark to read my watch. I've no idea what time it is. Six would know just by looking at the sky.

I try to keep one eye open, but it doesn't work. It never does. I slip down into sleep again as though the path were a log-slide.

* 3 *

When I next awaken, the sky outlines the black mountains in a gradient of blues from pale to indigo. Six and I have traded places. I squirm out from beneath his arm and sit up. The back of the pickup is not the most comfortable bed. My stirring rouses Six.

"My God," I shout. "We missed the Virgin. She came and we were asleep. *Hijo de la chingada*! Son of a bitch!"

"Easy, Antonio," he says, sitting up and folding his legs beneath him

I tug on my boots and jump down from the tailgate. I look for some sign of the Virgin's visit, some disturbance of the ground or a new pile of iron meteorites. Walking around to the front of the truck, I peer off into the distance. The first streaks of dawn are reflected in the glassy water of Bottomless Lake. There is no sign from the Blessed Mother.

"*Hijo de la chingada*!" I repeat, kicking the dirt. "*Pinche*! Damn!"

I jump when I realize Six is standing at my shoulder. He made no noise.

"You're crying," he says. "What's the matter, Antonio?"

He dries my cheeks with his thumbs.

"We're a couple of knuckleheads, you and me," I tell him.

"Speak for yourself," he replies, putting his hand on my shoulder.

He makes me smile even when I don't want to. We walk around to the back of the truck.

"I must've disappointed the Holy Mother, Six. That's why she didn't come. She promised she'd appear to both of us the night before we get to Los Alamos to deliver her letter. I failed her. I wish I was dead."

"Easy, amigo. Last night wasn't the night before we deliver her letter. It's three-hundred-fifty miles to Los Alamos. I don't think your Tio's truck is up to that much in one day. I don't think we are, either. We don't want the truck to overheat or blow a gasket or something."

"So what're you saying, Six?" I ask him.

"That we aren't going to get to Los Alamos until tomorrow, that *tonight* is the night before we deliver the Virgin's letter. She will appear to us tonight."

"I sure hope you're right," I tell him. "God I hope you're right."

"Of course I am. I'm always right," he says, "except when I'm not."

He makes me smile again. God bless my friend.

"Come on," he says. "Let's pack up. I'm cold."

We shovel dirt onto the campfire ashes and shake out our open sleeping bags. After rolling them up, we secure our gear at the front of the pickup bed. We take the ice chest with us into the cab. It is much lighter after I drained the water from it.

The engine is slow to turn over. It is a cold morning. It feels like autumn.

"There's a sign of the Virgin," Six says, pointing through the frosty windshield. "That's Venus rising over there, just above the horizon. The Morning Star was considered an emblem of the Blessed Virgin Mary."

"*No manches*. No kidding. I learned something from a Lutheran," I tell him, grinning.

"Martin Luther had a special devotion to the Virgin Mary," he remarks.

"I guess I learned another thing," I say, clearing the windshield with the squeaky wipers. "Thank you, amigo. I'm glad to know that."

I turn on the heater. It makes a racket, but it blows only cold air. I switch it off again and wait for the motor to get warm. Six unfolds part of the map and, turning it towards me, he draws our route with his finger. I nod, calling him the scout of our expedition. It makes him smile.

Putting the truck in gear, I take my time backing up and turning around. I do not want my uncle's truck to tumble down an arroyo or wind up at the bottom of Bottomless Lake. My hands tremble on the steering wheel.

Once we leave the state park and turn onto the gravel road, I breathe easier. The sun is behind us and I raise the visor.

"How far d'you think we'll get today?" I ask *mi compa*.

He unfolds another crease in the map and measures with his fingers.

"We oughta make it to Socorro, maybe a little further," he replies. "Do you wanna stop some place for breakfast?" he asks.

"I can't even think about food right now. *Qué tonto soy*! What a fool I am! I'm so upset we missed the Blessed Virgin's visit. She might not come back."

"We didn't miss her. Take it easy, Antonio."

Even with the pedal on the floor, I don't get much above fifty. My mind is not on driving except when I veer a little, sending up a spray of gravel and dust that jars me back onto the road. Six looks at me with concern. I smile to reassure him.

We pass no place to stop for breakfast and decide to press on to Carrizozo. Pooling our resources, we fill up at the Texaco and ask about someplace to get a bite to eat. The gas attendant recommends Tiny's on the main drag. By now I'm pretty famished.

The aromas wafting out of Tiny's make me as hungry as a wolf. Six beats me to the door, but winds up holding it open for me. I put a pretend quarter in his outstretched palm.

We take off our cowboy hats and hang them on pegs beside the door. The only other customers are two white-haired fellows with skin like tanned hide. One of them looks *mestizo*, with long braids tied with colored yarn. I nod to them and smile. They return the greeting.

Neither the waitress nor the cook at Tiny's is tiny. The waitress has *Fanny* embroidered on her blouse. We sit down at the counter. She pours two steaming mugs of coffee without asking.

"Thanks, Fanny," I say. "I needed that."

"Me, too," Six tells her.

"You're lookin' pretty hard-traveled," she remarks. "What can I get you boys?"

"A couple of burritos and hash-browns," Six replies without even glancing at a menu.

"Same here," I tell her.

"You got it," she replies, smiling.

Fanny slaps our order down on the pass-through counter to the kitchen. The blue neon clock says it is almost eleven o'clock.

"I wonder how Fanny gets her fanny into Tiny's tiny kitchen," my buddy says under his breath.

I swallow my coffee wrong and choke. Six slaps my back. He chuckles, then laughs, nearly choking on his own coffee.

Poking his thigh beneath the counter, I get up to use the restroom. If I don't leave now, we'll get into a laughing jag that won't end until we're rolling on the floor.

When I return, I see Fanny has refilled our cups. I try not to look at her embroidered name or glance over at *mi compa* for fear our hilarity will start all over.

At last Fanny brings our breakfast.

"Anything else, boys?"

Our mouths full, Six and I shake our heads. Fanny puts our check face-down on the counter between us. She takes off her apron and says goodbye to Earl, the cook. Her shift must be over. She tells us to come back real soon. We nod to her.

I do not remember eating any of my breakfast, yet it is gone. Six wipes his mouth with his paper napkin and shoots me a satisfied smile.

We pay our bill with dusty money. Then we collect our hats and go out to the parking lot.

No sooner do we get outside than Six repeats his line about Fanny getting her fanny into Tiny's kitchen. We double over with sidesplitting laughter.

I'm glad we didn't crack up inside the restaurant. I wouldn't have wanted to hurt Fanny's feelings.

I'm not sure how we held it in so long. Six and I hang on each other to steady ourselves. Tears stream down our faces. It's hard to get my breath.

Our gales of laughter diminish and trail off. Then we put on our sunglasses and head to the truck, pretending once more to be grown-ups.

"I can take over now," Six says, scooting around me and climbing in on the driver's side.

We agreed he'd drive for a while. Still, it makes me nervous to see him behind the wheel of my uncle's pickup, even though Six has done a lot more driving than I have. The boss always lets him drive the two-ton truck for Mila-Grow Tree Nursery.

He adjusts the mirror and pulls down the visor. The dust coating his face makes him look older—old enough to drive Tio's truck, I guess.

"Hang onto your seats, boys and girls," he remarks, chuckling.

He kills the engine before getting it in gear. Then he takes off like a jack-rabbit. I'm sure he put on the whole performance for effect. I punch his shoulder.

"Why don't you catch a few winks?" he suggests. "We'll stop again in Socorro for gas."

I lean against the door and pull my hat down. The door handle jabs my ribs and I can't get comfortable. I sit up and lean the other way, towards Six. I slide next to him and rest my head against his shoulder, tilting my hat over my eyes. I'm able to stretch my legs all the way out.

I feel the first few turns and the occasional pothole, but the road is pretty smooth. I slip away so gradually I'm not sure when I fall asleep, dreaming almost at once.

The Blessed Virgin stands on the shoulder of the road. Six stops the turquoise pickup and I get out. *Nuestra Madre* gathers her robes about her. Her feet are dusty.

"Where are you going, Holy Mother?" I ask, offering her a drink from my canteen.

"Thank you, my child. I am going to save my children, Antonio—all of my children."

I help her up into the pickup and close the door. I go to the other side. Six scoots next to the Virgin and takes her hand. I think, *What a kind thing he has done*, and smile at him. I take the wheel again and drive.

"Where are your children, Blessed Mother?" I ask, turning to her.

"They are coming, Antonio. They are just up ahead a little ways."

The sky grows dark all at once, as though sunset were a curtain-fall. I turn on the headlamps.

"There they are," Holy Mother says, raising her arm and pointing up the road.

A great racket descends out of the black sky. It is another storm of meteorites, big ones and small ones. They smash into the ground all around us, sending clouds of dust and dirt skyward. They smack the road, too, setting patches of asphalt on fire. The sagebrush bursts into flames. A large iron stone is headed straight for us. Holy Mother raises her hand to her mouth.

"Watch out," I shout, swerving to avoid its crashing into us.

I startle myself awake with a jerk, stomping on the brakes in my dream. My cowboy hat tumbles off my head and lands on the floor. Six steps on the real brakes.

"It was just a chunk of gravel flying up from the road, amigo," he tells me. "Nothing your uncle's can of paint can't cover over. We're almost there."

He pulls over on the narrow strip of gravel.

"You were really out, Antonio. Are you OK?" he asks, touching my shoulder.

"Yeah. Just a dream," I assure him. "It was another meteor storm."

I sit straight and put my hat back on. Six pulls back onto the road.

"We can switch again after we get gas," I tell him. "That nap did me good."

The scenery looks so dry and scrubby and desolate. There hasn't been much rain from this summer's monsoon. All of New Mexico is parched.

I take the roadmap from the dashboard, but I have no idea where we are and put it back. I'm fidgety. I can't wait to get out and walk around to stretch my legs.

Six pulls into the Texaco. I get out and pace twice around the station. As the attendant pumps gas, my buddy climbs out of the pickup and talks to him. There is a lot of pointing and sign language going on. Six must have asked for directions.

He pays the fellow and we are on our way again.

"What was that about?" I ask him.

"I got directions to the rock shop," he says. "It's just up the road a piece, not actually in Socorro. It's in Escondida—on our way."

"Are we gonna have time for that?"

"We're halfway to Los Alamos already," Six informs me. "It's only around three o'clock, right?"

I look at my watch.

"Yeah," I reply. "All right. We'll stop, but we shouldn't dawdle. I'm just curious whether our meteorites are worth as much as you say. I think we oughta drive on a little further after that in case we run into trouble tomorrow."

"You mean like the engine blowing up and all four tires falling off?"

My buddy's remark makes me laugh.

"Something like that," I say. He has a knack for making me forget my worries.

Rocks & a Hard Place is about twenty miles up the road. There's only one other old pickup out front. The wooden *Open* sign is hung out. We get out of my uncle's truck.

Six takes an oily rag from beneath the front seat. We lean over the side of the pickup, looking down at the bucket of meteorites in the back.

"Pick one," he tells me. "Not too big."

I choose the smallest one. Even so, it's awfully heavy for its size. Six holds out the dirty cloth, folding it around the meteorite.

"We found only this one for now, Antonio," he cautions. "Better let me do the talking."

"OK," I say.

A bell tinkles above the shop door. After coming from the daylight, it seems dim as a cave inside. There are several tall glass cabinets with glass shelves lighted from above. Each is crammed with rock and fossil specimens of an astounding variety. It's hard to believe they all came from Mother Earth.

An older guy, maybe in his forties, sits at a large worktable behind the wooden shop counter. The counter, too, is a large display case.

The man looks up from his work and peers down over his glasses at us. He twitches his gray moustache.

"What can I do for you fellas?" he asks, getting to his feet and coming over.

Six unwraps the meteorite. The shop owner switches on a gooseneck lamp and places a large magnifying glass on a stand over our specimen. He looks down, moving his head back and forth to examine it from different angles.

"Beautiful example of an iron-nickel kamacite," he says, after holding us in suspense. "Find it around here?"

"Near Bottomless Lake outside Roswell," Six tells him.

"Did you see the strike?"

"We did. It was back in June."

"I can tell it's fresh," the owner says. "No weathering to speak of. I assume you boys would like to sell it? I have ready buyers, you know."

"Yes. We'd like to sell it," Six tells him.

"Give me a few minutes to run a couple of assaying tests on it—with your permission."

"Sure," my amigo says.

The fellow first weighs our iron stone. He immerses it in a beaker of water to measure its volume. Then he files off a few flakes onto which he dribbles a few droplets of liquid from an eyedropper. He observes the results, marking them down in a lined notebook. He flips through a dog-eared paper catalog and runs a finger down the page. He looks up.

"I'm prepared to offer you one-twenty-five."

"I thought we'd get more than a buck-and-a-quarter," I remark to Six, whispering.

The owner of the shop must've overheard me.

"All right," the man says. "One-hundred-thirty bucks. But not a nickel more."

"Dollars?" I say. Six steps on my foot—hard.

"I mean... all right. One hundred-and-thirty dollars. Deal."

The man smiles. He removes his spectacles and wipes their lenses with a cloth.

"I don't keep that kind of cash on hand, though," he says. "I hate to put you boys out and make you come back, but the bank's already closed. Can you come back tomorrow?"

"Turns out we're on our way up north. We'll be coming back this way on Friday," Six says.

"Perfect," the man tells us, shaking our hands. He places our meteorite back in the dirty cloth and hands us his business card.

"I'd like to encourage you fellas to look for more specimens. I had an old fellow from the Acoma Pueblo outside Albuquerque used to find 'em for me. He had an uncanny knack for it. But the man passed away last year. I got buyers, but nothing to sell 'em. You boys take care. See you in a coupla days."

"Thanks, Mr. Carson. Adios," Six says, tipping his hat to him.

Outside, I act as though my legs are made of rubber and I'm about to keel over.

"Holy mackerel, Six. You were right. I thought you were talking through your hat."

He smirks in a sort of *I-told-you-so* way. I chuck his shoulder and we climb up into the cab. I take the wheel again and my buddy sprawls out this time.

"There's not gonna be any good place to get supplies until we reach Albuquerque in the morning," Six tells me. "We oughta look for some place to get food before we leave Escondida."

"All right," I reply. "Looks like a little farm stand up ahead."

I pull onto the gravel shoulder. I realize I'm getting hungry again.

* 3 *

We camp outside the small town of San Ysidro, near the Jemez Pueblo. I poke the coals of our cooking fire with a stick. Six returns with an armload of piñon deadfall he plunks down beside the fire.

My buddy and I polish off everything we bought at the farm stand outside Escondida: two ears of corn apiece, and a pair of potatoes that got burnt on one side while the other remained raw. Six opens the can of pork-and-beans from home. We're saving the two fat oranges for dessert.

After chowing down, we park ourselves on the open tailgate, watching the sky in the final half-hour before dark. Six puts his arm around my shoulder and feeds me a slice of orange.

The sky fades from red and gold above the mountains to a deep indigo that verges on black along the horizon behind us. The first stars and planets appear. I wait for Six to tell me which ones they are. He points.

"There's another one of those crazy zigzag meteors like we keep seeing," he says.

I watch the blazing trail across the heavens. It turns at a sharp angle before zipping off in yet another direction. Two more appear. They dart and skim across the sky like insects on a pond. The three meteors, now in formation, streak across the heavens so rapidly I can barely turn my head fast enough to watch them disappear behind a bank of clouds.

"I have no idea what they are," Six says, anticipating my question. "It's not a star or a planet or a meteor. I never saw anything move like that."

It is almost dark. The fire is nearly out. All the colors of sunset have turned to smudges of gray.

"Here comes another one," I say, pointing towards the horizon.

"I don't think so," Six replies. "It's not moving like the others did. It's steadier, more like a real meteor except that it's moving awfully slow."

We watch spellbound as the fuzzy patch of light approaches, growing brighter and larger. Like the meteor in my dream, it is headed straight for us.

"Could it be the Holy Virgin?" Six suggests.

"Yes. Yes, of course," I reply, jumping down from the tailgate. "It's the Holy Mother."

Six also climbs down. We drop to our knees. I cross myself and Six, surprisingly, does the same. He's seen me do it enough times, especially when he comes to mass with me.

"*Pray for us sinners, now and at the hour of our death*," I say aloud, looking up at the brilliance.

The Blessed Virgin descends on ripples of light that radiate from beneath her feet like gentle waves on the water. She looks down at us, smiling, warmth and light flowing forth from her in all directions. Once again, I feel calm and peaceful in her presence.

The Holy Virgin comes toward us, walking on the air, a sight so unbelievable and magnificent, my jaw drops. I am unable to get any words out.

"Oh, my God," Six exclaims.

"No," the Virgin says to him. "I am only His mother."

Six tries to stifle a chuckle but is not successful. He hadn't known what to make of it when I told him the Holy Mother had a sense of humor.

The Virgin's smile invites us to share in her mirth.

"You must be Sixtus," she says. "Please, get to your feet. You, too, Antonio."

We rise. Six reaches for my hand. I don't know what I should do. I let him take my hand.

"I thank you both for undertaking the mission to deliver my missive to Dr. Feynman. Tomorrow he will hold it in his hands," the Virgin says, glowing brighter.

"If you please, Holy Mother..." I say, shifting from one foot to the other. "What shall we do with the pile of meteorites you left for us at Bottomless Lake? They're worth a lot of money."

"It was not I, children. I remind you only to share your bounty with those in need as Our Lord commands us."

The Holy Virgin looks from one of us to the other, her eyes glowing intently.

"Have you mentioned my visit to anyone?" she asks.

"Only my Tia Ana," I reply.

"Yes, I knew you told her, Antonio. Your aunt prayed to me for your safety. I have conveyed her prayer to Our Savior. Was there anyone else you told?"

"I told Father Consuelo in confession," I tell her. "He did not believe me."

"Of course not," the Virgin replies. "No one ever believes any of my messengers until they have witnessed miracles. I am curious. What did Father Consuelo have to say?"

"He wondered why you would visit a pair of no-accounts like Six and me when there are many who are far worthier. He said you are likelier to be a sign from the devil to lure two innocent, but confused, young men into a pit of depravity."

"That sounds like Consuelo. Despite his name, he consoles no one. I pity those who have to sit through his long-winded sermons. Do not mind him, Antonio. There will be others who will want to silence you, too—permanently, if they can. I shall watch over you both. Speak the truth clearly and you will have nothing to fear."

I let go of Six's hand and take my Tia Ana's rosary from my pocket. I hold it out to the Holy Mother. It dangles from my fingers.

"Yes, dear child. I know about your aunt's prayer to spare her brother, your Tio Nicolás. He has cancer, Antonio."

The news shocks me. I had suspected it was my aunt, not my uncle, who was sick. I burst into tears, covering my eyes.

Six holds me and I sob into his shoulder.

"Easy, amigo," he says, stroking the back of my neck.

"I love my Tio Nicolás as much as I did my father," I say, choking on my words. "I can't lose him, too."

My chest heaves. It is hard to get hold of myself. Six hugs me harder.

"I have interceded on your uncle's behalf, Antonio," the Virgin says, "but it is not Our Lord's will, dear child. God answers all prayers, but sometimes the answer is *No*."

I break down again and Six gently rubs my shoulders until the squall has passed.

I tuck my aunt's rosary back into the pocket of my overalls. I can't recall whether the Virgin blessed it or not.

"Our Savior assures me Tio Nicolás will not suffer long, Antonio. His death will be peaceful. He will die in his bed."

"Thank you, Holy Mother," I tell her. "Please pray for us."

"Of course I shall."

"I also told Brother Asinus on the pueblo outside of Roswell of your visit," I confess to the Blessed Mother.

"He is a very devout man, Antonio, a holy man. He will help you. You must do as he advises."

"Yes, Holy Mother," I say. "If you please... Brother Asinus gave us question to ask you."

"Certainly, my child. What is his question?"

I take the slip of paper from the other pocket of my overalls so I do not get it wrong.

"*As the Queen of Heaven, are you also Holy Mother to other possible races among the myriad of stars?*"

The Blessed Virgin smiles and laughs softly.

"Perhaps Brother Asinus reads a bit too much Robert Heinlein," she says. "But you may assure him that I am Mother to all God's creatures, even little green men. I am here to save all my children."

It is what the Holy Mother told me in my dream of the meteor shower.

She holds out her hands and begins floating skyward.

"If you please, Holy Mother," Six says, delaying her ascent. "What are Antonio and I to do about... you know... about our strong feelings for each other?"

Six looks down at his feet and shuffles them in the dirt. The Virgin floats earthward again.

"You love each other, do you not?"

"More than I can say," I tell her. "More than my own life, Holy Mother."

"I would die if I lost Antonio," Six says. "He is my brother, the brother I never had."

"Your love is exemplary," the Blessed Virgin says. "I can assert that you will remain together for your entire lives."

"Thank you, Holy Mother. I think maybe Six is talking about... about... c-c-carnal... about, you know... We have those kinds of feelings for each other, too. What should we do?"

"I encourage all young people to refrain from premarital congress until it can be enjoyed within the bonds of Holy Matrimony."

"Yes, but..." Six begins.

"Go on, Sixtus," the Virgin says. "What you say to me is held in confidence."

"Um... Well..."

He takes my hand again and winks at me.

"If we were to have premarital congress, Holy Mother... Begging your pardon... that would mean that one day Antonio and I might get married. But we cannot marry each other in the Church. Therefore, it would not be premarital congress."

"Your argument is most convincing, Sixtus. You put forth your case with logic and conviction, as a Jesuit or a lawyer might. It is your love for each other that is most important, my children. The love of Our Lord shines through you both—in your tenderness towards one another. You are blessed."

Holy Mother glows in earnest.

"Be steadfast, Antonio, Sixtus. Many obstacles will be strewn in your paths. You must be brave and trust in Our Savior. He will give you strength.

"Remember. I shall visit you again once the war is over. You must say the rosary daily and pray for lasting peace so the next war never happens. God bless you and all my children."

Her aura flares and then subsides. She floats skyward.

We watch the Blessed Virgin rise up, fading and dimming until she vanishes, her blue mantle melting into the deep blue sky, her halo a pinpoint of light lost among the stars.

It is a couple of minutes before we realize we are standing in the dark and cold, still looking up. The campfire is all ashes. I shine my flashlight up into the empty sky where it is swallowed by the immense blackness.

Six and I hop up into the back of the pickup. We slide down into our sleeping bags and lie on our backs, our heads on our knapsacks. I switch off the flashlight.

"I told you we didn't miss the Blessed Virgin's appearance, Antonio. You worried for nothing," Six tells me, nudging closer.

I turn to him. There's barely enough moonlight to make out my buddy's features. It will be setting soon.

"You were right, amigo," I admit. "I'm so relieved we didn't disappoint the Holy Mother. Thank you for helping me."

As my eyes become accustomed, the roof of the sky fills with an arc of stars: The Milky Way.

"What did you think of the Holy Mother, Six?" I ask.

"I can still see her image when I close my eyes. You were right about how beautiful she is, Antonio. I felt so safe in her presence, as though I was under a mother's care once more. It's hard to explain."

"I know what you mean," I tell him. "All my worries seem so small when she's there. But as soon as I'm on my own again, I am full of doubt. I just hope we don't run into trouble on the road to Los Alamos tomorrow."

"Look," he says. "The Blessed Mother said Dr. Feynman would hold her letter in his hands tomorrow. So even if we get four flat tires and the engine blows up, we're still gonna make it to Los Alamos. She said so."

"Thanks for reminding me, amigo," I say, poking his thigh through our sleeping bags. "I hope I didn't draw the map wrong on how to get there."

"There you go again, Antonio. Where's your faith?" he asks, nudging me with his elbow. "Where's your faith in yourself? You did all you could. Let's trust in God and get some sleep. What d'ya say?"

"OK," I reply. "Thanks for being *mi dulce gringo*. I'd be lost without you, Six. I think that's why the Holy Mother didn't come to just me alone. She knew I'd need your help."

He chuckles and scoot's closer.

"I need you, too," he says, turning to me and kissing my cheek. "You mean the world to me, Antonio. And all those worlds sprinkled up there in the sky, too."

"I love you," I tell him, tapping his thigh. "Good night, Six."

"G'night," he mumbles.

I feel the rhythm of Six's breathing. My own slows to match his. I am content merely to be with him.

At last his breathing grows shallower and slower. I realize he's asleep. My eyelids grow heavy. I no longer have to fight to stay awake for fear we'll miss the Holy Mother's visit. My mind quickly trails off into dreaming, and dreaming inside of dreams.

My best friend and I sleep beneath our tent of stars.

* **4** *

I awaken as Venus, the Morning Star, rises just before the sun. Six has his arm around me, outside his sleeping bag, breathing on my neck. I nudge him. He turns to me and smiles.

"G'mornin'," he says. "What's for breakfast?"

"A long drive to the next place that might be open," I tell him, poking his ribs.

We sit up and unsnap our sleeping bags, ready to embark on the final leg of our mission to deliver the Blessed Virgin's letter to Dr. Richard Feynman in Los Alamos.

My amigo and I decide to flip for who gets to drive first. I reach into the pocket of my dusty overalls for a quarter.

CHAPTER FOUR

NIHIL HUMANUS MIHI ALIENUS EST
Nothing Human Is Alien to Me

We pack up our gear and secure it in the bed of the pickup. It was another night of heavy dew. Our sleeping bags are damp. The bed of the pickup is slippery.

Wanting to make a good impression on Dr. Feynman, we change out of our old, worn work clothes and put on our newest overalls and jackets. We climb down and close the tailgate.

Six and I stand holding each other for a moment, looking into each other's eyes. His smile makes me forget how cold I am.

We climb into the cab of my uncle's turquoise pickup. I take the wheel. It starts and stalls twice before catching. As the engine warms up, I take my Tia Ana's rosary out of the pocket of my overalls. I finger the beads and we recite two decades of the prayers.

I switch on the squeaky wipers to clear the dew from the windshield. The streaks are muddy with dust. Then I turn on the heater. I pour lukewarm coffee from my uncle's Thermos flask into the cup. We each take a sip before I drive off.

The heater roars but doesn't throw out much heat. The road is bumpy; the truck rattles like it's going to come apart. Tio's Thermos tips over, spilling all the coffee onto the floor.

"*Hijo de la chingada*! Son of a bitch!" I curse.

"*Pinche*. Damn," Six joins in. "I was lookin' forward to a little more cold coffee."

I laugh.

My amigo takes the folded map from the dashboard and consults it. He's better at reading maps than I am.

"It's about fifteen miles to the highway to Albuquerque," he informs me. "Maybe some place'll be open."

It is still foggy when we reach the intersection with the highway.

"Wanna stop for some fresh coffee?" Six asks as an electric sign emerges from the mist.

"Sure," I reply. "One sip didn't do it for me, either. I'm still groggy."

I pull into the lot out front of the diner. They have just opened and are still getting set up. Six and I take off our cowboy hats and sit on a pair of stools at the counter.

"What can I git you fellas?" the waitress asks.

Her voice is gravelly. She looks in need of some strong coffee herself.

"A coupla coffees, when you got some made," Six tells her.

"Oh, we got some," she says. "I turn on the coffee before I turn on the lights and git my coat off. I know what's important."

She smiles, setting two steaming mugs on the counter. The aroma clears the fog in my head.

"Thank you," Six and I say in unison.

"You boys wanna see a menu?"

"Nah. It'll just be the coffees," I tell her.

The front door jingles and a couple of really old guys walk in. They look like ranchers, but I'm not sure how they'd mount a horse. They seem barely able to climb the counter stools. The waitress calls them by name: Zeke and Charlie.

"That's gonna be us some day," I tell my friend under my breath.

He smiles.

"I sure hope so," he replies, tapping my thigh. "The Virgin promised we'd always be together. I *want* to grow old with you, amigo."

After a refill, we finish our coffee. Feeling generous, I leave fifteen cents on the counter and we get up.

"Safe travels," the waitress remarks.

The old guys look up. I nod to them. *Yeah, I hope Six and I do get to be that old. It'll mean we lived a good life.*

Six decides to drive until we get on the other side of Albuquerque. I doze off again, dreamlessly this time.

I'm startled awake by a deafening squawk from the radio. Some bump or jolt must have turned it on. Six grabs the knob and turns it down. He sings happily along with the Andrews Sisters.

> *Don't sit under the apple tree with anyone else but me*
> *Anyone else but me, anyone else but me*
> *No! No! No!*

It's one of my buddy's favorite songs. Six has a pretty good singing voice. He pays more attention to music and seems to remember whatever he hears. I like drawing and carving better.

The next bump in the road knocks the radio out again, but Six keeps on singing. He remembers the words and the tune and continues the song all the way to the end. Then he turns to me and smiles. I applaud.

"Maybe we could sell one of those meteorites to get your Tio's radio fixed," Six suggests. "He's been really swell to us. It'd be nice to do him a good turn, don't you think?"

"Yes," I reply. "That's a nice idea. The Holy Mother said to share our good fortune."

"We should stop for gas up ahead," Six says. "I don't think I'm ready for breakfast yet, though. How 'bout you, Antonio?"

"Nope. I'm as nervous as you are, amigo," I tell him. "This is our big day."

"I don't mind the butterflies so much as the guy chasing after them with his net," Six jokes, grinning.

"Maybe we'll stop for a bite to eat before we get to Los Alamos later," I say.

"OK," he replies, as he turns into the gas station. "We've got plenty of time."

* * *

On the way north to Los Alamos, the radiator overheats twice and we get a flat. I'm grateful Six thought to make sure the spare tire was filled before we left home.

I feel like a nervous wreck. I'm glad Six offered to keep driving.

"The Blessed Virgin warned us it wasn't always going to be smooth sailing," he remarks.

"I know, huh? I'm afraid we're going to be late, that's all."

"Did we have an appointment? Are we expected?" Six asks. "Please. Take it easy, Antonio. It's not far now."

I look out the window. Sundown approaches. It is hard to resist being transfixed by the golden light on the canyon walls. The layers of rock look as though they have been saturated with aeons of sunsets.

A single steep, winding road leads us into Los Alamos. We ask at the filling station how to find the government facility outside of town. The attendant points in the general direction.

"It's out where the old boys' ranch used to be. But you didn't get it from me," he cautions.

Six drives on. I refer to the map I'd drawn on the old gas receipt after the Holy Mother's appearance to us back in June.

It is soon dark. I turn on the flashlight from the glovebox and shine it on my map, telling Six which way to turn. Then I switch it off again.

The dirt road we follow isn't much more than a wide, rutted path cleared through the scrub. Red dust coats the landscape and gets into my uncle's truck. I can taste it.

The pickup jostles from one pothole to the next. The headlamps bounce and waver, projecting bizarre shadows that seem to leap out from the side of the road. My heart pounds.

We drive on despite the ever more threatening signs. The first says it's unlawful to enter the area without the permission of the installation commander.

"We'll be sure get his permission as soon as we learn his name," Six jokes.

I'm on the edge of the seat. Six acts as though we're out for a Sunday jaunt.

The next sign reads, *Off Limits to Unauthorized Personnel*.

"I get the feeling your roundabout map got us around a road-block or something, Antonio. It looks like we're already on government property."

"Oh, shit," I say. "What're we gonna do?"

He turns to me and grins.

"*Damn the torpedoes. Full speed ahead.*"

"Admiral Farragut," I respond. "The Spanish-American War."

"You get an 'A' in American History," he tells me.

For a minute, I've forgotten my worries.

U. S. Army Restricted Area: Warning, the next sign reads. The one after that says, *Trespassers Will Be Persecuted* (sic) *to the Full Extent of the Law*, but the lettering is too small for me to read which federal statute we're breaking. The last warning reads, *Trespassers Will Be Shot on Sight*.

"Guess we better stay invisible then," Six says, chuckling.

I realize he's trying to put a good face on our predicament. I don't imagine he's any less terrified than I am.

A minute later, we reach the government laboratory. There's only a small painted sign to identify it. A tall barbed-wire fence surrounds what we can see of the installation.

Six stops the pickup and we get out. Leaving the truck doors open, we stand next to each other at the front of the truck in the light of the headlamps.

"I know the Blessed Virgin promised to watch over us, Antonio, but I'm scared as hell."

"Me, too, amigo."

We step up to the security gate. I finger my aunt's rosary in my overall pocket.

Most of the buildings look like temporary two-storey clapboard barracks. A couple of them seem to be of sturdier construction with stone foundations. There is a tall guard tower and a guard station beside the gate. A wooden water tower stands a short distance beyond. What looks like an equipment garage occupies the opposite side of the road. Our headlamps reveal no more.

An army guard and his German shepherd approach. Neither of them looks very friendly.

"Maybe we can just hand the Virgin's letter over to the guard and be on our way," Six tells me.

The soldier withdraws his pistol and aims it at Six through the barbed-wire gate. The dog barks fiercely, slobbering spit.

"Hands behind your head," the soldier commands.

Six puts his hands up and cups them behind his head. I reach into my jacket pocket to retrieve the letter from the Blessed Virgin Mary.

I hear clicks behind me. I turn to see two rifles aimed at my chest from three feet away. I've no idea where they came from. A second guard and dog have joined the first.

"We have a letter for Dr. Richard Feynman," I say.

"Bite the dirt," the soldier barks. "You, too, buster," he says to me.

I turn to see Six already on the ground. I lie in the dirt and put my hands on my neck, my right hand still holding the Virgin's letter. They don't seem the least curious about it.

I am surrounded by dusty boots. More dusty boots approach from inside the barbed-wire fence. Someone's spit splatters in the dirt.

One pair of boots steps so close I see only one boot, wearing white spats.

"On your feet," he says. "Real slow, boys."

The harsh voice does not match the figure standing before Six and me. He's a slight guy, fair-haired, shorter than my buddy and me. His stern expression tells me not to mess with him. His armband and helmet say he is Military Police.

I feel like I'm in a Gary Cooper movie. I get up, covered in dust. The letter is now dirty, too.

The barbed-wire gate, on tracks with rollers, slides open. The MP swings the metal barricade inward.

Six and I are frisked, and lightened of our wallets, loose change, and my Tia Ana's rosary. They leave our pockets turned inside out. I'm annoyed that we got our clean clothes dirty when they made us lie on the ground.

A soldier drives my uncle's pickup inside the compound. Two more begin rummaging through our stuff both inside the cab and in the back. The barricade clangs shut behind us and the gate slides closed. An officer with more stripes on his sleeve comes toward us.

"They're my problem now, Corporal."

"Yes, sir," the MP says, saluting his superior.

The officer takes the letter from my hand. He glances at it. His name tag identifies him as Sergeant Bragg.

Six and I are escorted by the two MPs into one of the nearby barracks. The room is so dim it is hard to see at first after coming from the flood-lit courtyard outside.

"Sit down," the officer says gruffly, pointing to two chairs against the wall.

There's a narrow oblong table between them.

The officer turns on an overhead light that blinds me briefly all over again.

It doesn't look like I pictured an interrogation room. It looks more like an unused office. The clock says fifteen minutes after midnight.

Six hiccups, a sign he's anxious. The sergeant motions to one of the guards stationed on either side of the door. The guard returns with a glass of water. The kind gesture surprises me.

"Thank you," Six says. "Hic."

Sergeant Bragg remains expressionless.

"How'd you two get past the main gate?"

"I guess we got lost," Six says. "I don't remember a front gate, Sergeant. Hic."

"Uh-huh," the sergeant says. "How'd you two find this place?"

"We asked around," I reply. "The townsfolk watch trucks and construction equipment go by all the time. This place is no secret to them. They told us this used to be a boys' camp."

"Who sent you?" he asks, glowering down at us.

Speak the truth clearly and you will have nothing to fear. I answer without thinking.

"The Blessed Virgin Mary."

"Jeeze. You sure it wasn't the tooth fairy?"

Six hiccups faster. I know he's getting irritated. He takes another swallow of water.

"Which one of you nancy-boys has the fancy handwriting?" the sergeant asks, glancing down at the letter in his hand and tossing it onto the table.

We are silent. I grab Six's hand beneath the table, hoping to calm him.

"All right. How do you nancy-boys know Dr. Feynman?"

"We don't," I reply. "We're just delivering a letter to him."

"Ever heard of a three-cent stamp?"

"It's not from us, Sir," I say, trying the polite route. "It's from the Blessed..."

"Yeah, yeah," he interrupts. "Save it for your famous last words."

Sergeant Bragg snatches up the letter and goes out. The two guards follow him but remain stationed outside the door.

I put my hand at the back of Six's neck and stroke it. That usually works. His hiccuping slows down and then stops.

"We're in a lot of trouble, aren't we, Antonio?"

I shrug. I don't want to tell him that I think we're going to be saints because we're going be martyrs.

"Remember the Virgin's promises," I say, as much to remind myself as him. "She said she'd watch over us and that you and I would always be together."

He smiles. I feel better seeing him smile. I want to lean over and kiss him, but I'm sure the sergeant would barge in as soon as I did so.

I glance at the clock on the wall. It's one-thirty in the morning. It seems like hours have passed. Six and I look at the half-empty water glass on the table and decide to share it.

We finish praying the rosary we began this morning.

Six leans back in his chair and closes his eyes. I listen to the rhythm of his breathing. Scared as I am, I nearly doze off myself.

We jerk wide-awake when the door bursts open. It's not the sergeant. The man who enters is wiry and athletic, kind of handsome, with dark, wavy hair. He looks pretty young. His ready smile reminds me of Mr. Archuleta, our science teacher.

"You're kids for cripes sake," the man says. "What was the sergeant thinking? He may have won a medal for bravery, but he's never gonna get one for common sense."

Six and I smile. We get to our feet. The man extends his hand to each of us and invites us to sit down again.

"I'm Dick Feynman," he says. "I brought you some fresh coffee. Only one cup, though. Plus the other half of my lunch: pastrami on rye from Sid's in town."

"Thank you," Six and I say.

"We haven't eaten all day," I tell him.

Six and I drink some coffee from the Thermos cup and I rip the half-a-sandwich in half.

"You boys can probably guess they're entertaining the idea that you're a couple of spies," Dr. Feynman tells us, rolling his eyes.

"Sergeant Bragg wants to know who the Nazi agent is who lured you both to betray the United States of America at the tender age of sixteen. In the next sentence, he said you were a couple of 'pansies,' saw you holding hands. I can't imagine what *Mata Hari* used as bait, then, if you two like boys."

"Yeah, we do," Six tells him. "We like each other. We're best friends."

"*Nihil humanus mihi alienus est,*" Dr. Feynman says.

"Nothing human is foreign to me," Six replies.

"Why does it not surprise me that you know that?" the doctor remarks.

"We just had that in our humanities class, Doctor. It was Terence," Six says. "We both know a little bit of Latin from attending mass, too."

"I'm far more interested in the letter you brought me than in your private lives. You can trust that I do not report to Sergeant Bragg.

"The United States government has gone to great lengths to conceal the information in your letter," he says, laughing.

"But I'm curious. I'm a scientist. If you're not secret agents, where did you come by that information? Some things haven't happened yet."

"The Blessed Virgin Mary gave us the letter, Dr. Feynman. That is the truth," I tell him. "We never read the letter. I have no idea what's in it."

"But your contact told you about *The Gadget*, the project we're working on here?"

"No," Six and I say in unison.

"I never heard of anything called *The Gadget*," I tell him.

Six and I get up and sit next to each other on the edge of the table. Dr. Feynman drags over another chair and sits backwards in it. Resting his forearms on the back, he leans forward, facing us. He raises his eyebrows and looks back and forth at my amigo and me.

"I believe you and Sixtus saw *something*," he says.

"Call me *Six*," my buddy tells the doctor.

"All right, Six. Can you describe what you saw?"

"I saw a beautiful woman descend from the sky on waves of light. I thought she was on fire at first and ran with the fire bucket to put her out."

"*The first principle is that you must not fool yourself,*" Dr. Feynman says, "*and you are the easiest person to fool.*"

We all smile.

"Don't you think the odds are pretty slim, Doctor, that my amigo and I would imagine exactly the same illusion?" Six asks him.

"I like you two. I think it'd be hard to put one over on you. So I'm willing to suspend disbelief—for now."

"Thanks, Dr. Feynman," I tell him.

"I certainly can't argue with what's in the letter. There were two long number sequences that might be either atomic masses, quantum variables, or stellar coordinates. I'm not sure. I'd have to run them past my colleagues. There are a couple of interesting theories presented as well, but nothing useful to our work here. I'd need more time to look it over."

"Makes us kind of unusual spies, don't you think, Dr. Feynman," Six says, "*providing* information instead of *stealing* it?"

The doctor laughs.

"You've got a point there, too," he says.

"Do you think you could get us out of here, Dr. Feynman?" I ask him. "We didn't mean to pry into any secrets. We were just trying to do what the Holy Mother asked us to do: deliver her letter to you. We don't want our families to worry. They think we've gone camping."

"You're good kids," Dr. Feynman says, smiling. "I believe you don't know any more than you've told me.

"I'm sure the sergeant has gone back to bed. I've sent the two MPs for papers that are in my office safe. For security reasons, I certainly couldn't give them the combination, so they'll have to wheel the safe over here. It'll take them a while."

He smiles a sly grin.

"Sit tight, guys. I'll send you off with whatever grub I can rustle up from the commissary. I'm going to get your personal effects from the sergeant's office, too. I'm actually a pretty good lock-pick and safe-cracker."

We laugh, but I don't think he's kidding us. Dr. Feynman is a strange bird. I like him.

Six and I pace up and down the small room. I'm tempted to peek behind the blinds and look out the window. Six tries the doorknob. It's unlocked, but I don't think we'd get far on foot.

The doctor gets back with a paper bag of food in waxed cartons. The aromas make me instantly hungry. I smell chicken soup.

There's also a large manila envelope in the bag with my and Six's names written on it. We take our wallets and change. Six picks up his pocket knife and I put my aunt's rosary back in the pocket of my Levi's.

Six and I dive into our food. None of it tastes fresh, but I'm not going to complain.

A knock at the door scares me and my amigo out of a year's growth.

"At ease," the doctor tells us. "Situation under control."

He answers the door.

"Excuse me, Dr. Feynman. Where would you like us to put the safe?"

"That was awfully quick. Um... There's an empty office upstairs. Think you can get it up there?"

"I don't know, Dr. Feynman. That safe's pretty heavy and those steps are kinda rickety. Maybe we oughta get a block-and-tackle."

"All right. I leave it up to you, Murphy. Absolutely no hurry."

"Thanks, Doc."

He closes the door.

"Eat up, boys. I'm gonna get youse sprung from this joint," he says, doing a bad Jimmy Cagney imitation.

"You're not gonna get in hot water on our account, are you, Dr. Feynman?" Six asks.

"Believe me, it wouldn't be the first time. It's better than the cold showers we have around here."

We laugh. Six crumbles soda crackers into his lukewarm soup—enough that his spoon could stand up in it.

"What's the story with the bucket of meteorites they found in your truck?" the doctor asks. "They didn't know what they were."

"We saw a huge meteor shower just before the Virgin's first appearance last June," Six tells him. "There are no major showers in June."

"So you've learned some astronomy in school?"

We nod.

"The night before last, before the Holy Mother's second visit, we also saw those strange zigzagging meteors again," I say. "What are they, Dr. Feynman?"

"Darned if I know," he replies. "I've seen them, too. My eyes either deceive me or else the objects operate on a kind of physics I can't explain. In short, they're impossible," he adds, chuckling. "Do you know what the Indians on the Jemez Pueblo call them?"

We shake our heads.

"Fastwalkers," he says.

"They sure are," I remark.

"What do scientists call them?" Six asks.

"We don't call them anything," Dr. Feynman tells us. "I have no idea what they are, Six. No one else here has managed to witness a single one of them. I'm the only one. The army term for them is *non-reference targets.*"

"You mean they'd shoot at them?" I ask.

"It wouldn't surprise me, Antonio. But to a scientist, there is nothing more intriguing than a mystery."

"Religious people like them, too," I remark.

"Yes, I suppose," the doctor says, grinning. "Faith is fine, but it's doubt that gets you an education. *I'd rather have a question that can't be answered than an answer that can't be questioned.*"

His gaze is penetrating. He's a very intense but likeable fellow.

"So, back to the iron-nickel meteorites," he says.

"That bucketful is only a fraction of the whole pile," Six says. "It looked like they'd been plunked down in one spot by one of those big junkyard magnets."

"We asked the Virgin what we should do with them," I tell the doctor. "She told us she had nothing to do with gathering them up. It's sure a puzzle."

We re-pack the leftover food in the paper sack. Dr. Feynman opens the door. The bright lights in the courtyard are off.

He stands in the doorway and lights a cigarette. He looks up and down the narrow courtyard, puffing on his coffin-nail as though he hadn't a care in the world. The smoke curls around his head.

"I know how to get in touch with you boys. Your addresses are in the sergeant's report," he tells us, exhaling a cloud. "But if you want to reach me, this place is at P.O. Box 1663 in Santa Fe. Got it?"

"Santa Fe?" Six asks.

"More red herrings to put Nazi agents off the scent," Dr. Feynman says, laughing. "Keep in mind that anything you write me will be read by several pairs of eyes before it reaches mine.

"I advise you to keep a notebook. The mind plays tricks, especially with memory."

"I *have* a notebook, Dr. Feynman. Six gave it to me."

"Good. Be sure to use it. Nothing beats careful observation. Get ready to move, men," the doctor says.

He drops the butt of his cigarette in the dirt, crushing it with his shoe.

"This is your chance," he says at last. "Quick, but not in a hurry. It's a straight shot from the mechanics' garage to the front security gate."

"Thank you, Dr. Feynman," Six says.

He slaps me and Six on the shoulder. We sidestep the safe in the courtyard.

My amigo and I dart across the road to Tio's truck. Six and I open the doors of the pickup and put our shoulders to the task of pushing it to the front gate so we don't make any noise. I use my fear to give me strength. I steer as best I can. Dr. Feynman has already swung the barricade open and slid the barbed-wire gate aside.

Once we are beyond the gate, the doctor steps out of the guardhouse and walks toward the pickup. We wait for him, standing there with our doors still open.

The doctor reaches into his inside jacket pocket and hands me the Blessed Mother's letter.

"I don't need to keep this," he says. "I've copied it all down. You may need the letter to prove your case of a messenger from the heavens."

"Thank you, Dr. Feynman," I say, tucking the letter into my jacket pocket. "God bless you."

"It couldn't hurt."

Six comes over, holding one of the meteorites from the fire bucket. He hands the iron stone to Dr. Feynman.

"I'm sure the Holy Mother wouldn't mind if we gave you one," I tell the doctor.

"Thank you, boys, for *this* messenger from the heavens," he says, smiling. "Not so long ago, no one believed stones fell from the sky. It's always best to keep an open mind. I'll have the lab run some tests on it. I'll let you know what they find.

"Good luck to you both," he adds, shaking my hand and reaching over to shake Six's. "I'll be in touch once this endless war is over and I'm no longer under the microscope. Let me know if you hear or see anything else."

Six and I climb into the pickup. I take the wheel. My hands tremble. I'm still so scared. I'm afraid we're going to get shot escaping.

Dr. Feynman lights another cigarette with his Zippo and taps the driver's door. I roll down the window and start the engine.

"You might receive a visit from federal agents," he says. "But don't worry. You did nothing wrong except get lost and wander onto government property. I don't think Sergeant Bragg really believes you're a pair of Nazi spies, either.

Speak the truth clearly and you'll have nothing to fear."

I smile. It is the very thing the Blessed Virgin told us to do.

I roll up my window and drive off.

The last thing we see of the Los Alamos laboratory is the zigzagging red glow of Dr. Feynman's cigarette as he waves to us in the dark.

* 2 *

We drive and drive, taking turns every so often, hardly talking. I think it's only fear that's keeping us awake. I spend more time looking behind us in the review mirror than I do paying attention to the road ahead.

I take the back roads in a place where they're all back roads, heading in the general direction of home. Except for the road signs' occasional agreement with Six's maps, I'd have said we were lost.

At last the sun comes up. We are just a little south of Santa Fe. We haven't been followed—at least not so far. I pull to the side of the road under a clump of aspen trees and rest for a minute. Then we recite today's rosary.

I feel so much better now that *mi compa* and I have accomplished our mission for the Blessed Virgin Mary. A weight and a great responsibility has been lifted from our shoulders. I am both relieved and proud that we pulled it off.

Six offers to drive and I let him. Still sleepy, I lean against him and close my eyes. I am jostled awake by a series of ruts and potholes. The road is like a rusty washboard.

Realizing we're not going to make it to Rocks & a Hard Place in Escondida without taking another break, Six pulls over beneath a shady grove of cottonwoods.

We stretch out on the ground and get a half-hour's nap in. I awaken with Six's hand on my chest, his head on my shoulder. I try not stir so he can get more shuteye, but he soon wakes up, too.

"I can take over driving now, amigo," I tell him. "The nap helped."

"OK," he says.

At last I see a place to stop for breakfast outside of Albuquerque. It's one o'clock in the afternoon. Our times for eating and sleeping are all mixed up, scrambled. I order a *huevos rancheros* omelet with red chilies. My amigo orders his with green chilies.

Six dives into his *huevos*. He smiles at me with salsa dripping down to his chin. I realize how blessed we are to live in America.

I think of all the people in places ravaged by the war who went to bed hungry last night and who have nothing to eat this morning, either. Here we are, stuffing our faces.

We pay with our last dusty dollar and leave a dime on the counter.

Our big breakfast seems to energize Six. It makes me sleepy. He takes over driving again. I lean against him and pull my hat down.

I dream I am sitting beneath an apple tree, like in the Andrews Sisters song. Six sits beside me, our shoulders touching. He points and I look up. The tree is so full of apples the branches bend almost to the ground.

The breeze stirs. An apple falls and clocks me on the head. Six turns to me, laughing. He nudges me.

"We're here," he says.

"Here? Where?" I ask.

The apple tree fades. I open my eyes.

The truck jostles into the bumpy parking lot of Rocks & a Hard Place. My cowboy hat falls off my head.

"Feel better?" my amigo asks, smiling his dimpled grin.

"Uh-huh, a little," I reply, retrieving my hat from the dirty floor of the pickup.

We get out of the truck and walk to the *portál*. The bell above the door jangles. Mr. Jeremiah Carson looks up from his worktable and takes off his Coke-bottle glasses.

"There you are," he says, smiling.

He gets up, taking an envelope from a drawer in the table. He comes over. The envelope has our names on it. It looks a lot thinner than I was expecting a hundred-thirty bucks to look.

"Good afternoon, Mr. Carson," Six says to him.

The shop owner nods.

"You boys look kinda bedraggled. You been chased by a bobcat?" he asks, chuckling.

"Somethin' like that," Six says.

Mr. Carson takes our money from the envelope.

"A hundred-thirty simoleons," he says, counting out just three bills. "I thought you boys'd get a kick outta seein' a genuine Benjamin Franklin—*your* genuine Ben Franklin."

He holds up the hundred-dollar bill for our inspection, setting the ten and the twenty on the counter.

"Just think," Six remarks. "Ol' Ben Franklin was never even president and he's on the biggest bill of all."

"Not hardly," Mr. Carson replies. "They go all the way up to the $10,000 bill. Ever heard of Salmon P. Chase? It's his mug that's on the ten-thousand-dollar note."

"*No manches*," I say. "No kidding. I don't think we have to worry about ever coming across one of those."

The owner laughs. He puts our money back in the envelope and hands it to Six.

"Thanks, Mr. Carson," Six and I say.

My amigo puts the money in his dirty jacket. We turn to leave.

"Don't forget my offer to buy up any more meteorites you boys come across. If you can't make it up this way, you can always mail 'em to me. I'll send you a check. Here's my card."

I have one of his cards from the last time, but I've no idea what's become of it. I accept a new one.

"Adios," Mr. Carson says.

We return the farewell and go out.

Once back at the truck, Six takes out the envelope and removes the hundred-dollar bill. We each finger it and look at each other.

"After we get Tio's radio fixed," I suggest, "we can set aside whatever's left for any future missions for the Blessed Virgin Mary."

"Great idea," Six says. "It might be good to contribute twenty dollars to Brother Asinus's chapel to the Holy Mother, too, don't you think?"

"OK," I reply.

"There," Six remarks, brushing his hands together. "All spent. Easy come, easy go," he says, holding up his empty palms.

We laugh and climb into the pickup. I feel so lighthearted. I take the wheel again and turn back onto the paved road.

Six leans against me for a nap. Before long, I'm seeing double and can't hold my eyes open any longer. I nudge my amigo awake. I pull over and we trade places. He doesn't look any more awake than I feel.

"What d'ya say we just park here for a while so we can *both* catch a coupla winks?" he suggests.

Six leans against his door and I lean against him. He lays his arm over my shoulder, resting his hand on my chest. It feels awfully nice.

Tired as I am, I can't get my mind on track to getting a nap in. All I can think about is getting cozy with my best friend. It's been on my mind all day.

I never manage to quite fall asleep. Six squirms and I sit up.

"Feel better?" he asks.

"A little," I say.

"We oughta look for a pleasant place to pull over for the night," Six suggests. "We're not gonna make it back home until tomorrow anyhow. We've got almost a hundred miles to go."

"You're the official navigator of this expedition," I tell him. "I rely on you."

My amigo smiles.

"And you are *mi compás*," he says. "I can't be lost when you're with me."

His remark makes me smile. I'm so grateful for his love and friendship. I'd never have completed the mission for the Holy Mother without his help. I think the Holy Mother knew that.

In the eye-blink town of San Antonio, New Mexico, Six pulls into a filling station.

"What? We outta gas already?" I ask.

"No, but they got a public telephone," he replies, pointing to the Bell Telephone sign. "I want to call my grandpa and let them know we won't be home. I'll ask Gramps to go over and let your aunt and uncle know."

He gets out of the truck and fishes in his pockets for change.

"I have no idea how expensive a telephone call is, Antonio. You got any change?"

I slide forward on the seat and reach into my dusty Levi's, handing him a dime and three nickels. From my other pocket I pull out my Tia's rosary.

"I don't know if that'd work," Six says, smiling. "What number would I dial?"

"Et cum Spiri 2-2-0," I tell him, repeating our old joke that the Latin mass response is really God's telephone number.

We have a good laugh, the first since fulfilling the Blessed Virgin's mission. I feel so light and happy. I'm glad Six and I will have one more night to spend together before returning home.

He goes into the filling station office to use their pay telephone. I can see him through their big front window. I watch his pantomime as he talks to his grandpa with his hands. I don't think he's on the telephone more than a couple of minutes before he hangs up.

On the way back to the truck, he takes off his dusty work jacket. I'm getting warm, too, and remove mine, putting it over the back of the seat. Our T-shirts are no longer white. They're streaked with red dirt and sweat.

Six hops up into the truck. He hands my change back to me.

"Maybe we could get my uncle's truck cleaned up a little before we get back," I suggest.

"OK," he says. "Wouldn't hurt to get ourselves washed up, too. We oughta be coming up on the Rio Grande pretty soon. Maybe we can find a place to go swimming."

"That sure sounds good to me," I reply. "We'll get an early start in the morning and be home in time to take my aunt to mass."

"What's the hurry?" Six asks. "We completed the Blessed Mother's assignment. You can take it easy now, amigo. Let's enjoy our last day together."

He touches my bare arm. It sends a thrill though me that travels down to my toes. I picture snuggling up next to him with our sleeping bags snapped together. The thought conjures a delicious anticipation stirring in my blood. I pray to God I know what to do when the hour comes for me and *mi mejor amigo* to at last give ourselves to each other.

* 3 *

Six and I are dusty and sweaty and dirty. Everything is coated with grit from having the windows rolled down in order to stay awake.

Up the road, far outside San Antonio, the last town we pass, Six turns onto a dirt side road. It leads to a shady grove of cottonwoods and willows. They wouldn't be there if there weren't some source of water nearby.

Without saying a word, we decide this will be the perfect spot to have our supper and our night's rest. This will be our last night to sleep together beneath our tent of stars.

Six and I sit in the tall grass near the wide, swiftly-flowing river that splashes and gurgles over stones near the shore. We share our last beer and eat the grilled cheese sandwiches Dr. Feynman sent along with us. They are a bit mashed and squishy.

"A whole lot better than the prison food would've been," Six says, smiling.

"Maybe," I say, jabbing his ribs. "I don't think much of army cooking so far."

The escalation of our jabs and pokes leads to our wrestling on the ground. Neither of us gains the upper hand for long. Our match is more about struggling against one another, feeling the other's straining muscles, than it is about winning. We are both out of breath and lie back on the grass.

It would be so easy to fall asleep right here, lying next to *mi compa*, lulled by the rushing water. It is cool in the shade.

I sit up again. Six is already off in dreamland. I'm not surprised. He's done most of the driving today.

I'd like to get the back of the truck cleaned up before it grows dark. I don't want to disturb Six, though. I get up slowly, trying not to make noise.

Crouching down at the river bank, I put my hand in the water. It's pretty cold for the end of summer. It flows here from the mountains up north.

I hear rustling behind me. My billfold is lifted from the hip pocket of my overalls.

My amigo pushes me headlong into the river. The icy water takes my breath away. I stand up gasping. My Levi's feel like they weigh twenty pounds.

Six laughs his head off. I trudge towards shore and stand on the bank.

"You look a lot better," he says, chuckling. "You probably smell better, too."

I stand dripping.

"How could you possibly think you weren't gonna go swimming, too?" I ask him, grabbing hold of his shoulders.

"Sorry, amigo. You won't be able to push me in," he tells me.

"No, why not?"

"Because I'm gonna jump in," he replies, grinning.

With that, Six pushes me backwards from the bank into the icy water again. He lands on top of me, both of us completely submerged.

I'm glad the stones in the river are worn round and smooth. Downstream, the clear water grows cloudy with the dirt from our clothes.

Six jumps up out of the cold water, panting. Water streams down his face, plastering his hair to his forehead. His T-shirt is transparent. His Levi's glisten. My heart thumps.

As soon as he catches his breath, he wrestles me into the deep water, dunking my head. I swallow water and come up choking. I call a time-out before he wraps his arms around me and plunges us both underwater again.

My heavy wet clothes make it feel as though we are wrestling in slow-motion. We tumble in and out of the water. Six and I wear ourselves out as much from laughing as from our roughhousing.

We splash onto the narrow shore of the Rio Grande and climb out. I see Six's wallet next to mine in the grass. My aunt's rosary, in the pocket of my overalls, has not only been blessed by the Holy Mother, it has now also been baptized.

"That's one way to do laundry," Six says, laughing.

"It's a heck of a lot more fun this way, that's for sure," I tell him. "Except maybe in winter."

We strip out of our T-shirts and wring them out. We hang them in the sun over the branches of a hickory tree at the edge of the unfenced meadow. I think the sun will set before our heavy denim overalls get dry.

My amigo and I let down the tailgate and sit on the edge. We tug at our sodden cowboy boots. It's a lot easier to hang onto the tailgate and let one another pull our boots off.

We decorate a hazelnut bush with our white socks and put our boots on the front hood of the truck, angling them to drain downward.

Six and I take our knapsacks and dusty sleeping bags from the back of the pickup. We unsnap the sleeping bags and, each taking a corner, shake them out downwind. We lay them out to air in the meadow.

We each put a hand on the fire bucket laden with meteorites and lift it out of the back of the truck. Six dumps the iron stones onto the ground.

Taking turns, we walk barefoot to the river to fill the bucket, splashing water onto Tio's pickup. I nearly forget to roll up the windows first.

A few bucketfuls of water land wide of the mark and I accidentally-on-purpose douse my amigo. He's quite happy to return the favor. Our overalls are never going to dry out at this rate. But my uncle's truck is sparkling clean. Sunlight glistens on the glass.

We dip our kerchiefs in the red bucket and wipe the dust out of the cab. Six cleans off his grandpa's ice chest. He pours the last bit of dirty water from the bucket onto the floor to wash away the spilled coffee from the other day. We leave the doors open and sit on the tailgate. The sun feels good on my shoulders.

"That was refreshing," Six says. "Is there anything left to eat?"

"Just the apple at the bottom of the ice chest," I tell him.

"Wanna share it?" he asks.

"Sure," I reply, getting down to fetch what will be our dessert.

I toss the apple to him and he catches it.

He takes a bite of the warm apple and hands it to me. I jump up onto the tailgate and sit beside him. We pass the apple back and forth. He gives me a sweet apple kiss.

I rest my hand on his damp overalls. The wet denim does nothing to hide my buddy's growing arousal.

Six grabs my hand before I can pull it away.

"Please, don't," he begs. "I love it when you touch me, Antonio."

We look at one another. Six puts his hand on the back of my neck, pulling me to him for a long kiss. The apple core rolls out of my hand and lands in the tall grass.

Six jumps down and stands between my knees, facing me. Putting his arms around my waist, he pulls me to the edge of the tailgate. I get down and fold my arms around him. He kisses me for all he's worth.

Mi compa leads me into the still-sunny meadow. He lowers me onto the ground and lies down beside me. We turn and look at each other.

I climb on top of Six. He wraps his arms around me. We kiss so hard and so frantically it's hard to get my breath.

We exchange positions several times, tumbling back and forth across the rough grass and wildflowers. We roll in and out of the sun's slanting rays the way we splashed in and out of the water of the Rio Grande.

The grass is prickly on my bare back. It smells like mown hay as we crush it with our wrestling. Our damp overalls are flecked with seeds.

What started out as horseplay now feels like making love.

Sitting up next to me, Six rubs my chest and stomach. It feels awfully good. His hand is warm. He looks at me. I see myself in his eyes.

Little by little, his fingers follow the ridge of hair from my chest down to my Levi's. He undoes the top button and pushes his hand down inside. I give an involuntary moan.

Leaning on one elbow, he continues his exploration. I yank the rest of my buttons open. I pop up through the fly of my shorts. Six laughs.

Is today the day? I wonder. *Is this the hour when we finally give the rest of ourselves to each other?*

I sit up and push him gently back into the prairie grass. I feel his hard penis even through his wet overalls. I pop the buttons which he strains to escape, rubbing his wet boxer shorts against his hard-on. It throbs in my hand. I pull the waistband down.

Six reaches over and pulls my shorts down, freeing me. I roll over on top of him, putting my legs between his. I push my crotch against him. We rub up and down, back and forth. I come to the edge several times but do not tumble over it. It is a wonderful sensation, one I want to stretch out so it lasts forever.

"If we keep going, I'm not gonna be able to stop, Antonio," he says, his chest heaving against mine.

"I don't want you to, amigo," I tell him.

"You sure?" he asks, wrinkling his forehead.

"As sure as I am of anything, Six."

He folds his arms around my naked back. His touch feels so warm and wonderful. Grabbing my denim-clad butt, he pulls me closer.

We roll onto our sides and scoot next to each other. We resume our thrusting, lying side-by-side, chest-to-chest, dick-to-dick, skin-against-skin. I am so excited it feels like I'm going to fly apart at the seams or have a heart attack.

"Oh, Antonio. Oh, my God. Antonio," he shouts.

His eyes widen. I feel him throbbing against me as he spurts his warm sperm onto my belly. It sends me straight over the cliff of my own climax.

"Six," I exclaim, sucking air through my teeth. "Oh, how I love you, Six."

He smiles at me, flashing his dimples, as I come on him. He silences my moans with a kiss. His lips still taste like apple.

We wriggle together, enjoying the sticky, slippery mess we made on one another. Then we put our droopy erections back inside our undershorts and button up our overalls.

We sit up, leaning against the rough bark of one of the cottonwoods. He takes my hand.

"There," he says, leaning over and kissing me. "We've done it. We don't have to wonder any more what it will be like."

"Oh, Six. It was the most wonderful feeling I have ever known. I love you so much—more than ever.

"It certainly didn't feel like a sin to me, either, amigo," I tell him. "Instead, I think God gave you and me one more way to love each other."

Six smiles. He appears different—more handsome, more beautiful. He looks at me in a different way, too. His gaze is deeper, somehow darker. I've always known Six loves me, as best friends do. But now I see in his eyes that he also wants me. I think we have finally grown up. We are no longer boys.

He tickles my bare foot with his big toe.

"Come on," he suggests. "Let's get out of these wet overalls while there's still a little daylight left to dry 'em."

We strip to our boxer shorts, now streaked with indigo dye from our soaked Levi's. Standing on the running boards, we hang our damp overalls on the roof of the truck, the legs dangling over the windscreen. We strip out of our shorts and hang them from the door handles.

Naked, Six and I fetch our sleeping bags from the meadow and lay them down in the back of the now-clean truck, snapping them together to make a single bed. We put our knapsacks against the cab.

Six loads the meteorites into the fire bucket and we hoist it up into the back.

Taking the apple core from the ground beside the truck, he picks up the shovel and walks to the field. I follow him.

My amigo whistles the Andrews Sisters' apple tree song. I'm not sure he knows he's doing it. It makes me smile.

Striking the point of the shovel into the ground, he digs up two chunks of sod. He drops the core into the hole and flips the sod over on top of it.

"We'll come back in fifty years and pick a bushel of apples for a batch of *empanadas*. What d'ya say?"

"I don't think I'll ever forget this place, Six," I tell him, "*especially* the trees. I'm gonna draw them when we get home, just as I saw them: looking up from the ground, like their branches were holding up the sky."

We stand, holding hands, watching the sun go over the blazing horizon at the edge of the meadow. It grows chilly quickly.

After gathering our clothes from the trees and bushes, we toss them, along with our boots and overalls, into the cab where they will be protected from the dew. Our stuff is mostly dry.

My amigo and I slip naked into our joint sleeping bag and scoot down into it. His skin is cold. I rub him in as many places as I can reach with my hands and feet.

"Mmm," he purrs.

We fumble beneath the covers, touching one another, feeling our erections grow in the other's hand.

Six climbs on top of me. There is nothing between us this time but our skin.

We push and rub against one another. I hold onto him with all my might, feeling the muscles in his back and buttocks tighten and relax, tighten and relax, in the rhythm of a loping horse.

I see a fire kindled in his eyes as the crest of the moon rises over his shoulder. Our ejaculations come in the same moment.

Our moans sound like a pair of yowling coyotes. Six howls. I laugh and tickle his ribs. Anyone who hears us would think we've been drinking.

My amigo and I, breathless, lie back and hold hands. We turn to each other every so often, not saying a word, just smiling. When Six no longer does so, I know he is asleep.

As I drift to sleep, Brother Asinus's words come to mind: *You must do as both your heart and your conscience tell you. They need not contradict each other.*

I thank God for my friend's love and pray to be ever worthy of it.

I watch the sky, growing sleepier. The world is an awfully beautiful place.

The moon sets. More stars appear.

I fall asleep counting them—like beads on a rosary.

CHAPTER FIVE

ARS AMATORIA
The Art of Loving

I return Tia's rosary to her on our way to the eleven o'clock mass the next morning.

"You did not forget, Antonio. God bless you. Oh, my child," she says. "*Nuestra Madre* has blessed my rosary."

My aunt clutches the rosary in her right hand and touches her heart with the left. She holds her beads throughout mass. Her devotion inspires me.

After driving my aunt back to her house, Six and I return home to my house. It is good to be back after a whole week away. Everything familiar looks slightly unfamiliar.

My uncle slumps, asleep in his rocker, beneath the *portál*. He awakes when I close the truck door. He has difficulty getting up from the rocking chair.

"Did it rain?" my uncle asks. "The truck looks pretty good."

"No, Tio. We washed it," Six says.

"Thank you, boys. It looks almost good as new..."

We smile at him.

"...so long as you ignore all the dents and scrapes," he adds.

Though the rest of him appears frail, his eyes sparkle with humor.

"I am so happy to see you boys home again, safe and sound."

"We are glad to *be* home, Tio. We missed you, too."

I take his elbow and help him into the kitchen. Six holds the screen door. It is lunchtime.

* * *

Two weeks after our return from Los Alamos, Tio Nicolás got a visit from a pair of G-men in dark glasses. They left their card in case my uncle remembers anything else.

"Anything else?" I ask him. "What'd you tell them, Tio?"

"I said you are my nephew and Six is your best friend, and that you are both still in high school.

"I told them I loaned you my truck to go camping and said you must've gotten lost. I laughed out loud when they hinted you might be spies."

"'*No es cierto?*' I asked them. 'Are you kidding me? So how do they report to Nazi headquarters? We don't even have a telephone.'

"That seemed to convince them, but the one G-man still had to go outside to see that there were no telephone lines coming to the house.

"I offered them a beer, but they said they were on duty. I don't expect we'll see them again, *mi sobrino*."

I am glad my Tio did not ask me any more questions about our trip. I don't want to lie to him. I'm in enough trouble with Father Miguel after confessing to losing my virginity with Six at the end of our trip. He's not as strict Father Consuelo.

We received a short note from Dr. Feynman last week. It didn't come from the secret post office box in Santa Fe. It was written on the stationery of a hospital in Albuquerque where he has been spending every weekend visiting his wife Arline. She has tuberculosis and is very sick. My amigo and I pray to the Blessed Virgin for Mrs. Feynman.

The doctor also said he had some news about our meteorite and would write us again soon.

* 2 *

Our junior year of high school hasn't turned out to be the breeze my amigo and I expected. Our load of schoolwork is pretty heavy. It's the end of March, 1945. Thank God, there are only two months of classes left.

Six and I work at Mila-Grow Nursery & Greenhouse every day after school and on Saturdays now.

My Tio is very sick. He has gotten skinny except for his stomach. It's hard to get him to eat anything but soup from Tia Ana. She looks in on him when I am at school. My uncle can hardly do anything for himself. There is now a chamber pot in his bedroom and a cane hooked on his bedstead

Six and I get hardly a minute to spend together when we are not at work or school or doing our chores at home. When I don't get to see Six, I feel lonely and incomplete.

Though we haven't made love since the last day of our camping trip last autumn, all I can think about is getting cozy with *mi mejor amigo*. The strength of my desire for him scares me. I distract myself with my chores and reading and wood carving, but on some days, I feel ready to explode.

I dream every couple of nights about lying next to Six and awaken with a wet spot in my boxer shorts.

Father Miguel is now my confessor. He says that wet dreams don't count because I'm not awake.

Yeah, but aren't I me in my dreams? I want to ask him.

I am so confused. The only thing I know for sure is that I love Six more than anyone else on earth.

* * *

The war in Europe is winding down, thanks to the help of the Russians on the Eastern Front. Japan, though, looks like it might still be waiting for us after we graduate next year. Six and I talk about enlisting then, after we turn eighteen.

The longer the war drags on, the longer it will be until the Blessed Virgin's next visit. She promised to come to us again when the war is over.

Six and I are eager to set out on whatever mission the Holy Mother entrusts to us next. Though I cannot speak for Six, I do not fail to recite the rosary every single day. Sometimes we say it together.

My amigo has been spending a lot of time over at a schoolmate's house this past winter. Hypatia is a senior. Her father bought her a big Newtonian telescope. I got to look through it once, but Six has the real interest in astronomy and knows how to operate it.

Six wants to learn everything he can from Hypatia before she graduates in two months and goes off to Barnard College at Columbia University on her scholarship. She's already smarter than some of our teachers.

I don't tell Six how jealous his spending so much time with Hypatia makes me feel. I pray hard not to be that way, but sometimes I can't help it.

Six has been late a few times when he was supposed to come over to my uncle's house to spend the night with me, but, until now, he never stood me up.

This time I fall asleep at the kitchen table waiting for him. When I awaken, it is morning. My neck aches. I have to look in on Tio Nicolás and get ready for school.

Six does not show up for classes and avoids me at work. He seems unable to look me in the eye. My heart sinks into my stomach.

After work, when I drive him home in my uncle's pickup, Six still doesn't look well. He's pale and shaky. I want to ask him what happened last night, but, more than that, I want him to level with me and just tell me.

"Are we gonna talk?" I ask. "Do you got time to fit me in?"

"*Cierto*," he says. "I'm so sorry I missed you last night, amigo. Please forgive me. Can you stay over tonight? We'll talk about it."

"You know I can't, Six. I've got to make sure Tio is comfortable."

We arrive at his grandma's and grandpa's house. I call them *Grandma* and *Grandpa*, too, just like Six calls my uncle *Tio*. We feel honored to be included in each other's family.

"At least come in for a minute," Six says.

He puts his hand on my shoulder and we march up to the porch.

"There you are," his grandma says to him. "Just in time."

When she sees me behind Six, she puts another plate and napkin and silverware on the table. She smiles at me and hugs me.

"It's been so long since you ate with us, Antonio. We're having rabbit stew tonight after our neighbor's successful hunt."

"I love rabbit stew," I tell her truthfully, hanging my jacket on a hook beside the kitchen door.

"Will you be staying over?" Grandpa asks me. "It has been a while since you spent a night under our roof."

"No, Grandpa," I reply. "I can't. I have to make sure Tio is all right."

Grandpa is still handsome among all his creases and wrinkles and white hair. I think that is what my amigo will look like in his old age.

His grandpa pops a loaf of bread from its pan and slices it on the cutting board, placing it in the center of the kitchen table. The bread is still steaming inside.

Grandma sets a crock of butter on the table next to it. Next comes the Dutch oven full of rabbit stew. She removes the lid. The aromas make me want to drool like a hungry dog. I'm ready to dive in.

"Will you please say our grace tonight, Antonio?" Grandpa asks.

I am caught off-guard. We Catholics recite most prayers from memory. Six's Lutheran family always makes up their benedictions on the spot. At least I had no time to get nervous. I clear my throat and cross myself.

"Dear Savior, bless the food that is set before us. Bless those who prepared it and those who eat it. And bless those who go hungry. Amen."

They nod their heads in approval. Six taps my foot under the table and smiles at me.

Grandma brings a steaming bowl of egg noodles to the table, several chunks of butter melting and disappearing among the noodles. Grandpa spoons rabbit stew onto the mounds of noodles on our plates. Six passes the bread and butter. I put on the brakes so I do not devour my meal like a starving beggar.

"How *is* your Tio Nicolás?" Grandpa asks.

I swallow my mouthful before answering.

"His pain is worse, Grandpa," I tell him. "I feel so bad that I cannot help him. I hold his hand and read to him. It takes his mind off his pain for a little while."

I get in two more mouthfuls of stew and noodles before Six's grandma asks the next question.

"What do the doctors say, Antonio?"

"They say he shouldn't drink brandy with his medicine, but he says it helps. I think it just makes him sleepy. He doesn't like to talk about his cancer."

"I will ask your Tia Ana. Your uncle talks to her some times," Grandma says. "Eat up, boys. That includes you, Grandpa. There's enough for seconds all around."

Six and I puff out our cheeks and pat our bellies.

"No, Grandma. Thank you," Six tells her. "But if there were a slice or two of your hobo bread to spare, my amigo and I wouldn't turn it down."

He smiles at his grandma. I help clear the table and put our bowls in the dishpan.

Grandma Matilda raps the bottom of the coffee can in which she's baked the hobo bread. It is a kind of coffee cake with raisins. It comes out in a round loaf. She puts a slice on each of our plates. Six and Grandpa slather theirs with butter.

"We are working tomorrow, Gram," Six says. "We've both got to be there by eight. I'll fend for myself in the morning."

"I'll leave something for your lunch in the icebox," she tells him. "Make sure you don't forget it, honey."

When we've all finished our hobo bread, Six and I excuse ourselves from the table. I kiss Grandma good-night and shake Grandpa's hand.

"I'm going outside to say good-night to Antonio. I'll be back in a minute," Six tells his grandparents.

I take my jacket from the hook. Six's grandma hands him her shopping list, scribbled on the back of an old envelope. He puts it in his jacket pocket. I smile to myself, remembering our earlier jacket and letter mix-up.

"Your grandpa will pick you up after work tomorrow, dear, so you can get our provisions for the week."

"Yes, Gram."

We go out to the backyard. The glow from the kitchen windows lights our way. I open the truck door.

"So," I ask Six. "Are you gonna tell me what's up? Or do I have to go home wondering what I did wrong?"

Six rushes up to me, almost knocking me off my feet. He throws his arms around me and nestles his head against my neck and shoulder. His chest heaves with deep sobbing. His tears wet my cheek and neck.

"O... O, Antonio," he says, his voice catching. "No. No. It's not you. It's me. O, I'm so sorry... I... I..."

He steps back and looks into my eyes.

"That's all right," I tell him. "I forgive you."

"Don't you want to know what I've done before you forgive me?"

"Nope. It doesn't matter. I forgive you no matter what."

He hugs me tightly and puts his head back on my shoulder, crying harder than before. I rub the back of his neck.

When the storm at last blows over, we let go of one another. His face is red and puffy and tear-streaked. The shoulder of my workshirt is wet.

"I spent last night at Hypatia's house—on her floor," Six confesses, wrapping me in another bear hug. "I got very drunk and never made it home. Gram and Gramps don't know. They probably think I left for work extra early this morning."

I wonder if I haven't forgiven him too soon, but I can't go back on my word. I take hold of his upper arms and push him gently away, looking into his eyes.

"I forgave you, remember?" I tell him. "So what happened?"

My amigo sputters and stammers before finally getting the words out.

"Hypatia's parents were not at home. We looked at Jupiter, at two of its moons, actually. She put her arm around my waist as I peered into her telescope. It was cold, like tonight, and it felt nice. She knows you and I like each other. I thought she was being friendly.

"We got cold so she invited me inside to get warm. She said her father always drank a little brandy to warm up. She said she liked it, too."

"She came back to the living room with a bottle of Presidente brandy—like your Tio likes—and two glasses on a tray. It tasted like medicine. It took my breath away and made me choke. Hypatia laughed. She told me a real man knows how to drink and poured a little more in my glass.

"Her sofa kept getting smaller. She was right next to me, almost in my lap. I could feel her brandy breath on my neck.

"The other thing a real man knows how to do is make love,' she said. 'Do you and Antonio, you know, ever make out?' she asked.

"'Sometimes,' I said.

"'Show me,'" Hypatia dared.

"She closed her eyes and leaned toward me, puckering up. There was no more sofa left. I fell on the floor with a crash and hit my head, though I was pretty dizzy even before then."

"So where is this all going?" I ask Six.

"Oh, Antonio. I love you—more than I love anybody, amigo. You've gotta believe me."

My heart sinks into my stomach. He touches my shoulder.

"She got undressed and got on top of me. We had sex. It just happened. I couldn't help it, Antonio."

"The hell you couldn't."

I push him away so hard it knocks him to the ground. He reaches his hand up to me.

"*Vete al diablo!* Go to hell!" I say, turning my back and climbing up into the truck.

I slam the door so hard it surprises me I didn't break the window. In the mirror I see Six pick himself up from the ground and dust himself off. He holds his hand out.

I take off so fast down his grandpa's driveway that I spray Six with dirt and gravel.

My eyes swim with tears. I slam the steering wheel until my hands hurt. I pull over until I can see where I'm going again.

* * *

Unable to sleep a wink, I toss back and forth between clenched-fist anger that makes me wish Six were dead and a heavy, tear-filled sorrow that makes me wish I were dead.

I pretend it's a dream, but it's all too real. Six and I, despite the Blessed Mother's promise, have reached the end of our friendship. I feel so bad I want to cry until I'm all dried up.

I am useless at work the next day. At least I don't also have to avoid Six. The boss sends him on a round of errands and deliveries that keeps him out of my sight all afternoon.

Leaving work for the day before Six gets back, I notice his grandpa waiting for him out front of Mila-Grow Greenhouse. I say "Hello" to Gramps and drive off. I can't wait to get home and start my other job: taking care of my Tio Nicolás.

I hang my work jacket by the kitchen door. The house smells bad. I'd like to open a window, but I don't want my uncle to catch a chill.

I pass his bedroom on the way up to my room and poke my head in. My uncle has gotten tangled in the bedsheets and was unable to reach the chamber pot.

"I am sorry, *mi sobrino*. Please forgive me," he says.

"*Cierto*, Tio. It wasn't your fault."

I get him into the chair and wipe him off, wrapping the blanket around his shoulders. There are no more clean sheets or underwear for my uncle. Tomorrow is laundry day, the only day I have to do wash. I bring my sheet for him from upstairs.

After getting him situated on his pillows, I heat up the chicken soup Tia Ana left for us on the kitchen table. My uncle is not hungry. I get more soup in his scraggly beard and on the towel than I get into his mouth.

I boil water on the stove for my bath. I'm just about to step in when Tio calls me. Wrapping a towel around me, I go to see what he needs.

"Please, *mi sobrino*. It is time for *él Presidente* to pay me a visit."

"You know what the doctor said about drinking so much brandy, Tio."

"*Si*, but he does not love me, Antonio, and you do."

I go into the kitchen to pour him a glass. I stand sobbing at the sink. My hands tremble.

Dear God, show me what to do. I do not want to make Tio sicker. I only want to help him.

I know if I am stingy with the brandy, my uncle will only call me again in a few minutes. I fill the small glass more than halfway.

"Thank you, *mi sobrino*. Will you come read to me later?"

"Yes, Tio," I tell him, "if you are still awake."

My hot bath is now lukewarm.

Everything in my life is wrong. It has all come flying apart. Please, dear God, help me.

I lie back in the tub, letting the water and soap wash this day away. My bath turns cold before I finish.

I pull the stopper and listen to today gurgle down the drain.

* * *

There is enough time for me to make my confession to Father Miguel before mass.

I tell him about my best friend cheating on me and how I wish something really bad would happen to him.

"I can't help it, Father. I know I shouldn't, but he hurt me so much."

"Perhaps it is time for you and your friend to part ways, my son. It might be best for both of you."

"How can we, Father? We are in the same classes. We work together and our families know each other. What should I do?"

"Your anger is understandable, my son, but it is a sin to wish harm to come to someone. Whether you see your friend again or not, you must forgive him before you leave church this morning."

"I'm not sure I *can* forgive him, though I will try my best. I'm no saint, Father."

My heart pounds. My mouth is dry.

"And, please... What is my penance, Father Miguel?"

"I have told you what you must do, my son. You must forgive your friend. If we cannot forgive our friends, how shall we forgive our enemies as Our Lord commanded?"

"But, Father..."

My confessor begins reciting in Latin. I say the *Act of Contrition*. He raises his hand and blesses me. I leave the confessional booth.

There, in our usual pew, kneels Six. He sees my shadow and looks up. I can tell he's trying to hold back a smile. He can't hide his dimples.

Six sits back in the pew and scoots in further to give me room to sit beside him.

"What're you doing here?" I whisper.

"Confessing my sins," he replies.

"But you're not Catholic."

"So? I'm in God's house and I'm talking to God. I confessed my sin to you already. Now I told God."

We search one another's eyes. I want to frown at him, to be very angry with him still, but...

Dear Jesus, help me.

I sit down next to Six. My anger and hurt bubble up again.

I pray to Our Lord to know what to do. Fixing our friendship is up to me—the ball is in my hands. I love my amigo and feel the same way about him that I always did. I can't help it. I want to forgive him, but...

The sacristy bell rings and we stand for mass.

I feel like I'm sleepwalking. I hear the words, but they don't sink in, they don't mean anything.

We stand for The Lord's Prayer. Six and I place our hands on the back of the pew in front of us. Father Miguel recites the prayer in Latin. When he reaches the part that says, *And forgive us our trespasses, as we forgive those who trespass against us*, I am jolted as though shocked with electricity, awakened as though from dreaming.

The message cannot be clearer. God has shown me the way, shown me what I must do.

I put my hand on Six's and lean towards him.

"I forgive you, amigo," I whisper.

"Thank you, Antonio," he says, kissing my cheek, right there in church. "Oh, God, how I love you."

3

Tia Ana and her friend Miss Emelina from church offer to take care of Tio Nicolás every other Sunday so that I can have one day off from my duties.

My amigo invites me to stay over. My aunt says she will stay with my uncle overnight tonight. My aunt is so good to me. I know it is not easy for her.

After church, Six and I spend the day at his grandparents' house, helping his grandma plant her kitchen garden. It is late when we finish. His grandma sets a place for me at the table. Six asks his Gramps if I can spend the night.

"Of course," his grandpa says. "I was afraid you boys were having a dispute."

Six's face gets red. I feel mine grow warm, too, but my skin's too dark to register much of a blush.

My buddy gets us off the hook by changing the subject. He steers the conversation toward the Allies push into Germany from both the east and the west.

I can't keep my mind on anything anyone is saying. All I can think about is getting cozy with my best friend tonight—the first chance we've had since we patched things up between us.

After supper, we excuse ourselves and say "Good night." We go up to my buddy's room, my heart thumping all the way. I wonder if his grandma and grandpa imagine that we still share Six's bed like we did when we were boys. Or do they think one of us sleeps on the floor?

"Wanna sit outside?" Six asks.

"*Cierto*," I reply. "Sure."

Six pushes the screen up and we step out onto the tin roof. It's chilly. We stretch our legs out and lean back against the house. I rest my forearm on his thigh, my hand on his knee. He nudges closer.

More stars appear as my eyes get accustomed to the dark. I am glad to feel Six's warmth.

I wriggle my hand between his thighs. I see his smile in the starlight.

I notice the moon rising through the cottonwoods. I'm getting cold.

Six gets up. I think we are going back inside. He crawls through the open window and tosses out the quilt from his bed. We spread it out. The tin roof is rusty, otherwise we would slide right off and tumble into the back yard.

We sit down on the quilt and I lie back. Sitting next to me, Six unbuttons my workshirt and lifts my T-shirt. He rubs my chest and stomach. It feels awfully good. His touch is tender.

Little by little, his hand follows the ridge of hair from my chest down to my Levi's.

"Do you want me to stop?" he asks. "Or should I keep going?"

"Keep going," I tell him, smiling. "We haven't had a chance to make up after our fight."

Six looks at me as he undoes the top button of my overalls and pushes his hand down inside. Then he reaches for the fly of my boxer shorts and sticks a couple fingers between the buttons.

He leans on one elbow and continues his exploration. I yank the rest of my overall buttons open. My stiffie pushes against the fly of my shorts. Six laughs.

I sit up and push him gently back onto the quilt. I pop the buttons of his Levi's and pull down his shorts. My hands tremble. His skin is hot against my cold fingers.

I roll over on top of him, putting my legs between his. Six pulls down the waistband of my boxers, freeing me.

Lowering myself onto my elbows, I maneuver my penis next to his, against his belly. I feel his hard-on throbbing next to mine. We rub slowly against one another.

Beneath my shirt, he folds his arms around me. His touch gives me a tingle and a shiver.

We peer deep into one another's eyes to see where the other is on our journey. Several times we manage to pull back from the edge before finally tumbling over it. It is our third time giving ourselves to each other all the way.

I feel his warm juice spurt against my stomach. Closing my eyes, I shoot mine onto him, kissing him with all my might. Six and I moan.

My amigo and I make love in our boots and Levi's on the tin roof of his Grandpa's porch as the moon rises through the cottonwoods. It never happens how I imagine it will. It is always better.

My toes curl inside my boots in rapture. I think, for a minute, that I am no longer there, no longer anywhere.

Six releases me and takes hold of the quilt. He pulls it up over me on both sides. I see his smile and steaming breath in the faint moonlight. We wriggle together in our puddle of semen.

"It feels awfully nice to kiss and make up, don't you think?" I ask *mi dulce gringo*.

"I know, huh?" Six replies. "Almost makes me want to have another fight. What d'ya say? You get to start this one."

I tickle his ribs. He squirms and the quilt slides off my back. I feel the cold air and roll away from him.

We pull up our shorts and button our overalls. Sitting up, we hold hands.

"Look," Six says, throwing his other arm up and pointing. "One of those Fastwalkers."

I watch it zigzag among the cottonwood branches and then veer off almost faster than my eyes can follow it. If not for Six's confirmation that he saw it, too, I'd have thought I imagined it.

"Let's get back inside," he says.

Six gets up and offers me his hand. I roll the quilt into a ball and toss it through the window. We climb inside and close the window. Six turns on the electric lamp beside his bed.

We hold each other. I shiver. I don't ever want to let go of him. I want to put tonight in a scrapbook, pressed between yesterday and whatever tomorrow holds in store for us.

We each take a corner of the heavy patchwork quilt and toss it over his bed.

We scramble out of our clothes, slinging them together over the chair. We keep on our shorts and climb beneath the covers. The sheets are cold. My amigo is warm.

Six leans on his elbow and reaches over to switch off the lamp. The moon shines through his window. I roll onto my side and scoot next to him, spooning up against him. I put my hand on his chest. He purrs.

He falls asleep as I listen to his breathing, mine slipping into rhythm with his. I hear an owl outside the window and another further away who answers note for note. Their haunting duet becomes my lullaby.

* * *

I awaken when my buddy jostles the bed. He dangles his legs over the edge and sits up. Faint daylight shines through the window. I hear a truck in his grandpa's backyard.

Six stands and reaches for his overalls. He sits beside me to put them on. Pulling aside the curtain, he peers out the window.

"I wonder where Gramps is going so early," he says.

I roll out from between the warm covers and get dressed. His wind-up alarm clock says 6:30. We could've snuggled for another half-hour before getting ready for school.

Six opens his bedroom door. The smell of freshly-perked coffee drifts up from the kitchen.

His grandma has set the last of the hobo bread out for us under a napkin. He brings the butter crock from the larder and pours two mugs full of coffee. The aroma and the steam clear my head.

"You know, you laugh in your sleep," I inform *mi dulce gringo*.

He smiles.

"It beats crying, don't you think?"

He hands me a slice of hobo bread and takes one for himself.

There is a note on the table beneath the jar of honey. Six picks it up and shows it to me. It's in his grandma's handwriting.

Hitler is dead, it reads. *Going to town. Back soon.*

* 4 *

It is the last week of our junior year of high school. My amigo and I will be working six days a week for the rest of the summer at Mila-Grow Nursery & Greenhouse.

My Tio Nicolás has taken very ill and does not leave his room. Six stays with me nearly every night so we can help the old man. My uncle is so thin and frail. But his belly is like a watermelon. It is the cancer.

Tia Ana looks in on her brother when Six and I are at work and school, but she is also weak from an infection in her lungs. We bought her medicine. She is getting better.

After work on Saturday, Six and I drive home in my uncle's old pickup. Tio has not driven in half a year. I park in the shade in front of the old barn.

Six and I climb out with our lunch buckets and work jackets. He hangs an arm over my shoulder. I can't tell which of us smells sweatier.

"Do you mind if I claim first dibs on the trough tonight, Antonio?"

"No," I say. "I'm going to look in on Tio. Maybe I'll join you."

He hands me his denim jacket and lunchbox, and I go inside. I hear Six working the pump handle to fill the old horse trough. My uncle hasn't had horses since Six and I were little boys. The trough is our bathtub in summer.

I can't wait to have a bath myself. I hang our jackets on the pegs beside the kitchen door and set our dinner pails on the sideboard.

I peer into Tio's room. He's sitting up in bed. His eyes are open.

"Where's Tia Ana?" I ask him.

"She just left the front way. She heard the pump and knew one of you was taking a bath."

I smile.

"Is there anything I can do for you, Tio?"

"I'd like to lie down again. My sister bosses me around. I can't get any rest. You're lucky you never had a sister. Younger sisters are the worst."

He leans forward and takes my arm while I rearrange his pillows behind him. He lies back against them and I pull the covers up. His smile twists into a grimace, no doubt from a stab of pain. Then it passes, like the shadow of a cloud darting across the meadow.

"At least now you have a brother," he tells me. "I do not worry about you any more. I miss my brother very much, Antonio. Perhaps I will see your papa again. Who knows?"

Six has finished his bath. I hear the screen door slam. He pokes his head around the doorway to my uncle's bedroom but ventures no further. He's probably buck naked.

"*Buenos noches, Tio*," he says. "I will sit with you while Antonio takes his bath."

I hear him rush upstairs to our bedroom and down again a couple minutes later. Dressed in a fresh pair of overalls and moccasins, he appears in the doorway still tugging on his T-shirt.

"Your turn to wash up," Six tells me, shooing me out of the room.

I undress in the bathroom beside the kitchen, tossing my grubby clothes into the wicker wash hamper. Grabbing a towel, I wrap it around myself and go outside.

Six has drained his dirty water and refilled the trough for me. Water still gurgles through the sluice out to the garden. The air is warm but the well-water is always cold.

I toss my towel over the old hitching post and grab the cake of lye soap and washcloth. The freezing water takes my breath away as I sit down in it. I won't be taking a leisurely bath, that's for sure.

I get clean in near record time.

Climbing out, I knock the wooden plug out of the trough with the side of my fist. I dry myself as it drains. Getting dressed in the kitchen, I pull on clean overalls and a T-shirt and slip into my moccasins.

When I return to my uncle's bedroom, Six sits in a chair beside Tio's bed, a book in his lap, holding the old man's hand. My uncle's eyes are shut. It is a sweet scene.

I take the chair on the opposite side of the bed. My uncle hears me and stirs. I take his left hand.

Now that I am washed and in clean clothes, I notice how bad Tio smells. His sister, Tia Ana, tells us he will not let her see him naked and will not let her bathe him.

"It's your turn, Tio Nicolás. Six and I have had our baths."

"Are you boys trying to do me in? I'd get pneumonia in that icy water."

"No, Tio," I say. "I'll make a little fire in the stove and heat up some water for a sponge bath."

"Oh, leave that for the undertaker. It's his job to make me presentable."

I ignore his remark.

"Six will stay with you while I warm up the water," I say.

I bring kindling and three small logs from the barn. I fill the cast iron pot from the kitchen sink. The water takes forever to boil. The water is rusty.

When I return to my uncle's bedroom with the pitcher of hot water, Six no longer holds my uncle's hand. Tio is asleep. There are tears on Six's face. He jumps up from his chair and throws his arms around me.

"He's leaving us, Antonio," he says, sobbing into my shoulder.

"Tonight?" I ask, returning his hug.

"I don't know," he says. "But very soon."

Six moves the oil lamp from the bedside table to the dresser, and puts the washbowl on the table. I pour in hot water. My uncle opens his eyes.

"I am on my way, Antonio. I am going home, *mi sobrino*," he says.

I pull back the sheet. Six gives him an arm so he can sit up. We pull his dirty nightshirt from beneath him and lift it over his head. I toss it on the floor.

Six and I place two old towels beneath him. As my amigo soaps up the washrag and rinses it, I bathe my uncle. His belly looks like a melon about to burst. There is a large, smelly sore on his left side.

First I wash Tio's face and run the damp cloth through his hair. He smiles.

"Thank you," he says. "That feels so good. I'm ready to go now."

I laugh.

"There's a bit more to wash," I tell him.

I scrub his hands and arms, then his chest. Helping him sit up, I hand the cloth to Six who washes Tio's back.

"Have I died already?" my uncle asks. "That felt like heaven. Thank you, boys."

"Only half done, Tio," Six tells him. "Now comes the ticklish part."

Six tosses the scummy water out the bedroom window into the garden. I refill the wash bowl with warm water. I soap up Tio's legs and Six holds his feet up so I can wash the backs of his legs, then his feet.

I wash his privates next. He giggles, but I think he's doing it for effect. We roll him on his side and I clean his butt. I fling the dirty water out the window.

My uncle smiles with as satisfied a smile on his face as I have ever seen him wear.

With the last of the warm water, I shave my uncle. I am afraid to cut him, but he trusts me. I should trust myself.

Gingerly, I dress Tio's open sore with a salve for burns and a large gauze bandage, held in place with brown packing tape. It was all I could find. I expect him to wince, but he does not.

We remove the damp towels and Six takes the washbowl and washcloths out. I pull the sheet and blanket up to Tio's chin.

"Thank you, *mi amado sobrino*, my beloved nephew. Where is Six? I have something to tell you both."

"Here I am, Tio Nicolás," Six says, entering the bedroom.

Six puts his arm on my shoulder and we stand at the foot of the bed.

"I am leaving you the house and property, Antonio. When your Tia Monica died and we had no children, I had the *abogado* draw up papers. I hope Six will live with you. He is your brother."

Six and I go to opposite sides of Tio's bed, each taking one of his hands.

"Thank you, Tio," I say.

"I'm giving you my shotgun, Six. I keep it cleaned and oiled. Take good care of it. Antonio tells me you're a damned good shot."

Six smiles.

"Who is that beautiful woman who came with you boys? Is she a friend of yours?" my uncle asks. "You must introduce me."

Six and I look up. There is no one there. But—for the briefest flash—the glowing image of the Blessed Virgin Mary comes into my mind.

Six looks over at me. He is wide-eyed and his mouth hangs open. I know he must have caught a glimpse of *Nuestra Señora*, too.

"Yes, Tio," I reply. "She is a friend of ours."

"And what is her name, *mi sobrino*?"

"*Maria*," I tell him.

"Pleased to meet you, Maria," my uncle says, looking beyond Six and me.

There is an indistinct flickering in the doorway behind us.

"Oh... I know who you are, Maria," Tio says. "I didn't think I believed in you. You'll watch over my boys, won't you?"

A calm expression and a beatific smile emerge on my uncle's face. His eyes are clear again. His transformation is startling. I've never seen him look so content.

"Yes, thank you, Maria," Tio says, responding to a voice I do not hear.

"I've got to be on my way, boys," he adds, squeezing our hands with the last of his strength.

"I love you," I tell him.

Tio Nicolás closes his eyes. He fills his chest with a deep breath and exhales, never drawing another. His hands grow limp in ours.

I contain my own tears, but I see from his trembling lip that Six is about to break into a squall. I hold him. We both sob. I am so glad I am not alone.

Six lights the oil lamp on the dresser and we leave Tio's bedroom.

I send Six down the road to Tia Ana to bring her the sad news of her brother's passing. I go back to my uncle's bedroom and take my rosary out of my overall pocket. Sitting in a chair at the head of the bed, I recite the cycle of prayers, the Sorrowful Mysteries.

I close my eyes, calmed by the repetition of counting the beads and saying the prayers.

* * *

Six returns with Tia Ana around midnight. She has brought blessed candles with her.

Though it is difficult for her, my aunt gets down on her knees and takes out her rosary. I light the candles. Tears stream down her face. Six and I join her at the side of her brother's bed.

I recite the prayers with my aunt. Six prays silently.

When we have finished the second rosary, we take my aunt upstairs to my room and make her lie down on the bed.

Six and I sit up with Tio's body until we can let Father Consuelo know of his death in the morning. We take turns lying fitfully on the sagging couch.

At dawn, Tia stirs in the kitchen, making a pot of coffee for us, and burritos with eggs and ground beef.

After breakfast, Six and I drive Tia Ana to Nuestra Madre de Dolores Church to make funeral arrangements for her brother with Father Consuelo. I doubt she will be able to persuade the pastor to celebrate a requiem mass. My uncle never set foot in a church so far as I know. He was never a member of Nuestra Madre parish.

My amigo and I get back in the truck. We notify my uncle's doctor and go to have a talk with the undertaker. I am glad Six is with me. I couldn't do this on my own.

By the time we collect my aunt back at the church and drive home, they are already carting Tio Nicolás in a wooden coffin out to the horse-drawn hearse.

My buddy and I stand beside my aunt, our arms around her, until the black-and-silver hearse drives off. The fancy wagon does not go fast enough to raise a single mote of dust. It seems to have all the time in the world to reach its destination.

We drive my aunt home as the sun rises higher. Gusts of wind rustle the cottonwood trees. After helping her down from the truck, we walk her to her *portál* and up the steps.

"You boys made my brother's last days comfortable," she tells us. "He died at peace in his own bed. God bless you for giving him a bath. He wouldn't let me."

My aunt invites us inside to have lunch with her, but neither Six nor I are hungry.

"Thank you, Tia," he tells her. "I think we're gonna show up for work this afternoon."

"But there's been a death in the family. No one expects you to work, do they?"

"No, maybe not," I tell my aunt. "But I'd rather be busy, Tia. Besides, taking the day off isn't going to pay any bills."

"Then you must let me help you," she says, going inside her house.

She returns with an envelope stuffed with cash. I refuse it. She puts it in Six's hand and folds his fingers around it. He drops it into her apron pocket.

"Tio left us his house," I tell her.

"He told me he was going to do that. I'm glad he did. Let me at least pack you boys a lunch. You work hard. You're still growing."

Six and I wait on the porch steps as my aunt packs us a hasty lunch.

She hands us each a brown paper sack and kisses us.

"God bless you, *mis hijos*," she says. "Come by for supper tonight."

"Yes, Tia," I say. "We will."

We climb into the truck. I watch my aunt wave to us in the rearview mirror.

Six reaches across the seat and touches my arm. The gesture is consoling. The duties of becoming grown-ups are catching up with us awfully quick.

I pull onto the road for Mila-Grow Nursery & Greenhouse.

* * *

Father Consuelo refused to celebrate a funeral mass for my uncle since he was not registered as a parishioner of Nuestra Madre de Dolores Church nor any other church. He sent Father Miguel to bless Tio's casket and recite The Lord's Prayer at the graveside this Monday morning.

The funeral luncheon is held at Tia Ana's house. She and her friends from church cooked and baked all weekend. But it's not going to be much of a party without Tio.

It is a cool but brilliantly sunny day. There are far too many people to fit in my aunt's tiny *casita*. Funeral guests sit beneath the front and rear *portál*s and in the back yard beneath the cottonwoods. Six and I bring wooden crates from her barn for people to sit on.

"What will you and Six do after high school, Antonio?" my aunt's friend from church asks.

Miss Emelina has taught third-graders for over forty years. She corners my buddy and me near the fence.

"Are you boys going to enlist?"

"We talk about enlisting," I tell her, "if the war is still going on when we finish school."

"Yes, of course," she says. "It's most important to complete your schooling first."

Six shifts from one foot to the other. Miss Emelina must make him uncomfortable, too. It feels as though I am back in her class, afraid of giving a wrong answer.

"We all pray the war will be over soon. It will be nice to have a full larder again," she remarks. "You boys should go get more food. You both look kind of thin. Take some home."

"Yes, Miss Emelina," I tell her. "Thank you."

Miss Emelina goes to the table with all the desserts and loads up her plate. She motions to my amigo and me to come over. Luckily, Six's grandma interrupts our passage across the back yard.

"It looked like you and Six needed rescue," she says.

"Thank you, Grandma," Six tells her. "I think we will be going home soon."

"Of course, dear. Will you be staying at Antonio's house from now on or will you be coming back to live with your grandpa and me?"

"No, Grandma," I tell her. "Six and I will be moving in together. Tio left me his house."

Six's grandma is joined by his grandpa.

"I heard," Grandpa says, "Congratulations to you, Antonio. I know your uncle loved you very much. A father could not love a son more than he loved you."

Grandma Matilda takes her leave and goes among the tables of food to prepare a basket for me and Six to take home.

"Do you think you boys will start up your Uncle Nicolás's ranch again?" Grandpa asks. "If so, I'd like to help you out."

"I don't think so," Six tells his grandfather. "Antonio and I talk about owning a place like Mila-Grow some day. We both like planting things and taking care of them. We dream of having an orchard, too. But I don't know if Roswell is big enough for two tree nurseries."

"Of course it is," Grandpa says. "When that day arrives to set up shop, you boys let me know. I'll be happy to bankroll it for you—interest free. I've never seen a pair of harder working young men than you two. It'd be fun to stick Ol' Eduardo with a little bit of friendly competition, don't you think?"

He smiles and chuckles. Grandma brings us the laden picnic basket she packed to overflowing. The lid won't go down.

"Thank you, Grandma," I say, smiling. "I guess you think we don't know how to take care of ourselves."

"No, Antonio, dear. There is just so much food. I hate seeing food go to waste when there are so many people in the world who go hungry."

Six's grandma kisses us both good-bye. Gramps shakes our hands. I look around for my Tio Nicolás, forgetting for a moment that we are at his funeral luncheon. My heart breaks all over again and I burst into tears.

Six puts his hand on my shoulder and rubs the back of my neck. I want to hold him and kiss him so bad.

I settle down and we take leave of our assembled clans. It takes another half-hour for us to make it down the line of mourners. All of them in black, they look like crows perched on a telegraph wire.

My friend and I steal glances at one another as I drive the quarter-mile up to Tio Nicolás's house. It will always be Tio's house. And, as long as Six can keep it running, it will always be Tio's 1934 turquoise Ford pickup truck.

Back at the house, we put the lunch goodies away and plug my uncle's rattletrap refrigerator back in. It gives a couple of clunks and shakes like a misfiring engine. It sounds as though it is about to expire for once and all before settling into a regular rhythm.

I take two bottles of my uncle's Dos Equis from the larder for me and Six to enjoy later. I put them on the top shelf in the icebox, beside the tiny freezer.

We sit out back under the *portál*, sharing our memories of Tio Nicolás. We laugh and cry tears until I think there are no more of either kind to shed.

* 5 *

My amigo and I start work full-time at Mila-Grow right after our last day of classes at Roswell High, the end of our junior year. It doesn't look like we'll have any time for a camping trip *this* summer.

Hypatia gave Six her old telescope before she left for Barnard College in New York City. It's not her big telescope, but it is a beautiful brass spyglass on a tripod mount. They both cried. She and Six promised to write one another.

It's much easier not being jealous of her when Hypatia is two thousand miles away at college. I do my best to conceal my envy, but sometimes it nearly leaks out.

The letter-writing between Six and Hypatia has fallen off. It seems to me he's about due for another letter from her.

I don't want to hurt Six or make him feel bad. I have forgiven *mi mejor amigo* for being so easily lured by Hypatia, but I struggle still with forgiving *her* for seducing my best friend. I know I have to forgive her, too, and pray for strength to do what I must. A grudge is a heavy stone to carry.

According to our recent Saturday custom, Six takes the truck to go get our food and supplies for the week while I start supper. Next week we'll switch.

I walk out to the road first to see whether there's any mail.

I reach inside the rusty, squeaky mailbox—something else around here in need of oil and paint. Finding a letter in Hypatia's handwriting in the mailbox makes me bristle. I always fight with myself not to throw it away. So far, I have won that argument—narrowly.

There are two letters in her hand, one addressed to me. *Did she make a mistake?* I wonder. *No, Hypatia doesn't make mistakes.* Curiosity tempts me, but I wait until I get back to the house.

I set his letter at Six's place on the kitchen table, propping it up against the candle stand so he'll see it. *With any luck, it might catch fire.*

I say a *Hail, Mary* to distract myself from my unkind thoughts. Then I tear into her letter to me.

June 2, 1945

Dear Antonio,

> *I suppose that by now Six has told you I am carrying his child.*

"What?" I say aloud. "Oh, dear God. It can't be."

I slump into the kitchen chair. The letter shakes in my hand. I want to punch Six for not leveling with me.

I close my eyes before I start bawling.

In my imagination I watch Six pick up his bags from the *portál*. The taxi driver loads them in the trunk. Six emerges from the taxicab in New York City, a canyon of buildings ablaze with lights that disappear into the clouds.

He wears a suit and tie and polished shoes, and looks very dapper. Six doesn't see me.

Another taxicab rushes past, splashing him. I laugh. Six doesn't hear me.

I open my eyes and read on, fighting back tears.

> *I suggested to Six that we name the child* Nicolás, *in honor of your uncle, if it's a boy and* Ana *if she's a girl—but I have not heard back from him. In any case, will you be the child's* compadre— *its sponsor for Baptism?*

I'm surprised Hypatia gives me a second thought. It's more consideration than my so-called amigo gives me. He's back to his old tricks of keeping things from me.

> *While my Barnard College scholarship at Columbia University pays my tuition, and room and board, I do not have any money for a doctor. My father says I must pay for my own mistake.*

My parents are furious with me, but they want me to have the child at home. I have had to delay my attendance at school until after the child is born.

I also learned the baby and I have different blood factors. It is not serious if treated before birth. The regimen will require multiple blood transfusions.

"Oh, dear Lord. Help both mother and child," I say aloud.

But I feel phony for saying it. My only true concern is what this will mean for my amigo—and for me. I know that Hypatia must be so jealous of me that she'd do anything to come between me and Six. It might not even be his child.

Six told me you boys received an inheritance from your Tio Nicolás. I do not want to ask you for help paying for the doctor, but I have nowhere else to turn. I will repay the money to you with interest.

If you are the best friend Six says you are, you will not tell him about my financial situation. I shall tell him myself when the time is right.

God bless you.
Hypatia

I refold Hypatia's letter just as the pickup rumbles into the yard. I tuck the envelope into the hip pocket of my overalls.

Six comes in whistling, carefree, as though he were innocent. I want to punch him twice. He slams the kitchen screen door. I want to punch him three times.

He sets the sacks of groceries on the sink drainboard and kisses my cheek. I do not respond.

"What's got you so grouchy?" he asks.

He takes two beers from the icebox and opens them, handing one to me.

"Uh-oh," he says, noticing the letter from Hypatia on the kitchen table.

He picks up the envelope.

"Come on. Let's sit outside," he says, holding the screen door open.

We go out to the rear *portál* and sit down in the old wood rockers. Six tugs off his boots and puts his feet up on the porch railing. He takes a sip of his beer, ignoring the letter.

"Aren't you going to open the letter from Hypatia?"

"Yeah, I will," he replies. "I was just enjoying being home with you after a hard day's work."

He picks up the envelope and glances at it.

"This one sure took its sweet time getting here," he says. "It's postmarked two weeks ago."

He takes a sip of beer and sets the letter down again, in no hurry to tear open the flap.

Though Hypatia's letter was sent to him a week before mine, they both arrived today. I'm happy I didn't accuse him of hiding things from me when it was the post office's fault.

I'm curious to know what his letter says, though. He usually shares them with me. I wish he'd open it.

"It might be important," I suggest.

"It's waited this long," he says, taking another sip.

I want to take the letter from his hand and rip it open.

He takes his socks off first and wriggles his toes. He reaches into his Levi's for his pocketknife. He cuts open the flap.

Six unfolds the letter and takes a swallow of beer.

He sprays a geyser of Dos Equis across the page. He reads on. I watch the blood drain from his face.

My amigo turns and looks at me, searching my eyes. His color returns, all the way to bright red.

"I'm going to be a father," he declares.

I stare at him as expressionlessly as I can manage.

"I never figured on that one," he says, chuckling.

I can tell he's trying to suppress his dimples. He leans forward in his rocker and clinks my bottle of beer with his.

He hands me the letter. My heart sinks into my stomach. My eyes swim with tears. I cannot read the words.

"Will you be marrying Hypatia, then?" I ask him. "And moving to New York?"

My heart beats faster and my stomach somersaults, afraid what my buddy is going to tell me.

Please, dear Jesus, help me. I am alone in the world without him.

I am ready to cry. I am ready to die.

Six searches my face and bursts into laughter. His callousness crushes my heart.

"I thought you were joshing me, Antonio," he says. "I can't live in a city. I'm a small-town boy. Besides, I'm not in love with Hypatia. I'm in love with *you*. What a goof, you are."

He sets his bottle of beer down on the little table. Putting his bare feet on the rungs of my rocker, he tilts me forward. Resting his hands on my thighs, he leans to kiss me. My heart beats faster still.

"I want to live with *you*, Antonio—for the rest of my life as the Holy Mother promised."

He leans back in his rocker and takes another sip of beer.

"Hypatia does not want to get married. She does not want to be a mother, either. Her parents are really mad at her, but they can't force her.

"She's gotta attend classes or she'll lose her scholarship. She will have the baby at her parents' house and the child will live with them."

"But you are the child's father, Six. How can you send your child to live among strangers? You must take care of the child if the mother will not."

"Are you out of your mind, Antonio?" he asks. "How are the two of us are going to be able to raise a child? We've got jobs, amigo. We've gotta finish school. We'll probably be going into the army.

"Besides, grandparents are hardly strangers. My grandparents *are* my parents—the only ones I've ever known."

"Couldn't we give it a shot, Six? My family could help with babysitting while we're at work."

"Thank you, Antonio," he tells me. "You are generous to a fault. I love you more all the time—impossibly more.

"But we just can't do it, amigo. Hypatia's family would never stand for it."

Six leans forward in his rocker and touches my bottle of beer with his.

"Congratulations," he tells me, taking a sip.

"Me?" I ask. "For what?"

"On becoming an uncle," he says, grinning.

Six touches my cheek.

"May I do half as good a job as my Tio Nicolás," I say, getting choked up.

"You'll make a first-rate uncle, *Tio Antonio*. I'm absolutely sure of that."

He smiles at me.

I have invited him to live in my uncle's house and he has invited me to share his life. I haven't the foggiest idea how we're gonna work any of this out. We're probably both crazy.

By the time we finish our beer, it is nearly sundown. I pull off my cowboy boots and socks.

I flip with my amigo for who gets to take the first bath. I win.

The water drawn this morning before work and sitting in the sun all afternoon will at least be warm. The second bath, drawn after that, fresh from the pump, will be as cold as meltwater.

Mi dulce gringo, with his Norwegian blood, does not seem to mind the icy water half as much as I do.

* 6 *

Six drops me at the house after work. He's going over to Hypatia's to meet her parents tonight. I know nothing about the Montoyas. I'm really worried for him.

I wish I could've gone with Six and at least waited in the truck. But only our families and friends, and our boss and coworkers, are aware we share my uncle's house.

Everyone accepts that Six and I are best friends who care a lot for each other. But no one except my amigo and I knows we also share the bed.

I go outside and pace the porch. An entire hour goes by.

It's my turn to cook supper tonight. I put the pot on the stove but fail to put anything in it. It takes the smoke to get my attention.

What if they force him into marriage even if their daughter does not want to be his wife? I've heard of shotgun weddings. What if they hogtie and kidnap him, forcing his family to pay a ransom for him?

Another hour passes.

I wish we had a telephone like Six's grandpa. I'll bet Hypatia's family has a telephone. Six would've been able to call me.

Going out to the back yard, I stand in the driveway. Maybe I'll be able to see the pickup coming, or at least the cloud of dust chasing it down the road.

It's near sunset.

I put my hand in my pocket and finger my rosary, walking around the yard in circles while I recite the prayers.

It's nearly dark before I see the headlamps bouncing down the long driveway like a pair of zigzagging Fastwalkers.

Six parks the old truck and gets out. He comes up to me and kisses me. Taking my hand, he leads me into the house, whistling the Andrews Sisters "apple tree" song.

Seeing nothing on the stove for supper, he asks if I've already eaten.

"No, I'm sorry, Six. *Pinche*. I completely forgot. I was getting worried about you. Are you OK? What should I make for us?"

He smiles and touches my cheek.

"I already ate, Antonio. Mrs. Montoya is a pretty good cook—although not quite in the same league as my Gram and your Tia. Can I fix something for *you*?"

"I can take care of myself," I say, sounding harsher than I intend.

I take the loaf of bread from the breadbox and peanut butter from the larder. I cut two slices and stir the peanut butter with the butter knife.

I pour myself a glass of milk and sit down at the table. Six sits down across from me. I wait for him to recount his evening at Hypatia's.

"So, how do you like the in-laws?" I ask, chomping down on my sandwich, hoping the peanut butter will stick to the roof of my mouth so I won't be able to say anything sarcastic.

Six laughs.

"Nope, they're not in-laws, amigo. They're more like out-laws. There's no way they will ever get Hypatia to the altar. They would have to hogtie and kidnap her."

"Wha' 'bou' 'ou?" I ask.

"Huh?" he says. "Oh. Yeah, they'd have to hogtie and kidnap me, too. I wonder, would you pay my ransom?"

I chuckle, nearly choking on my peanut butter sandwich. I take a swallow of milk.

"It depends," I reply.

"On what?"

"On if I can get a bulk rate or whether I've gotta pay your ransom by the pound."

He smiles.

I finish my sandwich and rinse the plate. Six takes a bottle of beer from the icebox and opens it. We go out to the *portál*, our usual place for talking in good weather—which is most of the time. At meals, we're too busy getting food into us to carry on much of a conversation.

"Señor Montoya remembered me from all the times I came over to use Hypatia's telescope. It turns out my Gramps co-signed a loan for him a few years back, during the Depression. It helped him hang onto his shipping business. He never forgot Otto Thorson and welcomed me into their house."

"*No manches*," I say. "No kidding. But what's going to happen with the child, Six?"

"The *partera*, the midwife, will help Hypatia have the child at home," he tells me. "Hypatia will begin college right after the baby is born—early next year."

"Will you get to see the child?"

"*Cierto*, Antonio. Whenever I want. I knew that would make you happy."

He smiles and I smile. I pass the bottle of beer back to him.

"Señor Montoya and I shared a brandy and a cigar and a couple of dirty jokes under the *portál*. I poured the brandy in the bushes when he wasn't looking.

"He said he and the missus were looking forward to being alone again once Hypatia goes off to college. They're not so eager to have a toddler underfoot again.

"Hypatia's dad asked if maybe my Gram and Gramps wouldn't mind sharing some of the duties with them every now and again. They want to drive down to Mexico for a second honeymoon next year."

"That's not gonna be too hard for your grandma and grandpa, is it?" I ask.

He laughs, and passes the bottle of beer back to me.

"*No es cierto!* Are you kidding me? They'll be so proud they'll burst apart at the seams. I don't think they ever counted on becoming great-grandparents."

"Oh, amigo," I tell him. "Everything is working out. The Holy Mother is watching out for her children—*all* her children."

"She is indeed," he says, showing his dimples.

I finish our beer and we go into the house.

* * *

It took me a couple of nights lying awake to hatch my plan. I prayed for help and inspiration, and it came to me.

I want to help Hypatia and the baby with the doctor bills. But the little bit of money Tio Nicolás left me, Six and I plan to use on repairs. The house needs *enjarre*—re-plastering. The barn sags and leans. There are missing cedar shingles. We want to replace the rotted corral posts and cross-rails, too.

After work, while Six goes down the road to fetch some of Tia Ana's chicken and *posole* stew, I head out to the barn. It's hard to get the door open, the frame leans so much. The door scrapes the ground in an arc.

It's difficult to see, coming from the full sunlight into the dim interior of the former stable. Shafts of dusty daylight squeeze though the gaps and cracks between the barn boards.

In the corner is the small stack of meteorites from the bucket of them we collected at Bottomless Lake. I can tell at once, by the gleaming meteorite at the top of the pile, that one of them has recently been removed. The rest are covered in dust, their luster dulled.

I slip one of the iron chunks into the hip pocket of my dirty dungarees. I am careful. The heavy metal is sharp. I don't want to rip my pocket. Neither Six nor I can sew worth a darn. We're hoping my aunt, or Six's grandma, will give us lessons some time so we don't have to always ask them to mend our clothes.

I leave the barn and push the door shut. Six enters the yard, carrying the cast iron stew pot. I can smell supper.

As we go up the porch steps, Six pats my butt as he often does. There is no way he could not have felt the iron stone in my back pocket. Though he does not comment, I know he knows.

Six sets the stew on the stove. He banks the coals and puts in a small log. I pump water into the sink to wash my hands. My amigo takes a bottle of Dos Equis from the icebox that we will share. The ice-cold bottle drips with sweat.

We go to the kitchen table while the chicken stew heats up. I pour beer into our glasses.

There, on the checkered tablecloth, is an iron meteorite.

I look at Six, taking the iron stone from my pocket and setting it beside the first one. He looks at me; I look at him. We laugh.

Six hooks his arm around my waist and pulls me to him. He kisses my sweaty neck.

He takes Mr. Carson's bent and dirty business card from the front pocket of his Levi's and sets it on the table.

"I'm guessing both our meteorites are heading to Rocks & a Hard Place," he says, grinning. "And the money will go for Hypatia and the baby?"

I nod. He kisses me.

"Thank you, Antonio. Thank you for being my friend, my best friend," he says.

He puts his arm on my shoulder.

"Come on. Our beer's getting warm."

We sit down at the table and touch our glasses together.

"It means so much to me, amigo, that you want to help mother and child. It's more than I could have hoped for."

Six gets up to stir the stew, and sits back down.

"Believe me," I tell him. "I did a lot of praying. The child must be surrounded with love, Six, not resentments and ill will. I think we should send Hypatia the money from both meteorites."

He brings his lunch bucket to the table. He takes out a tiny cardboard carton, a scrap of brown paper, and some packing string.

"I got it from Louisa in the office at work, the owner's wife," Six says. "She said, when we bring the parcel back to her, that she'd use her postal scale and send it out with the mail."

Wrapping the meteorites in several sheets of newspaper, I place them inside the cardboard box and stuff more paper around them. Louisa's not going to believe how much the tiny box weighs. The postage might be our entire paychecks.

I tear a sheet of paper from my notebook and hand it to Six. He writes instructions to Mr. Carson and prints Hypatia's address at the bottom.

He puts the letter of instructions on top, using brown packing tape to seal it. Then he folds the brown paper around the tiny carton and I tie it with the string. He uses a black crayon to address it to Rocks & a Hard Place. Six puts the parcel on the sideboard.

"You are good person, Antonio, a kind person. I figured I could talk you into helping Hypatia with some of our 'meteor money.' But you came up with idea on your own. That means a whole lot more to me."

He kisses me. I breathe in his sweaty smell.

"Mothers are special, Six," I tell him. "We are motherless. We must help Hypatia. The Blessed Virgin would want us to. That's really all there is to it."

"Thank you," he says. "I love you so much, amigo—more than I think I even know how to do."

We toast each other with the last of our beer. His smile fills my heart.

* 7 *

It is almost the middle of August. In three weeks Six and I will start our senior year of high school. I feel like a big cheese, but at the same time I'm afraid like a little mouse. I understand so little of the world. It swirls around me in a whirlwind of confusion. I trust only that Our Savior will lead us all, in our roundabout ways, to salvation.

My amigo and I stop at Toribio's Market on Saturday on the way home from Mila-Grow. We get beef and chicken, tortillas, tomatoes, and onions.

Six adds a quart bottle of beer to our items on the counter.

Mr. Toribio looks at Six, then turns to me, glancing down at the bottle of Dos Equis.

"We're going to share it," Six tells Toribio. "Our age, totaled up, is thirty-four."

The merchant smiles. I wasn't sure we'd get away with it. Six thinks on his feet and seems to always come up with the right thing to say. He makes people laugh.

Since I forgot to check how much flour remained in the bin before leaving home this morning, I put a ten-pound sack of Gold Medal flour on the wooden counter. My aunt is going to show me how to make *empanadas* and *biscochitos*.

Toribio tallies up our meat and groceries with a pencil on a scrap of butcher's paper. He packs the sweaty bottle of beer in a separate paper sack and places it, along with the rest of our groceries, in a larger brown sack with handles.

Six and I hand him our dusty money from the pockets of our dirty Levi's.

"The beer's on me, boys," he says. "We all got something to celebrate. Too bad your Tio Nicolás didn't hang on long enough to see it," he adds.

"See what? Celebrate what?" I ask.

"You don't know? Where you two been?"

"Working and sleeping," Six replies.

Toribio slaps a copy of the *Roswell Register* on the counter.

"It's over, boys. The war is finally over," he announces, practically shouting. "The Japs surrendered."

The picture beneath the headline shows the cloud from a huge explosion over the city of Nagasaki. It is shaped like a poisonous white mushroom, an *amanita*—the Angel of Death.

The photo shocks me. I think of how many people must have been killed. My knees get rubbery and I feel queasy.

Toribio puts the *Register* in our bag of provisions. Six reaches into his pocket.

"That's on me, too," the owner announces. "The war's over. You boys lucked out. You know, huh?"

"*Gracias,*" Six tells him.

We go out to the pickup, placing the sack between us on the seat. Six starts the engine.

"What got you?" he asks me. "You don't look so good. Was it the newspaper?"

I nod.

We do not say another word on the short drive home.

Six parks the pickup. I take the sack of groceries. He holds the squeaky screen door open for me.

There is clattering in the cupboards and the larder as we puts things away. Six lays the *Roswell Register* on the kitchen table.

We stand beside each other as we read the front page account of the two atomic bombs dropped on Japan. I have to turn away, unable to bear the thought of so much death and destruction—even if , at long last, it helped bring World War II to an end.

We go out beneath the *portál* and sit down in our rockers. My workshirt sticks to me. I smell.

"Care for a little beer?" Six asks.

"Sure," I reply.

He goes back into the kitchen. He returns with the bottle of Dos Equis from the icebox and three short glasses from the cupboard. I do not have to ask him who the third glass is for.

Six pours just enough beer in Tio's glass to wet the bottom.

I take a swallow of mine. The beer is so wonderfully cool. I'm glad we plugged my uncle's icebox back in. I hope we can afford the electricity.

"*Salud*, Tio Nicolás," Six toasts.

"*Salud*," I repeat. "God bless you, Tio."

We smile and take a long swallow of our beer.

"Feel like talking?" Six asks.

I nod. The newspaper photo of the atomic blast flashes into my mind.

"I think Dr. Feynman had something to do with it, Six—with making that bomb, the atomic bomb. He called it *The Gadget*."

"I remember," Six remarks. "Kind of a childish name for something so frightening."

He unties his workboots, pulling them off and propping his feet on the railing.

"Do you think The Gadget is what could lead to the next war, Six, the one the Blessed Virgin warned us might happen?"

"I dunno," he replies. "I cannot imagine a war being fought with such weapons. Who could survive?"

"Part of me is happy for the terrible revenge that's been rained down on the heads of the Japanese, amigo. It is repayment for my father's death and those of all the other patriots at Pearl Harbor. I pray to learn forgiveness, but it is always so hard for me."

"Nothing worthwhile is ever easy, is it, Antonio?"

He gets up and goes into the kitchen, returning with a fourth glass. He pours in a tiny amount of beer.

"To your father," Six says, touching the fourth glass with his own.

"To my father," I reply, doing the same.

I fight to hold back my tears.

"Let's celebrate the end of the war, amigo, and thank God and the Holy Mother that even more lives were not lost."

"You're right," I say. "I was pretty sure the war would still be going on by the time we graduated next year."

"Yeah. So did I. I'm happy it's finally over."

We finish our glasses of beer and simply pass the bottle back and forth. The two extra glasses remain on the porch table until the beer evaporates in a couple of days.

I unlace my workboots and take them and my socks off. It feels good to be barefoot.

My amigo and I share our recollections of my father and my uncle, reciting our favorite incidents to each other and laughing. It lightens our heavy mood.

The shadows of the cottonwoods fill the yard. The evening breeze is cool.

It is time to take our baths in the horse trough before it gets dark. Then we have to make our supper. Tomorrow is Sunday, our free day, our day for laundry and chores at home.

* 8 *

After church, while the hot water for washing clothes comes to boil on the woodstove, I tell my amigo the idea that came to me during mass.

"I want to carve a statue of the Blessed Mother, Six. What d'ya think?"

"That's a great idea, Antonio. Her image is always in my mind, too. It would be a way of paying homage to her. It's got my vote—even though I can't vote yet."

I smile at him.

"There's a beautiful cedar log at work—if Eduardo will let me have it."

"I wish I could do something, too," Six tells me.

"Why don't you build a grotto for the statue, to keep it out of the weather? Eduardo always has you doing the stonework. You're pretty good at it, amigo."

"Thanks," he says. "Where am I gonna build this grotto?"

"I thought maybe beneath the grove of cottonwoods, overlooking the meadow. It was one of Tío Nicolás's favorite places."

"OK. You can help me choose the nicest, most colorful stones from the field and from the ditch. How big is the statue of the Holy Mother gonna be, Antonio?"

"Life-size," I tell him.

"That's a lotta stones for the grotto, buddy."

"Well, the price is certainly right," I tell him. "God provides them free of charge."

Six and I laugh. We each take one of the big pots of hot water from the stove. We carry them out to the wooden washtub in the backyard. Six goes to the barn for the wringer.

I'd much rather be working on our project to honor the Holy Mother than do laundry. I can't wait to get started on my carving. I'm glad Six is enthused about building the grotto.

* * *

Eduardo lets me have the cedar log. Six helps me carry it to my Tio's pickup.

"Thanks, boss," we tell him.

"You must let me see the statue of *Nuestra Señora* when you finish it, Antonio."

"*Ciertamente*," I say. "Six is going to build a grotto out of stones for the statue of the Holy Mother. I will ask Father Miguel to come bless it for us."

"You and Six are good boys. I am happy to see you both using the talents God has given you. Your uncle would be proud."

My amigo and I smile at him. We are so blessed to have such kind and loving people in our lives.

* * *

At last Six thinks he has gathered enough stones for the grotto. He arranges them in semicircles on the ground, largest to smallest. We buy sacks of sand and Portland cement and lime, and load up the pickup.

Six mixes the mortar in the wheelbarrow with a garden hoe. He takes his shirt off. His back soon glistens with sweat. I go back to carving the figure of the Blessed Virgin.

I watch Six out of the corner of my eye. The exact right stone comes to hand as he works. He drops the mortar onto the stones and smooths it into place with a mason's trowel. The trowel started out rusty but is already polished to gleaming from the sand. He forces more mortar between the stones.

"I'll mix the next batch," I tell him, stripping off my own dirty, smelly workshirt.

"I don't think we should go any higher today, Antonio. Too much weight. It might collapse. I can put up the last couple of courses of stones tomorrow."

"Fine by me," I say. "I don't mind calling it a day. We can have an early supper tonight for a change."

He puts a hand on my shoulder and we go back to the house.

* * *

Six finishes the stone grotto during the week. I work on my carving of *Nuestra Madre* as long as there's daylight. My amigo helps me lift the wooden statue into the grotto to see how it will look. We both smile.

On the way home from work on Saturday, we buy our customary two bottles of Dos Equis at Toribio's, along with our supplies for the coming week.

We put our provisions away and Six opens our bottles of beer. We take off our sweaty shirts and sit in the rockers, propping our booted feet on the porch rails. We clink our bottles and raise them to each other's health.

"You know," I say to Six. "Japan surrendered two weeks ago. The Holy Mother still hasn't visited us. She promised to appear to us at the end of the war. I wonder if I misunderstood her again. I'm getting kinda concerned."

"Take it easy, buddy," he tells me. "I read in the newspaper that the *official* end of World War II won't be until tomorrow, September second.

"Maybe the Holy Mother is just waiting for the papers to be signed at the ceremony, for all the *I*s to be crossed and the *T*s dotted," he says, repeating *Santa Madre*'s joke.

He has the knack for making me laugh no matter how glum I feel.

"Do you wanna drive out to Bottomless Lake tomorrow after our Sunday chores?" I ask him. "Maybe we can go for a swim."

"I thought you were going to finish your carving of the Holy Mother after mass," Six replies.

"I don't know, amigo. Has my carving really been inspired or do I just think it has? Like Dr. Feynman said, the easiest person to fool is ourselves.

"I wanted to free the figure of the Blessed Virgin from inside the cedar. Instead, I think I simply cut and pounded her shape into the wood from the outside. I'm not sure I can finish it."

"Of course you can," Six tells me, touching my arm.

"Maybe it doesn't resemble Holy Mother's face exactly," he says. "I can't describe what she looks like, either. Her face shimmers and shifts and changes. But your carving makes me *feel* as though I am standing in her presence. It makes me feel calm and peaceful."

"Thank you, Six. What you think means a lot to me. If you say it's worth finishing, I'll work on the carving after mass tomorrow."

"We'll go out to Bottomless Lake on Monday, Antonio. It's Labor Day, and we've got the day off from our labors."

We sip our beer.

"You want to take your bath first, Six?" I ask him. "The water should be nice and warm from sitting in the sun all day."

"I don't mind sharing," he says. "Let's bathe together in the warm water. And we'll share the cold water from the pump when we rinse off. It'll be faster."

"You sure?" I ask.

My buddy nods. He stands up and begins unbuttoning his dusty overalls. He steps out of his boxer shorts. I follow his example. We hang our dirty dungarees over the hitching post.

Six and I climb into the water trough. It feels like heaven. We take turns submerging ourselves. The water nearly overflows. We wash our faces and hair with the lye soap and dunk ourselves again.

He stands up and I scrub his back with the brush. He returns the favor and then continues washing himself. When he has finished, I take the soap and brush from him and go on cleaning myself.

I knock out the plug. After the water drains, we take turns pumping fresh cold water into the trough. I pour a pot full of icy water over his head. He sucks in his breath. By the third pot of water, he seems to have gotten used to it. After all, his ancestors came from Norway.

"Your turn," he says, grinning ear to ear.

My ancestors came from Mexico, a much warmer place. He dips the pot into the freezing water, but hands it to me to pour it over myself.

"I'd rather be surprised," I tell him, hunching my shoulders.

He douses me three times. I pant as though I'd been hiking up the mountain.

We drain the trough and refill it one more time for our next bath. Six and I go up to the porch.

I run inside to fetch our last clean towel and our last pairs of clean shorts from upstairs.

Six and I dry ourselves and pull on our shorts. We lean against the porch railing and take a couple of swallows of our beer.

The sky at the end of the overgrown field is the color of poppies and glinting gold. Behind us it is indigo with speckles of starlight.

We lean towards each other and embrace. Six rests his head on my shoulder. I enjoy the sensation of his naked chest against mine.

"Oh, my God, Antonio," he says, pulling away from me. "Your statue. It's on fire."

I turn to look at the stone grotto beneath the cottonwood grove where I have been carving the figure of the Blessed Virgin. Six jumps down the steps and runs to the old trough. He scoops up a bucketful of water.

I realize my statue is not burning. It is the Holy Mother, standing in the place of my carving. Her image glows like wood-coals when a breeze passes over them.

I approach, walking barefoot across the gravel drive. I barely feel it.

Six is soon at my side with the pail of water. He sets it down beside him. We both wear only our undershorts. I feel embarrassed.

"Please, come nearer, my children. You do not need to be ashamed. You need not cover yourselves. You are beautiful as God made you."

My amigo and I smile. She has made us feel comfortable.

"Your love for each other has been tested, *mis hijos*," the Virgin says. "It is your forgiving one another, as Our Lord asks, that has saved your friendship and made your love stronger."

Six puts his arm across my shoulder.

The air shimmers around the Holy Mother, lighting up the stones of the grotto as though they were jewels and gemstones.

"I thank you both for the devotional grotto you have erected here. Not many years from now, this spot will become a destination for pilgrims."

She smiles radiantly.

"There is something I must tell you *Santa Madre*," Six says, looking down at his feet.

"I know about the child, Sixtus," Holy Mother says, stunning both my buddy and me. "He will be christened *Nicolás Antonio*."

"He?" Six asks.

"Yes," the Virgin replies. "*Nicolás Antonio* would be a very odd name for a girl, don't you think?"

Six and I laugh.

"Nicolás Antonio will be born in late December," the Blessed Virgin says.

"On Christmas?" my amigo asks, his face lighting up.

"No," the Virgin says. "Not on Christmas."

"What about the child's mother, *Santa Madre*?" Six asks.

"I am afraid she will be a stranger to her child. It will be up to you and Antonio to make up for her missing love. You must spoil the child and spare the rod."

We smile.

"Do you have another mission for us, Holy Mother?" Six asks.

"You will learn about the next part of my mission for you through Dr. Feynman. I gave him information and instructions in my message to him. The doctor will be able to explain it better than I could.

"Please remember his wife Arline in your prayers. She succumbed to her tuberculosis. Dr. Feynman is heartbroken. They were high school sweethearts."

Six and I glance at each other.

"Though World War II is now officially over, the scars are indelible, my children. Many dangers remain.

"The draft will not be over for several more years. You will both be inducted into the army after high school. I shall visit you again just before you go into the army," the Virgin says.

"What must we do in the meantime, Holy Mother?" I ask.

"Recite the rosary every day as you have been doing, *mis hijos*. Pray for lasting peace.

"Let the Lord's love for you shine through you like light through a lens, magnifying it. Be kind, always and everywhere, especially when it is most difficult.

"Remember. It is forgiveness that will save the world.

"I shall continue to watch over you. All will be well. The Lord is with you."

The Holy Mother's smile radiates warmth in all directions. She glows, and slowly fades away, her form and likeness now burned into the wood statue. My carving smolders, as if it had been rescued from a fire. Tendrils of smoke curl around it.

My statue of the Holy Mother has been completed by *Nuestra Señora* herself. She has imbued my rough-hewn figure with her own fine features. The statue is beautiful beyond anything I'd be able to create.

I shiver. September nights are growing cold.

Six takes my hand and we walk gingerly on the sharp gravel back to the house. The only light is from the back porch. We follow it like a beacon. The fragrance of the singed cedar remains in my nostrils.

We wipe our bare feet on the straw doormat and hurry upstairs. I light the old kerosene lantern atop the dresser.

Keeping on our clean undershorts, my amigo and I scramble beneath the covers. His feet and hands are ice cold. He winces when I touch him with mine.

We lock our arms and legs around each other. Six shakes with shivers. I kiss him and I am no longer so cold myself. We roll onto our backs.

I hold his hand. The lantern light flickers on the ceiling.

"I love you," he says, squeezing my hand. "More and more all the time."

We turn to each other in the wavering light.

"I love you, too, Six. But most of the time I don't feel I deserve your love," I confess.

"Do you think I'd waste my time and my life loving somebody who wasn't worth it?"

"No," I say, "probably not."

"You're right. I wouldn't," he declares, turning to me and kissing me hard on the lips.

It is the first time I have been silenced with a kiss.

The moon hangs like ripened fruit among the branches of the tree.

As I close my eyes, the glowing image of *Nuestra Señora* comes into my mind, standing in the place of my crude carving in Six's grotto.

The wooden figure smiles. It reminds me of my own mother's smile.

CHAPTER SIX

GRATIA TIBI AGIMUS
We Give Thanks to Thee

Hypatia had the child at her parents' house with the help of a *partera*, a midwife, and missed only one semester of college.

Once I decided I must forgive her for my amigo's sake, it was not so hard. I have made my peace with her.

Hypatia said Six and I are what they call *homosexuals*. I couldn't find the word in any dictionary. Maybe she made it up.

I sent Hypatia a Christmas card I drew myself and another when the baby was born. She said the cards were "cute" and made her laugh.

Hypatia gave Six a very beautiful astronomy book, *The Backbone of Night*, about the Milky Way Galaxy. It is loaded with color plates. She called it her graduation present to him. He and I graduate in just over a month. We can't wait. She graduated last year.

I hate to think what the volume cost her. A book on child-rearing might have been more helpful, but I do not mean to complain. Hypatia's OK, I guess.

She and I agree on a couple of things. We both dislike nicknames. That's why I am *Antonio* and not *Tony*. I only answer to my name.

Six's and Hypatia's son, Nicolás Antonio Montoya-Thorson, was born on December 28th, the Feast of the Holy Innocents. The day commemorates King Herod's slaughter of the firstborn sons of Israel in order to do away with the infant Jesus whom Herod's astrologer saw as a rival to the throne.

The baby has his mother's brown Mexican complexion and his father's icy blue eyes. The combination is quite striking.

My amigo called his son *Nicky* as soon as the child arrived. To my Tia Ana, and everyone else in our families, including Hypatia's mother and father, he is *Nicky*, too. The baby had no say about it.

The infant's grandparents on his mother's side, the Montoyas, are on their way to Mexico. They brought the baby, now four months old, along with his truckload of paraphernalia, to Six's grandparents, the Thorsons. Nicky will live with Gram and Gramps for the couple of months that Hypatia's mom and dad will be enjoying their second honeymoon.

To give the old ones a break from minding their great-grandson, little Nicolás stays with my amigo and me on weekends. I cobbled together a crib for the baby out of willow branches lashed together with strips of leather. It made Six very happy—as though I'd made it for him. My Tia Ana sewed a little mattress for the crib and stuffed it with cattail fluff.

The child is a lot more work than I imagined, even for just two days out of seven. It's a good thing Six talked me out of thinking we could raise him.

We moved into my Tio's bedroom on the ground floor and put the infant's crib next to the dresser. It's better than running up and down the stairs to our old bedroom each time one of us hears the slightest whimper. We don't get any more sleep with this arrangement, but at least we can attend to little Nicolás before he works himself up into a proper fit.

No one in Hypatia's family except Hypatia knows Six and I share my Tio's house, which he left to us when he died. Sooner or later her family will find out. Six talks about telling them, but he has no idea how to phrase it. Neither do I.

Six is going to ask his grandpa to mention it to Hypatia's father. But, fortunately, Grandpa Otto doesn't have to say anything to Mr. Montoya about Six living with me.

"That's what some bachelors do, Papa," Hypatia told her father. "Once they move out and before they get married. Six and Antonio also work the same job."

I like Hypatia more than I ever thought I would. God bless her for helping us out.

Mr. Montoya still hopes his daughter might relent some day and marry Six—maybe after she graduates from college. I wouldn't get my hopes up if I was Mr. Montoya. Hypatia already talks about pursuing a graduate degree in astronomy.

I wish I had half Six's faith that any of us will be able to figure our lives out some day. They look as tangled as tumbleweeds to me. Sometimes I think my amigo is optimistic to the point of foolishness.

* 2 *

We get home after a backbreaking day at Mila-Grow Nursery & Greenhouse. Tomorrow is Sunday, thank God, though we will have plenty of chores to keep us busy around the house.

My Tia Ana sits in the rocker beside the empty fireplace, little Nicolás cradled in her arms, fast asleep. She puts her finger to her lips. Six and I take our heavy workboots off by the front door and slip into our moccasins.

We stand beside the rocking chair. Six bends to look at his son. The infant opens his eyes and smiles toothlessly.

"I'm happy to see you, too, Nicky," Six says, stroking the boy's pudgy cheek with his dirty thumb.

My aunt offers the child to him.

"I want to wash up first, Tia," he tells her.

My aunt props the infant up in her lap. His eyes follow us into the kitchen. We pump water for each other, scrubbing our hands with the cake of my aunt's homemade lye soap.

Six takes off his mud-splashed workshirt. His undershirt is sweaty, but at least it's not dirty. I do the same. I take two beers from our noisy refrigerator and we go back to the parlor.

"Would you care for a little beer, Tia?" Six asks, offering to pour some in a glass for her.

"No, thank you, Six. I'm going to go home. I'm very tired today, though it was not little Nicky's fault. He was a perfect angel."

"Did it make up for his being a perfect devil yesterday?" my amigo asks.

"Almost," Tia says, smiling. "Would you like me to stay to give him his bottle before I go home?"

"Thank you, Tia. We'll be all right," I tell her. "Let me walk you home. It's getting dark."

"That would be nice, Antonio."

She takes her heavy wool sweater from the hook beside the front door. I put on my clean denim jacket. It has a blanket lining. I take my aunt's arm and we go out.

There's no moonlight tonight so I light the kerosene railroad lantern from the front porch and hold it in my other hand.

My aunt and I chatter and laugh on the short way to her house just down the road. She invites me in, but I want to get back home. I wait on the porch while she prepares a package of her homemade *biscochitos*, a kind of butter cookie that she baked for us yesterday.

"They're not for Nicky," she admonishes. "He's too young. He'd choke on them. Good night, Antonio. God bless you, *mi hijo*."

"He already has, Tia. Too many times for me to count," I say, giving her a kiss.

She goes back inside her house. The aroma of the cookies in the paper sack wafts towards my nose. I realize how hungry I am and run home.

I am struck by the warmth and the smell of cooking as soon as I open the front door. I hang my jacket on the peg and take the bag of Tia's cinnamon and anise *biscochitos* into the kitchen.

I find Six cradling his son in the crook of his arm as they sit at the kitchen table. They both look up and smile.

The image that comes to mind is the old creased photo of my own father holding me in his arm, trying to push a spoonful of porridge into my mouth. My mother must have snapped the picture.

I burst into tears remembering the photo.

"What's the matter, Antonio?" Six asks, getting up from the chair.

Holding little Nicolás, he comes up to me and puts his free arm around my shoulders, drawing me to him. The baby puts his hand on my chin. I wrap an arm around Six's waist. He looks into my eyes. My tears continue streaming.

"It'll be coming up on five years since my father was killed, Six. I still miss him so much," I sob. "Seeing you and the little one reminded me of him."

"That's a good thing, isn't it?" he asks, wiping my tears with his fingers.

"Yes. It's a good thing, Six. But then I lost my Tio Nicolás, my second father."

"I miss him, too, amigo. But we have a new Nicolás in our life. And he's crazy about his Tio Antonio."

Little Nicky slaps my chin.

"Come on. We're all starving. You take Nicky," Six says, handing the baby to me. "I'll get supper on the table."

"Yes. That's your Tio," he tells the child.

The baby makes burbling, bubbling noises that sound like he said *Tio*. I'm sure I imagined it.

It still makes me nervous to hold such a precious package. The baby feels so fragile, so helpless—so breakable. He makes faces and fusses. I rock side to side and he quiets down.

After testing the temperature of Nicky's milk by squirting some on the inside of his wrist, Six hands me the baby's bottle. My aunt and Six's grandma taught us what we must do. I had no idea a baby was this much work.

"Hah! Just you wait until he starts walking," Grandma Matilda warned. "You'll see the very kind of mischief you and Six got into."

Nicky looks all around but is especially interested in what his papa is doing at the stove. I whistle a couple of notes and he looks up at me, my chance to get the nipple in his mouth. He sucks so hard I think he'll swallow the entire bottle. He comes up for air and burps.

Six takes our opened bottles of beer from the icebox and puts them at our places. He sets the table with two bowls, spoons, and two small plates and napkins. He cuts four slices off a loaf of cheddar bread with jalapeños, putting the knife and cutting board on the table. My mouth waters.

The soup is cream of celery, made with the first fresh stalks and roots from our kitchen garden. I am not looking forward to weeding season.

Six fills our bowls and slides his chair up to the table. He bows his head.

"It's your turn," I tell him.

He looks up at me, then lowers his eyes again.

"Dear God. Thank you for our many blessings and for the food you set before us. Bless little Nicky and help us raise him as Your child. Amen."

Nicky pushes the bottle away and gurgles.

"You can hand the little one back to me, Antonio, so you can get some food in you," Six says.

"We're comfortable," I reply. "You can butter my bread for me, though. It's hard to do one-handed."

"Sure," he says, smearing my two slices with butter from the crock on the table.

Six eats his own bread plain for once, dunking it in the soup.

Nicky watches me, following the spoon from the bowl of soup to my mouth. He is no longer interested in his bottle of milk. I dip the tip of my finger in the celery soup and put it in his mouth. He spits and makes an icky face. Then he lets out a loud burp. We laugh.

After I clear the table, Six puts Nicky in his crib in our bedroom.

I draw two big pots of water for our baths in the bathroom tub. I put the kettles on the wood stove, stirring the embers and adding two small logs. There is talk of a late frost tonight.

We polish off my aunt's cookies while waiting for the water to boil.

Six lets me take my bath first, adding the second pot of boiling water to the tepid water in the old porcelain tub. It feels wonderful. He scrubs my back.

I climb into bed naked and wait for Six, warming his side of the bed. The kerosene lantern atop the tall dresser flickers.

All day I thought of lying next to him, hoping we might both be in the mood to get frisky. I try to stay awake for him, but sleep overtakes me. His crawling between the covers awakens me, but I cannot get any words out. He kisses my neck.

The baby screeches and howls three times during the night, each time just as I was drifting off to sleep again. I am disturbed less by Nicky's crying than by Six's jostling the bed to get up and attend to him. He lets in cold air, too.

When I awaken near dawn, Six, his head resting against my shoulder, snores softly. I fall asleep again listening to his throaty murmurs.

* * *

I wake up and scoot over to Six's side of the bed. He must have gotten up a while ago. The sheets are cold where he has lain. I scramble into fresh long-johns and my moccasins, and pull on a T-shirt.

Six cradles Nicky in his arm at the kitchen table. They must have been up since dawn. Six is dressed except for his Sunday white shirt. I slept through it all.

"Good morning," he says.

The baby looks up at me, too, but keeps chugging on his bottle of milk. It is nearly empty.

"Mornin'," I reply.

I would die for a cup of coffee this morning. I fast before mass so I can receive Holy Communion, drinking only water after midnight. Six fasts out of sympathy for me.

"We're running kinda late. We'd better step on it," he says.

Six holds the baby against his chest and burps him, something Nicky does willingly. As Six changes the baby's diaper in his crib, I put on my socks and my newest overalls. I never ironed our white shirts from our last washday. Not much of them will be seen anyhow once we put on our new denim jackets that are only for Sunday and special occasions.

My buddy wraps his son in a sort of sleeping sack his grandma made from an old wool blanket. There is a spare in case the baby gets the first one wet. The sack has a flap at the top to cover the baby's head. I hold the squirming bundle while Six finishes getting dressed.

It is a cold morning for early May in these parts. Everything is coated white with hoarfrost, including the old pickup truck. I scrape the windshield. We climb in, me behind the wheel, Six holding the little one.

Though reluctant, the cold engine starts at last. It stalls again at the end of our drive. I let it run a couple minutes before putting it in gear. Six looks at his watch.

"There's not going to be enough time to drop Nicky at my Gram's and Gramps', Antonio. We'd better drive straight to church."

I look at him.

"Are you sure?" I ask.

He shrugs, and then nods.

"Nicky hasn't been to church since his baptism. He's being a pretty good kid today. I think we can chance it, Antonio."

"All right," I say. "Maybe Jesus would like to see him again."

There are only a few cars and trucks outside Nuestra Madre de Dolores Church. We are only a couple of minutes early for eight o'clock mass.

Mabel Nuñez, from one of the oldest families in the parish, stands just inside the door, in the chilly vestibule. She is still an attractive woman, though she's let herself get a bit plump. She hands out the church bulletins and hymnals. I take one for Six.

"Oh, my," she says, her broad smile lighting up her whole face. "This must be our newest member of the parish."

"Yes," Six tells her. "This is Nicolás Antonio—*Nicky* for short."

My buddy lifts the hood on the baby's blanket-sack. Mrs. Nuñez pokes his cheek and Nicky laughs.

"My," she says. "Such a happy baby."

"For now," Six tells her. "Let's just hope it lasts."

Mabel Nuñez's dresses always match her hats, always worn with the fishnet veil down. Summer or winter, she wears gloves. Mr. Nuñez was a sharp dresser, too. He died of pneumonia last winter. Six and I pray for him.

We bless ourselves at the holy water font. Six puts a drop on Nicky's forehead. There are about two dozen people attending, sitting mostly in the first few pews. According to our custom, Six and I take the last pew.

Father Miguel and the groggy altar boys enter the sanctuary. We stand. Mabel Nuñez enters from the vestibule and sits in the pew opposite us where she and her husband always sat. Miss Emelina, the old school teacher, pumps the pedals on the tiny organ and introduces the entrance hymn. Usually, there is no music at the early mass, only at the eleven o'clock high mass.

Nicky is prompted to join in with squeals and shrieks. I fight to keep from laughing out loud. He's inclined to help Father Miguel with his recitation of the prayers, too.

When the congregation answers with their responses, however, the low rumbling of our voices, echoing through the church like waves crashing on the shore, frightens the little one. He wails and squalls loud enough to turn his tiny lungs inside out.

Six manages to calm him before the next rumbles rebound through the church.

An older fellow in the first pew gets up and steps into the aisle without bowing or genuflecting or crossing himself.

"Come on, Estelle," he says in a loud voice, taking the hand of the gray-haired woman beside him. "I didn't come here to listen to that infernal cater-wauling. Church is for grown-ups. What's next? A nursery in the choir loft?"

Mabel Nuñez steps into the aisle beside her pew, hands on her hips. She is a very outspoken woman, afraid of no one. The man and his wife, visitors to Nuestra Madre de Dolores Church, attempt to step around her.

"Excuse me, sir," she says in a lowered voice that only Six and I can hear. "Before you stomp out of here *por despecho*, in a pique, I'd like you to consider that maybe that's what *we* sound like to God."

The man harrumphs and pulls his wife along beside him. They leave the church. Mrs. Nuñez nods to us.

"There," she whispers. "Nobody talks mean in *my* church."

We smile at her and she resumes her place. Fr. Consuelo may be the pastor of *Nuestra Madre*, but Mabel Nuñez is our mother—all of us, the entire parish.

After the Epistle and Gospel, Father Miguel steps over to the lectern for his sermon, an occasion Six and I often make use of to catch up on sleep.

Perhaps prompted by the old fellow's cranky outburst, Father Miguel's topic for this Sunday's sermon is, *Suffer the little children to come unto me.*

Six nods off nearly as soon as Father Miguel begins speaking. I nudge him, afraid he and the baby will tumble out of the pew.

For the rest of mass, there is not another peep out of Nicky, fast asleep in his sleepy father's arms.

* 3 *

Hypatia told her friend Ginnie, who's in my and Six's graduating class, not to tell a living soul about her pregnancy or to reveal the identity of the father. As a result, the gossip spread like a prairie-grass fire.

My amigo and I thought that might have put to rest the rumor circulated so gleefully by the class bully, Jorge Carbón, that Six and I were more than "just friends." But the news of Six's fatherhood didn't stop "Big George," as he likes to be called. He's been picking on us, on and off, since sophomore year. He's not happy unless he's making someone's life miserable.

There are thirty-five seniors in our graduating class, lined up alphabetically on the two front rows of bleachers in the gymnasium. Six and I—Thorson and Sanchez—get to sit next to each other.

I thought I would be more excited than I am. It feels like what our literature teacher, Mrs. Dowdy, called an anti-climax.

The principal and assistant principal both like to talk. I'll have to fight twice as hard to stay awake through their speeches.

Jorge sits down in front of us, in the first row of bleachers. He turns around, smirking. He doesn't bother to whisper.

"Awww, the sweethearts," he says, puckering his lips and blowing a kiss. "We been classmates all this time, you know, huh? And I still can't tell which of you plays the boy and which of you is the girl."

Even sitting half-a-foot away from my amigo, I can feel Six's muscles tense.

"Not now, Six," I whisper. "You've kept your head. This isn't the time to blow your stack. Please, amigo."

He smiles.

"I asked you nancy-boys a question. Don't I get an answer?" Big George says.

"George," Six replies. "Put an egg in your shoe and beat it."

The bully's jaw drops, but nothing comes out. He looks shocked. Everyone who hears Six's remark chuckles.

The public address system squeals and squawks. Everyone stands.

Principal Lujan taps the microphone. He invites Father Miguel to say a benediction for the Roswell High School Class of 1946. Then we recite the Pledge of Allegiance.

It finally sinks in. My amigo and I are going to be free at last. For Six and me, school's gonna be out forever. I want to shout.

But first we have to listen to the buzzing, droning speechifying. My mind wanders.

After the school chorus sings the national anthem and our school song, we resume our places on the uncomfortable bleachers.

Six hooks the hem of Big George's graduation gown over a corner of the seat behind the bully's back. Those behind George see what my amigo has done. The nudging of elbows goes up and down the line of students. There is quiet laughter and twittering.

Big George turns around. Everyone stares straight ahead.

"How will you explain that to the Holy Mother, Six?" I whisper to him. "She said, *Be kind, always and everywhere, especially when it is most difficult.*"

Six nods and looks down, a little bit ashamed of himself, I'm guessing.

"Yeah," he says. "It's pretty difficult this time."

He unhooks the hem of George's graduation gown from the corner of the bleacher seat.

Someone says, "Aw, darn." There's chuckling on either side of us.

Principal Lujan calls, "Jorge Alphonso Carbón."

George gets up. In his hurry to receive his diploma before someone thinks better of awarding it to him, he steps on the hem of his black gown. Everyone hears the loud rip.

Big George lands head first on the wood gym floor. His mortarboard skitters into the free-throw zone.

The class bully is helped to his feet by one of his henchmen. He has a bloody nose. The entire gymnasium, down to the last girl and boy and even a few teachers, erupts into laughter that is loud and long. There is applause. George is helped out of the gym by the school nurse.

Six gets many slaps on the back and congratulations from our classmates who must still think he had something to do with Big George's falling on his face. Though it wasn't his doing, Six has his revenge for being called a sissy since sophomore year.

It is quite a while before order and quiet are restored. As they resume calling names, our row on the bleachers stands up.

"Juan Antonio Sanchez."

My heart flutters. It's hard to swallow. My mouth is dry. I'm glad I won't have to say anything more than, "Thank you, sir."

"Sixtus Otto Thorson."

My heart skips a beat to hear my buddy's name called, too.

I feel like I'm walking in my sleep. Nothing seems quite real.

We receive our diplomas in their spiffy leather folders. I look at mine again on the way back to my place. They even spelled my name right.

I stop at our row. Six plunks his mortarboard on an empty bleacher seat and pulls his graduation gown over his head. He rolls it up and sets it beside his cap. He begins walking out.

"You coming?" he asks, pausing in the double doorway.

I don't know if I should go or stay.

"What're they gonna do?" my amigo asks. "Expel us?"

I laugh. I take off my cap and gown and set them beside Six's.

He puts his arm on my shoulder and we walk out to the parking lot before the graduation ceremony ends.

I think Six encourages me to take more chances than I otherwise might. I hope my influence on Six is to make him more cautious. God knows, he doesn't need to become more daring.

We fling our arms up, shouting the old singsong from grade school:

> *No more pencils,*
> *no more books,*
> *no more teacher's dirty looks.*

Six and I dance a kind of crazy jitterbug all the way back to the truck.

"Thank God Almighty," Six shouts at the top his lungs. "Free at last."

* * *

Six and I had hoped for a quiet evening at home—as quiet as Nicky will allow us, that is. But Tia Ana insisted that graduating high school is *una gran cosa*—a big deal.

She has invited everyone but the people I would most like to see at our graduation party—my mother and father and my Tio Nicolás. I know my uncle would be proud enough of me to burst apart at the seams. He never graduated high school.

Neither Six nor I was up to having breakfast this morning. We had a good case of the jitters. But now we're ready to chow down at the first sign of food on the table.

Our graduation party is held at our house because Tia Ana's *casita* is too small. There is a battered army Jeep parked beside the barn in back.

"Uh-oh," I say. "Looks like they finally caught up with us, amigo. What're we gonna do?"

"Take it easy, that's what," he replies. "Let's not jump to conclusions. Let's just wade into 'em, OK?"

He goes up the steps.

"What do you think they could do to us, Six?"

"Probably shoot us at sunrise," he says, smiling. "So let's enjoy our last meal."

I take Six's arm and hold him back. I feel we are walking right into a trap set by Hoover's G-men.

"No, amigo. You have a son to think of now. Let me go in first and see what's what."

"Why you, Antonio? We're both gonna have to face the music sooner or later."

Six grabs the knob and opens the kitchen door.

We are greeted with the wonderful aromas of my aunt's and Six's grandma's cooking and baking. They got here at dawn to prepare.

"Whose Jeep is that out back, Tia?" I ask.

"Jeep?" she says, wiping her floured hands on her apron. "I think it belongs to Dr. Feynman."

"Dr. Feynman?"

The doctor steps from the parlor into the kitchen, grinning like the Cheshire cat. He's gotten a little gray on the sides since we last saw him in Los Alamos.

"Hello, men," he says. "Congratulations on your matriculation into the real world."

We smile and shake his hand.

Six takes his good work jacket off and hangs it beside the kitchen door. I hang mine on the peg next to his.

"Your Aunt Ana wrote me a couple months back. I knew I owed you both a letter or two, so I thought, *Why not?* I'm on my way to closing out my office at the lab. Otherwise Uncle Sam is going to start charging me rent."

"We're very glad to see you, Doctor," I tell him, smiling. "Aren't we, Six?"

Six's grandma catches him lifting the towel on her lattice-work pie and spanks his hand. I hope it's a raspberry pie. Grandma knows that's my favorite.

"Care for a little beer, Doctor," I ask him.

"That would be great. Thanks, Antonio."

Six picks up Dr. Feynman's leather flight jacket and his gray hat from the kitchen chair and sets them on our bed. Though Six tiptoed, Nicky awakens and screams out a lungful.

He takes the infant from his crib and comes into the kitchen, cradling him in his arm. Little Nicky quiets down.

"Meet Dr. Feynman," he tells the baby. "And this is my son, Nicolás Antonio, *Nicky*, for short."

"I see," the doctor says, "but I guess I don't. I mean... I thought..."

"Let's go out to the *portál*, Dr. Feynman," I suggest, trying to deflect him.

"Yes, please, Antonio," Grandma says. "The kitchen's getting crowded."

I hand the doctor his bottle of Dos Equis. We go out to the rear porch. I carry Six's beer, handing it to him when Nicky gets nestled into his other arm.

"I guess a second congratulations are in order, after your graduation today," the doctor says, tapping Six's bottle of beer with his own.

The baby looks up at the clinking sound and smiles.

"Nobody's story is without a few twists and turns, but I'm lost," Dr.

Feynman says. "Help me out, Six. I thought you and your buddy were, um..."

"We are, Doctor. But... I made a serious mistake with a girl we knew from school."

I know Six is trying to be careful of my feelings, but it still hurts to remember it. I look down.

"The girl and I had lotsa help from a bottle of her father's brandy. Hypatia was a year older. She taught me most of what I know about astronomy."

The doctor smiles and says, "Well, astronomy... is *like sex: sure, it may give some practical results, but that's not why we do it.*"

We all laugh, even the baby. He reaches for Six's bottle of beer.

"The mother wants to continue her education at Columbia University," Six explains. "So Nicky's grandparents will raise him—with plenty of help from my grandma and grandpa and Antonio's aunt, too."

The baby gurgles. The doctor tickles his chin.

"There's a third celebration today, Doctor," I announce. "It's also Six's birthday."

"Well. Congratulations, Six," the doctor tells him, raising his bottle of beer.

"I turn eighteen next week," I say. "On Tuesday."

He raises his bottle of Dos Equis to me, and takes a swallow.

"How'd you get here, Doctor?" I ask him. "My aunt didn't breathe a word of your surprise visit. She kept your secret."

"The army flew me from upstate New York to Roswell Army Air Force base. They provided me a Jeep to drive up to the lab in Los Alamos."

"That's a long drive," Six tells him. "Antonio and I have done it."

"I drove every weekend from the lab down to the clinic in Albuquerque to be with Arline while she was sick. I was privileged to be with her when she died."

He sighs.

"So what are you boys going to do about the army?"

"We're going to enlist early next year, after Nicky is a year old," Six tells him. "We've already signed up. It's a two-year stint whether we enlist or wait to be drafted. But if we enlist, we might get to choose our training and be stationed closer to home."

"Sounds like you boys thought this all out."

"It only looks that way," I tell him, grinning. "I think we just bumble along and get lucky sometimes."

Dr. Feynman laughs.

"It's no different for any of us, Antonio. You're just more honest about it."

"I've gotta change Nicky," Six says. "Then he'll want his bottle and then a nap. Can I get you another beer, Doctor?"

"Sure," he says. "*Gracias.*"

Six and Nicky go inside.

Grandpa's tan Chevy pickup pulls into the back yard. The horn honks.

"It's Six's grandpa and our third-grade teacher, Miss Emelina," I tell the doctor. "Grandpa Otto is the baby's great-grandfather."

I go into the yard to greet them. They ascend the steps and I introduce them.

Miss Emelina carries a paper bag. She is famous for her *galletas de suero*, buttermilk biscuits. I hope she's made a batch. She nods to the doctor and goes into the kitchen.

Grandpa extends his hand.

"Pleased to finally meet you, Dr. Feynman," he says. "Are you a medical doctor or an egghead doctor?"

"The egghead kind, I'm afraid."

"Don't be," Grandpa tells him. "Nothing to apologize for so long as you don't let it go to your head."

"I try not to," the doctor says, grinning.

"I understand you helped the boys out of a scrape that might've gotten serious," Gramps remarks. "They're good boys, but a little hare-brained sometimes."

"I remember being their age," Dr. Feynman says.

"Me, too," Grandpa replies. "That's what's got me worried."

Six comes back onto the porch with another bottle of beer for Dr. Feynman.

"How long are you staying, Dr. Feynman?" Grandpa asks. "Where you headed, if I may ask?"

"I'm going up to the lab in Los Alamos. I've got to pick up a few things."

"That's where they figured out the A-bomb, isn't it? You know anything about that?"

"A little," the doctor replies.

"Good. Maybe you can explain it to me then."

"I'd have to explain how it works to myself first," he says.

Gramps chuckles.

The kitchen door opens and Tia Ana calls us in to supper.

The spread before us is worthy to be called a feast. There are so many serving bowls and platters of food on the table that there's barely room for our dinner plates and soup bowls. Six holds Nicky, who is drawing on his bottle hard enough to turn the glass inside out.

Dr. Feynman joins us as we stand behind our chairs for the grace. I will sit between Six and his grandpa.

After my Tio Nicolás died, Grandpa Otto became the oldest man in our families. He will say grace. We bow or heads. I watch the steam rise from the hot food.

"Dear Lord, thank you for the time you shared Nicolás with us before calling him home. Thank you for bringing a new friend to us," Grandpa says, nodding to Dr. Feynman. "Thank you for the love we at this table share. And thank you for the wonderful meal you and Ana and Matilda and Miss Emelina have set before us. Oh. And God bless America."

Our *Amens* are mixed with the scraping of chair legs as we all sit down. Food is passed and conversations started up without anyone directing the hubbub.

We begin with one of my favorites: my Tia Ana's spicy acorn squash and apple soup. Little Nicky pushes the nipple out of his mouth, looking up to watch his father each time he puts the spoonful of soup into his mouth. I think it's cute.

I stand to carve the first chicken. Grandpa opens a bottle of red wine and fills our glasses. We all say, "Just a little, Grandpa," but he ignores everyone.

The bowls and platters of food are passed around the table with no one directing traffic. There are tamales and tortillas, and a tomato salad with corn and green onions. Grandma Matilda takes a tray of Miss Emelina's buttermilk biscuits from the oven and puts in a tray of cherry jack *empanadas*.

I put food on my plate and then on Six's as it goes past. I take Nicky from him so Six can get some of the delicious meal into *his* mouth. The baby fusses at first. I dip my finger in the soup and offer it to him. He makes a face and spits. Grandma looks at me sternly over her glasses.

Dr. Feynman pushes his chair back and gets to his feet. He proposes a toast with his glass of wine. We raise ours. Nicky watches me and reaches for the bottom of my glass.

"I am sorry my late wife Arline is not here to join us, either. But I am enormously thankful to be with all of you at this table. To our good health. *Salud.*"

He swallows his glassful. Grandpa reaches over and refills it. I do not care for wine. I put it to my lips but don't drink any. Six doesn't seem to mind the taste.

It's hard to get food in my mouth with the baby cradled in my left arm. I stand up to walk around the living room with him and burp him. I still marvel at how much work it is caring for a child. Both our entire families seem like hardly enough people for the job.

Placing Nicky in his crib, I rub his tummy. He smiles and yawns. His eyelids flutter and close. I tuck the blanket beneath his chin and leave the bedroom.

"Thank you, Antonio," Six tells me. "I put your plate on the stove to keep it warm."

"What about you, Six? Were you waiting for me?"

"Nope," he replies. "This is my second helping. Better hurry up."

"What should I do with the little three-cornered colonial hat things you brought, Dr. Feynman?" my aunt asks.

"They're *hamantaschen*. It's a dessert pastry. My mother baked them for all sorts of celebrations. I picked these up in New York."

Grandma and Tia take the plates of desserts to the table, including the lattice-crust raspberry pie. Six cranks the eggbeater furiously to make whipped cream. The kitchen seems crowded again.

Dr. Feynman and I go onto the back porch. He lights a cigarette with his Zippo lighter. We look up at the setting quarter moon. He makes the cigarette seem like it tastes awfully good. Six and I never had an inclination to try smoking.

"Do you and Six ever wonder about life beyond Earth?" he asks, blowing smoke and the steam of his breath into the cool evening air.

"You mean like maybe on Mars?" I suggest. "That's like science fiction, isn't it?"

"Maybe," he replies. "It's best to keep an open mind, don't you think?"

He crushes the butt of his cigarette on the ground and picks it up.

"I hope you and I and Six will have the opportunity to have a long talk tomorrow," he says. "I'm eager to tell you about your meteorite. I'll have to drive up to Los Alamos early on Sunday. I won't have time to stop on the way back."

"We plan to leave little Nicky with my aunt tomorrow and drive out to Bottomless Lake. We have something to show you, Doctor."

Six opens the kitchen door and calls us inside. The warmth and aromas and laughter make me feel very blessed and happy.

The table is set with all the pastries and cookies and Dr. Feynman's fruit-filled *hamantaschen*. I feel like we should say another grace just for the desserts.

Tia Ana sets the teapot on a trivet and Grandma Matilda brings the coffee pot. Grandpa Otto pours some of his hot spiced wine, called *glögg*, into two glass mugs for himself and Dr. Feynman. Grandma raises her eyebrows and looks down over her glasses at her husband.

Six slices the pie, plopping whipped cream on each wedge.

Grandpa Otto's *glögg* smells fragrant and fruity. It reminds me of an autumn farm stand.

Dr. Feynman raises his clear mug and asks, "To what shall we toast?"

"To the past," Grandpa says. "And to the future."

"Let's not forget the present moment," the doctor says. "Cheers," he adds, taking a healthy swallow.

Grandpa take a sip. The rest of us raise a cup of tea or coffee.

"This is good. What's in it?" Dr. Feynman asks.

"Red wine, port, rum, and brandy—plus almonds, raisins, cloves, and cinnamon," Grandpa replies. "Gotta watch out for them raisins, though. They pack a heck of a wallop."

We laugh. Grandpa refills the doctor's mug.

Dr. Feynman's tongue gets a bit slippery around the edges of some of his words. It's kind of funny because he's trying to be so serious. He rambles. Only Gramps seems to follow him.

No one wants seconds of the desserts. Six and I sampled a little of everything. I'm stuffed. Grandpa and Dr. Feynman haven't touched their desserts, getting by instead on the mulled wine.

We leave them at the kitchen table and go into the parlor.

Six and I open our graduation envelopes from our families. Our gifts make our graduation *official*.

Miss Emelina has given us what feels like a book. We each collect five dollars inside our graduation cards.

"Thank you," Six and I say in unison.

"That's for you both to buy new overalls so you don't have to look like vagabonds on Sunday," Grandma says.

"They're not for work, either," my aunt adds.

There will be almost two bucks apiece left over for me and my amigo after we buy new Levi's.

"You may think the book I selected for you is a children's story because it is an allegory," Miss Emelina tell us. "But I assure you *Animal Farm* is quite a serious work. I think you boys will have no trouble understanding Mr. Orwell's intention."

"Thank you, Miss Emelina," Six and I say.

"You should leave little Nicky with me tonight, *mis hijos*," my aunt says, "so you won't have to come by with him in the morning."

"I don't want to disturb him, Tia," Six says. "He's sound asleep. Who knows if he'll ever fall asleep again for the rest of his entire life?"

We laugh. There's nearly simultaneous laughter from the kitchen. Dr. Feynman and Grandpa talk above one another.

"I hope the doctor remembers the good time he's having tonight in the morning," Grandma remarks. "Otto is used to his *glögg*. I'll loan you an ice bag for Dr. Feynman."

"I think I would like to be going home, Matilda dear," the old school teacher announces.

Grandma helps Miss Emelina put on her coat. Gram goes into the kitchen and announces to Gramps that they are going home. He and the doctor swallow the last of the spiced wine in their mugs and stand up. They're both a little giddy and wobbly.

We kiss Tia and Grandma goodnight, and shake Miss Emelina's hand. Six takes his grandma's elbow. I latch onto my aunt's and Miss Emelina's. It is dark and we walk slowly down the porch steps.

Grandma starts the engine of their pickup, turning on the headlamps and putting it in gear. She is not about to let Grandpa drive them home. He does not argue with his wife. Six and I go back to the house and wave to them from the porch.

Gramps lets down the tailgate and rolls into back of the truck. They will drop Tia at her house and then Gramps will get in the cab.

The kitchen is a mess. Dr. Feynman sleeps in his chair, his head tilted back. Six and I smile at each other.

"Think we oughta clean up the kitchen tonight or make a racket in the morning?" I whisper to Six.

"I vote for doing it in the morning," he tells me. "We don't want to wake Nicky up."

"What about the doctor?" I ask.

"I think we'd better get him up to your old room, Antonio. I don't think it'd be safe to leave him in the chair without strapping him in."

We chuckle.

Six takes the doctor's leather bag upstairs. I pump water to fill the empty cooking pots at the sink. It's hard to be quiet about it. The noise wakens the doctor.

"Are we there yet?" Dr. Feynman asks jokingly.

He stands. We steady him on either side and get him to the stairway.

"Where're we going," he asks.

"To the interrogation room," Six remarks.

"In that case, I confess," Dr. Feynman says. "I confess to knowing very little about much of anything."

His tongue slips on his words. He chuckles at himself. I like that. He hasn't let his brains go to his head.

Six and I position ourselves above and below Dr. Feynman as he goes up the narrow staircase to my old bedroom. Six walks backwards up the steps, ready to catch the doctor if he topples forward. I wait behind, ready to push him if he totters backwards. He does better than I expected.

He hums an odd tune I don't recognize. I wonder if it might be a Jewish nursery song his mother taught him. I'm not sure why I think that.

I light the old railroad lantern that sits atop the tall dresser. Six pulls back the quilt and we lower Dr. Feynman onto the bed. He lands like a sack of seed. I untie his shoes and tug them off. Six pulls the quilt over him.

The doctor goes back to humming himself to sleep. I turn down the kerosene lamp and Six and I go out.

I leave an oil lamp burning on the kitchen table in case Dr. Feynman needs to find his way downstairs to the bathroom during the night.

Six grinds the coffee beans and sets up the coffee pot for the morning. I bank the coals in the kitchen stove. Then we turn in.

The little one hears us and turns his lungs inside out. Six picks Nicky up and cuddles him.

They go into the kitchen. I hear clattering as my amigo gets a bottle of milk ready for his son. He makes up a bedtime story for Nicky while the water boils.

I fall asleep listening to Six's story to his son. I don't catch all of it. There is something about three wanderers and three ships and three treasure chests. I'm not sure when Six came to bed.

I lost count how many times he got up during the night to check on the baby, whether Nicky cried out or not.

Maybe I should've built a larger crib so Six and the infant could sleep together and let me get on with my night's rest. I'm going to suggest it to my amigo in the morning.

* 4 *

It is barely light out. Six jostles the bed and hangs his legs over the side. I feel the cold air. He reaches for his longjohns on the post of the old brass bedstead. I kept mine on.

"Let me get the fire going and make us some coffee," he whispers.

"I'd rather have your heat," I say.

Six smiles and ruffles my hair. He slips into his longjohns and stands up. He doesn't put a shirt on. I shiver, and roll over onto the warmth he has left in the mattress.

He peers into the crib and pulls up the blanket, tucking it beneath Nicky's chin. He turns to me and smiles before leaving the bedroom.

The noise in the kitchen does not prevent me from drifting off to sleep again. I awaken to the sound of the chattering coffee pot on the wood stove, encouraging me to get up at last. I don my new workshirt from yesterday and my moccasins, and go into the kitchen.

Six has done most of last night's dishes and has put things back in the larder. I hear Dr. Feynman splashing water in the bathroom, a small curtained enclosure separating it from the kitchen.

I set three coffee mugs on the table. Six fills them. Our guest emerges from the bathroom.

"Good morning, men," he says.

He's still in his clothes from yesterday. He grimaces as he sits down, as though movement caused him discomfort. He puts the mug to his lips with both hands, inhaling some of the coffee aroma before taking a healthy swallow. I know the signs of a hangover from when my Tio Nicolás overdid his tequila or his Presidente brandy.

I feel bad for him, but both of Six's grandparents warned him about the glögg. He drains his coffee mug and Six refills it.

"Ahh. That's better," the doctor remarks, rubbing his eyes.

"We'll be leaving little Nicky with my Tia Ana today," I remind the doctor. "We'll go down there for breakfast."

"Good," he replies. "I left lox and bagels in her icebox. Think she'll have some eggs on hand?"

"She'd better," I tell him. "She raises chickens."

"Do you remember the song you were humming last night, Dr. Feynman?" I ask. "Is it a Jewish lullaby?"

He takes a sip of his coffee and pauses.

"No, it's Swedish, actually. Or maybe it's Norwegian. God knows where my mother learned it. There were three strangers in three ships bringing three treasures. I remember very little of it now."

I recall some of Six's bedtime story to Nicky last night where there were things in threes.

Six gets up from the table. We swallow the last of our coffee and return to the bedroom to finish getting dressed. My amigo bundles his son up in his woolen sleeping-sack. Dr. Feynman goes back upstairs for his leather bag.

We find him standing next to the hearth, looking at the photos arranged on the mantle. He's changed his shirt, and holds his flight jacket beneath his arm. He carries a camera in its leather case, the strap slung over his other shoulder.

Six and I take our jackets from the front door. We go outside, Six carrying little Nicky.

"We're going to take our pickup out to the lake later, Dr. Feynman," Six tells him.

He hands the baby to me. Dr. Feynman and I decide to walk. Six drives the pickup down to my aunt's *casita*.

The morning is brisk. The doctor walks as fast as a roadrunner. It's hard to keep up with him, especially since I am carrying the little one. Six gets to the house only a minute before with the truck. The walk helped me wake up the rest of the way.

"Yaah," Nicky hollers as we walk through the front door and into the kitchen.

"Good morning, gentlemen," Tia says, turning around from the stove.

"Yaah," the baby repeats as Six takes him from me and rocks him in his arms. Nicky's smile takes up half his face.

"How do you feel Dr. Feynman?" my aunt asks.

"As good as can be expected under the circumstances," he replies, smiling. "Not bad, actually. Let me help you in the kitchen, Tia Ana. Do you have any capers?"

"I don't know what they are," she admits, "so I guess I'm fresh out."

"How about shallots?"

"No, but I've got green onions."

"They'll do," the doctor says.

Six and Nicky sit at the kitchen table. The baby yawns.

I pour three coffees, handing one to Dr. Feynman, and set the table. Tia prefers her rosehips tea and honey.

My buddy and I watch his son's eyelids slowly set. The noise from the stove and sink do not disturb him. He sleeps an innocent sleep, surrounded by love and untroubled by care. I think of the baby Jesus in the cradle his father

Joseph carved for him, the Holy Mother looking down at her child and smiling her radiant smile.

The food coming to the table awakens me from my reverie. Nicky stirs, too.

Dr. Feymnan's smoked salmon, rye toast, toasted bagels, and cream chcese sit in the center of the table. He's made two enormous omelets with diced green onions and goat's cheese.

I don't know how I could be hungry again, but the spread before us has made me famished. I make the sign of the cross and ask God to bless our meal.

Six has gotten to be very good at putting food into his mouth with Nicky squirming in his other arm. The baby reaches for each forkful Six brings to his mouth. I smile.

"Will you boys be back in time for supper?" my aunt asks.

"Pretty sure we will be, Tia," I tell her. "We're just going out to Bottom-less Lake. We want to show the doctor where we found the meteorites."

My aunt puts the last potato pancake, made with last night's leftover mashed potatoes, on the doctor's plate. He looks much better than when he first got up.

My amigo hands Nicky over to me so he can finish his breakfast. Dr. Feynman watches us.

When the doctor finishes his breakfast, Six gets up from the table. He brings the dishes to the sink and begins pumping water. I get up to help him

"Leave that for me, *mis hijos*," my aunt says. "You must show your guest a good time."

She takes the apron from my hand and gives us each a kiss on the cheek, including Dr. Feynman. She takes the baby from me and kisses him, too. We put on our jackets, hanging on the backs of our chairs, and go outside.

My aunt has a wicker laundry basket with a pillow in it sitting on the porch. She puts Nicky into it and covers him with the tiny blanket she knit for him. She and the baby go back inside.

"My Tia takes the basket with her throughout the house so she can keep an eye on Nicky," I tell the doctor.

"That's a clever idea," he says.

"I think we ought to invest in a wicker basket, too," Six says. "Several women from the pueblo make baskets and sell them at the farmers' market."

"It's got my vote," I remark, "though Nicky will probably outgrow it before anyone can finish weaving one. He's growing like a weed."

My remark reminds me that weeding season has begun.

I take the wheel of my Tio's old pickup. Six scoots beside me. Dr. Feyn-man climbs up and sits on the outside. I crank the engine and let it warm up before stepping on the clutch and putting it in gear.

We head into the blazing late-morning sun. It warms up the cab in no time. I decide to go the long way around to Bottomless Lake, coming in from the east. We want to see what's on the other side of the pile of meteorites. We have plenty of time.

The ruts and potholes seem deeper on this side. There are three craters in the dirt road that we have to drive around. Maybe Dr. Feynman's Jeep would have had an easier time of it. I slow down. I don't want to bottom out my uncle's pickup, even though it belongs to me and Six now.

I stop the truck at the crest of the dead-end dirt road and pull off to the side. We get out.

"Where is it?" Six asks. "Where are the meteorites? Did someone steal them?"

My amigo looks at me, confusion on his face.

"Maybe I got turned around coming in the back way," I suggest.

"No. This is the spot, Antonio. There's our tire tracks. Here's the crater. But the meteorites are gone. Damn," Six says, kicking dirt into the crater.

"Hold on," Dr. Feynman says. "Don't destroy the evidence. The impressions left in the ground tell me something of great weight was parked here."

"We haven't had rain, either," I tell him, "so the marks haven't been worn down."

He takes his camera from his shoulder and hands it to me. Then he takes off his heavy flight jacket and lays it across the truck seat. Six and I remove our jackets, too. It's getting warm.

The doctor removes his camera from its leather case. It is a Kodak Retina. He pops open the little door to reveal the lens. There are rings with numbers on them, and all sorts of buttons and levers. I remember my parents' Kodak Brownie camera: a box with a hole in it and a knob to advance the film. Dr. Feynman motions me and Six into the picture.

"As a size reference," he says.

He takes photos of the empty crater from every angle. Crouching down, he takes several pictures with his camera practically resting on the ground.

"To get an idea of the depth of the impressions," he explains. "It might help determine the total weight of the pile."

He returns to his jacket in the truck for another roll of film. After reloading his camera, the doctor instructs me on how to use it so he can get into a couple of the shots. It's not quite as complicated as it looks.

"I was hoping to take a couple more meteorites back to the lab with me," Dr. Feynman says. "A colleague suggested he might be able to estimate the size and shape of the original object if he had more pieces—like an archeologist with pottery sherds."

"We still have about a dozen meteorites in the barn," I tell him. "We can give the doctor a couple more samples. Right, Six?"

"Sure," my amigo replies. "I'm curious about where they came from, too."

We walk to the brink of the precipice above Bottomless Lake.

"This is a beautiful spot," the doctor says. "I see why you like it up here."

He opens the lens cover door and takes several photographs of the lake, urging Six and me into one of the shots. Six nearly takes a step too far.

"Careful, Six. My God. Is this where you fell in the lake?"

"Yep. This is the spot, Dr. Feynman."

"You're lucky you didn't kill yourself."

"I guess someone was watching over me," my amigo says, smiling.

We sit down on the wood barricade at the end of the dead-end road.

"So what can you tell us about the meteorite sample we gave you, Dr. Feynman?" Six asks.

"I'm sorry," the doctor says. "I intended to write you. It was at the time my wife was so sick and I was immersed in my work for the government.

"Your sample is indeed a form of kamacite, but not a form anyone has catalogued. It is almost certainly of extraterrestrial origin."

The doctor stands up. He takes his pack of Pall-Mall cigarettes and his lighter from his trouser pocket. He glances at his watch.

"Pretty good," he announces. "Eleven o'clock. My first cigarette of the day. I'm trying to cut back."

He lights his coffin-nail and takes a drag.

"So did your tests on the meteorite answer your questions, Dr. Feynman?" Six asks.

"Yes, they did," he replies. "And they raised just as many new ones. That's the way science works most of the time. I'll fill you in on the rest of the lab report when we get back to the house. I made a copy of it for you."

"Do you think the army stole the pile of meteorites, Dr. Feynman?" I ask.

"The thought did occur to me," he says, "especially since the way you described the pile, it sounded to me like a salvage operation. My army connections are stretched pretty thin these days, but I'll ask around"

"Antonio drew a couple of sketches of the stack of meteorites in his notebook," Six tells the doctor.

"That'd be a terrific help," he says, "another piece of the puzzle."

The doctor draws on his cigarette and exhales into the wind. He crushes the stub against the barricade and puts the butt in his trouser pocket.

We walk back to the truck and climb in. Six takes the wheel and turns the pickup around, going back the long way, the way we came into the state park.

We don't try to be heard above the clunks and thumps as the old pickup goes into and out of ruts and potholes, kicking up dust and stones. I'm relieved once we get back on the paved road into town.

Six pulls the pickup into the back yard in front of the barn. We climb out and go into the house for our late dinner, our midday meal. It's nearly two o'clock.

Our icebox is stuffed with leftovers from yesterday's party: an array of luncheon meats, salads, and fried chicken. I take tortillas from the larder and bread from the breadbox. Six sets the table. Dr. Feynman fills all our glasses with beer and puts the quart bottle back in the icebox.

I slice the loaf of bread and Six makes three sandwiches. There is lots of potato salad left from our graduation party.

We stand before our chairs and I say grace. The doctor looks down.

Taking our places, we shuffle things hither and yon, passing bowls and platters back and forth as though dealing cards in a poker game.

Six and I do not say much at mealtimes. Dr. Feynman has not yet caught on to our habit. We finish our dinner while he's just getting started.

"Have you and Six thought about what you'd like to do in the army," Dr. Feynman asks.

"We'd both like to learn to fly," Six tells him, "but it takes more training and dedication than I think we're up for. It seems like a really neat idea—flying *into the wild blue yonder*—but we have duties here at home on the ground, doctor."

"That's too bad. You're smart fellows. I think you'd make excellent pilots. I might be able to put in a good word for you—as much as my word still counts for anything."

"We're pretty set on taking over Mila-Grow Nursery & Greenhouse when we get out of the army," I say. "The owner, Eduardo, will be ready to retire and he's going to sell the business to us. Six's Grandpa Otto is going to loan us the money."

"So I guess we'll do what ever the army asks of us for a couple years and go wherever they send us," Six adds.

"What about little Nicky?" Dr. Feynman asks.

"There are five grown-ups, including the mother's parents, to look after him while Antonio and I do our stint in the army. I just hope it'll be enough people for the job."

We laugh.

"But they are all getting on in years," Six says. "It's not fair to ask so much of them. I'm going to have to figure out how to raise the kid once we get out of the army. He's my son. I'm responsible for him."

I look at Six and smile. The doctor raises his eyebrows.

"I wish you all the luck in the world. You're going to need it," he says, grinning.

We get up and clear the table. Six washes the dishes, I dry. Six asks Dr. Feynman if he'd care for a little more beer.

"Sure," the doctor replies.

I take a bottle of Dos Equis from the icebox and Six brings three short glasses. He and I will share a bottle of orange Coke.

We go out to the *portál* in back. It is a glorious late spring afternoon: warm and not too windy.

"Is there anything else you can you tell us about our meteorite, Dr. Feynman?" Six asks. "It's not classified, is it?"

The doctor smiles.

"No, it's not classified," he says, "though maybe it should be. I'll leave you a copy of the official lab report for your 'archive.' I don't mean to be so mysterious, boys. But your meteorite *is* a mystery."

"How so, Doctor?" I ask, taking a sip of my orange Coke.

"It's an alloy that clearly came from out there," he replies, raising an arm to the clear blue sky. "But the metal in that sample contains no impurities. It appears it was smelted. And machined, too."

"What?" Six says. "Machined?"

"Yes," Dr. Feynman replies. "I don't know what to make of it."

"People from outer space?" I suggest.

The doctor shrugs and sips his beer.

"Maybe," he says. "I was hoping we'd uncover evidence of intelligent life here on earth first."

We smile. He looks back and forth at my amigo and me.

"What other explanation can you come up with?" the doctor asks, addressing neither of us in particular.

Six and I raise our shoulders.

"Well," Six says, "maybe, that somebody made something out of meteorites they collected here on Earth. Then maybe they fired it back up into space. It might have fallen down to earth again and broken into pieces."

"Not bad," Dr. Feynman says. "But it's not a very straightforward explanation, is it? *The truth always turns out to be simpler than you thought.* Besides, who has the ability to put a big chunk of metal up into space from down here?"

We shrug.

"Exactly," he says. "No one, not even the Army Air Force, I'll wager. That's why I'm hoping a couple more samples from your pile might provide us with more clues."

"All right," I say. "Let's go have a look in the barn."

We stand up and down the rest of the beer or Coke in our glasses. The doctor fetches his camera and its flash attachment from the truck.

Six pries the barn door open and we go inside. It is dark and dusty. I point to the stack of meteorites in the corner.

The doctor attaches the flash to his camera and pops in a bulb. The bright burst fills the whole barn. He takes three more shots of the pile from different angles.

"Take however many more of the meteorites you need, Dr. Feynman," Six tells him.

"My colleague tells me two more ought to do it. I know they are worth some money, so I'll pay you for them. I'd just like to get some answers to this riddle."

The doctor takes his time choosing which iron fragments he wants. I look for an old gunny sack in one of the stables. There's a rusted horseshoe at the bottom. I hang it on a nail on the post among the others that have turned up from time to time.

Dr. Feynman puts the two chunks of meteorite in the sack and rolls it up. We go out into the daylight. He puts the iron stones on the floor of his Jeep. I push the barn door shut and we go back to the porch.

Dr. Feynman sits in my rocker. I bring a kitchen chair for myself.

"The Holy Mother told us that you would explain the next part of her mission for us, doctor," I say to him.

He rocks forward and smiles.

"I did as instructed, boys—not my usual habit. It must be the result of my couple of years working for the army, following orders and all that. Your celestial informant requested that I wait until you asked me."

The doctor rests backward in his rocker as Six and I lean forward expectantly. He takes a sip of beer, teasingly leaving us on the edge of our seats.

"The letter said you two will be the emissaries selected to greet important visitors from far off."

"Us? Why us?" I ask.

"How far?" Six asks. "Africa? China?"

"I don't know why you boys were chosen, Antonio. I suppose you are as strangely qualified to represent Earth as our ambassadors as any two individuals could be."

"Earth? Where are the visitors from? The moon?" I say, laughing.

"A bit further out."

"Mars?" Six asks, raising his voice. "Are there people on Mars, Dr. Feynman?"

"Not so far as anyone knows. How about farther out still?"

"There's nowhere else people *could* live. Every other place is either frozen or boiling," my amigo says.

"How about visitors from another sun?"

Six jumps to his feet, nearly tipping his rocker over.

"You're kidding us, Dr. Feynman, right?"

"Not intentionally. Remember. I'm only reporting what was in the letter. You have to decide how reliable your correspondent is."

We take a sip of beer.

"Does this other sun have a name," Six asks.

"It's a star only visible from the Southern Hemisphere—*Alpha Carinae*. It's just over three hundred light years distant."

Six and I whistle.

"How would they ever get here, Doctor?" I ask. "One light year is almost six trillion miles."

"I can't even guess at the physics, Antonio. It's unknown. If visitors do arrive, I expect you to ask them all the questions I would. I'll provide you a list."

The doctor smiles. Six goes into the house to get the astronomy book given to him by Hypatia. He brings it out to the porch and sets it in his lap.

After checking the index, he flips to a color plate and turns the heavy book towards Dr. Feynman and me.

"There it is," Six says, pointing. "That little dot. Alpha Carinae is real."

"Yes, it most certainly is," the doctor replies.

"This is unbelievable," Six says, nearly shouting.

"Did Holy Mother say *when* we would meet these visitors?" I ask. "We never read the Virgin's letter. The letter was for you, Doctor."

"No," he replies. "The letter contained no mention of a time or place for the meeting."

"Why should we be Earth's ambassadors, Dr. Feynman?" I ask. "We're just a couple of pretty ordinary guys."

"I can't answer that, Antonio. But *ordinary* is not a word I think of to describe you two. I'd give anything to be there with you if could, to witness the encounter for myself. It will be you and Six who will welcome them after their long voyage.

"You've received a tremendous honor. I hope you boys realize that."

A huge raven lands on the round finial of one of the hand-railings up to the *portál*.

My buddy goes into the kitchen for a treat. Dr. Feynman watches the bird like a hawk.

"'Edgar' is one of Six's pets," I tell the doctor. "Named after Poe."

He seems fascinated by Edgar's antics.

Six returns. He holds both closed palms out to the raven. Edgar points with his beak to Six's left hand. It's empty. He caws indignantly.

The bird chooses his right hand. It's also empty. Six laughs.

Edgar squawks madly. He rocks back and forth on the finial, pointing left and right and back again, giving Six a piece of his mind.

Six has a grape in his mouth. He pushes it between his teeth and leans forward. The raven walks up the hand-railing and takes it from his mouth.

Edgar flies up to the gable of the barn to enjoy his juicy treat.

"Perhaps that's why you two were chosen," Dr. Feynman says, chuckling. "That was a wonderful example of interspecies communication."

We smile and finish the last of the beer in our glasses.

"I'm going to go collect Nicky," Six announces. "I'm sure Tia has had enough of the little varmint by now."

"I'll go," I tell him. "There's something I want to ask her."

"All right," he says. "I'll get supper going, then. Ask Tia if she can spare a coupla onions, Antonio. We forgot 'em."

I go through the back yard and down the *calle* to my aunt's house. She sits in her rocker beneath the front *portál*, little Nicky cradled in her lap. She is singing to him, *La Araña Pequeñita*, The Itsy-Bitsy Spider. She sees me approach.

The baby follows the movements of her mouth and is beside himself with glee at the music coming from her lips. My Tia finishes the children's nursery song and looks up at me.

Nicky looks up, too. He grins to see me. It makes me feel good.

"I used to sing that to *you*," my aunt tells me.

It makes me smile.

"I remember," I say.

That makes her smile.

My aunt has the baby in new sleeper pajamas with feet that she has sewn for him. She leans forward and hands Nicky to me before getting up out of her rocking chair.

I don't want to tell her how silly the baby looks. The material she used, no doubt a remnant from Woolworths, is emerald green, as gaudy as the paper grass in an Easter basket.

His complexion taking after his mother's Mexican side, and his blue eyes after his father's, Nicky looks like a sun-browned leprechaun. I want to compliment my aunt on her effort, but I don't want to lie. I smile instead.

"Nicky has not yet had his bottle, Antonio," Tia says. "He stayed awake all afternoon."

"Good," I say. "Maybe the grown-ups can have a conversation tonight."

I feel a little bit funny calling myself a grown-up. I don't think of myself as one most of the time.

"You were no different, *mi hijo*," she tells me.

We walk into her front yard where the buds of her tea roses are blooming in great numbers. There is more red than green on her bushes.

"Did my Tio ever talk to you about three shooting stars he and my papa saw one night, when they were boys? I only just remembered my papa's story. I wondered if Tio Nicolás ever talked about it."

She closes her eyes.

"Not that I recall, Antonio. But those two were always making things up. It was hard to believe them when they *were* telling the truth," she says, laughing softly. "Please take my good-bye to Dr. Feynman. He is a nice man. I'm glad he came to your graduation."

I am out her gate before I remember the onions for our supper.

"You know where they are, child," my aunt tells me.

She takes Nicky from me and I go into her kitchen.

The onions are too big to fit in my overall pockets. I take a paper sack from beneath the sink and go back out.

Nicky hears me come down the steps. He squirms in my aunt's arms and reaches a hand out to me. My aunt kisses us both.

"Where are your manners, Nicky?" I tell him. "Say, *Adios*, to Tia."

I put him against my shoulder so he can see my aunt wave to him.

"Bah," he screeches, right in my ear.

We turn into the lane. I jiggle him up and down like a horse trotting as I walk home. He turns his head to look at everything on both sides of Calle Alegre.

As I walk into the kitchen, Six is frying strips of beef in the iron skillet. Dr. Feynman slices peppers. They both look up and smile.

Nicky reaches for his papa.

"Gort," the baby squawks.

Six sets the skillet aside.

"Well, well," he says, wiping his hands on his apron. "If it isn't my little green man."

We all laugh.

Six takes Nicky from me and I wash my hands at the sink.

Supper smells pretty good even before the addition of the onions.

* 5 *

As usual, Six and I fast before mass on Sunday morning. Dr. Feynman decides to skip breakfast, saying he'll find some place to stop on his way up to Los Alamos. He plans on making the entire trip today in his rough-riding Jeep.

The little one is fussy this morning. I wouldn't be surprised if he suspects that someone is leaving.

Six changes Nicky's diaper in his crib. I make a small pot of coffee for Dr. Feynman. He smokes a cigarette beneath the rear *portál* as my amigo and I get dressed for church.

The doctor comes in from the *portál*. He sits down at the kitchen table and I pour him a cup of coffee. It sure smells tempting.

Six props the baby in his arm and feeds him his bottle of warm milk.

"I want to leave my camera with you boys," Dr. Feynman says. "It's my graduation and birthday present to both of you."

"No, doctor. We couldn't accept your camera," I say. "We're both kinda clumsy sometimes, you know, huh?"

"Speak for yourself," Six says, repeating his familiar line.

"Everyone is clumsy at times, but neither of you is careless. You'd be doing *me* the favor. If visitors from Alpha Carinae do, in fact, show up, I expect you to ask them to pose."

Without waiting for us to reconsider, Dr. Feynman takes his Kodak camera from his leather bag next to the sideboard. He flips open the camera cover and stands next to Six and the baby. I get behind Six's chair so I can see the doctor's demonstration, too.

"It's really very simple once you've studied advanced optics and calculus," the doctor says, smiling.

Nicky pushes the nipple of the bottle away and looks up, too.

When the doctor finishes instructing us on using his camera, he takes a group photo of me and Six and Nicky. Then he takes a folder from his leather bag and zips the bag back up. He sets the file on the kitchen table next to the camera.

"The folder contains a copy of the Los Alamos lab report on your first meteorite sample."

"Thank you," Six says. "Will we be able to understand it?"

"I think so. It's pretty straightforward, not too technical."

"I've got to get going," I tell the doctor. "I have to pick my Tia up for church. When the baby stays with us, Six and I don't attend church together. Nicky thinks he's a member of the choir. Six stays home and minds Nicky. Then we switch."

"Of course," he says. "The best of luck to you, Antonio. I look forward to hearing from you boys. You can write me at Cornell University."

He puts his card on the kitchen table. The university seal is like a coat-of-arms.

"Thank you, doctor," I tell him. "You've been a huge help to us. You've given us an awful lot to think about, too."

"It's just part of my job," he says, smiling. "I hope to get back to teaching."

I put on my jacket. Dr. Feynman slaps my shoulder and I go out to the truck.

* * *

Though it makes me nervous, I watch Nicky while Six goes off to church. He and I will have our lunch—our breakfast, really—when he gets back home. Then we'll do our usual Sunday chores, which include laundry. I always hope it will rain.

While Six attends church with his Gram and Gramps, I decide to practice with Dr. Feynman's camera. Maybe I should have waited for Six in case I forget something about how to operate it. I guess I could ask Nicky. He was there for the doctor's instructions, too.

I carry the baby to the far end of the yard, the camera strap slung over my shoulder. Nicky seems happy to be outdoors. He looks around him until I think his head might swivel off.

We stand before my statue of *Nuestra Señora* in the grotto, in the shade of the cottonwoods.

"This is Nicolás Antonio, Holy Mother," I say.

"Yaah," Nicky shouts.

While nestling the baby in my left arm, I open Dr. Feynman's camera. It's not so easy balancing both. Nicky's curiosity keeps him amused while I fumble with focusing the lens.

I snap a photo of the Blessed Mother's statue. In case I goofed something up the first time, I take a second shot. Then I close the camera. I don't want to waste film.

"Come on, Nicky. Let's get back to the house. Time to make breakfast before your papa gets home. I don't have to ask you. You're just like your papa. You're always hungry."

I set Nicky in his crib in the bedroom and put the camera on the sideboard.

I take out the skillet and dice a couple of peppers. Then I scramble four eggs and grate some cheese..

* * *

Since I forgot to show it to him during his visit, I will make a copy of my sketch of the meteorite pile at Bottomless Lake and send it to Dr. Feynman. I have been using drawing paper instead of notebook paper for all my sketches.

After we use up the film in Dr. Feynman's camera, I take it for developing. One of the two photos I took of my statue in the grotto is quite ordinary. It shows my wooden carving just as it is, except that it's in black-and-white and a little blurry.

The second shot, taken only a minute later, shows the Holy Mother herself in all her splendor and beauty, glowing and radiant and smiling. Though I'm not sure how it could happen, it is the only color photo on the roll. It is almost overexposed by the brilliant light.

The black-and-white photo of Six and me and little Nicky was also on the roll. It's one of my favorites. We're going to send prints of all the exposures to Dr. Feynman.

I wonder what he will make of it when he sees the photo of the Blessed Virgin Mary.

CHAPTER SEVEN

QUI GLADIO FERIT
He Who Wounds with the Sword

Yesterday was our last day of work at Mila-Grow Nursery & Greenhouse. We signed up with Uncle Sam after high school last year and now he's expecting us to show up. Our buddy Tomás and the other guys at Mila-Grow, as well as Eduardo, the owner, threw me and Six a little going-away party. There was plenty of beer and tequila but not much food.

Today my stomach tumbles like a cement-mixer and my head feels as though it were packed with sand. Either Six has a better tolerance of liquor or else he took it slower than I did. I would like to lie down in the shade of the back yard and die, letting Six roll some sod over me and put up a tombstone. I don't even care if he spells my name right.

It is two months after little Nicolás's first birthday on December twenty-eighth. It is time for me and Six to say good-bye to our families this morning.

Six holds his son against his chest, bouncing the infant slowly up and down or rocking him back and forth. The boy is having none of it. He's been fussy and fidgety since we got up this morning. He screeches whenever his papa is out of sight. I wouldn't be surprised if he suspected something was up. He doesn't like people going away.

"They're here," my amigo announces, passing Nicky to me. "I gotta finish getting dressed."

The boy squirms and squalls, reaching his arms out for his father. He hollers as though he'd been stuck with a diaper pin. His face turns red as a ripe tomato. There is such a long pause between wails and screams that I'm afraid he's stopped breathing.

He was merely refilling his lungs.

My Tia Ana and Six's Grandma Matilda swoop to the crying baby like a pair of cooing doves.

"There, there, little one," my aunt says, taking the wriggling infant from my arms.

She kisses him and he stops fussing. I'm not sure what her magic trick is.

"It's almost like he knows we're going away," I tell Tia.

"Of course he does," Grandma remarks. "Just watch how he follows a conversation. It won't be long before he starts chiming in."

"Yaah," Nicky shouts.

"See?" Grandma says.

Six returns in his new denim jacket and fresh overalls, but his boots are still muddy from work. He looks slowly around the kitchen at his grandparents and at my aunt holding little Nicky.

"If I get homesick," he says, "this is the scene I will remember."

His grandma wraps her arms around him and leans her white head against his chest. She sobs.

"I remember when I cradled you in my arms and sang lullabies to you and gave you a bath in the sink. Now you are a man and leaving your home and family."

My aunt joins them, adding her tears to the weepy gathering. Nicky is only too happy to show them he can outdo them all. Six remains dry-eyed, but there's a cloud drifting in.

"Now, come on," Grandpa says. "What's everybody so all-fired glum about? This is a happy day, a proud day. Our boys have become men, prepared to die for God and country."

I don't think it's a speech that gave much comfort to the weeping women.

Tia, Grandma, and Nicky open the floodgates. I take Six's elbow and pull him from the huddle.

"I think we'd better be heading out, Gramps," I say to his grandpa. "We don't want to be late."

"Does your amigo ever *not* worry?" he asks his grandson.

"Maybe when he's asleep. I'm not sure," Six says, punching my shoulder.

He kisses my aunt and his grandma quickly on the cheek. Tia passes Nicky to his papa. I see tears welling up in Six's eyes, but only one breaks free.

"I love you, my little green man," my amigo tells his son, even though the child outgrew his green sleeper pajamas months ago. "I'm putting you in charge while I'm away. You don't have to take guff from anybody."

His remark makes everyone laugh. That was the right kind of good-bye speech to give.

Six hands Nicky over to his grandma. I kiss the child and the women good-bye, and hurry out to the porch before I start crying. Grandpa Otto and Six follow me.

It is a foggy morning like it was a couple weeks ago when Six crumpled the front fender of his grandpa's tan Chevy pickup driving into town. He's promised to send his grandpa the money for the body work from his army paycheck.

We climb into Grandpa's truck. He takes the wheel and turns onto the county road leading into town. He's not about to let Six drive again just yet.

We get to the recruitment center on Main Street in Roswell a few minutes early. Gramps walks with us across the parking lot to where a beat-up olive-drab bus waits. He uses his cane.

"You boys be good," he says. "Don't do anything I wouldn't do."

His eyes glisten.

"I'm sorry, boys. I'm no good with words. I love you. That's all."

Six's grandpa hugs us both and turns quickly away. He waves to us from behind the wheel of his pickup and drives off.

I swallow a lump in my throat. I don't think I'd be able to go through with this if not for my amigo's standing beside me. He puts his hand on my shoulder and smiles. God bless him for always making me feel better.

The recruitment center looks like a combination post office and police station: gray and drab and utilitarian. This is where we signed up for the army right after graduation. Today's the day we have to report and make good on our promise.

There are around forty of us inductees all told. Most of us milling about are dressed in blue denim or gray twill work pants. The only colorful things are the American and New Mexico flags on the pole aloft and the enlistment posters taped to the inside of the windows.

A soldier opens the door at exactly eight o'clock and calls us inside. He recites the letters of the alphabet in a gruff voice. It feels like I'm back in school—grade school. We assemble ourselves in a ragged line.

"Oh, brother," the soldier remarks, shaking his head.

Behind the counter is a desk manned by a soldier with two stripes on his upper arm. I don't know yet what rank it signifies—less than a sergeant, that's all I know. A sergeant has three stripes.

My amigo and I are in the last group to be called: S to Z. Six stands behind me, behind the white line painted on the polished wood floor. It feels like we're back in school in the principal's office, waiting to take our lumps.

We are asked our names, and date and place of birth. The army clerk—a corporal, as it turns out—ruffles through the stack of papers on his desk. He pulls out a form with my name on it.

He looks me up and down, and checks boxes on the form. Then he signs and dates it at the bottom and asks for my autograph. It feels like I'm signing up at school to play baseball for the Coyotes.

"You'll get your pre-induction physical at Fort Sill," the corporal says. "Get on the bus."

He gives me a copy of the form.

"Don't lose it, meathead," he warns.

The corporal has a different insult for everyone without ever running out of them. Those in front of me were *blockhead, knucklehead, bonehead,* and *dunderhead*. It sounded like he was calling out the names of Santa's reindeer.

When the last civilian has been handed his form, we're told to line up again in our former order, reciting our names. A couple of guys appear lost.

The corporal wags his head.

"I seen more sense in a fence post."

Six asks one of the lost his name and points him toward a spot in line.

"What's your name," the corporal asks my amigo.

"Thorson, Sir."

"Mind your own goddamn business, Thorson."

"Yes, Sir."

We file out and climb up into the bus. It smells like hospital disinfectant and fresh paint. It makes me queasy.

There is no one after Six alphabetically. We get into the last seat. Six takes the aisle and I lean against the window. The seat across from us is vacant, the only one.

The driver adjusts the mirror and starts the engine. It is loud even all the way in back. He grinds the gears. It makes Six wince.

We pull onto a paved road I've never driven down before. The driver is going at a pretty good clip. The sun is coming up strong. The glare on the window glass makes it hard to see out unless I squint. It's too cool out to have the window open.

Six turns to me and smiles. He punches my shoulder.

"You act like you're looking forward to this," I remark.

"I'm not sure about that," he says. "I wanna do my part, that's all. I'm proud to be an American. I'll do whatever they ask me to do.

"But if they said I didn't have to enlist, that would suit me fine, too. How 'bout you?"

"I'm afraid, Six. My father got killed in the service. He was just taking care of patients in a hospital. He didn't even have a weapon on him. I don't want to die."

"Neither do I, amigo. But you're getting way ahead of yourself. There's not even a war going on right now.

"Relax. Just enjoy the ride. Enjoy the scenery."

We turn to look out the window again. The highway is as straight as a line drawn with a ruler. The landscape is flat and dry and scrubby as far as I can see.

"Well... Then at least enjoy the ride," Six says.

He makes me laugh.

We take turns leaning against one another but can't get comfortable. Six nearly falls in the aisle when the bus hits a big bump. The boring scenery makes it hard to stay awake. The back roads Six and I usually take are far more interesting than the highway.

Though I don't recall dozing off, I awaken when the bus comes to a jolting stop outside another recruiting center in Albuquerque. Six is already standing up in the aisle stretching his legs.

The driver opens the door and gets out. He stands beside the bus and lights a cigarette. A sergeant, as I can tell by his stripes, climbs on board. His voice booms.

"I will not repeat myself. You. In back. Siddown."

My amigo takes his seat again.

"It's Bragg," Six whispers to me. "Sergeant Bragg, the guy who had us detained in Los Alamos. Can you believe it?"

I hunch my shoulders, trying to look small and inconspicuous. But it's no joke. I'm scared as hell.

"What're the odds we'd run into Sergeant Bragg again, Six?" I ask. "Especially here."

"Close to astronomical," he replies, looking skyward. "So... I'm guessing there's a reason for our meeting him again, you know, huh?"

"You mean like something the Holy Mother arranged to happen?"

He shrugs.

"I don't know. Maybe. Nothing's ever just a coincidence, is it, Antonio?"

The sergeant looks up from his checklist.

"When I call your name, step into the aisle," he says. "If you don't hear your name—or if you're not sure what your name is—stay put. You lucky fellas will get to ride on with me to Fort Sill."

He calls names from a sheet on a clipboard, making check marks. My heart beats loud enough for everyone to hear it.

My amigo and I talked often about the scary possibility that the army could ship us off to different places and bases. We hope we get to stay together, at least through basic training. But this could be the moment when we won't see one another again for a very long time. We don't have much to say about it.

My heart jumps into my throat. It's hard to swallow. Six touches my hand.

Sergeant Bragg calls about a dozen names. Six and I are not among them. I say a silent *Hail, Mary* in thanksgiving.

The guys the sergeant called step off the bus and walk across the parking lot to another waiting olive-drab bus. It spews clouds of oily exhaust. It's an old bus, but I'm sure the army oughta have plenty of mechanics to keep it in better shape.

"You two nancys in back. Move forward."

"Oh, shit," I whisper.

Six taps my thigh and gets up. I follow him.

The sergeant looks right at us, but there is not even a faint glimmer that he recognizes us from our run-in at the Los Alamos lab. That was over two years ago. Can my amigo and I look *that* different that he doesn't remember us? I say a silent prayer that he *never* remembers.

We sit in the last empty seat, about halfway back, doing our best to look invisible.

"When you hear your name, you will stand and repeat it. If you don't hear your name, you're in big trouble. Your ride just left."

He nods his head toward the other bus as it pulls out of the recruiting center parking lot.

"You two. In the back. Do I know you?"

"I don't believe so, Sir," Six replies.

"I can't think from where," the sergeant says, "but it'll come to me. You can count on it."

We sit back down.

"Thorson, Sixtus."

Sergeant Bragg must've started at the bottom of the list this time. My buddy gets up and recites his name backwards, then sits down again.

"Sanchez, Antonio."

I stand and repeat my name. My tongue sticks. There's so much pounding in my ears, I hardly hear the other names.

When the last civilian is called at the front of the bus, the sergeant tells us to pick up box lunches inside the recruitment center. He advises us to use the latrine, too, before our ride to Fort Sill, Oklahoma, departs in thirty minutes.

"Your first taste of army cooking, boys. Enjoy it," Sergeant Bragg says, laughing heartily.

Actually, it will be the second taste of army cooking for Six and me. Our first was the mushy grilled cheese sandwiches from the commissary at the lab in Los Alamos. I was not impressed.

Going inside, we take a leak and get our box lunches. Everything in the army so far is a form or a checklist or a line. We return to the bus and take our seats. We're pretty hungry, not having eaten all day. We were too nervous to eat breakfast this morning.

Sergeant Bragg gets back on the bus and takes his seat across from the driver. The bus pulls out.

Six and I open the lids of our waxed cartons, ready to chow down on whatever the army has given us. Right now, I'm not fussy.

Our late dinner is a mushy grilled cheese sandwich, an apple, and three pickle slices apiece. The sandwiches are only slightly fresher than the ones we had at Los Alamos. We laugh so hard everyone turns around to see what the ruckus is. The sergeant turns around. We duck down.

We decide to save our apples for later.

* * *

It's nine o'clock according to Six's wristwatch. The rest of the guys, if they speak to each other at all, talk in whispers. Everyone seems sunk in his own thoughts.

I'm happy to have someone I know sitting right beside me. It's a comfort even when we can't think of anything to say.

The sergeant and the driver chatter and chuckle long into the night. Theirs is the only conversation besides our own that Six and I can hear.

Before long, my amigo's head bobs. He slouches against me. I look hard out the window, but there's nothing to be seen.

At last Six and I manage to doze off.

* 2 *

I lean in a cramped position against the window, Six resting against my shoulder. The glass is no longer cool. It feels warm.

There's not a star in the sky. It is utterly black out. I sense no motion and wonder if the bus has pulled over or broken down. I heard nothing.

The eerie green glow from the instrument panel lights up the driver's and Sergeant Bragg's faces, but they don't seem to be moving, either. I wonder if they're asleep. It is absolutely quiet.

There is a dim flash from the back of the bus. Somebody's in deep trouble if they've tried to light up a cigarette. The sergeant warned us.

I nudge Six and try to sit up with him lying against me. He mumbles. I drop my apple core under the seat. I poke Six again.

My amigo shoots bolt upright and jumps to his feet. His apple core rolls onto the floor. He stands in the aisle, blocking my view.

Six's silhouette is outlined in tongues of flame. The bus must have caught fire. He falls onto his knees.

"H-H-Holy Mother," he says, almost shouting.

I'm afraid Six will wake the sergeant up and disturb the whole bus, but I don't think they can hear us. I kneel down in the narrow aisle behind him, reaching into my overall pocket for my rosary. I cross myself.

The Holy Mother stands at the rear of the bus, hovering just above the floor. She seems nearly transparent at first and so bright it hurts my eyes to look at her. I worry her blinding radiance will rouse everyone on the bus in a fright. Her shimmering resplendence glows like a flickering fire. Her beauty exceeds that of any depiction I have seen.

"*Mis hijos*," the Blessed Mother says, smiling. "Please, get to your feet."

Six and I stand side by side in the aisle. I realize the bus is not moving, otherwise we'd have been tossed to the floor. Everyone and everything seems frozen in place like in a museum diorama.

The lights outside the windows remain stationary, too.

"You are about to render the coin of tribute unto Caesar, my children. I know you would not intentionally harm a soul. You are both gentle and forgiving.

"Do not forget your allegiance to God Who has given you life and Who asks you to respect all life.

"I do not mean to scold you, *mis hijos*. You are grown-ups now. Choices will be neither clear nor easy. They will be complicated and confusing.

"Pray for guidance and continue to recite the rosary every day."

"*Si, Santa Madre*," I say.

Though this is the fourth time the Blessed Virgin has appeared to us, it always makes my knees tremble and my hands shake. I know it is a great honor of which I will never feel worthy.

"I shall visit both of you next at the time of the visitors' arrival."

I do not feel worthy of that honor, either: welcoming emissaries from another world.

"What must we do to prepare for the arrival of the visitors, Holy Mother?" Six asks.

"You and Antonio have done all you can in preparation. Be who you are *mis hijos*: friendly and kind and natural. That is the best way to welcome strangers: to make them feel at ease, to feel at home."

"Yes, Holy Mother," Six says.

"May you give us some idea when the visitors might arrive, *Santa Madre*?" I ask. "What if we're out on maneuvers or... or something?"

"Please do not worry so much, Antonio," the Blessed Mother tells me.

Her smile, and the sonority and gentle timbre of her voice, comfort me.

"Do not look over your shoulders for the visitors, my children. Live your lives and do not wait for them.

"Did Dr. Feynman explain the many complicated factors involved in their getting here from so far away?" she asks. "I believe they must set out from their home world long after they arrive here. They must travel forward in time and backward in space—or something like that. Maybe it's the other way around."

"Dr. Feynman couldn't quite explain it to us, either, Holy Mother," Six tells her.

"I'm not surprised. Only God knows what He had in Mind making everything spread out so far apart."

The Blessed Virgin laughs softly.

"I shall do my best to watch over and protect you both during your time in military service. I am sorry for what you will soon have to endue. Our Lord will give you strength. You need only ask Him—in the name of His Mother.

"God be with you, Antonio and Sixtus. Please know that my protective wing enfolds you both, *mis hijos*."

The Blessed Virgin Mary turns and takes the handle of the rear emergency exit.

"If you please, *Santa Madre*..." I say.

She turns and smiles.

"We're pretty sure Sergeant Bragg from Los Alamos recognizes us," I explain, "but he doesn't remember from where. Should we tell him? It might not go so good for us if we admit how he knows us."

"It is always best to be forthright, my children. Even an innocent thing looks suspicious when it has been hidden. Is that all of your questions for now?"

"Yes, Holy Mother," I say.

Nuestra Señora nods, and steps out the rear exit of the bus. She closes the door behind her, melting into the night as easily as the shadowed folds of her deep blue mantle.

The bus lurches. Six and I nearly fall down trying to reach our seats. Everything is in motion again, both inside and outside the army bus.

Our apple cores tumble down the aisle towards the front. Sergeant Bragg stands up and turns into the aisle, taking a few steps toward the back.

My pounding heart will awaken everyone on the bus.

The sergeant stops, and returns to his seat. It's too dark to see a thing except the bus's fan of headlights shining onto the road ahead.

I don't know when my amigo and I will get the next chance to have a private conversation. We whisper loud enough to be heard above the engine, the transmission, and three styles of snoring: wheezy, snorty, and whistler. It makes me think of Snow White's dwarves in the cartoon.

I want to take my composition notebook and pencil from my gym bag, but it's too dark to see what I'm writing. We try to recall everything the Blessed Virgin said to us. We repeat whatever we can remember.

"What do you think *Santa Madre* meant by being sorry for what we'd have to endure, Six?"

"The army's no picnic, amigo, especially basic training."

"I know, huh? The guys at work sure didn't sugar-coat it," I remind Six.

"I'm far more nervous about meeting ambassadors from outer space, Antonio. What if they look like octopuses or something? It'd be hard not to stare at them."

I laugh, forgetting myself and where I am. I clap a hand over my mouth.

After reciting everything we can recall of the Blessed Virgin's latest visit, Six and I lean against one another. We try to squeeze a little more sleep out of an anxious, uncomfortable, and restless night. I am relieved remembering that the Holy Mother has kept each of her promises to us. I touch my rosary in my overall pocket.

I am rocked to sleep by the swaying bus, knowing *Santa Madre* will watch over and protect us.

* * *

The olive-drab bus screeches to halt outside the main gate to Fort Sill. Six's watch says it's seven in the morning. The day is overcast. The puddles the bus splashes though suggest we just missed a downpour.

Everyone is awake and peering out the windows. The driver winds down a couple of narrow roads and pulls out front of rows of olive-drab clapboard barracks. They are surrounded by so many identical ones it would be easy to get hopelessly lost if not for numbers and insignia to identify them.

We all stand and file into the aisle. The sergeant checks names off yet another list on his clipboard. Six and I find our apple cores under the first seat. We are the last to climb off the bus.

The air is thick and humid, not something my amigo and I are much used to except after a cloudburst. I think if you twisted the air with your hands, you could wring water out of it.

My heart is in my throat as we stand facing Sergeant Bragg. He makes us recite our names yet again and dutifully checks them off his list.

"Excuse me, Sergeant Bragg," Six says.

I don't how he found enough air to get the words out. The sergeant looks up.

"Yeah, Thorson. What is it?"

"We remembered where we met you before, Sir."

The sergeant looks surprised.

"It was at Los Alamos. We were delivering a letter for Dr. Feynman at the lab."

"You didn't think I'd really forget you two after all the headaches you caused me, did you? I had paperwork up the keister—in triplicate.

"I remembered you two as soon as I laid eyes on you. But I didn't figure you and your buddy would fess up. It took guts.

"I might have been wrong about you two. I say *might*..."

He smirks.

"Doesn't mean I'm not gonna keep an eye on you, looking for the slightest slip-up. You can count on it.

"All right, you two. Fall in."

We rush to catch up to the ragged, wavering line of new recruits, none of us with any idea where we're headed. We just follow the guy in front of us.

* * *

From the conversations Six and I overheard, several guys on the bus figured, since today is already Friday, that, after a restless night, we'd have the remainder of the day off. Our transformation into soldiers would get off to a good start on Monday morning, bright and early.

My amigo and I chuckle to ourselves about what some of our fellow recruits think induction is all about. We have no such illusions. Tomàs, our co-worker at Mila-Grow Greenhouse, and Diego, the boss's nephew, filled us in on what we could expect.

"An army physical is the most embarrassing thing a young man can go through," Tomàs warned us.

"You will have no more secrets," Diego added, chuckling. "Not even from yourself."

It seemed like Tomàs and Diego wanted to scare us, preparing us for the worst. But I saw them nudge each other and wink. Still, Six and I do not exactly expect a Sunday picnic on the lawn.

* * *

My amigo and I take our jackets off and stuff them into our gym bags. I feel that we overpacked by having a single change of underwear, but some guys carry suitcases. Six and I wind up in different lines. After one, there's always another line to get into. Six and I cross paths a couple of times, but then I don't see him any more.

We talked about the army sending us to opposite sides of the globe, but I'm not ready for that just yet. My amigo and I hope to at least go though basic training together before getting split up. But it's not up to us any longer. Nothing is. Our lives are not our own any more. That thought scares me more than anything else.

"You. Move up."

It takes me a minute to realize he's talking to me.

The first stop that doesn't involve filling out a form or answering questions, is the "barbershop." There's one style for everybody: bald as a cue ball. The floor seems about ankle-deep in hair.

Six and I have had pretty short hair since we were boys. Crew-cuts last longer and they are much cooler in summer. But now, at the end of winter, we're giving the barber a lot more to clip off this morning.

"Why do you gotta shave *all* our hair off?" a recruit asks.

There's quiet laughter.

"That's 'cause some of you come in here with 'mechanized dandruff.'"

"*Mechanized dandruff?*" the recruit asks.

"Head lice, you rummy," the barber replies. "Next."

I wonder how far ahead Six might have gotten. I look around for him. There's hair down the back of my shirt. It itches and scratches.

A recruit at the opposite end of the room keeps looking at me. I can't imagine where I know him from. I don't think he was on the bus. He waves.

It is Six. I recognized his shirt. He looks so funny. His head looks so much bigger without hair hiding the top of it. He smiles at me and is urged to move forward in his line.

The next room looks like the gym locker room at school except that there are no showers. We are told to strip to our *drawers*, our undershorts, and to stash our *civvies*, our civilian clothes, in the cubbyholes behind the benches.

There are little cloth bags on a cord inside the cubbyholes. The number on the bag matches the one on the locker. We're instructed to put our wallets and valuables in the bags, and hang them around our necks. We each carry a folder with our enlistment papers in it.

Six stands next to me. He doesn't seem the least bit self-conscious.

"Remember those dreams where you don't have any pants on?" he whispers.

I nod and smile.

"We're embarrassed 'cause we're the only ones in the dream running around without any clothes on. Here, no one's got any pants on."

It makes me laugh. I'm no longer as nervous as I was. Maybe it has something to do with seeing my amigo again.

"Cut the chit-chat. Get going," a gruff voice urges.

We are marched into an adjoining building. "Infirmary," the sign reads.

They pass out small glass bottles on which the soldier distributing them writes the number from the tags around our necks. We line up next to each other at the trough urinal to fill them. I really had to go.

"Filling out forms and filling up bottles," Six remarks, grinning.

We get separated again after our chest X-rays.

Then we recruits are lined up again and told to drop our drawers.

"Uh-oh. It's the 'pecker checker,'" someone jokes.

I can't help it. The remark makes me laugh.

"You. Quiet," a corporal tells me.

The doctor goes down the line. He touches my privates. He must've immersed his hand in ice water first. I wince and suck in my breath. The doctor tells me to turn my head and cough.

Another doctor examines me from behind.

"Bend forward and spread your cheeks," he says.

One fellow, whether being a smart-aleck or just plain stupid, leans forward and pulls his face cheeks apart. The doctor swats his behind. There is laughter.

In the next room are three army dentists. One examines my mouth and teeth.

"Not a single cavity or filling. What's your secret, son?" he asks, looking over his glasses.

"I never visit the dentist."

He laughs. I think some of Six's quick sense of humor has rubbed off on me. I like making people laugh.

I am then given an eye exam which I pass, too. Another doctor examines my ears and nose and throat. I feel like I'm undergoing a thorough inspection by mechanics on an assembly line.

"Next."

The blood test makes me anxious. The fellow in front of me passed out after getting up too soon. I wait until they tell me I can get up and leave.

The next part of my exam takes place in a small room with only a fellow in a suit and tie sitting behind a desk. There is a second door on the other side of the room.

The man invites me to sit down in the chair opposite. I hand him my folder. The name plate on his desk says he is a doctor: Dr. Mallow. He informs me this is a psychological examination and instructs me to answer honestly and to the best of my ability.

The doctor asks me a whole bunch of questions that have nothing to do with one another. He jots notes in my folder, open on his desk.

"Do you ever hear voices?"

"Usually just when someone is talking to me, Sir."

He remains expressionless. I wonder if this guy ever cracks a smile. What a sourpuss.

"Do you get along well with your father, Juan?"

"I go by my middle name: *Antonio*, Doctor. *Juan* was my father," I tell him.

"You're evading my question."

"My father is dead, Sir," I say. "He was killed at Pearl Harbor."

He does not look at me. He writes in the folder.

"Do you like girls?" Dr. Mallow asks.

"*Cierto*," I reply. "Sure I like girls. I had two girl friends in high school."

I hope he doesn't hear the difference between *girl friends*, two words, and *girlfriends*, one word. Six and I talked about what we should say if the question about whether we liked girls came up. We didn't want to have to lie if we could help it.

Dr. Mallow scribbles more notes. Then he stamps the file and the folder, and hands it back to me.

"That's all. You may leave by the other door."

My heart thumps like a tom-tom. Incredibly, I must have passed the psychological exam. I am at the back of the line again. I'm told to move up.

We file next into the Quartermaster's where we will be given our army clothing and uniforms—*everything from the skin up*, as one of the officers put it.

It looks like an assembly-line tailor's shop.

"Step up."

A soldier with a tape-measure hanging around his neck, measures me top to bottom, barking out numbers to another soldier behind the counter. Behind that soldier are racks and stacks of clothing, all of it either olive-drab or khaki. The soldier slaps a shirt on the counter. I'm told to put it on, buttoning all the buttons and stretching my arms out. My tailor pulls and tugs the shirt, seeing that it fits properly.

Next come the fatigue pants. My tailor-soldier holds them up against me before flinging them back onto the counter.

"Let's try inseam thirty-four," he says.

Another pair of pants appears on the long wood counter. Meanwhile, other recruits are being fitted up and down the line. There's quite a hubbub.

I try on the pants. The soldier-tailor tugs and yanks them in every direction before deciding they are my size. He makes checkmarks and writes numbers on my yellow card, Form 20. The card contains everything about me.

The shirt and pants and jacket, for which I am fitted next, are pretty comfortable—no more stiff and scratchy than a new pair of shrink-to-fit overalls. I look at myself in the full-length mirror on the wall behind me.

"Not too bad," I say to myself, though I hardly recognize me.

Without hair, my face looks so much bigger. My eyes are wide, as though I've been startled. I have to laugh at myself.

Down the line, I am fitted for boots and told to walk around in them to see how they fit. They're about like a new pair of workboots.

"Not bad," I say.

I think "Not bad" is the proper response for everything around here. You're not saying you actually like something, but on the other hand, you're not complaining.

"All right. Next. Step up."

We are given caps and helmets and huge canvas "barracks bags," also called "duffel bags."

At the next station, a soldier checks my Form 20 card and begins calling out items and sizes of underwear: five sets of drawers, undershirts, and socks. I stuff it all into my duffel.

In the next room we are given our vaccinations, all recorded on our yellow cards, too. One fellow passes out before he's given a single shot. At the next station, we are fingerprinted—not to check whether we've committed a crime, but to identify our bodies... *in the event*, as they say.

Finally, all of us are assembled in a large room with an enormous American flag tacked to the wall. Except for slight differences in height and color, in our identical uniforms and shaved heads, all of us recruits look alike. There is one Negro fellow. I think I see Six on the opposite side of the room. I try to get his attention.

"You got a nervous fit or something?" an officer asks me.

"No, Sir."

He steps to the front of the room.

"You will all raise your right hands and repeat after me, inserting your own names where appropriate."

"I, Juan Antonio Sanchez, *do solemnly swear that I will support and defend the Constitution of the United States against all enemies, foreign and domestic; that I will bear true faith and allegiance to the same; and that I will obey the orders of the President of the United States and the orders of the officers appointed over me, according to regulations and the Uniform Code of Military Justice. So help me God.*"

My heart races. I am nervous, but also very happy. I am now a soldier in the United States Army. My father would be so proud of me. My Tio would be proud of me. I'm proud of myself—and of Six, too.

After our oath, we file outside into the dim sunlight. I stand with the other recruits at the side of the road. We are no longer civilians though I'm guessing we're a long way from being soldiers.

When the last of us emerges from the infirmary, a soldier barks orders at us, instructing us in the basics of marching—how to put one foot in front of the other. There was a coach at Roswell High who taught the boys of our class the basics of military drills and formations. He knew what we'd be facing.

"You'll thank me some day," Coach Martinez had said.

"Thank you, Coach," I say under my breath. "Today's the day, I guess."

I see Six further up in our ranks, trying to help a fellow-soldier with two left feet get into the cadence. I wonder how long it will be before the instructor tells Six to mind his own business.

"Mind your own damn business, Thorson. I'm the drill instructor here."

"Yes, Sir."

They know his name already.

We are marched up a couple of roads. The last stop on our induction train is a building marked "Insurance and Allotments" on a sign above the door.

It looks like another classroom with school desks. Six takes the desk next to me.

A corporal stands at the front of the room. We're instructed to fill out the forms naming our beneficiaries in case we are "killed in the line of duty." It's another reminder that this is more than six weeks at summer camp.

"Those of you with dependents back home will need to fill out this form," the corporal says, waving it in the air. "You'll need to provide a copy of their birth certificate."

Six has the copy of Nicky's birth certificate in a frame on our bedroom wall. I know he's proud of being a father. He'll have to write and ask his Gramps to send it.

I glance across to see Six busily checking boxes and filling out the form. I'm reminded what a serious obligation being a father is.

It's much easier being an uncle.

* * *

We stand in the cafeteria line. We're served spaghetti with meatballs that aren't too bad, though the red sauce has tomatoes only in its name.

In addition to the plate of spaghetti, I take two slices of garlic toast, and a plate of lettuce with a slice of real tomato. At the end of the line, I put a cup of coffee on my tray. I feel like I'm going to have to fight to stay awake for the rest of the afternoon.

Six and I sit across from each other in the mess hall, the *mess*, for short. Six eats and enjoys whatever is set in front of him. Since learning to cook for my Tío Nicolás when I went to live with him, I am more picky. But I'm also very hungry.

After a hurried meal, the roster sergeant collects us from the mess and leads us to our barracks. We are assigned our bunks alphabetically. There are two more of us now: the Negro fellow named Jackson and a Mexican named Zamora. I think Zamora is one of the guys Six tried to help earlier.

I get the bottom, Six is assigned the top bunk. There is a folded blanket, top and bottom sheets, and a pillow with its cover on each mattress.

We newly enlisted men are given a demonstration by the sergeant on the proper way to make a bed according to army specifications. I have been making my own bed since I no longer fit in my crib. There are three ways of doing things: the right way, the wrong way, and the army way. I guess I've been doing it wrong my whole life. I pay attention.

After I have made and re-made my bed enough times to last another the week, the roster sergeant makes his way down to our end of the barracks.

"What's your name, soldier?"

"Thorson, Sir," Six tells him.

"Do you know what a forty-five-degree angle looks like, Thorson? Corners are folded at exactly forty-five degrees. Do it over."

After he harasses Six and Jackson and Zamora, the sergeant returns to inspect my efforts. He wags his head.

One corner at a time, he takes me through the proper techniques for making a bed in the army, doing most of it himself. The bed is as tight a trampoline. The sergeant bounces a quarter off of it and nods his approval. He smiles.

Then he yanks everything off the bed, even taking the pillow from its case. He throws all of it on the floor.

"Now you do it," he says, and turns on his heals.

Six chuckles.

"Just you wait," I whisper to him. "Your turn's coming up."

"Fall in," a voice barks. "On the double."

I never finished re-making my bed.

"Guess we're gonna face the firing squad for sloppily-made beds," Jackson jokes.

Instead, we are grouped for another march. We go up this road and down that one until I am completely turned around and lost. All the buildings still look alike to me.

"Company, halt."

We are back at our barracks. I wonder if we simply circled the block ten times.

"Company, dismissed," the instructor says.

We go back inside. No one is sure what comes next. There's lots of murmuring and commotion.

The blankets and linens have been pulled from all the bunks, as though it were some kind of fraternity prank or initiation. I guess in a way it is. We begin re-making our beds for the umpteenth time. Six and I make sure we do it right, so we're ready for the next inspection.

"My name's Jackson," the Negro fellow says to us, extending his hand. "Ezekiel Jackson. I go by *Zeke*."

Six and I introduce ourselves and shake his hand. Carlos Zamora, his bunkmate, joins in our huddle.

"How'd you wind up back here with us, Jackson?" Six asks.

"I guess somebody thought *Zeke* was my last name," he says, chuckling. "I wonder how long it'll take to get *that* straightened out."

We laugh, and go back to making our beds, checking one another's corners for deviations from the army standard.

The roster sergeant gets our attention with a shrill whistle. He reads announcements from his clipboard.

"Evening mess is in one hour. You may take showers after mess. Tomorrow is Saturday. That is all."

A few of the recruits choose to use the spare hour to lie down. With all the hubbub, I'm not sure how they'll ever manage to doze off. Most of the guys gather in clusters of two or three, talking and joking around. It's good to see everyone so friendly.

Six and I dump the contents of our barracks bags on our beds. The duffels are deep and narrow, making it hard to find things.

We put our civvies at the bottom and organize the bundles of clothing we hastily stuffed into the bags when it was issued to us. Six draws nearer and whispers.

"Congratulations, amigo. I guess we made the team," he tells me, smiling. "Here we are: soldiers in the United States Army."

He chucks my shoulder.

"Thank God," I say. "I really want to serve my country, Six. I know you do, too. I was afraid they'd turn us down because of... because of you and me being best buddies, you know?"

"I had that army psychiatrist going in circles," Six tells me, chuckling.

"Dr. Mallow really had me nervous, too," I confess. "He asked me if I liked girls. I'm glad you and me practiced what we were gonna say. I told him I had a coupla *girl friends* at school. I don't think he heard my pause between the words. I didn't wanna lie."

Six continues re-folding his government issued clothing and stuffing it into his duffel. He leans in closer.

"The doctor asked *me* whether I liked boys."

"*En serio*?" I ask. "Are you serious? What did you tell him, Six? We didn't practice that one."

He pulls the drawstrings on his duffel shut and hangs it from his bunk at the foot of his bed. I'm still packing mine.

"I said, 'Of course, I like boys. My buddies from school and work are all guys. Don't you like your friends?'

"'I'm the one asking the questions, smart-aleck,' he said, glaring at me.

"I was really starting to sweat my answers. The doctor jotted in my folder and handed it back to me, telling me I could go."

I smile at Six.

"How do you always manage to think so fast, amigo?"

"Nah," he replies. "Other people are just kinda slow sometimes."

I laugh loud enough to turn heads. Everyone grins at us. I wonder if Six and I are the only two who know each other.

* * *

We file out of the barracks at 17:00—5:00 pm in civilian time—for the *To the Color* bugle call. It is also known as *Retreat*, when the flag is lowered at day's end. It is the first time I have saluted the flag as a soldier in the United States Army. I am proud enough to pop the buttons off my olive-drab field jacket.

The next bugle call is at 17:30, the evening mess call. The new recruits enjoy a supper of roasted chicken with mashed potatoes and gravy, peas and carrots, dinner rolls, and banana pudding. My opinion of army cooking has improved somewhat during the course of the day. I must be hungrier than I thought.

We return to our quarters after supper. The roster sergeant makes his way back up the center of the barracks, stopping more to chat than to offer advice. Maybe he's not such a bad guy after all. He strolls down the rows of bunkbeds, asking if there are any questions.

"You'll find out soon enough," is his reply to most of them, followed by a sly chuckle. "Your *Life of Riley* is about to end," he adds.

I wouldn't have known what he meant—that we've got it easy—except that *The Life of Riley* was one of my Tio Nicolás's favorite programs on the radio. My life isn't even my own any more, and it sure doesn't have many idle moments in it.

The rest of the evening is finally our own. Many of the men simply sack out or take a shower; some re-pack their duffels. Others take out a book or converse with the other fellows. A couple guys write their first letters back home. I haven't had a chance to get homesick yet, especially with Six nearby.

I decide to have a shower. The loose hair in my neck from my haircut still itches me. I take a pair of my new army undershorts, my bath towel, and my toothbrush with me.

Six and I figure it will be best if we don't shower at the same time. He and I will avoid spending too much time together or getting too friendly. We don't want to start tongues wagging.

We're both used to showering with other guys in the gym showers at school. I admire their form and handsomeness, but it does not excite me particularly to see naked men. Only one naked man gets my attention: *mi mejor amigo*.

The shower is hot. I close my eyes and let it run down over me. It feels wonderful. It sure beats our often cold baths at home.

Two more men come into the shower room as I leave.

Returning to my bunk, I see four guys nearby sitting on a bottom bunk playing cards, probably poker. There is a pile of pennies in the center of the mattress. They look up as I pass.

Six talks to Jackson, leaning an elbow against his bunk. They nod when they see me.

I do not feel like getting dressed again, only to get undressed in a couple of hours. Pulling on an undershirt from my duffel, I climb into bed wearing my underwear.

Though it's two hours before they'll call *Taps*, I'm bushed. I am not the only one to turn in early. Today was a pretty big day for all of us. I wish the guys, *Good night.*

Six's upper bunk provides me some shade from the lights in the center aisle of the barracks. I'm so exhausted I drop off to sleep almost at once, like spiraling down a whirlpool.

I am vaguely aware when Six jostles the bed climbing up to his bunk. I hear when *Taps* is played, but it sounds way far off. It strikes me as a sad tune. Like a train whistle, it is mournful and plaintive, the sound of leaving.

* * *

Though it is Saturday, *Reveille* is still at 6:30. We made our beds well before the first bugle call. I hope I'll have the chance to tidy mine up. I could barely see what I was doing.

We assemble in the courtyard, facing the flag and saluting it. Then we break ranks and return to our barracks.

"How'd you guys sleep?" Jackson asks.

"Like a stone," Six says. "I don't think I rolled over once all night. I dreamt about making my bed, over and over, while I was still in it."

Jackson, and his bunkmate, Zamora, both laugh.

Six takes his kit from his duffel, telling us he plans to shower. He takes out his razor and toothbrush and comb.

"Any of you guys know what this thing is for?" he asks, holding out his comb.

They laugh again. Six has such an easy time making friends. I have to work a little bit harder at it.

* * *

Our Saturday is hardly a "free day," but then they weren't free days back home, either. If we weren't working at Mila-Grow Nursery, we had enough chores around the house to last a month of Saturdays.

Our day consists of more drills and marching and demonstrations of army etiquette. We learn the proper form of saluting and how to fold the American flag in case we didn't know already. The army thinks none of us knows anything.

When no activity has been assigned, we "pull" various unpleasant "details" to keep us out of trouble. I don't mind. I'd rather not have time on my hands. That's when my brain works overtime concocting things to worry about.

After the *To the Color* and evening mess bugle calls, we are "encouraged" to attend a film in the Recreation Hall. In other words, it's an order.

The movie is all about induction into the United States Army, the very thing we just went through the day before.

"Boy, they sure cleaned up the dialogue " Six jokes. "They didn't show any privates' privates, either."

I laugh. If he and I get shipped off to different places, I guess I'm gonna have to learn how to tell jokes to myself.

* * *

My second night in the army is not as restful as my first. I hear every noise, from loud to soft, from the bugler calling *Taps* to guys throughout the night walking barefoot to the latrine.

Though I manage to get back to sleep after each interruption, it is shallow sleep, not deep enough to dream. My ragged rest has me on edge, afraid I'll slumber through all the bugle calls in the morning.

Without a watch or an alarm clock, I have no idea of the time. Minutes pass like hours, hours like minutes. I hear what sounds like whimpering. Maybe it's just the sighing of the wind or someone's style of snoring. I listen harder.

I'm sure it is someone crying. It is muffled weeping, as though he has his face buried in the pillow. I feel bad for him, whoever it is. I'd like to help, to offer a couple words of encouragement, to say a prayer with him. But the best advice around here seems to be, *Mind your own damn business.* I don't think either Six or I is very good at ignoring those we might be able to help.

I fall back to sleep at last, not awakening until Six shakes my arm well before *First Call*. I think I could sleep standing up today, like a horse.

* * *

We manage to scramble into our fatigues and make our beds before the roster sergeant blows his piecing whistle. There is no rest, not even on Sunday.

At *Reveille*, as I raise my arm in salute, the limp flag unfurls, filling with the wind the way my chest fills with a swell of pride. *God bless America*, I think.

We learn that, during the night, one of the recruits tried to cut his wrists with his government-issued razor blades. Another guy found him passed out on the bathroom floor. The soldier will be discharged—dishonorably discharged—adding mental grief to his physical wounds. I guess the army can do you in before the enemy even has you in his sights.

I am so sorry I didn't try to help my fellow recruit when he was in trouble. I want so much to be a good person, but I always seem to fall short.

* * *

After morning *Mess Call* at 8:00 o'clock, Six announces his intention to shower. He strips to his shorts and takes his bath towel and shaving stuff with him into the shower room. He returns fifteen minutes later, clean-shaven, with the towel wrapped around him.

We look for our olive-drab serge coats in our barracks bags. They're a little dressier than our field jackets for church. We've each been issued two mohair neckties. I'll have to help Six tying his. He never wears ties, not even Western ties.

I slip the necktie beneath his collar and attempt to tie it for him from the front.

"I can't do it this way," I tell him. "It's backwards to me."

Stepping behind him, I reach around him to fumble with the necktie. I am getting aroused just pressing up against him. I don't want anyone to see.

"Maybe we'd better find some other way to do this, Six."

I put the tie around my own neck and tie it. Then I loosen it and slip it over my head, handing it to Six.

"That's cheating," Jackson says.

"I won't tell if you don't," I say.

He smiles a big, toothy grin.

We inspect each other's appearance before the next bugle call. The *Church Call* is at 10:00.

Mass is held in a large paneled room in the chapel building. It's well-attended. Two soldiers are the servers. The priest's voice is awfully faint for such a big guy. Maybe he's just being kind, not wanting to wake anybody up.

After mass, we have a little bit of free time before the noon mess call. One of the guys heard we'll be getting the entire afternoon off today. Six and I ponder what we'll do.

We needn't have wondered. The roster sergeant, whose name is Moore, leads us across the courtyard into the room where we took our oath of enlistment on Friday. There's a movie screen pulled down in front of the American flag. We sit in the desks. Six moves up front and sits next to Jackson and Zamora.

"Who brought the popcorn?" someone jokes.

There is laughter.

"Anyone who doesn't care to watch these excellent U. S. Army training films can go around base picking up cigarette butts for the next four hours," Moore says. "Snoring is an infraction the same as talking. So shut up."

The lights dim and the screen flickers. The projector clicks and clacks. Then the sound comes on.

The movie is the same one about army induction we sat through yesterday. It hasn't gotten any more interesting. It's even harder to stay awake knowing how it all turns out.

During an "intermission" necessitated by the sergeant having to change movie reels, the head of one fellow near the front of the "theater" begins to bob. He verges on tumbling out of his seat.

Sergeant Moore, stealthy as a cat, stands beside the recruit. At the first snort and snuffle from the soldier, the sergeant slams the wooden desk with his palm.

The soldier starts—and finishes falling out of his desk. The room erupts into laughter.

The prank is sort of funny, more entertaining than the movie we just watched again. But I feel sorry for the guy. I can imagine picking myself up from the floor with a roomful of people laughing at me. Six reaches his hand out to help the recruit get up.

"Thorson? What d'ya think I'm gonna say?" the sergeant asks.

"I can't imagine, Sir," my buddy replies.

"Mind your own damn business, that's what," Sergeant Moore says.

I think Six's answer is funny, but I don't dare crack a smile. I stare straight ahead and wait for the lights to go down.

* 3 *

Our basic training will not begin for another week. I am disappointed. I'm eager to become a soldier, not just someone wearing his uniform.

In the meantime, we recruits are assigned various tasks around the base and barracks, what's called "pulling a detail." Two lucky fellows are given the opportunity to clean the latrines. I am given KP, the kitchen patrol, where I learn—in case I didn't know—how to scrub pots with steel wool until my fingers bleed.

Six pulls the warehouse detail. That job involves loading and unloading equipment and supplies from the trucks. Boxes and crates have to be stacked or marked for distribution to other facilities on base. He tells me he's going to apply to get an army driver's license. That way he'll get to drive the trucks instead of loading and unloading them.

Those told to "police" the area around the barracks are given brooms and told not to leave even one cigarette butt behind.

By day's end, we are all sore and fatigued in different ways. We'll be assigned different positions each day, so we "get to experience all the army has to offer."

The remark at least makes everyone smile.

* * *

The rest of our first week, in addition to our assigned duties, involves marching with brooms and wooden sticks in close-order drills. It seems each step some of the recruits takes is a mistake. Under my breath, I thank Coach Martinez again.

My boots get broken in somewhere along the route. By midweek, they no longer hurt my feet. They're almost as comfortable as my old workboots.

One of our examinations is the Army Classification Test, a written exam to determine in what job we would be the most use to the United States Army— and to ourselves. We are advised to answer honestly and completely so we don't wind up in the wrong job for the rest of our stint in the army.

I take my time. I don't want to be assigned to a position I'll hate and from which I won't learn a darned thing.

Though their order is often different, each day consists of bugle calls, saluting, mess, marching, tests, movies, forms, interviews, more movies, and more marching.

It pains me to be in a darkened room during a string of gloriously mild and sunny days. I fall asleep during one of the films and get yelled at. I don't think I even snored.

None of these movies is ever repeated. Most of the soldiers with speaking parts seem like actors to me. I am beginning to think that the United States Army has made more movies than Hollywood.

* 4 *

The weather was beautiful during our week of indoor testing and watching training films inside a darkened room. Today, the beginning of our six weeks of outdoor basic training at Fort Sill Military Reservation, it is overcast, humid, and drizzly.

After morning mess and marching drills, we are ordered to pack all our gear in our barracks bags. Anything left behind will be disposed of.

We recruits climb up into canvas-covered troop trucks. Six and I, and our new chums, Zeke Jackson and Carlos Zamora, are the last to load. The other truckloads of men follow their own instructors and head off in different directions. Someone closes the loading gate and slaps the side of our truck.

From our trove of official army brochures and pamphlets, we learned Fort Sill was built during the Indian Wars. Geronimo is buried here. The fort is almost a hundred-thousand acres. We are headed for a post and barracks in the northwest quadrant near Ketch Lake.

Sitting at the rear, it is the bumpiest ride I ever experienced. It's hard to hold on without getting flung to the floor. The shoulder straps don't really help. My rear end slaps against the slatted wood seat.

After maybe a mile or so, the truck stops. Six thinks there may be mechanical trouble.

"All right," our sergeant hollers. "End of the line. It's a beautiful day for a hike."

If I'd known we were going to get out so soon and march the rest of the way—about twelve miles—I might not have minded the bumpy ride so much. Our packs weigh about thirty-five pounds.

It is raining when we climb out, not hard, but steady. I packed my rubber rain poncho at the bottom of my duffel. In getting to it, I knock my spare fatigue pants and a change of underwear into a puddle.

"Doing wash already?" Jackson quips.

He has a quick sense of humor like Six. He helps me pick up my soggy stuff and put it in my bag. I suspect everything I own will be soaked through before long.

The trail to camp is only wide enough for two abreast. Six and Carlos march next to one another. I bring up the rear with Zeke.

My duffel contains all my possessions in the world at the moment. I feel like a pack-mule or a hobo who carries his kitchen with him. I struggle to get my poncho on over my duffel. Zeke gives me a hand. I'm hoping to keep the rest of my stuff dry, but it's probably a wasted effort.

In less than a half-mile, I am soaked and clammy: not from the rain so much as from sweating beneath my rubberized poncho. It is like a steambath inside. I am muddy halfway to my knees.

The drill instructor, Sergeant Wagner, does not let up. He's got an easier time of it: he only has to lug himself, not thirty-five pounds of gear as well. The sergeant had his stuff sent on ahead.

"Rank has its privilege," he said, smirking.

Jackson and I try to carry on a conversation, but the rain pelting our hoods and helmets, makes it hard to be heard and we give up.

I reach into the pocket of my fatigue pants. I want to recite today's rosary.

It is not there. I try to remember when I last held it—last night, in bed. When I finished saying my prayers, I put the rosary beneath my pillow—and forgot it when we packed up in a hurry this morning.

I feel as though I am cut adrift and anchorless without my rosary, even though I know all the prayers and could count them just as well on my fingers. It makes me very sad to have lost it. My mom and dad gave the rosary to me for my First Communion when I was seven years old.

Please, Holy Mother, I pray silently. *Help my rosary find its way back to me.*

We trudge on. My mood becomes as gloomy as the weather. I don't think I'll ever see my prayer beads again. I feel so stupid for forgetting them back at the barracks. *Qué tonto soy.*

At last we break for our late midday meal beneath a grove of hickories and crab apples.

"The army assumes none of you knows anything at all," Sergeant Wagner says. "I agree with them. So listen up if you don't want to be left in the dust."

"What dust?" Jackson mutters. "It's all mud."

We are instructed in how to open our cans of rations, how to use a knife and fork and spoon as though for the first time. There's no place to sit that isn't wet. I eat standing up.

Our march seems a lot longer than twelve miles, but maybe that's because I don't know the local landmarks. The landscape seems pretty featureless in the fog.

By late afternoon, we reach the site of our bivouac on a rise above a shallow valley filled with pine trees. Tonight we will be camping outdoors without benefit of tents or tarpaulins. It will take me a week to dry out.

Six and I are intent on learning all we can from our instructors. But there's not much anyone can teach me and my amigo about open-air camping. We've been doing it since boyhood.

Someone wants to know where the bathroom is. He is pointed in the direction of a hazelnut bush and reminded to flush.

A couple of recruits ask about wild animals. Our instructor says it's been nearly a week since anyone was mauled by a mountain lion in these parts. Bobcats and wild boar are more common, as well as *sidewinders*, rattlesnakes.

The sergeant's accounts are only somewhat accurate. He exaggerates as though he were telling ghost stories around the campfire. He's trying to scare us.

It's easy to tell who believes his tall tales by the looks of concern on their faces. Everyone else is trying to hide their grins. I'm surprised the sergeant didn't mention *jackalopes*, an aggressive cross-breed of wild hares and antelopes.

At 17:30, the same time as usual, we break for supper: more rations from cans: crackers, peanut butter, and smoked sausage. The second tin contains stale biscuits—hardtack—and jam. I guess that's dessert. I'd gladly settle for two-day-old cafeteria food.

The rain has trailed off to a persistent drizzle. The recruits set up "camp," scattered lean-tos made with our raingear strung between branches or saplings. One of the men carried Sergeant Wagner's pup tent.

The sergeant offers plenty of advice, often delivered with his tongue in his cheek.

"Not like that, knucklehead. Were you always that stupid or were you born that way?"

Everyone finds it funny until it's his turn to be made fun of.

Six and I choose to sack out away from each other. We find dried leaves, ferns, moss, and pine needles to provide dry beds to lie down on beneath our shelters.

"Looks like you two have done this before," our instructor remarks.

"Yes, Sir," Six replies. "The last time we went through basic. Practice makes perfect."

It takes Sergeant Wagner a few seconds to realize Six is joshing him.

"Wise-ass," he tells Six, but he is grinning.

I help Carlos set up his lean-to next to mine. It's going to take me a while to get used to calling everyone by his last name, his family name.

"By any chance, did you lose a rosary, Sanchez?" he asks. "I found one on the floor near your bunk on the way out this morning."

He takes my rosary out of his pocket and holds it up.

"Oh, my God. Carlos... I mean, Zamora. Yes, it's mine. Thank you. I can't believe you found it. I only just realized I'd lost it."

I cross myself and kiss the crucifix, saying a silent prayer of thanks to the Holy Mother in my heart for returning my rosary to me. I thank Zamora again, too.

"Don't mention it," he says, touching my shoulder.

In the last of the gray daylight, Zamora and I stow our gear beneath our lean-tos, made from our rubber ponchos. Near nightfall, the recruits gather what we can find of dry kindling and smaller chunks of deadfall to make a small fire in our midst. The rain has let up and it is our chance to dry out a little before turning in.

There are stories and jokes and wisecracks going around—as well as a lot of complaints, mostly about blisters. Six sits on a log with three other recruits on the opposite side of our camp circle. I see his eyes sparkle in the firelight when he looks over at me. My heart skips a couple of beats.

I was never in the Boy Scouts, but I think this is what it must have been like. The teasing is mostly good-natured. I feel like I'm part of the gang, both giving and taking the gentle ribbing. Zamora and I stand up to get our backsides dry against the fire.

Jackson tells us about the Negro Buffalo Soldiers who served on the western frontier after the Civil War, many of them here at Fort Sill. They got their name from the Indians who thought their dark skin was like that of the buffalo. The Indians admired the Buffalo Soldiers for their courage and skill.

"Who cares?" one of the men says, interrupting Jackson's tale. "You stupid cotton-pickers don't know anything anyway."

"You can stop right there," Sergeant Wagner says, jumping to his feet and confronting the soldier.

The sergeant clenches his fists but he does not raise them.

"I don't care what cockamamie ideas you chuckleheads entertain on your own time. But for the next two years, your time—every minute and second of it—belongs to your Uncle Sam. The only thing he cares about is how good a soldier you are. That is *all* that matters."

I wish I could be that brave: to speak up for what is right. Even if I don't like him much, I admire Sergeant Wagner—his quiet strength. He's the kind of man I want to be, a man like my father.

The expression, "Sharpen your sword and keep it sheathed," comes to mind, though I can't remember who said it.

"Dismissed," the sergeant says gruffly.

Six passes me and smiles. We haven't had much chance to talk.

"How's it going, amigo?" he asks, chucking my shoulder.

"Not bad," I reply.

"Is that your answer for everything these days?"

"It doesn't get me in any hot water, you know, huh?"

"Hot water sounds pretty good to me right now," he replies, smiling.

Jackson offers Six a cigarette and offers to light it for him. My buddy looks at me as if he needed my permission. I shrug.

After Jackson lights it and hands it to him, Six takes his first drag of a cigarette. He grins at me, his eyes glinting in the firelight.

Then he exhales all at once, a cloud of smoke and breath like an explosion. He coughs his head off. Jackson slaps his back but it doesn't help. Everyone nearby laughs, even me. Sergeant Wagner shakes his head.

Still holding the coffin-nail between his fingers like an experienced smoker, Six hands it back to Jackson. The Negro recruit smokes it to the nub and flicks it into the fire. Our little campfire is nearly burned out.

After directing two recruits to shovel dirt over the embers, the sergeant orders us to turn in. I was just getting warm.

Zamora and I get nestled beneath our adjoining lean-tos. We talk mostly about our families, switching back and forth between English and Spanish. But we're bushed. We've got plenty of time to get to know each other. Tonight we need our sleep more than anything.

"Buenas noches," he says.

"Buenas noches."

* * *

Before dawn, the rain begins again, not too hard at first. By the time Sergeant Wagner blows his whistle, it is a cloudburst complete with lightning and thunder. His whistle must be galvanized.

Hunching beneath our raingear, we open our tins of "breakfast" using the correct can-opening technique. It tastes remarkably like yesterday's dinner and supper.

Rather than proceeding directly to the outpost barracks, our instructor, Sergeant Wagner, decides today is the perfect weather for learning how to dig foxholes with camping shovels. The sergeant is greatly amused at our useless efforts to shore up the crumbling walls of our holes in the downpour.

I believe I will never be clean or dry again. Six seems to be enjoying himself, flinging mudpies out his foxhole one shovelful at a time. He nearly splashes the sergeant's gaiters.

"You get any of that on me, soldier, and it'll be your grave you're digging."

He says it without the slightest smirk of humor.

"Yes, Sir," Six says.

I wonder what my amigo is actually thinking and—wisely—not saying aloud.

* * *

The outpost barracks are more primitive than those during our first week of training and testing. I hear mice scurry beneath the floorboards. The window screens have holes. The showers run out of hot water very quickly. Six and I decide we are "camping in a hard tent."

There are both indoor and outdoor courses of instruction. The general rule seems to be that on days of fine weather we will be shut away inside, learning first aid or figuring out how to read maps and charts, and plot a course.

On days of spring rain in Oklahoma, of which there are eight per week, we slither and squelch over and through obstacle courses. We scale walls and fences, weave through mazes, jump over water-filled trenches, and swing across a pit on ropes designed to fall short of the opposite side. The sloppiest days are saved for learning how to crouch down in bomb blasts and crawl beneath barbed wire under fire.

Our company is not without injuries. One recruit dislocated his shoulder. Another soldier had his helmet shot off. If the bullet had been a half-inch lower, it would have parted his brain instead of just his scalp. Another recruit burned his hands badly on a shell casing.

If there is this much pain and suffering in our training, how much more in fighting an actual war? I cannot imagine it. Will I ever be as brave as my father was—or any of the other men around me?

My buddy and I get a rare couple of minutes to chat at the end of what we hope is our last live-fire obstacle course. Six and I each got a nasty gash on the barbed wire trying to slither beneath it.

"Everything I've seen of the army so far, Six, just reminds me of school or work, you know, huh? There's not much that's new," I tell my amigo.

He grins. I go on.

"It's tests and forms, marching around, standing in line, stiff new clothes, cafeteria food, bosses and bullies, getting really, really dirty, and showering with a lot of other guys."

"There's one big difference," Six tells me. "This time we're getting paid for it."

I laugh.

"You know what's not the same, though?" he asks. "There's nothing here that reminds me of home—except you, *mi amigo*."

His smile lights up my heart.

"All right, meatheads. Fall in."

Brief as it was, our moment together was as precious to me as a whole night spent with him beneath our tent of stars.

* * *

Though we do not have a second face-to-face with Sergeant Bragg, our nemesis from Los Alamos, he appears often at the edges of things, a pair of binoculars hanging from his neck. I get the creepy feeling he's watching us—Six and me in particular—checking up on us even when we can't see *him*.

Sergeant Bragg has received a promotion to staff sergeant. I hope it will also mean he's up for a transfer. I'd rather not have any more run-ins with him and I don't like being observed.

On Monday of our third week of basic training, we are taught techniques of camouflage—ourselves, our equipment, and our encampments. Later in the week, we recruits learn hand-to-hand fighting before we are issued weapons. Then we're taught how to assemble and clean our rifles before receiving instruction in firing them. Once more, Six seems to be in his element. I keep pinching my fingers.

I'm happy we have lots of "dry-fire" practice first without ammunition. When we are issued live ammunition, it's a good shot when I hit the target at all.

Though we are shooting only at straw targets, they have the outline of a human torso painted on them. Strangely, when I shut my eyes before firing, I do much better: good enough to get a passing grade.

Six, on the other hand, draws the instructor's admiration for his accuracy.

"Where'd you learn to shoot like that, Thorson?"

"I used to go squirrel hunting with my Gramps."

"Go on."

"Nailing 'em wasn't too hard, Sir. The problem was sneaking up on them till you could see the whites of their beady little eyes."

The instructor laughs.

"Make sure you give me your yellow card, Thorson. I'm gonna put you down for the marksmanship course—if you want to try out for it."

"Thank you, Sir."

I am happy for Six, and proud of him. *Holy mackerel—an army sharpshooter.* But I am struck by how different we are. I cringe at firing a rifle—though I do it well enough, just enough to squeak by. Six, I'm pretty sure, wouldn't mind shooting off a double-barreled cannon. It's funny that it took our going into the army to realize our differences.

For Six and me, our friendship is as easy as falling off a slippery log in an obstacle course. I fell for him head over heels, too.

I don't know how I can love somebody so much who is so different from me. We're like opposite poles of a magnet, I guess: attracting each other, even at a distance.

And I love him more than anybody else in the world.

* * *

Six asks our roster sergeant about our army pay during one of the sergeant's countless inspections of the barracks. I'm guessing Six is eager to give his Gramps the money he promised to send him for the wrinkled truck fender.

"Don't you fellas think you oughta do a little work around here before you get paid?"

He steps into the center aisle between rows of bunks and raises his voice.

"For those of you who don't know, Uncle Sam figures your services as a private are worth fifty-four dollars a day."

"Wow. No kidding, Sergeant?" someone asks.

"No kidding," he replies. "Fifty-four bucks a day, one day a month."

It makes everybody laugh.

* * *

Though the hours are long and the days endless, the six weeks of our basic training almost race past, each more quickly than the week before it. Six and I would've had a much tougher time of basic if not for our jobs at Mila-Grow keeping us in pretty good physical shape. Even so, it was the hardest thing I've ever done. I am sore but stronger, still fearful but bolder—and a little braver. I am proud of myself for sticking with it. I have proved me to myself. *Yes, now I am a man.*

We recruits spend our last day of basic training, the Friday of our sixth week, in long interviews with officers who go over our many test results with us.

"How does it feel to be a soldier, Private Sanchez, and no longer a raw recruit?"

"It feels very good, Sir. My family will be very proud of me."

"I hope you are proud of yourself, son," he says, looking up and smiling.

Sergeant First Class Ramirez looks through my file, spread out across his desk. His jet-black hair is turning gray on the sides.

"Your family's down in Roswell, correct?"

"Yes, Sergeant," I reply.

"Lucky for you, Sanchez. You scored exceptionally high on flight aptitude skills. I'm going to recommend you for flight training at the Roswell Army Air Field."

"Flight school?" I say, nearly jumping out of my chair. "I never flew anywhere before except in my dreams."

"Well, apparently the skills carried over."

I laugh.

"Now, it doesn't mean you'll make it to pilot, only that you've demonstrated a proficiency in the necessary skills and aptitudes. The only way to find out is to give it a try. I hope you'll consider it, Sanchez."

"Oh, yes, of course I will, Sir. Yes. Sign me up. Please."

"Enthusiasm goes a long way in the army, son. I'm happy to see you've got plenty of it. If you'll sign below—here —I'll get the transfer papers drawn up for Monday."

I take the fountain pen he hands me and sign my life away. *Flight school. Holy mackerel. I can't believe it. I can't wait to tell Six.*

I stop in mid-thought. This might be when my amigo and I get shipped off to different bases and different careers in the army. It scares me that we might not see each other for two years. And it'll be my fault. But I can't turn down a chance to become a pilot, can I? Six will be happy for me.

"Something wrong?" Sergeant Ramirez asks.

"No, Sir. I'm just wondering if a coupla my buddies made the cut, you know, huh?"

"What're their names, Sanchez? Maybe I interviewed them. There's only one more private to interview after you."

"Their names are Thorson and Jackson, Sir."

He laughs.

"I can't forget Private Thorson. He did about as miserably on flight aptitude as you did well. But he aced every exam for mechanical skills. The army needs three times as many mechanics at Roswell as they do pilots. And I think Jackson will make a damn good radio operator.

"Your buddies will be on the bus to Roswell with you come Monday morning, son."

"Yahoo," I say, perhaps a little too loud.

I don't care. I'm excited.

The sergeant hands me a large manila envelope with my paperwork in it. "Anything else, Sanchez?"

"Yes, Sir. Some of the guys said the Army Air Force might become its own branch of the service—maybe soon."

"Like every rumor, Sanchez, it may or may not be true."

"Yes, Sir. Thank you, Sir."

"Good luck to you, Sanchez."

I salute him and turn to leave.

The last guy waiting in the hall is Zamora. He smiles in passing. I wish him good luck.

I'm going to miss him if he doesn't get transferred to RAAF with Six and me and Zeke Jackson. Our friendship is off to a good start—especially after he found my rosary. Our families have a lot in common, too.

I feel light enough to fly back to the barracks. I can't wait to share my good news with Six—now that I know we'll both be stationed at Roswell Army Air Field. *Yahoo.* I can't believe our good luck. I'm sure the Blessed Virgin Mary must have had something to do with it. It's certainly no coincidence.

It is drizzling again. The late afternoon sun shines an enormous triple rainbow against the wall of gray clouds to the east. I saw only one other in my whole life: when I was a boy and my father called me outside to come see it. It lasted a long time.

The second rainbow is inside out from the first one and a little dimmer. The third rainbow, dimmer still, is again inside out so that it matches the color order of the first rainbow. I'm not sure how it works.

Like God's promise to Noah, I take it as a sign of His many favors and blessings and mercies to the human race.

CHAPTER EIGHT

GLADIO PERIT
He Perishes by the Sword

Yesterday Six and Zeke Jackson and I arrived at Roswell Army Air Force Base on a slow bus from Fort Sill that took two days to get here. It might have been the same rundown army bus that dropped my amigo and me at Fort Sill for our induction and basic training two months ago.

It's already near the end of April. Everything is leafed out with the tentative yellowish-green of early summer. The ditches are full of wildflowers and the first clusters of dandelions dot the meadows.

The old bus stopped at every military base and outpost along its roundabout route, dropping soldiers off to their new assignments. Even without a horse, I am saddle-sore. I'm cranky from ragged sleep.

The three of us check in with the duty officer who has our names on his list. He tells us to report to the roster sergeant at the B Company barracks. The sergeant is not there.

"What now?" I ask.

"Nothing," Jackson says. "There's no one here to tell us what to do for a change. We wouldn't want to go looking for the roster sergeant, would we?"

"Certainly not," Six says. "Taking initiative just gets you into trouble. Taking orders is a lot simpler."

We smile and step back into the shade beneath the shallow eaves. By now we are expert complainers about nearly everything in the army. Complaining is an old army tradition.

The Negro sets his duffel bag on the ground and reaches into the pocket of his wrinkled shirt for his smokes. He carries his Zippo in his pants pocket. I am happy Six decided not to have a second try at getting the hang of cigarette smoking.

Jackson does not get to finish his coffin-nail before the roster sergeant returns, carrying his dinner from the post exchange, the PX. It smells good, what-ever it is. We salute him.

"Are you the three sent down here from Fort Sill?"

"Yes, Sir," I say.

"I'm having my lunch. Come back in half an hour. In the meantime, get lost somewhere. Don't be standing around idle. It drives Staff Sergeant Bragg crazy. Dismissed."

I glance at Six. He seems surprised, too. From our looking back and forth at each other, Jackson sees we know something.

"We had a couple of previous run-ins with Sergeant Bragg," I tell our new chum. "I don't think he likes me and my amigo very much."

"At Fort Sill, he had us constantly under his eagle eye," Six adds.

"What? Did you say his *evil eye*?" Jackson asks.

"No, *eagle eye*," I say, chuckling. "Thorson and I heard he was being re-assigned. It's our darned luck that his transfer was to here in Roswell. It's almost like he's following us around. Stay out of his way, Jackson—if you can."

"Thanks for the warning," Zeke says. "I'll do my best to steer clear of him."

* * *

Our new advanced training—airplane mechanics for Six, the radio school for Jackson, and flight training for me—does not begin until next week. That's not to say we have nothing to do until then. The army never has too many pot-scrubbers or grounds-rakers.

Six applies to get his military driver's license, but, in the meantime, we both pull the warehouse detail, loading and unloading the trucks, not driving them.

We continue our combat training, too. We get thrown in with another company doing exercises in formation with their rifles. The drill sergeant in-troduces us to tactical training in small units: how to fire and move as teams in combat. We get assigned to the Survival, Evasion, and Escape course, too.

All in all, it seems to my amigo and me that we are back home. It's like we're taking a full load of classes at school, training to play for the football team, working for the tree nursery, and doing chores around the house. Nothing much has really changed.

On Saturday, the three of us—me and Six and Zeke Jackson—agree to meet at the PX for a couple of beers after the evening mess. It will be the first beer I've had in over two months. It's a hot day. I'm looking forward to it.

We are sized up and down and sideways by every soldier in the place, as though undergoing yet another inspection. It makes me nervous.

"Welcome," one of them says. "Lemme buy you fellas a beer."

Six and I and Jackson accept. We raise our bottles of Dos Equis and toast the other guys. Everyone seems friendly enough. I relax some.

"Where you boys from?" one of the G.I.s asks.

"I grew up outside of Norman, Oklahoma," Jackson says. "My family got here last century—during the land rush. I'm here to have a crack at your radio school."

"Another *Sooner*," one of the fellows says, smiling. "Me, too."

Six tells them, "My buddy and me—Sanchez here—grew up right here in Roswell. I'm enrolled in mechanics school."

"A fellow grease-monkey," one of the soldiers remarks. "What about you?" he asks, nodding to me.

"I'm gonna be taking flight training," I say.

"You're gonna need a bigger head, kiddo," one of the older fellows suggests. "They're gonna fill your brain with so much stuff, you'll outgrow your helmet."

Another soldier buys another round. Six objects, but he's told he can buy the round after that. I decide to buy the one after *that*.

Four beers is more than I have ever drunk at one time in my life. I don't feel so good. I'm wobbly and woozy. I need to use the bathroom again. Six goes in with me.

"You don't look so hot, amigo," he tells me, standing at the next urinal.

"Too much beer," I reply, letting most of it go down the drain.

"Wanna go back to the barracks?" he asks.

I nod, but nodding makes me dizzy. Six puts his hand on my shoulder and leads me back to the "bar" at the PX.

The soldier who told me I'd need a bigger head for flight training has another quip ready for me.

"Betcha thought you bought that last round, eh, Sanchez? You don't buy beer, son. You only rent it."

Everybody laughs.

"We're gonna head out," Six announces. "You coming or staying, Jackson?"

"I think I'll stick around a while," the Negro says.

My amigo puts an arm on my shoulder and steadies me.

"Can I call you boys a cab?" someone jokes.

There's laughter.

Six and I leave the PX. I just want to lie down until the world stops spinning.

* * *

Our class load is a lot heavier than our work load, especially for me. I study the manuals I've been given until the lights-out *Tattoo Call* at 22:45. One day seems like another, except for the weekends. They are the only chance I have to spend time with Six.

My amigo and I work half-days every other Saturday, too, and our schedules seldom coincide.

We agree to meet at the PX for our usual two Saturday beers before evening mess at 17:30. Two beers is definitely my limit. Six can sometimes handle three before he gets silly.

The soldier-clerk behind the counter greets us. His name is Álvarez. He's here on most Saturdays.

"*Qué pasa?*" he asks.

"*No mucho,*" I reply.

"*Lo mismo,*" Six says. "Same old, same old."

Six plunks his money down for our beers. His hands are stained black with grease no matter how much he scrubs them.

"A coupla Double Xs, *por favor,*" he says to Álvarez.

My amigo has gotten so good shifting gears between English and Spanish that it's hard to follow him at times, especially if he talks fast.

Álvarez opens our Dos Equis and gives Six change.

"Sorry about how a couple of the guys treated your buddy Jackson last Saturday. I heard about it. They won't pull that kinda stuff when I'm on duty, I can tell you that."

"*Gracias,*" I say.

"How'd you guys handle it?" the clerk asks.

"I told them, *You're being awfully rude to my buddy,*" Six says. "*And I don't like it.*"

"*Oh, yeah? What're you gonna do about it, soldier?*"

"*I'm gonna ask you to kindly knock it off,*" Six says, going on with his story.

"The big guy laughed. I was waiting for him to back off or back it up, you know, huh?"

"Six promised never to take the first swing," I tell Álvarez.

"I didn't need to lift a finger," Six remarks. "The guy came at me nearly flying. I just stepped out of his way and he landed on a table, turning it into kindling."

"So that's what happened to the table. I don't think I can fix it," Álvarez says.

"Ask my buddy Sanchez here before you throw it out. He's pretty good at woodworking."

Six turns to me and smiles.

"The soldier was out cold," I say, finishing the story. "His buddy had to dump water on him. They left with their tails between their legs and Six never lifted a finger."

Álvarez laughs.

The front door opens and Private Jackson enters. He's earned his private's insignia—a single stripe—but it is one more than Six and I have earned.

Jackson turns on his high-beam smile, happy to find us at the PX, I'm guessing. I wave him over. Six puts a dollar on the counter.

"No, boys. This round is on me," Álvarez tells us. "You're all real regular guys. I'm glad to know you."

He goes in the cooler and returns with three bottles of beer. He opens them, then reaches into his trousers and puts money in the cash register to cover his generosity.

The three of us raise our bottles to him and toast to his health.

"*Salud*," he tells us.

Everywhere we went, Six and I encountered unexpected kindnesses. They made up for a lot of the crap we took the rest of the time.

The three of us sit at one of the tables and make small talk, mostly griping about our army workload. When we finish our beers, we nod to Álvarez and head back to our barracks.

Jackson walks between me and Six as we go down the middle of the road.

"I had an interesting encounter with your Sergeant Bragg," Jackson says, whispering, even though there's no one nearby.

My amigo and I stop in our tracks. Jackson lights a cigarette and exhales.

"He said he hoped you two appreciate everything he's done for you."

"Done for us?" I ask.

We step aside to let an MP in a Jeep go past.

"Bragg said to me, *I've seen you palling around with Thorson and Sanchez, Jackson. Maybe you won't mind delivering a little message to them from me.*"

Six and I stop again and look at Jackson.

"*Your buddies couldn't possibly think their both getting stationed here was just a happy coincidence, could they?*

"He chuckled. *We're all here so I can keep a close eye on 'em. You can tell them that. I'm not letting you outta my sight, either, Jackson. You can count on it.*"

"Holy crap," I say. "What're we gonna do, guys?"

"Nothing that's outta line, buddy, that's for sure," Six tells me. "We don't wanna give Bragg any ammunition."

I notice how much of our talk has an army reference: *giving him ammunition* and *keeping us in his sights*. We cross to the other side of the road, to our barracks.

"Thanks for delivering Bragg's little message," Six tells our friend.

"I'm gonna finish my smoke," Jackson says. "I'll catch you guys at mess."

Six and I nod to him. We walk to our bunks. We're alone at the rear of the barracks. It's my turn to shower first. I unlace my boots.

"I guess we're gonna have to watch what we say in front of Jackson," Six says. "It's too bad. I really like him."

"Me, too," I reply. "You don't think Zeke would squeal on us, do you?"

"No, not for a second," Six replies. "But he might just let something slip. Bragg's a weasel. Nothing would get past *him*."

I continue undressing.

"We can't breathe a word about the Blessed Virgin's visit or Dr. Feynman's visit or anything else that's happened to us, amigo," Six says. "We can't chance Bragg's finding out about something he doesn't already know."

I finish undressing down to my shorts.

Six watches me. I see a bulge in the front of his fatigues. I wink at him and turn away before the same thing happens to me. I take out my towel and toothbrush and razor, and walk to the shower room.

* 2 *

As if our workdays weren't full enough, Six and I find plenty to do in our free time, too. I like the Company Day Room where there is a small library and also a billiard table. I'm learning how to play pool, but I'm a lot better at baseball. I just joined the Roswell Romeos baseball team on the base as third-baseman.

Sometimes my amigo and I go to the Recreation Hall when they show a movie we want to see. At other times, they have dances with local girls. Six has danced with a couple of girls. I just watch them. He has a pretty good sense of rhythm, not at all like me.

We notice Alicia from our graduating class one Saturday. It's a good thing our hair has grown back. Otherwise, she might not have recognized me and Six. We stand as she approaches our table in the corner.

"It's so good to see you boys. What're you doing here?" Alicia asks, smiling.

Six holds up his permanently grimy hands.

"Airplane mechanic," he tells her. "And from all I've learned so far, take it from me: there's no way an airplane will ever get off the ground. They're far too complicated."

She laughs.

"What about you, Antonio?" she asks.

I hold up my lily-brown hands.

"I'm enrolled in the flight school," I tell Alicia.

"*No es cierto,*" she shrieks.

I smile at Alicia. She seems impressed.

"I haven't gotten anywhere close to a real cockpit yet," I remark. "But from what I've learned, if a plane did manage by some fluke to get airborne, there's no way I'd be able to fly the contraption without crashing it. They're way too complicated."

We laugh. Alicia throws her arms around my neck and kisses my cheek. She smells like lilacs. Her hair is as soft as goose down. It tickles my ear.

"Care to ask me to dance, Antonio?" she asks.

"I've only grown another left foot since high school," I tell her.

She wrinkles her nose and frowns.

"What about you, Six?"

"Sure, if you don't mind my fancy dancing shoes," he says, looking down at his Saturday spit-polished boots.

My amigo never shies away from trying something new. He's not afraid to make a fool of himself, either, which is why he seems so confident.

He takes Alicia's hand and they go to the area designated as the dance floor. They have not put any music on yet. They are waiting for requests.

Alicia offers my amigo pointers for the first dance, a slow dance. He watches their feet and nods his head.

Then Six dances a waltz with Alicia without stepping on her feet. They wave to me while waiting for the next record to be put on the phonograph. It is "Boogie Woogie Bugle Boy," another of Six's Andrews Sisters favorites. It sure doesn't call for any slow dancing.

I have no idea where Six learned to swing, but he and Alicia clear the dance floor with their moves. It looks as practiced to me as a Fred Astaire and Ginger Rogers routine, though not as flashy. The other girls and soldiers urge them on with hoots and hollers.

Someone says, "Play it again," but Six and Alicia shake their heads. They are out of breath when they return to the table.

I get up until Six has pushed Alicia's chair in. He orders three Cokes for us.

"I guess it's time to level with both of you," Six says, grinning ear-to-ear, showing his dimples. "They offered a Sunday afternoon dance class in the Company Day Room. There are only four of us enrolled and I haven't missed a single class."

"You're a very good dancer, Six," Alicia tells him. "Couldn't you rub some of it off onto Antonio?"

"I'm not sure how I'd do that," he tells her, winking at me on the sly. "Antonio is good at lots of other things."

I think our conversation has gotten to be very grown-up. Nobody is saying what is really on our minds. We beat around the bush.

I know Alicia wants to dance with me in the worst way. I've got a pretty good idea Six would like to dance with me, too. Even with my two left feet, I'd love to dance a slow dance with my amigo some day—though I know it couldn't ever happen in a thousand years.

* 3 *

Six and I enjoyed our birthdays at the end of May, surrounded by all the new chums we made in just over two months here at Roswell Army Airfield. We both turned nineteen, Six on the twenty-forth, me on the twenty-eighth. Our buddies baptized us with their beers.

There has been no rain in Roswell in three months. Everything is dry as dust. I'm hopeful God will send some rain during monsoon season, soon to descend on us.

I was finally introduced to the Army Air Force's flight trainer. The training cockpits are left over from the war. They look like stubby midget airplanes. All pilots train on them, so I feel I'm in pretty good company.

Yahoo! I am so excited to have my hands on actual controls—instead of just holding manuals open with them. Huge bellows and mechanical arms move the tiny cockpit according to how we handle the controls. The instructor sits at his station, issuing commands over my headset and tracking my progress on his map.

There is no way I can forget I am not actually flying. There are no windows in the pretend cockpit. There is nothing to see anyhow except the hangar in which the three trainers are set up. They are teaching us how to fly at night and in poor weather, relying only on our instruments.

The Link Trainer—what our instructors call the "Blue Box" because of its color—gets unbearably hot inside, especially with the door shut and the hood down. It's nearly the end of June and it's sweltering. They make us drink lots of water, but I never have to pee. I sweat it all out.

When I come out of the flight trainer, I'm wobbly at first. I'm soaked with sweat. Even the uncomfortably hot hangar feels cool compared to the *Link's Oven*. That's what I call it. I'm glad I won't have to bake again for a couple of days. It's Friday.

I trudge back to the barracks, ready to stand in the cold shower in my fatigues. I couldn't get any wetter than I am. I feel two sizes skinnier.

There are two announcements on the bulletin board from the base commander, Major Sanford. In the first, the Major shares news that the National Security Act is winding it's way through the United States Congress. The act will establish the Air Force as a separate branch of military service. Come September, Six and I and Jackson, and most of the other guys on base, will have a new boss, though we'll still be working for the same company.

The second order concerns the cancellation of all leave over the Independence Day weekend, coming up next week.

"Yeah, ain't that a bite?" someone says over his shoulder on the way out.

"Crap," I say. "My buddy and I had three-day passes."

Another soldier wags his head. "Me, too," he gripes.

It was going to be our first time off base for Six and me since we got here two months ago. It's been four months since we saw home. Our families planned a big party—and a barbecue like my Tio Nicolás used to throw every Fourth of July. My amigo and I were looking forward to it like boys anticipating Christmas. He even crossed the days off the calendar.

Six and I plan to meet at the PX after work today. I delay my shower and go to see if he's already there. Jackson told us he pulled an extra detail today and can't join us this week.

My amigo is out back where most of the other guys have a bottle of Dos Equis in one hand and a Camel cigarette in the other. Six comes over and hangs an arm across my shoulder. He gives me a swig of his cold beer.

I feel comfortable being chummy with Six in front of the other guys. Everyone knows we're buddies. Six and I don't do anything we haven't seen plenty of other soldiers do. On the whole, everyone is pretty friendly. I've seen only two fights. Both were stopped quickly by the nearest officer. Six had concluded his fight with the two soldiers harassing Jackson without lifting a finger.

I can tell Six has not visited the showers, either.

He wrinkles his nose and sniffs. "Is that you or me?" he asks.

"It's you," I reply, not skipping a beat.

"Wow. You're getting pretty fast, Antonio. That pilot's training is starting to pay off."

I smile at him.

"I suppose you've heard the news?" I ask Six.

"We all did," another soldier remarks. "A lot of us had plans, you know, huh?"

His name is Ramirez.

"I wonder what's up?" someone else asks.

"We'll prob'ly be the last to know."

"Every time a Russian farts these days, somebody issues an alert."

There is laughter.

"But our next war is prob'ly gonna *be* with Russia, don't you guys think?"

There is shrugging and nodding, but nobody has a firm opinion. We are training to be ready for whatever happens.

"I think I'd better call my Gramps," Six tells me, "and let them know our passes got cancelled."

We say good-bye to the crew and go inside the PX to use the pay telephone. I reach into my pocket for change. Six already has two nickels in his palm. We stand on either side of the telephone. He feeds it a nickel and dials his grandpa's number. The nickel clinks into the belly of the telephone.

"Hello, Gramps?"

Everyone looks up from his beer or his Coke. Nothing on a military base is exactly private, except the lowest-ranking soldier.

"How's little Nicky?"

Six listens. I'll have to wait for his report unless I can figure out from Six's reply what his Gramps is saying to him on the other end of the line.

"He didn't. Really?"

Six chuckles. Nicky could have done almost anything and he would find it cute or funny. I recall the Blessed Virgin's admonition to, *Spoil the child and spare the rod*, when she told Six he was going to be a father. I smile remembering her advice.

"No, Gramps. I'm afraid not. Our passes are cancelled for the Fourth of July weekend."

There is silence on this end. Six shifts from one foot to the other.

"Sure, Gramps. I'll let you know as soon as we find out. Antonio says, *Hello.*

"Sorry. No time. We want to shower before mess. Please take our greetings to Gram and Tia Ana. And kiss the little one for me. Tell Nicky how much his papa loves him. God bless you all."

Everyone standing around in the PX looks away. Though they probably overheard a lot of names, I doubt anyone would be able to figure who any of us is to each other. The idea of their puzzlement makes me smile. We are sure a hodge-podge family.

Though I wouldn't mind my own beer, Six gives me the last of his brew and we head back to the B Company barracks. We want to shower before mess call. We have only a half-hour.

It is the first time I have showered at the same time as Six in the two months we've been stationed here at Roswell. There are two other soldiers under their streams of water, talking to each other.

Six turns on his spigots and steps beneath the spraying water, closing his eyes and smiling. It is how I picture joyfully receiving grace and being washed of our sins. The water cascades over his skin, rippling and glistening, from his ears to his toes—and every curve and hollow in between.

I have to turn aside. I do not want to get excited in front of the other soldiers.

Turning on my shower, I close my eyes and picture myself sailing among the clouds—towering clouds of rain. The rain is cold at first. I am startled in my reverie by a blaze of lightning.

Someone has switched on the lights in the shower room. The water is now hot. I open my eyes and begin washing away the day's sweat and grime.

I thank Thee, Dear Lord, for the Blessing of Water. With the most Precious of Elements, wash away my sins.

* 4 *

I am asleep but not soundly. The duty officer's whistle startles me out of my skin. The lights flash on.

Two dozen soldiers scramble into their fatigues and boots in their sleep. I can get undressed pretty fast, but this is the fastest I have ever gotten dressed.

It is just after midnight on the Fourth of July. *Happy birthday, America.*

"Come on. On the double," the officer barks. "You men go any slower and you'll be going backwards."

Sometimes, my Uncle Sam expects a lot, I think.

It is windy out as we climb up into the waiting troop transport. Faint flashes of lightning glimmer on the horizon, but any storm is miles away.

From the often contradictory orders being tossed back and forth, I get the idea no one is sure what's going on.

Six and Jackson are already aboard, towards the front. I thought they were behind me. The only light inside the truck shines from someone's flashlight.

The troop truck takes off like a jackrabbit. Six careens towards me and lands on the seat beside me with a jolt.

"Well, I guess we get to go off base on the Fourth of July after all," he says.

The soldier next to him laughs. I smile, though Six probably can't read my face in the dim light.

It's clear we have left both the army base and any paved roads in the vicinity. My helmet gets knocked over my eyes.

From mouth to ear, gossip gets passed down the line of soldiers along the two wood benches. I hear, "...to investigate the crash of an unidentified airplane. The radio operator said it might be a Russian spy plane. That's his guess."

"I wonder who pulled radio duty tonight," Jackson asks.

"I didn't catch the name," the G.I. replies.

Even through the heavy canvas top and sides of the troop truck, I can see that an awful thunderstorm is flashing and crashing over our heads. Six lifts a corner of the canvas flap at the back of the truck. The rain and wind whip inside and he lets the flap down.

My amigo and I get let off with two other privates we don't know. The truck headlights show we're at the bottom of the rise we're supposed to secure. Six and I look around, but Jackson is nowhere to be seen. He must have been ordered to stay on the transport with the other G.I.s.

The shallow arroyo has become a rushing stream. My boots soon fill with water. The gusts of wind from every direction fling our rubberized ponchos over our heads and all around us. I'm soaked before I can get it down again. The ponchos ought to be weighted at the bottom with shot.

Lightning crackles overhead and streaks down to the horizon. The flashes are so frequent we don't need our flashlights.

The slope of the ridge is steep and muddy. We take turns slipping forward and falling to our knees, then sliding backwards again almost as far as we'd come.

The crashes of thunder seem to be getting closer. It seems dangerous to be climbing higher. There are bright lights illuminating the thick fog on the other side of the rise.

"I think I know where we are," Six tells me, shouting above the howling wind. "We're on Foster's Ranch outside Corona."

"You sure?" I holler.

"Yeah, pretty sure," my amigo replies.

At last we reach the top of the ridge. I'm out of breath. So is Six. My boots carry ten pounds of mud each. I no longer see the other two soldiers who got off the truck with us. I don't think anyone is in charge of the situation.

The scene below us, on the far side of the steep ridge, is madness and chaos. There is shouting and barking of orders. Lights flash in every direction. Two Jeeps with their canvas tops up race past Six and me, churning up gobs of mud that splatter us. The Jeeps skitter down the other side of the ridge. I'm surprised they don't roll over.

An arc of four other Jeeps, their headlamps blazing, illuminate a silvery kind of airship or blimp. It's definitely not one of ours. The craft is edge up, at the bottom of a wide arroyo. It looks like a huge chrome hubcap, one crumpled in an accident.

The airship, though not on fire, smoulders. No one seems to know what they ought to be doing. They run around like my Tia's chickens.

I see what looks like Sergeant Bragg's familiar silhouette outlined by the vehicle headlights. He scouts the ridge with his binoculars.

A shot rings out. Then two more. Six jumps in front of me, knocking me to the ground. At least the muddy ground is soft.

"Hold your fire," someone shouts from below. "Hold your fire."

I nudge Six and get up. "The coast is clear," I tell him.

He does not get up. I cannot move in my poncho as the wind whips it around me. Removing my helmet, I pull my raingear off and over my head. The rain is cold and pelting. I fall to my knees next to Six.

"Get up," I shout. "Get up, amigo."

I do not see anything on Six's muddy, rain-slick poncho. I slit it open with my knife and take off his helmet.

"No! Oh, no," I scream. "It can't *be*. Six has been shot."

But there is no one nearby to hear me. My voice is drowned out by the wind and thunder.

The bullet has ripped a deep wound into his neck. His field jacket is blood-stained—a whole lot of blood. I strip off my jacket and, folding it up, tuck it beneath his head The mud beneath his head is puddled with his blood. His eyes stare at me. *Oh, God. No.*

I remove my shirt and rip off my undershirt. I hold it against the ragged wound, but there's no more blood coming out. His blood glistens all around him on the ground.

"No, no, amigo. You can't die," I shout. "The Holy Mother promised we'd always be together. Come on. Get up. I'll help you."

Sitting on the ground I prop him up, leaning his back against my chest. I fold my arms around him and rock him.

"Oh, my Dear Lord Jesus. If a life must be collected today, take mine. I will gladly give my life up for Six's. I will bear any death that he might live in my place and give You glory. I give myself to You. Thy will, not mine, be done."

The other two G.I.s from our transport tumble past, almost airborne in their ponchos. I shine my flashlight up into their frightened faces.

"Help!" I holler at them. "My buddy's been shot. Get a medic here on the double."

"Yes, sir," they reply, saluting, though I'm no higher in rank than they are.

My hands are sticky with Six's blood. He is limp in my arms. My amigo is so much heavier than when he breathed. Perhaps the air he took in when he lived made him lighter.

I sent the other two privates on a pointless errand. I know Six is dead. It is too late. I watch as the G.I.s slide over the edge of the ridge down to where the airship crashed. A tent has been set up. There is another troop truck beside it, mired in the deep mud.

I look up into the sky crisscrossed with lights and flares and lightning. The rain pelts me, streaming down my face, mixing with my salty tears. I tug my soaked shirt back on.

"Holy Mother, help me," I wail. "Help me. You said Six and I would always be together. Please, come. Please help us, *Santa Madre*."

"*¿No estoy yo aquí que soy tu madre?* Am I not here, I who am your mother?" comes the gentle voice.

A warm light shines behind me. I turn to see *Nuestra Señora*, the glowing rain and fog wrapped about her but not touching her. She looks down at me. Her expression is downcast, sad.

"Were you and Sixtus not always together?" the Virgin asks.

"Yes, but now he's dead. I am here and he is not. We are no longer together, *Santa Madre*. Please... your promise."

"Oh, *mi hijo*," she says. "I feel the pain you feel, the sharp stab of separation, the wound that refuses to heal. But I do not have power over life and death, my child. You and Sixtus will be together again in the bosom of Our Lord."

The Holy Mother looks down at me. She tries to smile. A tear glistens on her cheek.

"Please pray for me, Holy Mother. Help me to accept the Lord's will. It is a hard judgment for me to bear."

She holds her hands out to me. Her skin looks translucent, like alabaster.

"Perhaps there is someone who can help, Antonio," the Blessed Virgin says. "You must carry Six and follow me."

I stand up and heft my amigo up to my shoulders in a fireman's carry. Leaving our rifles and packs behind, I follow Holy Mother's faint glow in the fog. As she gets further and further ahead, I shift Six's weight on my shoulder. I'm afraid that, if I set him on the ground again, he will be truly dead and the earth will reclaim him. I don't think I can carry him much farther. My footing is slippery and unsure.

"Lord, help me," I blubber. "I cannot let him go. I am lost in the world without him. Take me instead, Lord. Please."

I sense someone behind me. I turn around, half-expecting to see Sergeant Bragg or the overdue medic—the medic who is too late to do any good.

A nearly-naked child stands before me. His skin is ashen gray, his head hairless. He looks malnourished.

"Good Lord," I exclaim, bending to look at him, nearly losing my grip on Six.

It is not a human child. The being is neither a boy nor a girl. He resembles one of Tia's plaster garden gnomes. He wears a cape with a hood. The child stands just over three feet tall. The wind-lashed rain does not land on him, as though he were under an enormous bell jar.

The creature's head is oversized compared to his body. His dark eyes are overly large, his mouth and ears tiny. There is a long thumb and three fingers on each hand.

Oh, my God. It must be the important visitor from Alpha Carinae. My heart beats as though it were trying to leap out of my chest.

"Do you have any strawberry ice cream?" the singsong voice asks. "I like strawberry ice cream."

"Welcome," I say, trembling in my boots. "W-w-welcome to Earth."

An older Visitor steps from behind the child whom he dismisses with a two-fingered gesture of his hand.

"You may go now, Korporal Kukla."

The second Visitor also stands just a bit over three feet tall, but he looks ancient. His skin is brown and wrinkled like a walnut. He pulls back his cowl, the hood of his cape, to reveal his face. It is creased with many lines that look like tattoos.

He produces a greenish light that shines from his palm. He turns his un-seen lamp on me. His dark eyes grow smaller, seeming to focus on my face.

"You would give your life for your friend?" he asks.

The voice, though speaking clear, if slightly mis-accented, English, sounds mechanical and artificial, as though it had been written on a typewriter for speech. I don't know how else to describe it. I shiver.

"You would exchange your life for your friend's?" he asks again.

"Yes," I say. "Gladly. Ten times over. Please, help me."

He touches my forearm. His touch is cool and dry on my sweaty, bloody skin. His eyes grow larger. I take it as a smile.

"Perhaps it will not come to that," he remarks. "I am Kaptain Kosmos, the closest I can express my name in your language."

"Were you on that crashed airship?" I ask. "Are you OK? Can I help you, Kaptain?"

"You have helped already, Antoniosanchez."

He pronounces my name as one word

"You know who I am?" I ask. My voice trembles.

"Yes, the Holy Mother asked us to help you—if we are able."

My shock almost makes me drop my amigo. I set him down as gently as my sore muscles allow, and kneel beside Six's body on the muddy ground.

I put my head on his blood-soaked chest and sob. My heart is broken in pieces like a clay pot. It is empty. Six's life, and my life, have leaked into the ground.

"Your friend gave his life to save you, and now you offer yours in order to have his life restored to him. I did not believe the Holy Mother that such love existed except in long-ago legends from places that no longer exist. You have refreshed my belief in the nobility of your species—and ours. God bless you, *Antoniosanchez*."

"Please, sir," I say. "You may call me *Antonio*."

The Visitor nods, his hood slipping forward. He bends to look at my ashen friend and takes a closer look at the gaping wound in Six's neck. Then he stands up.

"I cannot make promises, Antonio Our physicians have so rarely worked on Earthlings. Our knowledge is incomplete. We promised the Holy Mother we would help—if we can."

"My amigo is dead," I tell him. "It is too late for help."

"Perhaps not," he says.

"Since when can visitors from *out there* perform miracles the Holy Mother could not?" I ask the Kaptain.

"We can do many things that might seem like miracles. We have existed so much longer than your people, Antonio."

His voice is sing-song with a pleasant timbre.

"My people? How long have you been around, sir?" I ask him.

"Do you mean me personally or my race?" Kaptain Kosmos asks.

"Either," I reply. "Or both."

"By your reckoning, our civilization had over a million-year head start. And I am nine-hundred-sixty-nine years old."

"Can it be true?" I ask. "So many impossible things have happened today. I'm not sure I believe any of them."

"I understand," the Kaptain replies, his eyes widening. "You have not yet had breakfast."

I'm pretty sure he's referring to *Alice in Wonderland.* The White Queen encouraged Alice to believe six impossible things before having her breakfast.

Six... I think. *Six impossible things.*

A last ember of hope ignites in my heart—but I'm not sure I should trust it. I do not want to fool myself just because I want something so much—more than I have ever wanted anything in my life.

"I cannot help your friend out here, Antonio. We must move Sixtus to our craft, to our ship. Do you trust me?"

"Yes, of course," I tell the Kaptain. "Any friend of the Holy Mother's is a friend of mine."

The Kaptain smiles with his eyes. He shines the glow from his hand over Six's body. My amigo is lifted up from the ground but remains flat on his back, as though being carried on an unseen stretcher. He is shielded from the pelting rain by an invisible umbrella.

"There is something you could help us with, Antonio," the Kaptain says, "something you could do for us—if you would be so good."

"*Cierto,*" I say.

Kaptain Kosmos nods. I guess he knows Spanish, too.

"We lost two of our fellow officers in the crash of our scout craft, the broken ship you see down there."

"I'm very sorry to hear that," I tell him. "How can I help if your doctors could not?"

I look over at Six, motionless on the floating, glowing-green stretcher.

"We have recovered the body of Kolonel Klaatu, but the other officer was found by your soldiers. They hold his body in that canvas tent you see below."

I look down at the olive-drab army tent at the bottom of the ridge, glowing with lantern light from inside. A bluish streak of lightning crackles in the air above us, answered by another along the far horizon.

"It was your atmospheric disturbances that caused our scout ship to fall out of the sky. We travelers are not yet ready to reveal ourselves to your world, Antonio. You must recover the body of our companion and commend it to the sky or the water or the ground according to your customs."

"But the army has seen your airship," I say. "You can't hide *that.*"

"Well... perhaps they'll decide it is really just a weather balloon, after all," Kaptain Kosmos replies, his eyes widening in a grin.

"But the tent is under armed guard, Kaptain Kosmos, sir."

"If you close your eyes whenever anyone looks in your direction, they will not see you, Antonio."

"I'm afraid that trick stopped working when I was a little child," I tell him.

"Then you must become a little child again, Antonio, as Lord Jesus Christ advised."

The Kaptain turns aside and shines his palm down into the wide arroyo behind us. I can hear the water rushing in a torrent.

A glowing disk, enormous—maybe five times the size of the crashed airship—slowly solidifies and takes shape. Outlines appear first. It looks like a chrome-plated hub cap, perfectly smooth, with no features or fixtures, no way to get in or out. I have the idea it was sitting there all along, hovering a few feet above the ground, imperceptible to me.

"Do you see, Antonio? When everyone on board closes his eyes, our ship becomes invisible."

I do not know whether Kaptain Kosmos is serious or joshing me. Nothing seems real to me right now. Nothing—especially the death of *mi mejor amigo*. Maybe nothing was *ever* real and I'm just now waking up—in my own Wonderland.

Silently, a door appears on the side of the ship. The light from within illuminates the brown floodwater rushing beneath the gleaming craft.

Two Visitors descend a rampway. Their palms also glow with greenish light. The floating stretcher upon which my dead amigo rests, drifts toward them. I grab the corner. It stops moving.

"Please," I ask Kaptain Kosmos. "May I have a minute with my friend?"

He nods.

I lean over Six and kiss his cold, muddy cheek. I try not to look at his wound. *Dear Lord*, I think, *I don't see how anyone can help him. Into Thy Loving Hands I commend his spirit.*

The stretcher floats up the ramp, remaining perpendicular. My tears flow as plentifully as the pelting rain. I hold myself, shivering.

Dear Lord, help me. Help Six. Help the Visitors. Help me accept Your Will.

Kaptain Kosmos waves his glowing palm and the rain stops falling on me. It streaks down the sides of an invisible shield. Six, on his stretcher, disappears inside the gleaming ship.

A Visitor, lying on his back upon another floating stretcher, appears from behind the airship. I learn it is Kolonel Klaatu. There is an attendant on either side of his bier, guiding it without laying a finger on it.

The Kaptain stands beside me.

"You shall see and hear what no human has witnessed before, Antonio."

More Visitors stream forward from behind their silvery ship. Each wears a billowing white cape with high pointed collars. Unknown symbols decorate the hems. They file two abreast past their fallen fellow, one column on either side. They flow past the corpse, lying upon its floating bier, like a stream rippling around a stone.

Kaptain Kosmos raises his hand. All the Visitors stand still.

From beneath their robes the mourners produce what look like musical instruments: coiled trumpets of various lengths, and an array of strangely shaped gongs and chimes and bells. Others carry cymbals and drums.

The Kaptain hums a deep, vibrating note that the other Visitors pick up. They turn it and twist it into a swelling chord, a bizarre but harmonious chorus. The chanting seems too deep and resonant to be coming from such small beings with such small mouths and thin lips. They hold their notes longer than any human voice would be able to sustain them.

The tubas and trumpets and curlicue horns, from deep to high-pitched, blast out their discordant notes and trills. It sounds as though each instrument plays a different tune at a different tempo. They bang the metallic percussion instruments on their heads, playing each in its own distinct rhythm, too.

The result is a great racket capable of waking the dead they are laying to rest. Perhaps that is its intended purpose. But the deceased remains motionless atop his elaborate, luminous catafalque.

The chanting, for all its strangeness, is mournful and solemn. It touches my heart. Tears stream down my face. I feel so bad for Kolonel Klaatu and for his dear ones back home on Alpha Carinae. I mourn for my amigo and myself, too. Life is such a fragile gift.

The raucous cacophony gives me chills and hurts my ears. The music is almost tuneful at times, but it makes up for that with a renewed blast of dissonance which, if unable to raise the dead, will at least raise the hackles of every mourner in attendance—especially me.

The trumpets and tympani are happy sounds. The voices and cymbals are sorrowful ones. I hum one of their notes before it veers off and becomes a tone I can neither reach nor maintain. The sound makes my head vibrate.

"While, like you, we mourn the deaths of those we love," Kaptain Kosmos says, "we also celebrate the peace of death— when the time of struggle and wanting is over."

The phalanxes of attendants separate, drawing into two concentric circles around the floating bier. The Visitors continue to circle the gleaming casket in opposite directions while the entire procession moves forward at the same time. It is a wonder they do not trip each other up, especially in their long flowing robes.

The funeral procession winds forward at a stately pace. The mourners withdraw into the ship and disappear, along with the Kolonel's bier. Kaptain Kosmos and I are the last two remaining outside, standing at the crest of the steep embankment.

"I wish you could have met Kolonel Klaatu, Antonio. He had a most amusing sense of humor. I shall miss him.

"Kolonel Klaatu is the one who coined the term the *Holy Mothership* for our main vessel, the one the Holy Mother uses to get from here to there or some place else."

He laughs, but to my ears it sounds like shrill screeching.

"Do you mean *Santa Madre* travels in a spaceship?" I ask him.

"Yes," Kaptain Kosmos replies. "She says it is vastly superior to getting around upon floating clouds or in fiery chariots."

I hope he doesn't laugh again.

"So you and the Blessed Virgin Mary often travel together?" I ask him. "Things are getting stranger by the minute."

The Kaptain's eyes widen.

"Yes, Antonio. We both have humankind's welfare in mind. We both want to help your species get through a very rough patch. We and the Holy Mother are on the same team, so to speak—*your* team, the human race."

I can't think of anything to say. My mind is boggled—double-boggled.

"May I rely on you to retrieve our fallen companion from the tent below, Antonio?"

"Yes, Kaptain Kosmos. You can count on me."

"Gracias, Antonio."

He bows to me and turns away. He floats up the ramp to his gleaming airship. Once he is inside, the doorway vanishes behind him. The ship itself disappears a moment later, probably when everyone aboard closes his eyes and makes a wish.

I wonder whether I will ever see Six again—either dead or alive.

* * *

Sliding down the far side of the ridge on my rear end, I spread my arms and legs out to brake my descent in the slippery mud. I don't want to crash into the side of the tent and topple it.

I slither beneath the bottom of the tent, listening for any noise from within. I hear only rain spattering on the canvas—and my pounding heart.

Two kerosene lanterns, hanging from the center supports, light up the tent. Their glow seemed so much brighter outside. I crawl out from beneath a metal examination table.

It looks like a hastily-assembled field hospital. There is equipment and trays of surgical instruments along the walls of the tent and in the corners. There is no one here, so I stand up slowly, cautiously.

On one of the three operating tables lies a reclining figure—not very tall. My heart has been pounding at a fast trot for so long I almost don't notice it any more—until I lift the sheet. Then it nearly leaps out of my chest.

The rib-cage of the Visitor from Alpha Carinae has been cut open, exposing a jumble of unrecognizable organs. There is deep purple blood on the sheet and on the gray corpse.

The body of the unidentified Visitor is mangled on one side, his arm and leg mauled and twisted in unnatural ways. There is a gash on his head on the same side. His deep black eyes reflect the lantern light. My hands trembling, I reach to close his eyelids—but he hasn't any.

I find a duffel bag lying beneath one of the other tables. I dump out the clean linens and place the body of the small being, cocooned in its bloody sheets, into it. He is already stiff with the rigor of death.

A man in a long white doctor's coat walks into the tent. He folds his umbrella and shakes it. He looks up and freezes where he stands.

I can't imagine what sort of creature I look like to him. I am caked head to foot with thick mud. The doctor's jaw drops. His eyes widen.

Without a second to decide, my army training kicks in. I hurl myself at the doctor and tackle him to the ground, knocking the wind out of him. He is out cold. My muddy imprint is stamped on his laboratory coat.

The doctor moans. *Thank God I didn't kill him*, I think.

I get up and retrieve the body of the Visitor. Drawing the canvas bag closed, I skedaddle before the doctor awakens the rest of the way.

Slipping beneath the bottom of the tent, I crawl out, dragging the duffel with the Visitor's body behind me. Though still raining, it is no longer falling so hard. The lightning has trailed off, too.

The body of the Visitor doesn't weigh much—maybe forty pounds. I carry him in the duffel bag, the strap slung over my shoulder.

Realizing I am not going to be able to climb the steep, muddy embankment to go back the way I'd come, I follow the rushing water in the arroyo. Knowing I am on the Foster spread—if Six was right—helps me get my bearings. Occasional breaks in the clouds reveal a nearly full moon. I can see where I'm going for a few minutes before the clouds pass across the moon again.

I do not get very far when I hear a great clamor of sirens and whistles, and see flashing lights behind me. A confusion of shouting voices adds to the uproar. The doctor I knocked out must have raised the alarm. They will know the Visitor's body is missing, too. I keep going. It is the only thing my fear permits me to do.

I hear grinding gears and tires spinning in the mud, but none of the Jeeps or trucks seems to be getting anywhere but stuck.

By walking in the rain-filled arroyo, I realize I have effectively erased my tracks. I turn east, following the rising moon, though I have no idea where I'm going. I walk without a destination in mind. My only goal is to get away unseen.

The noise and lights are soon far behind me. There is what looks like the flickering glow of a kerosene lantern ahead. I don't know what it is, but I follow it. I have no other idea what I should do. I keep walking, plodding forward in the mud—one foot in front of the other. There is so much mud on my boots, I stand a half-foot taller.

The body of the fallen Visitor grows heavier. I do not seem to be getting any closer to the lantern light. I'm not sure how much longer I can go on. *Dear Lord, help me. Holy Mother, pray for me.*

The rain stops again, but the wind does not. The lantern seems to be drawing closer as though the person carrying it was walking towards me. Then I realize it is actually me getting closer to the light. Nothing has been what I expected tonight, from the moment the army duty officer woke us up with his shrill whistle.

I feel like I awakened into another dream—a nightmare—in which I walk alone in the world, a gloomy world without my best friend to walk beside me.

I reach the light at last.

The kerosene lantern hangs from a hook on the porch of the chapel at Nubes de Tormenta Pueblo. Brother Asinus's chapel is nearly twenty miles from where the Visitors' scout ship crashed. I don't understand how I could've walked that far.

As I ascend the steps with the small corpse of the Visitor in my arms, the doors of the chapel swing wide open. Brother Asinus, in his white habit and black cape, holds his arms open.

"Come, Antonio," he says, in a soothing voice. "I have been expecting you."

He shows me to the first pew, nearest the altar, and I set the wrapped body down on it.

Facing the altar, I fall to my knees and crouch down, holding my head in my hands. I sob and wail until I am empty, drained of all hope.

Brother Asinus touches my shoulder and urges me to my feet. Though my fatigues and field jacket are still mud-soaked, the friar enfolds me in his black cape. I feel his warmth. I shiver, and weep into his shoulder.

"Six is dead," I tell him, choking on the words.

I hear me say them with my own ears. It must be real. I said it. *Mi mejor amigo* is dead.

"Yes, I know, my son," the Brother says. "At times, the Lord asks us to bear more than we think we can carry. We must pray for strength to hold up beneath the weight. God will hear your prayer."

"How did you know I was on my way, Brother Asinus?" I ask. "I didn't know myself where my wandering was leading me."

"I had a dream, Antonio. *Nuestra Señora* came to me and showed me what happened."

The friar makes me sit down on the wooden bench opposite the one where the Visitor lies. He takes a bottle from a shallow cupboard against the wall. It is a bottle of brandy.

Brother Asinus pours a little into two small glasses and makes me drink some. I choke on it, but the warmth flowing into me on its way down makes me feel better.

After gently removing the Visitor's corpse from the canvas bag, the brother takes off his black cape. Carefully, lovingly, he tucks and folds it around the body as though it were a practiced ritual. He ties the black shroud with the black cord from around his waist. I have gotten his white habit very dirty.

"This is what *Santa Madre* told me to do in the dream, Antonio. Will you please give me a hand?"

Brother Asinus pivots the altar aside. He lights a candle and descends the few steps to the "crypt" below, the former friar's root cellar. I carry the corpse of the Visitor down into the tiny room. It is not deep enough for me to stand upright. The cellar is surprisingly dry, not at all damp.

The friar instructs me to lay the Visitor's corpse to rest on one of the slatted wooden shelves. Our meteorite sample, my notebooks and sketches, and the photos we took with Dr. Feynman's camera are all stored here. Each time Six and I visited the brother, we brought another item for the Blessed Virgin Mary's "archive" for safekeeping.

We go back up the steps. Brother Asinus and I push the altar back to its usual position.

I sit down heavily in the front pew, exhausted, placing my head in my hands. Brother Asinus places his hand on my shoulder. The gesture comforts me. It feels like a blessing, a consolation from one heart to another.

"You mustn't give in to despair, Antonio."

"But I have disappointed the Holy Mother," I whimper. "Six, my best friend in all the world, was killed by a bullet meant for me. I have let everyone down. Everybody, *mi Hermano*."

"*Tonteria*, Antonio. Nonsense. You have done all *Nuestra Señora* asked of you. You have done as the visiting ambassador asked, too."

Brother Asinus offers me a little more Christian Brothers brandy. He smiles.

"Though it's from a competing outfit, my son, the effect is still the same," he says.

I sip it slowly so I do not choke on it this time.

The brother takes his rosary from the pocket of his besmirched white habit and holds it in his hands. He kisses the crucifix.

"Let us pray the rosary together, my child."

We begin reciting the cycle of prayers. We come to, "Glory be to the Father, and to the Son, and to the Holy Ghost, as it was in the beginning, is now, and ever shall be, world without end. Amen."

The repetition of the prayers comforts my mind. They are like gentle waves lapping at the shore of a bottomless black ocean.

CHAPTER NINE

AD TE SITIVIT ANIMA MEA
For Thee My Soul Hath Thirsted

Brother Asinus fetches his spare black cape for himself and a blanket for me. He puts it over my shoulders. The passing thunderstorms have left a chill in the air.

"You should try to get some sleep before you go back, Antonio. If you wait until morning, I will have one of the young men from the pueblo drive you in his wagon."

"Just let me close my eyes for a few minutes, *mi Hermano*."

"Certainly, my son."

The brother sits down at the opposite end of the short pew. He and I lean back. My heart feels as weighty as an iron stone, heavy enough to sink down to the center of the earth.

As soon as I close my eyes, I see Six's lifeless figure lying in a pool of his blood. His eyes stare up at me, but there is no one looking at me from behind them. I will not be able to get any rest with his image in my mind. But as soon as I open my eyes, my tears flow again.

The latch on the front door of the chapel clicks. Brother Asinus and I turn around to see who is coming in at such an ungodly hour.

The hinges creak in a drawn-out moan, but there is no one there. It must have been a gust of wind.

A clap of thunder booms as someone steps slowly from the darkness. A lightning flash illuminates the figure. Another deep roll of thunder follows. Brother Asinus makes the sign of the cross.

"Oh, Holy Jesus. Holy Mother of God," I exclaim, jumping to my feet.

My heart leaps; my body sings. It is *mi dulce gringo*, my beautiful friend, restored to me. I want to rush to Six and throw my arms around him, to squeeze him as hard as I can and pull him to me.

Brother Asinus holds me back.

It is Six in form, but he is ashen pale, expressionless. He wears only his ripped, muddy, and blood-stained khaki underwear. His T-shirt is torn from the neck nearly to the hem, but there is not a mark or a scratch on him except for a raised white scar on his neck.

He walks stiffly, mechanically, his arms hanging limp at his sides—as though he were a puppet under someone else's control.

"Dear God, help us," I cry out.

I take a step toward Six. Brother Asinus walks behind me, praying the rosary.

I fold my arms around Six. His skin, while not cold, is not warm, either. He does not react to my touch.

"It's me, amigo," I tell him. "It's your Antonio."

There is no light in Six's eyes. He doesn't seem to know who I am. His eyes look beyond me. My amigo has what the army calls a *thousand-yard stare*, as though from shell-shock. He drools.

In my heart I pray to God for strength. I feel sorrow that this is how my amigo is returned to me, but I am grateful to God that my friend has come back to me at all.

I put my head on his shoulder and weep. If I must, I will take care of Six the same way he and I took care of my Tio Nicholás. I love Six with my life, the life he spared with his own. He was, and always will be, my best friend and my true love. Nothing will change that.

I lean forward and kiss him on his unmoving mouth.

Six parts his lips and sucks in a great gasp of air—as though he'd been holding his breath underwater and finally breaks to the surface. His eyes flash wide. He chokes and coughs, collapsing into my arms. I would have toppled beneath Six's dead weight if not for the friar's standing behind me, catching us both.

Brother Asinus and I each put an arm around Six and help him walk to the front pew. We lay him gently down across the wooden seat. The brother folds his ample black cape in half to cover Six.

He begins reciting the psalm, "*For thou, Lord, art good, and ready to forgive...*"

"*and plenteous in mercy unto all them that call upon thee,*" I continue.

In the flickering candlelight, I see color returning to Six's face. He shudders, and opens his eyes. His gaze follows me. He looks into my eyes.

"Oh, *mi dulce gringo*," I sputter, leaning over him. "You have come back to me. Oh, Six, you are my life, my everything."

My heart overflows with joy and gratitude. I thank God and His Holy Mother for the miracle they have granted to Six and me, for restoring the Gift of Life to my friend.

Still shocked by his appearance, I attempt to wipe some of the dirt from his face with my damp shirt cuff. There's something different about his eyes. I rattle questions off at him.

"Where did they take you, Six? What happened to you? What did the Visitors do to you, amigo?"

My barrage of questions seems to confuse Six, but I can't help myself. I want to know everything that happened to him.

"How did you know where I was?" I ask. "How'd you get here?"

Six takes his hand from beneath the black cape and places a finger on my lips, hushing me. Smiling, he closes his eyes, holding my hand in his hand atop the cape. I delight in the warm touch I never thought I would feel again. I rejoice at the faint smile on his lips.

Brother Asinus and I kneel in front of the pew where Six rests. We face the altar. As Six snores, we recite the prayers.

Hail, Mary, full of grace, the Lord is with thee.

* * *

After completing our recitation of the rosary, Brother Asinus offers me more brandy. He fills his own glass nearly full.

I sip it. The alcohol quickly goes to my head, making me even more bewildered.

"I do not understand how the Visitors can raise people from the dead, *mi Hermano*. Has God given them the power over life and death? Are they God's messengers? Are they angels?"

"I do not think they are angels, my son. Angels do not have a physical body. Perhaps Six was not yet in the bosom of Our Lord, his soul still residing in his body. I do not pretend to understand, *mi hijo*. What I *do* know is that you and Sixtus are blessed by God and His Holy Mother."

The brother takes my hand, smiling ear to ear.

"I'd invite you to stay here, Antonio, but it might be best if you return to the base. They will think you've gone *Absent Without Leave*, too. I urge you to return before you get in trouble, my son."

"How can I leave *mi mejor amigo*, Brother Asinus? I did not think I would ever lay eyes on him again. I cannot desert him again so soon."

"But you must. The soldiers must not come looking for you here. They will find Six and the Visitor's body in the crypt. I shall pray for your safety."

"What will I say, *mi Hermano*? How can I explain anything that happened tonight when I can hardly believe it myself?"

The friar looks at me, peering into my eyes. His eyes smile.

"Please, rest your mind, Antonio. God will help you find the right words. Our Lord and His Holy Mother are with you. They will protect you. Please. You must go now. I will take care of Six for the time being."

"Thank you, Brother Asinus. God be with you, too."

I return my blanket to the friar. Then I lean over Six and kiss his cheek. It is flushed with warmth.

Brother Asinus and I go out to the chapel porch. I hug the friar and go down the wood steps. The brother stands on the porch beneath the glowing lantern and raises his hand.

His smile assures me that things will be all right, though I haven't a clue how we will get to that place from here any more than I know how I will walk the twelve miles from the pueblo back to Roswell Army Airfield before they declare me AWOL.

* * *

The first streaks of dawn appear at the horizon like gentle ripples on a pond.

I hear a grinding engine draw closer. The vehicle pulls onto the side of the road, splashing me with mud.

"We been lookin' all over creation for you, soldier. How'd you get way the hell out here?"

Two GIs with MP insignia on their armbands and helmets sit in the Jeep. They lean towards me.

"Where's your buddy at, Sanchez? Sergeant Bragg has offered a bounty on your heads—dead or alive. We aim to collect it one way or the other, see?"

Like a lot of things in the army, the MPs might be joking or they might be serious. I don't wait to find out. I don't put anything past Sergeant Bragg. I make a run for it.

The Jeep takes off after me, straddling the ditch with two tires on either side. I want to jump into the field, but there's too much barbed-wire for me to scramble over. I'd never make it before they shot me in the back.

Stopping just up the road, the two MPs leap out of the Jeep. They come running for me and fling a tarpaulin over me. I try to get away and get tripped up in the canvas.

"Why you makin' this difficult, pal? Just get in the goddamn Jeep, will ya?"

I can't find my way out from beneath the tarp. The MPs both jump on me. I manage to land a couple of punches before they hit me with their nightsticks. They're not fooling around. I kick one of them and he moans. Then one of their "batons" connects with my noggin.

I see a most brilliant display of celestial objects at the bottom of a muddy ditch.

* * *

The light hurts my eyes. It seems to be coming from every direction. I try to see where I am, but my head is too heavy to hold up. I close my eyes again.

I hear whispers but the words do not make sense the way they are strung

together. It's as though two people were taking turns reciting Webster's dictionary frontwards and backwards.

My head aches as though I'd been hit with a brick. I try to remember.
*Sergeant Bragg's bounty on my head—dead or alive. The two MPs in the Jeep.
One of them hit me with his wooden baton.*

Where am I? Am I in jail? I wonder. It feels like I'm in a bed. *Where is
Six?*

I must find him and ask him where I am. *Where is he?*

A deep voice whispers, "This one made it, but we still don't know where
his buddy is. He's gotta be dead by now. It's been three days since the crash."

"No!" I shout. "It's not true. He's alive... someplace... somewhere. I've
got to find him."

I try to get out of bed to go look for Six. A needle goes into my arm.

Then someone turns off the lights and it is quiet again.

* 2 *

Though the voices are gone, my dreams keep me awake. *Six is dead and
Six is alive. Yes, that's it. He is alive, but he has been wounded. I must find him.
Dear God, please help me.*

A gentle hand touches my wrist. It is my nurse. She carries a kerosene
lantern that she sets on the bedside table. She turns it down so it does not hurt my
eyes.

"Thank you," I tell her.

"You are welcome, Antonio."

I know by her sonorous voice that it is the Holy Mother. I manage to sit
up, but the movement makes me dizzy. I look up at her. Her face glows with a
beautiful smile.

"*Santa Madre...*" I say. "*Santa Madre...*"

"Yes, I know my child."

"Please. Where am I, Holy Mother? Where is Six?"

"You are both in the infirmary. Sixtus is in the next room."

"I must go to him," I say, struggling to swing my legs over the side of the
hospital bed, but I am so weak I cannot stand.

"How long have I lain here, Holy Mother?"

"It is the middle of August, *mi hijo*. You were in a coma until now—for
six weeks."

"What is wrong with me?" I ask.

"You were knocked unconscious by one of the military policemen and
received a severe concussion, my child."

"Please, *Santa Madre*. You must help *mi amigo*."

"I have looked in on Six already. He sends you his love."

Her smile lights up the whole room. I'm afraid someone will see and think there's a fire.

"I am here to tell you what I told Sixtus, Antonio. They will be administering truth serum to you. They want to know what you saw on the night the Visitors' ship crashed. The drug is called *Sodium Pentothal*, I believe."

"What will the drug do to me, Holy Mother?" I ask.

"Nothing, my child, since you already do your best to speak the truth," she replies, smiling. "But it will also make you confused and drowsy. I know you are strong. You will resist all suggestions to confess to things that you did not witness. Speak the truth clearly and without hesitation. All will be well, *mi hijo*."

"What about Six?"

"They have already questioned Six several times. But he was shot before he witnessed anything they do not already know about. He will be discharged soon."

"Thank you, Holy Mother."

I take my rosary from beneath my pillow and hold it up to her.

The Holy Mother holds my wrist and takes my pulse. Smiling at me, she places my hand, still holding the rosary, gently beneath the blanket.

Taking the old railroad lantern with her, she leaves my room and softly shuts the door.

* 3 *

I awaken to bright daylight filtered through drawn window shades. It's hard to focus. I don't know whether it is hours or weeks later. For all I know, I have awakened before I even fell asleep. That would fit in with everything else strange that's been going on since the Visitors arrived.

Sergeant Bragg sits in an armchair beside the window, a copy of *Time* magazine in his hands. The chief Russian delegate to the United Nations is on the cover with the word "Veto" above Mr. Gromyko's head. The date on the cover is August 18, 1947. The details seem too real to be dream images, but I'm not positive. The last I remember, it was the Fourth of July.

Bragg looks up and puts the magazine down. He stands, and scrapes his chair across the floor to sit beside my bed.

"Have a nice nap, Sanchez?" he asks, smirking.

"I'm not sure, Sergeant. I get the idea that maybe *this* is the dream, you know, huh?"

"It's gonna become a nightmare, buster, unless you cooperate. You can count on it."

Pushing myself up on my elbows, I sit up. Though I'm not as woozy as when I first awoke, I can tell I've been drugged. I look over and see a rubber tube in my arm.

"You're gonna answer a couple questions for me, right, Sanchez?"

I haven't given a minute's thought to anything I should say. I begin hiccuping. Stalling for time, I reach for the water glass on the bedside table and drain it. My hand shakes.

If they've already questioned Six, I need to make sure my answers jibe with his. *Speak the truth clearly and without hesitation*, the Blessed Virgin advised me.

"What happened to your buddy Thorson the night that Russian spy plane crashed?"

"Oh, is that what happened? A Russian spy plane? It looked more like a blimp to me."

"My friend was shot, sir—in the neck. Maybe he was shot by one of our own guys. *Friendly fire*. I can't be sure. It was crazy out there. Nobody knew what was going on. When I saw Thorson had been shot, I called out for help."

"Do you think the Russians shot him, Sergeant Bragg?"

"I ask the questions around here, Sanchez.

"So... Your buddy got shot. We have other witnesses to that fact. Your pal Jackson said he thought he saw you talking to somebody up on the ridge—somebody kinda short. Any ideas who he saw you with, Sanchez? Dwarves? Kids? Little green men, maybe?"

"I don't know what Jackson thought he saw, Sergeant. But I did not see any midgets or little green men that night."

I'm glad he didn't ask me about little *brown* men.

"OK. Follow me, Sanchez. After your buddy was shot, two MPs found you ten miles from base. How the hell did you get out there? You tried to outrun the MPs.

"Then Thorson shows up three days later when some brave from the pueblo dropped him at the front gate wrapped in an Indian blanket. He was almost naked and streaked with his own blood. The wound that should have severed his carotid artery was now completely healed. What am I missing, Sanchez?"

"I left him there on the ground, Sergeant, by the crash site. I have no idea what happened to Six after I left him. Their medicine must be more powerful than ours."

"The Injuns' medicine? Don't make me laugh," he says, laughing.

I spoke the truth to Sergeant Bragg. I feel no obligation to correct his misunderstanding.

"OK, witch doctors aside, we're dealing with serious issues here. Answer me this: I was told by army intelligence that you and Dr. Feynman have been in communication. I want to know what you know, Sanchez. What did he tell you? If you don't wanna come clean, we can always increase the dosage. You're gonna tell me one way or the other."

"Dr. Feynman gave me a copy of the lab report on the meteorites we found."

"Yeah, I've seen that. Nothing much in it. What else?"

"He gave us his very nice Kodak Retina camera. Thorson and I turned nineteen. It was a graduation and birthday present to my amigo and me."

"I knew about that, too. The druggist gave us a copy of the negatives. What else?"

I'm not sure what the sergeant suspects me and Six and Dr. Feynman of being up to. I wish he'd just come out with it. I can't think of anything else to tell him.

"Dr. Feynman brought lox and bagels and *hamantaschen* to our graduation."

"You're just like your buddy, you know that?" Bragg remarks.

He looks disgusted.

"You're two of kind, you and Thorson: full of all sorts of information and details. But none of it is worth a damn to me. It's useless. But I know you and the Doc are up to something anti-American, and I'm not giving up until I've got the goods on all of you."

Sergeant Bragg gets up from his chair and slaps the magazine down on the seat. He rounds the foot of the bed, mumbling all sorts of cuss-words to himself. Leaving my room, he slams the door behind him.

I surprise myself by staying so calm, especially under fire. Maybe the army has turned me into a soldier after all.

Reaching for my rosary beneath the pillow, I close my eyes. I am sleepy again. My head spins. I'm still pretty confused myself about what really happened that night and what didn't.

* * *

Judging by the shadows on the wall, it's only a little later that same afternoon. Though I'm sure guards must be posted outside my door and Six's, I decide to check my guess. For all I know, this is just a U.S. Army movie set. I pull the tube from my arm.

The corridor is empty except for a single soldier, his back to me, who turns the corner at the end of the long hallway.

I have no idea which room is Six's. Wearing only my backwards hospital gown, I try the nearest door first. It is unlocked. I stick only my head in. It's a storage room. The next is an empty hospital room. The one after that is Six's room. I say a prayer of thanks.

Daylight filters through the window shade. My amigo is asleep, lying on his back. My heart, already pumping with fear, shifts into higher gear at seeing *mi mejor amigo*.

I approach his bed. Barefoot, I do not make a sound, but I'm sure my thumping heart will wake him. I lean in closer.

Six has an apple in his hand, probably left over from his lunch. He's taken only a couple of bites.

This is the first I have laid eyes on Six in two months—since the night he was shot. Maybe he is still not right. I steel myself for whatever God has ordained.

Thy will be done, I pray.

I bend down to kiss Six.

My amigo's eyes flash open as soon as my lips touch his. He sits up in bed. He has one blue eye and one brown eye. They were both blue before.

"My best friend in all the world," Six says, grinning his familiar dimpled smile.

"What happened to your eyes?" I ask, nearly shouting. "Oh, dear Jesus. Can you see all right, amigo?"

He nods and smiles. Letting go of his apple, he reaches for my hand. He places his fingers beneath my palm and rapidly taps out a message in Morse code.

THEY WATCH.

THE VISITORS? I tap back.

BRAGG, he responds.

Meanwhile, we also carry on a spoken conversation for the benefit of any eavesdroppers. It's hard for me to keep track.

"So what do they think happened to your eyes?" I ask aloud.

"The army doctor called it *heterochromia*. It's a birth trait."

"But you didn't have different-colored eyes before," I say.

He taps, MAYBE I'VE BEEN *RE*-BORN. OR MAYBE I'M PART VISITOR NOW.

He shrugs. "They can't explain it," he says aloud, smiling.

At the same time he taps, MAYBE THE VISITORS DIDN'T PUT ME BACK TOGETHER RIGHT — LIKE FRANKENSTEIN'S MONSTER.

He smiles at me on the sly.

"Jackson's come to see me a couple of times," he says aloud.

"That was awfully nice of him," I reply.

THEY'RE LEANING ON HIM TO TELL THEM WHAT HE SAW, Six taps. I SAID TO TELL THE TRUTH AND DON'T GET IN TROUBLE ON MY ACCOUNT.

BUT ISN'T THAT WHAT FRIENDS ARE FOR? Jackson asked.

"Do your Gram and Gramps know where you are?" I ask out loud.
"Sergeant Bragg said he notified them," he replies.

In code, he informs me, **I DON'T BELIEVE HIM. I HAVEN'T HEARD A WORD FROM THEM.**

"I'm going to be discharged soon," he tells me, smiling. "They want to keep me under observation a while longer, though."

UNDER BRAGG'S EVIL EYE, I remark in code, squeezing his hand, unseen beneath the blanket.

"That's great news," I say aloud.
"I'm being discharged from the army, too," my amigo tells me.
"*Cierto*?" I ask.
"*Cierto*," he replies. "An honorable discharge 'for severe injuries and impairments received in the line of duty.'"
"No, Six. I just got you back. You can't leave me again already. We can't get separated again."
"Maybe you'll be up for an army discharge, too, amigo," he suggests. "You were out cold for a month-and-a-half—in a coma. You may never be right in the head again. Who knows?"

THEY THINK I'M OFF MY ROCKER, he taps, pointing to his head with his other hand.
ME, TOO,"I respond beneath the blanket.

"So what else is new?" he asks out loud.
His remark makes me laugh.
"*No mucho*," I say. "Maybe I'd better be getting back before somebody misses me."

I MISS YOU, he taps.

"Stop by anytime," he says. "If you find the door's locked, feel free to use the window."
It seems his blue eye and his brown eye have switched sides. I'm not sure. I can't remember.
I never thought I'd see his smile again except in memories as faded as old photographs. His smile is worth the whole world to me.

* 4 *

After a month of physical rehabilitation, psychological counseling, and endless tests and examinations, I am told my discharge papers—both from the infirmary and from the United States Air Force—are drawn up. The attached letter, from the army physician, says I received serious physical and psychological trauma in the line of duty. The doctor stated I could no longer reliably perform my duties for the United States Air Force.

I am elated and disappointed at the same time. I wanted to learn to fly, but I am happy to have my life back—my life with my best friend. My joy easily wins out.

Once Six was discharged, he was no longer permitted to visit me in the infirmary. We could not get a good answer as to why. I suspect Sergeant Bragg might have had something to do with it.

"No, there's no reason for it," the corporal at the front desk told Six. "It's policy."

So Six and I communicated through the regular old U.S. mail. I received a letter from *mi mejor amigo* every day and answered each one.

We never wrote anything important or gushy—nothing we didn't care that many eyes would read.

Without knocking, Sergeant Bragg barges into my room to present my discharge papers to me personally. I'm in the middle of packing my duffel bag.

"I don't mind telling you that you're being released over my strong objections, Sanchez. But it's not a good idea to argue with the base commander's orders. I figure somebody higher up must've leaned on Major Sanford."

I stuff my folded fatigues into my bag and look up. It feels good to be wearing my civvies again—my newest Levi's.

"You and your buddy might think you're off the hook now, Sanchez, because you're civilians again. Nothing could be further from the truth. You may not be under my scrutiny any longer, buster, but I've turned everything over to Hoover's men at the FBI. They got all my notes on you two during your time in the army and those from your little visit to the Los Alamos lab.

"Army Intelligence will be turning over their files, too. You're gonna be under Hoover's watchful eye from now on. They'll get to the bottom of what you're up to. You can count on it."

The sergeant slaps the folder with my discharge papers on the bed. Turning on his heels, he reaches for the door. He flings it wide and storms out.

Before I go back to packing my bag, I take a look at my Honorable Discharge papers. I smile. They even spelled my name right.

* * *

Six picks me up in my Tio Nicolás's turquoise pickup at the Roswell Army Airfield front gate. This is a day whose arrival I both dreamed of and despaired of. I thought they were going to hold me forever. But there my amigo is, big as life, sitting behind the wheel. His smile is so bright in the glaring sunlight that I think I ought to put on my sunglasses. I fling my heavy duffel bag in the back.

"Looks like you packed enough for the rest of your life," he tells me.

"I sure hope so, Six," I reply, climbing up into the truck.

I want to lean across the seat and kiss him, but not in public. He drives out the front gate. I reach for his hand, but then he's unable to shift. Scooting closer, I rest my hand on his thigh.

Six turns and looks at me, suppressing his dimples. But he can't suppress the outline of his arousal in his overalls.

"You looking to cause an accident?" he asks, grinning.

"No," I say, "just start a fire."

He chuckles. I take my hand away. It has been seven months since I touched my amigo in an intimate way. My skin is hungry for him. The twelve miles to the house seem like two dozen in a donkey cart.

Six parks the truck beneath the cottonwoods in back beside the barn. It was late winter when I left and it is now early autumn. The leaves that had not yet unfurled are now turning golden yellow around their edges.

My amigo takes my hand and we go up the porch steps to the kitchen, my heart pounding louder and louder. He opens the screen door. Every familiar object looks so peculiar—as though I'd seen them before but can't recall where.

The screen door slams behind us.

"Welcome home," Six says, spinning in front of me and throwing his arms around me.

"Where is everybody?" I ask. "Isn't anybody happy I'm back?"

"I'm sure happy you're home, amigo. I told our families you'd probably want to lie down a while first. They'll be over later."

"Thank you, Six. You are so considerate."

"Maybe I have ulterior motives, you know, huh?"

"I hope so," I tell him.

"Yep," he says, "you're definitely faster on the uptake."

I smile at him.

"I guess I appreciate everything I learned in the army, Six, and *most* of what I experienced. But I'm sure glad our stint for Uncle Sam wasn't any longer than it was."

"Me, too," he says. "*Thank God Almighty. Free at last.*"

Mi mejor amigo and I lead each other by the hand through the parlor to our bedroom.

I glance up at the crucifix above our bed, where it has hung since we moved into this bedroom. I think about going first to the grotto with my amigo to pray the rosary in thanksgiving for our being reunited. But I know I wouldn't be able to concentrate. I hope Jesus and the Holy Mother will understand. We will pray later, when we can keep our minds on it. My mind is here now—with Six.

There is no use pretending. The more I try *not* to think about my desire for him, the stronger it grows.

Six and I sit at the edge of the bed. I unbutton my shirt and pull it off my arms. He takes off his own shirt and undershirt. My amigo and I kiss and canoodle until I think we will set something on fire. My arms and hands tremble; my breathing is short and deep, in the rhythm of a gallop.

We let go of one another and sit looking at each other a moment. It will take me a while longer to get used to his two-color eyes. Now I think they are back the way they were—blue on the right, but I'm not sure. I don't remember.

Before I can unlace my other boot, Six topples me backwards onto the bed. He pops open the buttons of my overalls. My throbbing penis pushes against my khaki undershorts until I think it'll rip them. Six smiles and pulls my army drawers down.

My hands shaking, I reach for his Levi's and yank open the buttons. His hard-on pushes past the waistband of his civilian undershorts. I slide them down and he leans forward on top of me, nestling his legs between mine. I feel his erect penis next to mine.

"Oh, God, Antonio. I love you so much. I love you with everything I've got, amigo—all of me."

We rub up and down, pulling back from the edge a couple of times, but our descent into climax is assured. It is not far off.

I watch his blue eye and his brown eye watch me. Then they switch sides. I'm sure of it this time. The more excited he becomes, the faster the colors flash back and forth. It reminds me of a theater marquee. It makes me laugh.

Six laughs, too, his chest and stomach bouncing up and down against mine.

"Are you doing that on purpose, Six? How do you even do it?"

He kisses me quiet. I roll over on top of him, switching positions with him. We continue our rubbing.

"I love you, amigo," his eyes blink in Morse code. "More than ever."

I laugh out loud. Our wriggling and laughing, our jiggling and howling and wrestling lead to our tumbling quickly down the hill of our thrilling but brief ride. I want to pay another nickel and go around again.

For a moment, I think I see me through Six's flashing eyes. I am far more handsome than I see myself.

Each time, our love-making is the best I can remember. We pull up our shorts and Levi's, and scoot closer. I fall asleep next to him, in his arms. I get to have my nap after all.

* 5 *

Slowly, I return to work at Mila-Grow Nursery & Greenhouse—just three days a week at first. Six already works a full week of five-and-a-half days. I am pretty out-of-shape after lying in the infirmary for nearly two months.

Little Nicky stays with Six's Gram and Gramps most of the time. The boy, now almost two years old, rarely stays with us any more. On most weekends, Six stays with his grandparents, helping them with chores and repairs, and, of course, pitching in to help take care of his son. I miss Six when we are apart, even though it is only two days a week. Sometimes I feel we will never make up for the time we were separated in the Roswell Airfield infirmary.

One Saturday, while Six is away, there is a rap on the front screen door. It startles me. The front door is only for company.

The man who stands there is a well-dressed Mexican fellow with nearly completely silver hair and a bushy mustache. He holds his hat in his hand. I unlatch the door and invite him in.

"I'm Mr. Montoya, son," he says. "Is Sixtus at home?"

"He's taken the truck into town, Mr. Montoya. He might not be back for a while."

"And what about little Nicky? I'm Hypatia's father, the boy's grandpa."

"Nicky is at the other end of the road, sir—at my Tia Ana's house. Six and I just got home from work."

"Well, the child is certainly being introduced to a lot of different people, isn't he?"

"Yes, and he seems to like all of us. You must be very proud, *Abuelo*."

If Señor Montoya had been wearing a vest, he would've popped at least one of the buttons.

"I am Six's friend," I say, "Antonio Sanchez."

Little Nicky's grandpa extends his hand.

"I am happy to finally meet you," he says. "You boys work together, no?"

"Si, Señor Montoya."

"So there are two incomes in this house?"

I nod.

"And Six pays you rent?"

"Um... no, sir. We're friends. He works it off by helping out with chores and errands and stuff."

"I see."

"May I get you a beer, Mr. Montoya?"

"Yes, thank you," he says.

I snap the caps off two Dos Equis and we go out to the *portál*. We toast to the child and his grandfather.

"So... if you don't mind my saying so, young man, I think there is enough money in this household to afford a telephone. It would save a lot of running back and forth and all around."

"I agree, sir, but Six says telephones are a bother and a constant interruption. He doesn't want one."

I don't tell him Six is afraid our phone would be wiretapped by Hoover's men.

"But this is your house, no?" Mr. Montoya asks, shrugging and raising his eyebrows.

I smile. "Well, I guess we will be getting a telephone very soon then," I say.

"How much influence do you have on your friend, Antonio?"

"A little," I reply. "We've been friends since we were boys in first grade."

"I ask because I am desperate," Mr. Montoya says.

He takes a long swallow of his beer.

"My daughter refuses to marry Sixtus. She is a stubborn child—*testarudo*. I have talked until I am green in the face. She has decided to be a famous astronomer and will not listen to her mother or me. She's already too smart for her own good. She will be in school for the rest of her life.

"Perhaps you can ask Six to put a little pressure on Hypatia. He is the only one she listens to at all. They should be married for the child's sake."

"I'll be sure to mention it to him, Mr. Montoya. Would you like another beer?"

"No, thank you, Antonio," he says, getting up from the porch rocker. "I'm glad I finally got to meet you. I don't mind telling you I think you're a fine young man. I think you're a good influence on Sixtus. He's a little stubborn at times, too. He and Hypatia would have been a good match."

I smile. I can just imagine the fights they'd be having, neither of them giving an inch.

Mr. Montoya puts on his hat. It's almost as wide as a sombrero. His spotless pickup truck looks as though it has never done a day's hauling in it's life, as though Mr. Montoya just drove it from the dealer's lot.

If we had a telephone, I would be calling down to Tia Ana right now to let her know she is about to get a visitor. Of course, we'd have to get her a telephone, too.

I admit I like Mr. Montoya. But his talk of Six and Hypatia getting married makes me nervous. What if Hypatia changes her mind about marriage? What then?

I take a deep breath and wait for Six to get back.

* 6 *

Two Saturdays later, Six drops me off at my aunt's house after work. I go over to my Tia Ana's when Six is away at his grandparents' house—nearly every weekend now. I help my aunt with whatever needs doing. She cannot walk without her cane and, in the seven months I was away in the army, she has grown stooped.

I am just in time for lunch. My aunt is ready to enfold me in hugs and kisses.

"No, Tia," I say. "Let me wash up first."

I take off my dirty, sweaty workshirt and hang it over the back of my chair. I pump water into the kitchen sink and scrub my hands with Tia's home-made soap.

She invites me to say our grace before we sit down. Then she takes the lid off her tureen and ladles her wonderfully cold *gazpacho* soup into our bowls. She has made a salad with watermelon and grapes from her garden and vines.

"I am so happy to see you, *mi sobrino*. How is Six? How is the little one?"

"Everyone is well, Tia, thank God."

My aunt does not wait for me to finish my bowl of chilled vegetable soup before she ladles more into it. It is the best meal I could think of for the unbearably hot late summer weather we've been having. It has been dry, too.

"Did you see the men in black suits?" my aunt asks. "They are in Vigil's field today."

"No, I didn't notice," I tell her, spooning more *gazpacho* into me.

"What do you suppose they are up to, *mi hijo*?"

I don't want to tell her they are probably government agents keeping an eye on me and Six. My amigo made up a story and told his grandparents they were probably prospectors.

"Maybe they're prospecting, Tia," I say.

"In suits and ties?" she asks.

"They must be high-class miners," I reply.

"Oh, go on," she says, laughing. "You're always making jokes. You're getting to be just like Six."

"Maybe Vigil is thinking of selling, Tia. They're probably just surveying his property."

"*That* I might believe."

My aunt lifts the lid of the tureen. I hold my hand over my empty bowl and slide it up to the watermelon salad instead. I spoon some in.

"I see your appetite is returning," she says, smiling at me.

"Yes," I say. "It seems that the more I work, the hungrier I get. Your cooking will make me fat, Tia."

"You have long way to go, *mi sobrino*," she tells me.

After I help clear the table and wash the dishes, my aunt takes out a bottle of ice-cold beer and two glasses. We go out to the rear *portál*. Her thermometer says it is still ninety degrees. I fill our glasses, hoping my beer doesn't evaporate before I get to swallow some.

I see the man in the black suit. He slips behind a tree whenever I look his way. My aunt notices I am watching something. She turns around to see.

"Oh, my," she cries, getting to her feet. "The man has just fallen down. I think he's fainted, Antonio. You must go help him."

I jump up out of my chair and dash down the back steps. I don't see how I'll be able to carry him very far. The FBI agent is a pretty big guy.

Spying my aunt's wheelbarrow at the edge of her garden, I dump out the radishes and race down the path to Vigil's field. Though his and my aunt's meadows are still fenced in, the gate between them long ago fell off its hinges.

I find the man in the black suit slumped beneath one of the cottonwoods. I wheel the barrow up to him and, tilting the front of it down towards him, I hoist his legs into it. Then I go around behind him and lift him up beneath his arms. I push him into the wheelbarrow and right it. His legs dangle out the back.

When I get him to my aunt's back yard, Tia helps me get the man's black suit jacket off. I fling it over the porch railing. He has a short-nosed pistol in a holster beneath his arm. It's lucky that the gun didn't go off during his bumpy wheelbarrow ride. I remove the revolver and set it on the porch table. Then I loosen the agent's tie, and take off his dark sunglasses.

My aunt and I laugh. The government agent has received no sunlight around his eyes. He looks like a negative raccoon. As she goes into her kitchen for water and a cloth, I dump the agent backwards out of the wheelbarrow—as gently as I can—and onto the porch. I drag him beneath the shade at the rear of the *portál* and put a chair cushion beneath his head.

Tia returns with a washbowl of cool water and a washcloth. She daubs the man's face with a sprinkle of water. I take the washbowl from her and douse him with it. He sputters and sits up, startled and disoriented.

"What's going on?"he asks. "Where am I?"

"The United States of America," my aunt says.

I smile at her. The agent gets to his feet, still unsteady. Looking around, he probably realizes he is not far from his stakeout beneath the cottonwoods.

"I'd like to use your telephone," the man says.

"I have no use for one," Tia tells him. "But my nephew lives just up the road. He has just gotten a telephone put in."

The man takes a plain white card from his shirt pocket. Using his fountain pen, he writes a telephone number on it.

"Just tell them where I am," he says.

Forgetting myself, I salute him. "Yes, sir," I say.

I go around to the front of my aunt's house and enter the *calle* down to my house and Six's. It feels so wonderful to be able to say that once more. It seems nothing less than miraculous to me. My heart leaps.

This is the first time we have a real use for our new telephone. I wonder if I shouldn't call for an ambulance instead.

By the time I get back to Tia's house, the agent who fainted is sitting in a chair with a glass of water in his hand.

"Don't gulp it, mister," she advises. "Just sip."

I hear a car pull up out front. Two more men in black suits enter Tia's yard. They got here awfully quick. They must've been waiting somewhere nearby. I look at their identification tags, pinned to their jacket pockets. Neither of their names has any vowels in it, just a jumble of random letters I'd never be able to remember. Maybe that's the idea.

"Nice work, Mxyzptlk," one of his colleagues says to the agent who passed out. "Instead of observing, you manage to *be* observed—caught in the act. Very professional."

They help their colleague into his jacket. It's pretty dirty. There are radish leaves stuck to the back of it. I try not to laugh. Agent Mxyzptlk puts his revolver back in its holster and pulls his jacket closed to hide it. He brushes off his name tag.

Without saying another word, the three men in black suits leave Tia's yard.

"*Eran muy groseros*," my aunt says. "They were very rude men. *Gracias*, never came to their lips."

I do not know what to tell her. It isn't their manners I am worried about, but what they'll put in their reports to FBI headquarters. Our lives are so ordinary, they will probably have to make things up to make it interesting.

"Perhaps I should not be so unkind," my aunt remarks. "Surveying is a hard life—always at the mercy of the weather. But, for goodness' sake, this is not a day to be wearing all black."

I smile.

"Why do you suppose the surveyor was carrying a gun, *mi sobrino*?"

"Well... "

I'll have to think awfully fast—as fast as Six.

"Well, you never know when some ornery prospector or farmer is going to disagree with where you've drawn the lines on your map."

"That makes sense," she says. "But why does he hide the gun? I think people would behave themselves better if they could see the gun, no?"

"Yes, Tia," I say. "You're probably right. Surveying is an awfully tough way to make a living."

We touch our glasses and sip the rest of our warm beer, enjoying the first cool breezes of the evening.

* * *

It has gotten much cooler—more like a proper autumn. There was a little rain this week, too. When I visit my aunt after work the next Saturday, she rushes out to the back porch before I have even climbed the three steps. She takes my hand and leads me into her kitchen.

"Oh, *mi sobrino*. I have something to tell you," she says, out of breath. "Something important."

She sits down at the kitchen table, putting a hand on her heart. I bring her a glass of water.

"With maybe a little brandy, *por favor*," she says. "And a little for yourself."

"No, Tia. I have not had my dinner yet. I don't want to get sleepy. I came here to help you in the garden. But first, tell me. What's got you so excited?"

She can barely sit still in her chair. She is still winded from her excitement and can barely get the words out.

"*S-s-santa M-madre* came to me, *mi hijo*—in the grotto."

I pour a splash of brandy into her water glass. My aunt touches my wrist, causing a little more to pour out. She takes a sip and rushes to tell her story.

"The Holy Mother stood in the place of your carving, Antonio. She was flesh and blood, though she was not entirely solid. She glowed like a candle flame. *Santa Madre* smiled at me. Oh, my heart fluttered. She is so beautiful—like a statue."

"What did the Holy Virgin tell you, Tia? Or was it a private talk?"

I sit down next to her and hold her hand. She trembles.

"Oh, my child," she says, weeping.

"What is it, Tia?" I ask, squeezing her hand. "What happened?"

"I saw the Holy Mother's lips move, Antonio, but I could not hear a word. I thought I had gone deaf, but I could still hear the meadowlarks in the tree. She reached her arms out to me, but I could not hear her. Oh, *mi hijo*."

I lean towards her and she sobs into my shoulder.

"You mustn't feel bad, Tia. A visit from the Blessed Virgin Mary is a tremendous honor. Maybe it is best to be grateful for what we've been given and not expect more."

"You are right, my child," she says, forcing herself to smile. She dries her eyes on the flowered handkerchief from her apron pocket. "But I wonder what *Santa Madre* said to me. It must have been important. Otherwise, why would she have come?"

She swallows the rest of her brandy in water and gets up from the table. She paces around the kitchen.

I wonder if the Holy Mother's silent visit to my aunt means that Tia is going deaf. I do not want to speculate out loud in front of her. I don't want to frighten her or make her feel bad.

"I don't know what it means, Tia. *Santa Madre's* voice is very soft. Perhaps you simply did not hear her."

"Perhaps," she says. "It was very windy and I wore my heavy wool shawl."

"There. That explains it," I reassure her. "But I will go with you next time. We will pray the rosary together."

"You are such a good boy, Antonio—a good *man*, I should say now.

"Are you hungry, child? Let me make your dinner. Vigil brought me some fish he smoked—a whole school of them."

"I do not care for smoked fish, Tia. A little bread and salad will be enough. I will take some fish home for Six for our supper. He will eat anything that doesn't eat him first."

We laugh.

As my aunt prepares our dinner, our midday meal, I look out the window at her garden to see what I will have to help her with today. There is talk in the *Farmers' Almanac* of an early frost this autumn. Half the time, their forecasts are often right.

* 7 *

Six and I get home from work after dark on Hallowe'en. We left a plate of Tia Ana's *biscochitos* under a napkin on the porch in case there are any early Trick-or-Treaters. Their costumes are all homemade. Six and I look forward to seeing their clever get-ups.

Six checks how many cookies are left. It looks like none of the kids in costumes has come by. I'm not too surprised. We live a bit outside of town. My amigo takes one of the *biscochitos*.

"Trick or treat," I say.

He puts the anise cookie in my mouth. It's hard to smile.

"The trick will come later—after supper," he promises.

I take the plate of cookies and we go inside. After hanging our dirty work jackets on their pegs, we pump water for each other at the kitchen sink to wash our hands. Six gets a fire going in the stove and brings Tia's pot of *posole* from the larder. I open a bottle of Dos Equis we will share and set the table.

Tomorrow night and Sunday, little Nicky will stay with us. This is our last chance to get frisky with each other. The boy is still a little too young to sleep alone upstairs in my old room. He still sleeps in our bedroom, in his crib.

Six hangs an arm on my shoulder and kisses my cheek. His sweaty work smell makes me want to get frisky with him right now. Then, facing me, he puts both arms around me and kisses me hard on the mouth. He slips his hands into the back pockets of my overalls and squeezes my butt. I close my eyes, waiting for the next kiss.

There is a knock at the kitchen door. We grin at each other. It's probably a couple of trick-or-treaters.

Six takes his hands out of my Levi's and opens the door. He laughs.

"And who might you be, kiddo?" he asks, bending forward. "A leprechaun?

A troll?"

I have to step around him to get a glimpse of the child in his costume.

"Holy mackerel. Kaptain Kosmos," I shout. "Quick. Come inside."

I'm afraid the FBI men, if they're still lurking in the field, will see our Visitor. He steps into the kitchen and the door closes behind him.

"How'd you get here, Kaptain?" I ask.

"In the usual way, Antonio," he replies, his eyes widening in a smile. I believe he knows his laughter hurts my ears.

"I am honored to meet you at last, Kaptain," Six tells him. "Antonio has told me a lot about you. I'm happy for the chance to thank you in person for restoring my life to me, sir."

"I understand very little of medical practice, Sixtus. You are here in good health because I referred you to our medical experts."

"Then thank you for the referral, Kaptain Kosmos," my amigo tells him, smiling.

Standing directly behind Kaptain Kosmos is another Visitor I did not see at first. He is even more ancient-looking than the Kaptain. His wrinkles have wrinkles. It appears to be their custom that the one of lesser age or rank precedes his superior or elder. Kaptain Kosmos holds his arm out to the side.

"This is Kommander Koskob," he says. "Kommander of our Holy Mothership."

They both smile with their eyes. Six and I bow to the Kommander.

"The honor is mine," he says. His voice is deeper than the Kaptain's.

"May I offer either of you a beer?" Six asks. He remembers his manners sooner than I do.

"No, thank you, Sixtus Otto Thorson. But if you were to offer us strawberry ice cream, we would be unable to resist."

Kommander Koskob shakes his head. I think he means to nod.

"I'm afraid our icebox freezer isn't cold enough for ice cream, Kommander," I tell him.

"Too bad, Juan Antonio Sanchez. Your strawberry ice cream is one of the most delectable treats to be found anywhere in our galaxy."

"That's incredible," Six tells them. "In the whole galaxy, huh? I'm glad to hear you enjoy it. Maybe we can have some shipped to you."

My amigo and I laugh. The Visitors screech.

"I am pleased to meet you both," the Kommander says.

"Sir, their friendship is exemplary," Kaptain Kosmos tells his superior officer. "The Holy Mother is quite taken with Antonio and Sixtus."

"Please, Kommander Koskob," I say. "My friend and I are neither unique nor special among human beings. We're really just a couple of pretty ordinary guys."

"*Ordinary* is not a word that adequately describes you and Sixtus," the

Kaptain tells us. "It is your saying you are ordinary that makes you special."

I think I am blushing. I turn to look at Six. *His* face is certainly red, even his ears.

"They are without guile, Kommander. They are who they profess to be, neither more nor less. It is a rare trait."

Kommander Koskob bows to us.

Six takes the camera Dr. Feynman gave us from the sideboard.

"Our friend, Dr. Feynman, asked us to snap a couple of photos of you, sir, if you don't mind," Six tells the Kommander. "I'm afraid we didn't have the camera with us on the night your scout ship crashed."

The Kommander looks at Kaptain Kosmos.

"It will be all right, sir," the Kaptain tells his superior. "I trust them completely. We have the answers to Dr. Feynman's questions for them, too," he says.

"But we didn't have the doctor's list of questions with us that night, either," Six tells the Kaptain.

"No matter. As Dr. Feynman's diagrams will soon make clear, it's possible to move both forward and backward in time. We're simply answering his questions a little before he asked them."

"Thank you, Kaptain Kosmos, for explaining that to us," the Kommander says.

Their "letter" for Dr. Feynman is folded in intricate ways and looks like an origami crane or a heron. One wing moves when I touch the paper bird. I set it on the sideboard. The other wing flaps and the long neck juts forward.

Six and I ask the Visitors to draw closer together for our photograph.

"Perhaps the two of you would like to be included?" the Kaptain asks.

"Yes, but then who'll snap the picture?" Six puzzles.

The Kaptain's eyes widen. He lifts his hand, his palm glowing green. The camera floats out of Six's hands and hovers above the kitchen table. My amigo and I look at each other and smile. We stand behind the Visitors and place a hand on their shoulders.

"Shall we consume some moldy curds?" the Kommander asks. "I believe that is the custom, is it not?"

The remark makes me laugh—as good as saying, *Cheese*, I guess. The camera flashes.

"Can you please take one more photo, Kaptain?" I ask. "Just in case."

The Kodak camera clicks again. Then it floats down onto the table.

There is a rap at the back door.

"Oh, please, Antonio and Sixtus. May we observe your custom of Hallowe'en. May we?" Kommander Koskob begs.

Kaptain Kosmos waves open the kitchen door. There stand a bedraggled hobo and a fairy princess with gossamer wings. They resemble our neighbor Vigil's grandchildren in every other respect.

"Trick or treat," the tiny voices say, their faces registering astonishment at beholding the wrinkled Visitors in their flowing capes.

Six covers his mouth and chuckles to himself.

Both the Kaptain and the Kommander reach into our Hallowe'en visitors' bags and take out some of their candy and fruit. They clearly misunderstood the custom.

"Hey," the hobo says, indignantly putting his hands on his hips. "What's the big idea?"

His sister, the princess, waves her wand at them. "Be gone, ye knaves," she commands.

Without further ado, Kaptain Kosmos and Kommander Koskob vanish into thin air.

"Pretty neat trick," the hobo declares.

We put two anise cookies into his bag of goodies. His sister holds out her paper sack.

Satisfied now, the princess and the hobo turn to leave. "Adios," they tell us.

They descend our porch steps, the lights from the kitchen shining on the path. Grandpa Vigil, at the edge of light and shadow, waves to Six and me. It's a good thing the old man didn't come to our door with his grandchildren. He'd have had a heart attack as soon as he laid eyes on the Visitors.

I close the door. My amigo and I look at each other and break into laughter.

"Think they're coming back?" I ask him.

"Probably not until next Hallowe'en," he says. "I wonder who they'll be next year."

"I'm talking about the Kaptain and the Kommander."

He shrugs. His dimpled grin tells me he knew who I meant in the first place.

"Aren't you worried the FBI agents might have spotted our Visitors, Six?"

"On Hallowe'en?" he replies. "Even if they saw them, so what? The Kaptain and the Kommander looked like Kids in Kostumes."

"What if they do come back? It will look suspicious coming to our house twice."

"Yeah, especially when they didn't leave in the normal way the first time," Six says, chuckling. "Take it easy, amigo. Didn't the Holy Mother tell us we should just get on with our lives and not wait around for the Visitors to show up?"

"Yeah, but.."

"But nothing," he says. "Let's eat. It's late. If the Kaptain and the Kommander show up again, we've got enough to feed them, too."

Six stirs the pot of *posole* and I slice the bread. We glance at each other. I get the idea we're both thinking of dessert already, which will be served in the bedroom after our meal—if we can wait that long.

* 8 *

A letter, a glittery postcard from Zeke Jackson, and a telegram arrive on Christmas Eve while Six is out. He is getting oranges and dates, and a bottle of Presidente brandy for Hypatia's visit. It's her favorite brand. I'll have to work hard at forgetting all over again about that episode when she seduced Six with help from her father's brandy. Six has avoided brandy ever since. I think his hangover cured him. I don't care for it because of the unpleasant memories it stirs up.

Since all the mail and messages are addressed to both me and Six, I feel free to open them. I'm eager to read the telegram first. It is from Hypatia. She is not coming for Christmas. Instead, she will be with her parents in Mexico. *Then why did she promise she would be here?*

Six will be so disappointed. So will little Nicky. His papa has been telling him for weeks that his mama will be coming specially to be with him for Christmas. I feel bad for both Six and his son—and for Hypatia, too—that they will not get to be together as a family at Christmas.

I don't want Six to feel glum. I set the telegram on the sideboard, covering it with Zeke's Christmas card, until I can figure out how to break the news to him.

The letter is from Dr. Feynman. It's a long letter and he has tiny handwriting. A quick glance tells me it has mostly to do with the strange origami letter from the Visitors we forwarded to him. There are enough equations and diagrams in the doctor's reply to fill the blackboard in math class. I leave the doctor's letter open on the kitchen table. Maybe Six will be able to make more of it than I can

I set the pot of water for the potatoes on the stove. I'll have to fetch more wood.

I look in first on little Nicky in his crib. He is happily playing with his fingers and does not see me. Then I go out to the barn.

Six drives the pickup into the yard as I go back up the porch steps. He blasts the horn and I drop the load of wood. I think he was trying to startle me on purpose. Living with Six is never dull: I'm never sure what he'll do next.

"Can I help?" he asks.

"Sure," I reply.

When I bend over, he gooses me with one of the logs. It makes me drop the ones I re-collected all over again. He grins.

"That wasn't exactly the kind of help I had in mind," I tell him.

"No? Maybe you can show me the proper technique for a good goosing, then. Practice makes perfect."

He makes me laugh. We go inside. The warmth feels nice. Six puts his half of the bundle of firewood beside the hearth in the parlor. I set mine beside the kitchen stove.

Six goes back out to the truck and returns with the groceries and the bottle of brandy. He takes it from the paper sack and places it on the kitchen table.

"I hope Hypatia appreciates this. It sure cost enough," he says.

"Maybe she has sworn off brandy, too," I tell him.

"Then I'll give the bottle to my Gramps for his *glögg*. He always makes spiced wine at Christmas."

Six hangs his jacket by the door and looks in on the little one. He returns with Nicky on his shoulders, galloping into the kitchen. He races around the table with the boy. Then they stop next to me at the sink.

Nicky reaches his hand out to me. "Tio, Tio," he says.

Six hoists the boy from his shoulders and sets him down. Nicky toddles over and hugs my knee. He shines his blue eyes up at me. I cut a slice of raw potato and hand it down to him. Six puts him in a chair at the table and gives him another potato slice.

"Go slow, my little green man," Six tells his son. "You don't want to choke."

The boy shakes his head. "No," he says.

Six moves the bottle of Presidente to the sideboard. He finds the telegram.

"What's this?" he asks. "When did it arrive?"

"While you were out. I was getting around to telling you," I say. "I got sidetracked with supper."

My amigo sits down at the table, putting Nicky in his lap. I hand the child another piece of potato.

"Gracias, Tio," he says. The boy has a bit of a lisp, making his Spanish sound Castilian.

Six unfolds the telegram from Hypatia.

"It's from mama," Six tells Nicky, looking down at his son.

"Mama," the boy declares. "Mama coming."

The boy discards his potato slice and reaches for the yellow paper. I watch Six read the telegram. I rinse my hands and place them on his shoulders. I know what's coming.

I feel his shoulders heave as he stifles his weeping. I sit down beside him and watch his tears flow. Nicky looks up at him.

"Papa," he says. "No cry, Papa. Me loves you."

Six wraps the little guy in his arms and stands up. They walk around the table as my amigo rocks his two-year-old son. It looks to me as though they are consoling one another. I'm sorry, too, at their disappointment. It makes me want to hold them both and weep with them, but I don't. Someone's got to get our supper going.

I place the pot of sliced potatoes on the stove. I even take on Six's job of cleaning and breading the fish. I don't think he's up to it right now.

Our meal is very spare on Christmas Eve according to his family's custom. Tomorrow, with our families, we will feast like lords and ladies and little princes.

After Six gets hold of himself, he hands Nicky over to me.

"Down, Tio," the boy tells me. "Me play."

We watch him from the doorway as the toddler pulls out his box of wooden blocks I made for him. Six painted the letters and numbers on them.

My amigo picks up the telegram and crumples it into a ball. I pull him towards me and fold my arms around his waist. He looks so unhappy.

"Please, Six. For little Nicky's sake. This is a joyful season."

Nicky hears his name and looks up from his tower of blocks. Six tosses the wadded telegram to his son who chases after it.

"I don't really care for my sake," Six tells me. "But I've been talking up Hypatia's visit for weeks. How could she be so selfish? How can I explain it to him."

"I have an idea," I say. "Why don't I get the fish in the oven? Then we'll all go out to the grotto and Nicky will see his mother—the Mother of Us All."

Six kisses me and smiles.

"Thank you, amigo. That's a wonderful idea, an inspired idea. I love you so much. I could never get along without you."

Six gets little Nicky first in his sleeper pajamas, then a cotton blanket, and finally his woolen sleeping sack. All that's visible is a small circle of the boy's face.

I get the pan of breaded fish in the oven and put on my jacket. As usual, Six wears neither cap nor scarf nor gloves, only his jacket. I hand Nicky over to him while I bundle up. The thermometer says it is only twenty degrees.

We go outside and cut across the yard to the grotto to the Blessed Virgin. Six carries Nicky.

"We're going to see mama," he tells his son.

"Mama."

The three of us stand before my carving of the Holy Mother in the stone grotto Six made for it. There is a bouquet of roses, wrapped in green floral paper, and a bundle of daisies at the feet of the statue. They are frozen to the ground and dusted with snow.

"Do you think your Tia left the flowers?" Six asks.

"I doubt it," I reply. "She doesn't go out when it's this cold. Besides, she doesn't have any flowers this time of year. Maybe it was our neighbor who left them."

"I thought Vigil doesn't go in for anything religious."

I shrug. "Maybe he makes an exception at Christmas."

The sky is a band of orange and red at the horizon and a speckled blue bowl above. The ground and trees are a black silhouette against the final blaze of sunset. They look like hands reaching for the last of the daylight.

"This is your *Santa Madre*," Six tells his son. He pulls the flap of Nicky's sleep-sack back so the boy can see the statue.

"*Madre*," Nicky says.

Six and I bow our heads and recite the *Hail, Mary*. Nicky repeats a few words, though I doubt he understands what most of them mean.

"God be with you, Nicolás Antonio."

We raise our heads. The Blessed Virgin stands in the place of my wood carving, glowing and translucent, as though refracting the sunset. She smiles at us and holds her palms out to us.

"God bless all my children," she says. "Peace to all the world. And Merry Christmas to you and your families, Antonio and Sixtus."

"*Madre*," Nicky says.

"*Mi hijo*," the Holy Mother replies.

Nicky somehow wriggles one of his arms free from his winter wrappings. He reaches out for his Mother. She leans forward and extends her hand towards the little one. There is a flash of light, a blue spark, for the instant their fingers touch. I expect Nicky to screech in fright. Instead he laughs. I suspect that children only rarely do what you expect.

"Do you have a message for us, *Santa Madre*?" I ask.

"*Madre*," Nicky pipes in. The Virgin smiles.

"Continue to pray the rosary, my children. Pray for peace. Peace, like life, is so very fragile.

"The coming year will be a most difficult one for you both. Be steadfast in your love for God, and for each other and all those around you. Pray for guidance and strength and He will grant it to you. Do not despair.

"Merry Christmas, my children."

"Merry Christmas, *Santa Madre*," Six and I say.

"Merry *Madre*," Nicky adds.

The Blessed Virgin's aura gives a glow to the frosty air and the snowy ground. Imperceptibly, gradually, she fades into the wood carving. Her smile is the last feature to disappear into the cedar statue.

The sun sets behind us as we hurry back to the house, Nicky giggling all the way. At the opposite horizon, the crescent moon, symbol of the Holy Mother, rises. Six points it out to his son from the back porch before we go inside.

"Mama," the boy squeals. "My mama."

CHAPTER TEN

DUO CONTRA MUNDI
Two Against the World

It was nearly a year ago that Six and I enlisted in the army and reported for our induction. To me, it seems so much longer ago than that, as though it had been in another lifetime. I still have nightmares of holding a lifeless Six in my arms. I awake sweating and panting.

"I'm-m here," Six mumbles, stroking my arm, and drifting back to sleep almost at once.

It takes me a while to fall sleep again. There are more than enough thoughts and worries to keep me awake until dawn.

Six and I learned that the Montoyas, his son's grandparents, have extended their long vacation in Mexico permanently. They sold their house here in Roswell and have moved to the outskirts of Mexico City. Hypatia, the boy's mother, has accepted a teaching position at the *Observatorio Astronómico Nacional* there. That explains why Hypatia did not visit over Christmas. She missed little Nicky's second birthday on December twenty-eighth, too.

No one's plans include little Nicky—except my amigo's. He is a good father.

Six's Gramps is sick with a heart condition. His doctor tells his Gram it is not too serious. The doc says it's to be expected for a man in his eighties. But the drugs they prescribe for his Gramps leave the old man weak—and sleepy a good deal of the time. Taking care of her husband is wearing out my amigo's Gram. Her face looks lined with new worries each time we go over there to help.

Six now spends every weekend with his grandparents, taking little Nicky with him. Now that we have a telephone, too, we can at least talk to each other.

Lately, Six has been staying with his grandparents a couple of nights during the week as well. I'd stay with Six overnight, but we're not boys any longer. We wouldn't fit in his old bed.

One of our neighbor Vigil's daughters, Hermione, babysits Nicky when there is no one else. She is so sweet with him that the boy is always excited to learn he will be going over to her house. I suspect she bribes him with cookies and stories.

My Tia's health is slipping as well. Winter is always hard on her, but this year she has not left her house once. She is weaker and more frail, and she requires coaxing to get her to eat her own soup. She no longer accompanies me to mass. Father Miguel looks in on her and brings her Holy Communion.

I remind myself that, after the Fall of Man, this is the Cycle of Life God has ordained for all of us. But when we see the old ones in our families bent and stooped and frail, it becomes awfully personal. I remember when my Tia teased me and chased after me in her yard. Six's Gramps took him squirrel hunting in freezing weather. It hurts me to see them so weak.

My amigo and I help the *ancianos* all we can, but we are unable to make them stronger or even one minute younger. We say our daily rosary for one or two or all three of them. Their bodies may have forsaken them but not their minds and wits, thank God. I look into their wrinkled faces and see their eyes shining as bright as ever. I makes me want to cry—for them, for all of us walking along the path of life.

It is little Nicky, the generation after my amigo and me, who lessens our sorrow and fills our hearts with joy and laughter, beginning the Cycle anew. Our families show us both who we once were and who we shall become.

* 2 *

Our snowy winter made up for some of last year's drought. Spring rains, combined with melting snow, made for a very sloppy start to the growing season. Six and I couldn't keep up with laundry. We'd whack the dried mud out of one pair of overalls over the porch railing with a broom. Then we wore that slightly cleaner pair of Levi's the next day.

It is the last day of April 1948. Eduardo, the boss and owner of Mila-Grow Nursery & Greenhouse, asks us at least once a week when we are going to let him retire. We promised to buy the business from him when we got out of the army. Six's Gramps is going to loan us the money.

This Saturday after work, Eduardo brings it up again.

"Please, boss," Six tells him. "If Antonio and I hadn't gotten our discharges early, we wouldn't even be having this conversation for another year, you know, huh?"

"Yes, but now that you and your amigo are both here, Louisa and I want to sit on the beach. We have worked hard. Every other day there are more color brochures in the mailbox for little houses on the beach in Florida. If I miss one, there's another pamphlet beside my plate at the table."

"Maybe the missus is trying to hint at something, Eduardo," Six tells the boss, trying to hide his dimples.

"Well, of course she is, Six. Even I am not that thick-headed."

We laugh.

"Maybe you could ask your *abuelo* for just a small loan, Six—just enough so Louisa and I can take a vacation down in Florida to see if it agrees with us."

"Six's Gramps is very sick, Eduardo. We do not want to ask him now."

My amigo and I talked about owning our own place like Mila-Grow since we first worked for Eduardo after school. We were fourteen. At last our goal seems within reach, but there are still many roadblocks.

"And what about your *abuela*?" the boss asks my amigo.

"Gram manages the household account, Eduardo. The rest is up to my Gramps. We'd have to ask *him*, boss. I'm sorry. Maybe we could give you some of the money we saved up. We didn't want to have to ask my grandpa for the whole amount. It's about a hundred-fifty bucks, right, Antonio?"

"Yeah," I reply, "give or take a little."

"We can stop at the bank on the way in on Monday morning," Six tells Eduardo.

"That would be a big help, boys. Louisa tells me I should be a bossier boss. Do you care for a sip of tequila?"

"No, thank you," Six says. "We wanna get home."

Six and I head for the door of Eduardo's office.

"Before I forget to tell you," he says.

We turn around.

"I hope it was all right. I have been telling my friends, who have been telling their wives, about the grotto you built, Six, and the beautiful statue you carved, Antonio. Though I know it is wood—I gave you the cedar log, after all— *Santa Madre* looks like a real person to me."

"So that's how everybody found out," Six says.

"I almost blamed my Tia," I remark. "She said she only told two of her friends from church who come to visit her. Often, that's as good as announcing the news with a megaphone. I am happy I did not accuse her or her friends."

"Some days there are so many cars and trucks and wagons that our neighbor opens up his field as a parking lot and charges a nickel per vehicle," Six tells him.

"I'm very sorry, boys," Eduardo says, hanging his head. "I meant no harm, believe me. I like you both very much. You are hard-working young men.

"I think it is a beautiful grotto and a beautiful likeness of *Santa Madre*. I thought my friends would appreciate your workmanship and your devotion. Please forgive me."

"Of course, Eduardo," Six and I say at the same time. "No harm done."

We all smile. The boss puts a hand on each of our shoulders.

"Come on, Six, Antonio. Have a drink with me," he says. "We all have something to celebrate."

He produces a bottle of tequila and three shot glasses. He fills them so full it's impossible not to spill when we raise them.

"To Florida and the missus," Eduardo toasts. "And to Mila-Grow Nursery & Greenhouse for you boys. Good luck to everybody."

Eduardo downs his in a single gulp. Six takes two swallows. I lost count how many sips it took to finish mine, but I didn't choke on it.

* * *

We stop first at Tia Ana's house to see whether we can help her with anything.

There are a half-dozen cars and pickups in Señor Vigil's meadow. A Cadillac limousine is parked in the road in front of my aunt's house. I wonder how it was able to turn the tight corners on our narrow road. A colored man in a chauffeur's uniform—from cap to gloves—waits beside the long black car in the shade of the cottonwoods. He is immaculate. We are both dirty from work. Six sneaks the truck into Tia's back yard. We go around to the front of the house.

As we turn the corner of her front *portál*, a stout man in fancy clerical attire leaves my aunt's house. He wears red satin, so he must be important, a bishop at least. *Oh, my God. It might be Archbishop Abelardo,* I think.

"Thank you for the lovely tea, Miss Ana," he says, leaving my aunt's house.

He lifts his robes as he descends the steps. There is enough lace at the hem of his surplice to cover all of Tia's windows.

"There's my nephew now, Your Highness," my aunt says to her visitor. She smiles at me. Fanning herself excitedly, my aunt goes back inside her house, closing the front door. I see her peek from behind the curtain. One by one, the pilgrims return to their cars in Vigil's field.

The fancy cleric turns to us when he catches sight of Six and me. I'm a little embarrassed for my dirty appearance.

"Antonio Sanchez?" the cleric asks.

"Yes, sir," I reply.

"I am Archbishop Abelardo."

"Oh... Your Excellency," I say, flustered. "I... I..." But nothing comes out.

The archbishop extends his hand so I may kiss his ring. Six gooses me and I shoot upright, interrupting my homage. My amigo's Protestant upbringing does not approve of the showy honorifics we Catholics go all-in for. I have another go at kissing the ring, steeling myself for another hard pinch. It does not come.

I stand up and look at the archbishop. He does not waste a minute getting down to the purpose of his unexpected visit.

"I am here to address certain matters that have come to my attention regarding the unauthorized shrine you have erected here."

He turns to his chauffeur, whom he addresses as Withers, and tells him, "I won't be long."

We cross the road to the grotto at the edge of my aunt's field. The archbishop holds up his hems. There are several bouquets of flowers lying at the feet of my wood carving of the Virgin, from a child's nosegay of dandelions tied with yarn to a dozen red roses bundled in a red satin ribbon and bow.

The archbishop does not look at my statue to the Holy Mother for more than a few seconds. He keeps his back to the statue the entire time he talks to us. The dappled sunlight falling on the face of the statue makes it look like *Santa Madre* is making faces behind the archbishop's back.

"Begging your Excellency's pardon," Six says, "Our humble efforts to honor the Mother of Jesus are hardly a shrine. Antonio carved the figure of *Santa Madre* from a cedar log he got at work. I built the grotto with stones from the field."

"That may be, but the site is attracting pilgrims. There must first be an investigation. Procedures and protocols must be followed for any purported apparitions. Father Consuelo has received numerous complaints."

"Complaints?" I ask. "From who? Lucifer?"

Six turns to me and smiles.

"Several of the faithful have reported incomplete apparitions," the archbishop says.

"Incomplete?" I ask.

"Yes. They say they hear a voice but see no one speaking. Or else they see a figure speaking, but can hear nothing."

"Like my Tia," I remark to Six. "My aunt said such a thing happened to her," I tell the archbishop.

"There. You see?" he remarks. "The devil wants people to be disappointed with their *Santa Fe*, their Holy Faith. That is his opportunity. You must take down the shrine and burn the graven image. It is a sacrilege."

"Please, Your Excellency..." But I don't know what else to tell him. *That Santa Madre completed the carving herself? That she told us one day pilgrims would come? That even little Nicky saw his Mother?* The archbishop would never believe any of it. The Holy Mother told us there would be those who would try to silence us. For all I know, he'd order my exorcism.

We follow the archbishop back across the road. Withers opens the rear door of the limousine for him.

"I have made my position on these unauthorized appearances and devotions crystal clear, Sanchez. If you fail to comply, there are legal remedies that can also be pursued. The archdiocese retains sterling legal representation. Good day."

Withers tucks in the archbishop's voluminous garments and closes the rear door. The chauffeur looks at me in his mirror before pulling away. I puzzle over his expression. *Is he sad? Weary? What? No,* I think. *He is resigned.*

We watch the Cadillac limousine wind down our narrow road. Six and I look at each other and go around back.

"The Right Reverend Windbag," Six remarks. "It was prelates like him who put the wind in Martin Luther's sails."

I smile at him. "You're right," I say. "He's pretty puffed up with himself."

"You're not considering taking down the grotto, are you, Antonio?"

"No, of course not," I tell him, touching his hand. "We dedicated it to the Holy Mother. The statue has been blessed. It belongs to her now—and to the pilgrims who visit."

"Good," he says. "What's Archbishop Tubolardo gonna do, amigo? The grotto is on private land, built with stone's provided by God Himself to honor His Mother."

I smile at him, but it falls quickly from my face.

"He could excommunicate me," I say.

"But doesn't he have to take that up with the High Cockalorum or something first?"

I laugh. "I've never heard of it, but there are a lot of dark corners in the Church."

I go up the porch steps to my aunt's house. Six takes the pickup to the babysitter's house to bring little Nicky home. He will stay with my amigo and me over the weekend.

I go inside Tia's kitchen. I find her at the table, her rosary in her lap.

"Please, come in. I have finished praying, *mi sobrino*. The archbishop said I should pray for you—for the rescue of your eternal soul. He's a very nice man, don't you think? Oh, and to think her drank tea in *my* kitchen—such an important man."

"I'm glad he was nice to you, Tia," I say. I don't want to disillusion her by giving in to my unkind thoughts and gloomy outlook.

Only once do I recall being really cross with my Tia. I was twelve. She said that I should persuade Six to become a Catholic. I told her the best conversions were those led by example not by argument. My rebuke made her cry. I gave her fresh flowers I picked from her own garden. I scuffed up the flower beds to hide what I'd done—hardly leading by example, but I hadn't thought of that at the time.

My aunt gets up, still bent, as though she had taken on the shape of her chair.

"I came to see if you needed anything. How can I help you, Tia?"

"I tell all my friends how good you are to me, *mi sobrino*. Perhaps you could bring in a little firewood. That way, you could hang out the wash on your way to the barn."

She smiles at me. I carry the laundry basket inside the log carrier—two birds with one stone.

I come out of the barn with the load of wood just as our turquoise pickup drives up.

Six narrowly misses hitting the washline with the truck. He holds Nicky in his lap, telling him to hold onto the steering wheel and help his papa drive. The boy is only too willing.

They climb out of the old truck. Six closes the door with his rear end and sets little Nicky on the ground.

I put down the laden log carrier and crouch down to catch the tyke as he barrels toward me. He falls down, skidding in the dirt like the guy at third base sliding into home plate. I laugh despite trying not to. Just like his papa, he can't stay clean for two minutes.

I pick Nicky up before he has a chance to squall. He screeches anyway. It reminds me of the Visitors' laughter.

Six joins us, kissing us both, the boy first.

"We're gonna have to wrap you in rubber, little man, so you bounce," he tells his son.

"Wubber," the boy repeats, forgetting his tears. He makes me laugh almost as often as his papa does.

Six picks up the firewood for me since I have my hands full with Nicky. We go into my aunt's kitchen. We are greeted by the smell of onions frying in the skillet. She wipes her hands on her apron and takes an envelope from her apron pocket. It has stamps and stickers pasted all over it.

"It came while you were at work this morning, *mis hijos*. The archbishop's visit made me forget," Tia says. "He sat right in that chair. *¡Dios mío!* What an honor."

The envelope has both our names on it. It is Registered Mail. Since I am holding Nicky, my aunt hands the letter to Six. He waves it at his son, teasing him by snatching it back at the last instant. The boy laughs.

Six sits at the table. I pass Nicky down to him. He sets his son in his lap. Then he rips open the envelope and pulls out the letter. I crane my neck and squint to read it over Six's shoulder, but he is too far away.

I relieve my aunt at the stove. I add sliced peppers to the onions.

My aunt sits down next to Six and makes faces at the baby. Nicky squeals with delight.

The letter shakes in Six's hand. It falls onto the table.

"Oh, boy," he says. "Oh, boy, are we ever in trouble."

His voice shakes.

"What is it, *mi sobrino*?" my aunt says, putting her hand on his. She calls him *nephew*, too.

I move the skillet off the heat and rush to the table. My heart pounds wildly as I pick up the letter. The registered letter is from an attorney. I rest my other hand on Six's shoulder. Nicky looks up at me. I don't know whether I can hold the letter steady enough to be able to read it.

"Please, Antonio," my aunt pleads. "Tell me what it says, *mi hijo*."

"It is from the lawyer for the man who bought our iron stones, our meteorites," I tell my aunt. "He says Mr. Carson learned from a customer that the meteorites were man-made. The lawyer says we defrauded his client out of nearly a thousand dollars."

My aunt puts one hand over her heart and the other over her mouth.

"What will you do, *mis hijos*?" she asks.

"Pay him back—or go to jail," Six says.

"Is it true, Antonio? Did you lie to the man who bought your stones?"

"Not on purpose, Tia. We saw the stones fall from the sky. We thought they were meteorites. We will have to pay him back. We've already given most of the money away."

"I will help you. I have two-hundred forty-seven dollars, *mis hijos*. It is my life savings."

"God bless you, Tia," Six tells her, squeezing her hand, "but he expects the full amount."

"Si, but a hundred dollars will tell the man you are serious about paying him. Maybe he will be quiet for a while."

Six and I look at each other and smile.

"Thank you, Tia," I say. "That's a good idea. We'll see what the man has to say. It doesn't hurt to ask."

"There," she says. "Problem fixed. Let's make your dinner now. You boys must be starving. It's almost two o'clock."

We usually have our midday meal at noon. My aunt stirs the skillet as I cut and toss in thin strips of beef. I don't have much of an appetite. Even the smell of onions cooking does not make me hungry. I am very worried about the letter from Mr. Carson's lawyer. Nothing ever hurts my amigo's appetite.

After lunch, Six takes his son for a stroll back and forth on the porch, holding the boy's hand. I want to set aside my worry, to trust in God the way little Nicky trusts his papa.

* 3 *

Two Saturdays later, already halfway through May, the telephone rings in the middle of the night. The way Six shot out of bed, I'd have thought it was our old roster sergeant's whistle that awakened him. Nicky screeches and I turn on the bedside lamp. I lift him from his crib and nestle him against my shoulder. He quiets down as we walk into the kitchen. I wear my longjohns. My amigo is naked.

"Gram, calm down. I can't understand you," Six says. "No. Hang up and call for an ambulance. The number's in the phone book. Never mind. I'll call from here. I'll be right over."

He hangs up and flips to the front of the telephone directory. He asks for an ambulance to be sent to his grandparents' house. Then he goes back to the bedroom.

"Let's watch papa get dressed," I tell Nicky.

By the time we make it to the bedroom, Six is already in his Levi's and is pulling on his boots. He reaches for a clean workshirt on the chair. It's my shirt he takes.

"She thinks Gramps had a heart attack," he says. "I'll call you from there."

He kisses me and Nicky, and flies out the screen door, letting it slam behind him. The boy and I watch him switch on the headlamps and drive off fast enough to spit gravel.

"Come on, kiddo. Let's go back to sleep. You want an animal cracker?"

He nods.

"But only if you get the name right."

I take one of the little *biscochitos* out of the colorful cardboard box that looks like a painted circus wagon. I hold it out to him.

"Cow," he declares.

"No, I'm sorry, Nicky. That's a camel. Can you say *camel*?"

He snatches the cookie from my hand and takes a bite out of it, then gives it back. He's bitten the camel's hump off.

"Cow," he says, looking up at me with his bright blue eyes.

I can't help laughing. *Like son, like father*, I think.

He eats the "cow." I take his hand and turn down the kitchen light.

"Sleep with Tio," he says, struggling to climb up onto the bed.

"Just for tonight," I tell him. "Just while papa's gone."

"G'night, Tio."

"Buenas noches, Nicolás Antonio Montoya-Thorson."

"Me," he shouts in my ear.

"The one and only," I tell him.

I turn off the bedside lamp. In the dark, I worry for Six. I hope his Gramps is all right. I keep one ear attuned to the telephone, in case it rings. Somehow, despite keeping an ear open, I manage to sleep straight through to morning.

* * *

I awaken in early daylight when the pickup pulls into the yard. The engine's running pretty rough, but Six hasn't had a minute to work on it. I crawl out on the opposite side of the bed so I don't disturb little Nicky.

Six stands motionless just inside the kitchen door. His expression reminds me of the night he was revived by the Visitors. It is blank, emotionless. I'm not sure he sees me. Maybe the same remedy will work this time, too.

Wrapping my arms around him, I kiss him hard on the mouth. He sucks in his breath and collapses into my arms. His chest heaves with sobbing. I pull him closer.

"Gramps...He... Gram..." he says, choking. "I'm an orphan, amigo. An orphan all over again."

"Oh, Six," I say, wiping his tears with my fingers. "What happened? How's your Gram?"

He takes my hand and leads me outside to the rear *portál*.

"So we don't wake Nicky," he explains.

We put our hands on the porch railing. Dawn's red and orange streaks are reflected in the barn windows. I reach for Six's hand. He turns to me.

Six looks horrible—like he hasn't slept in a week. Though it's probably tear streaks, his face looks lined, care-worn.

"Oh, Antonio," he says, fighting back a new wave of weeping. It takes him a while to get hold of himself.

"The ambulance pulled away just when I got there. Sheriff Pease was still on the scene. He came over when he saw me drive up. He put his hand on my shoulder and said, I'*m real sorry, Six*. He couldn't look at me. He stared at the ground.

"I realized Gramps was already dead by the time I got there.

"When I asked the sheriff, *How's my Gram taking it?* he said, *That was her in the ambulance that just drove off, son. I'm real sorry. She got very upset, very agitated, when they took your grandpa away. She fainted and they couldn't revive her. The ambulance driver said she's gone, too. I'm real sorry.*"

Six sobs again after finishing his story. I wrap him in my arms and kiss his wet cheek.

"I feel so bad for you, Six. Oh, amigo."

He trembles in my arms. I kiss his other cheek.

"Let's get you to bed, Six."

We go back in the house and tiptoe into the bedroom. Seeing his sleeping son, Six sits down on my side of the bed. I help him pull his boots off, then his shirt and undershirt. He seems content to roll over onto the bed wearing his overalls.

"No, come on, Six. Just one more. I'll help you out of 'em."

He is already asleep when I unbutton his Levi's. He's already snoring by the time pull them down his legs. I cover him.

Little Nicky is awake. He reaches his arms up to me.

"Papa," he says, as I lift him up.

"Papa sleeping," I tell him.

"Kiss papa g'night."

I hold the boy over his sleeping father and lower him slowly so he can kiss his papa's forehead.

"Bye," he tells his father.

We go into the kitchen. I give Nicky a slice of apple while I make a pot of coffee and boil water for oatmeal.

* 4 *

We didn't find much to celebrate on our birthdays last month. Next May, we will turn twenty-one. That will be *una gran cosa* as my Tia likes to say.

Since his grandparents' deaths, I often find Six staring off into space, a downcast look on his face. He seems somewhere far off.

After I drop my amigo's son at the babysitter's to spend the night there, I find Six standing on the rear porch. He has his hands in his overall pockets. He jumps when he hears me, as though suddenly jerking awake again.

"What's the matter, Six?" I ask him. "You look so exhausted."

"I am, amigo, tired enough that I could sleep forever."

"Please, don't say that. We'll work this out together. We have each other, right?"

"Yeah, we do," he says, smiling. "But between us we don't even have enough money for the ink to *print* dollar bills."

"Something will turn up. It always does."

"I'm not used to your optimism. Do you feel all right, Antonio?"

He puts his palm on my forehead and grins.

"The Blessed Mother told us it was going to be a difficult year, Six. Fore-warned is forearmed."

"What am I supposed to do with four arms?" he asks.

"This," I say, lifting his arms and putting them around my waist, then wrapping my arms around him. We stay that way a while, offering wordless warmth and comfort to one another.

"I think I'm gonna go over to my Gram and Gramps again, Antonio."

"I thought we were just going to enjoy a night alone at home."

"I have to find their will, amigo, or we're gonna go down the drain. We don't have enough to meet the payroll more than two weeks out. We're sending every spare nickel—both of them—to keep Eduardo happy until we can pay *him* off for the business."

I put my arm around his shoulder as we go out the back door.

"Gramps showed me his will one time, but I was ten years old, you know, huh? I remember he was very proud of it. Where would he put it? You got any new ideas where to look, Antonio? I'm fresh out."

I shake my head. Six climbs up into the pickup. He leans down and kisses me. We see another car pull into the neighbor's meadow on the other side of the road. A man and woman walk towards the grotto to the Blessed Virgin. Six closes the truck door and rolls the window down.

238 BRIAN ALLAN SKINNER

"I didn't like the idea of Vigil charging pilgrims to park their cars in his field," I tell Six. "I said he should count the number of cars and we'd pay him."

"That's a wonderful idea, amigo," he says. "It's very generous of you. But where's *that* money gonna come from?"

"I thought maybe we'd send Mr. Carson only fifty dollars this month."

"And where's *that* money gonna come from?"

"What if we each take a little bit of a pay cut for the next coupla weeks?"

"A pay cut down to what, Antonio? *Nada*? We earned more as privates in the army. We're just robbing Peter to pay Paul."

"No, we're not," I say. "We're robbing Paul to pay Peter."

He laughs. It is deep and resonant. It reminds me of a cello.

"Quick comeback," he says. "No question, amigo. You've got the reflexes of a pilot even if you didn't complete the Air Force training."

His remark makes me blush—or at least I feel I am blushing.

"I'll be down at Tia's then," I tell him. "Don't be too long. I miss you already."

He smiles. Then he rolls up the truck window and drives off.

* * *

My aunt is not at the kitchen table. I told her I'd come by to make our supper. She is not beneath the *portál* out front, either. Perhaps she's resting. She sleeps an awful lot lately.

"Tia," I call. "Tia?"

I call two more times, louder, before entering her bedroom. She is on her bed atop the covers. She raises her hand weakly and tries to sit up. I help her and put two pillows behind her.

She touches my hand and looks over my shoulder.

"*Santa Madre*," she says, out of breath, a look of wide-eyed astonishment on her face.

I turn to see what she is looking at. Holy Mother stands at the foot of Tia's bed. I have to shade my eyes with my hand to really see her. She stands inside the brilliant aura of light. Even the late-afternoon sun with the shades rolled up cannot outshine her. My aunt squeezes my hand.

"Do you hear me this time, Ana?" the Blessed Virgin asks her.

"Si," my aunt says.

"I was not playing a trick on you, dear heart," Holy Mother tells her. "But if there was someone you needed to forgive or amends that had to be made, then your heart was not pure. You could only hear me or see me, but not both at once. Now that you have made your confession to Father Miguel, I am here to accompany you on the last part of your journey, *mi hija*. Come."

My aunt releases my hand. She holds up her arm and *Santa Madre* takes her hand. Tia stands effortlessly and walks with her, their feet not touching the floor. They both turn to me and smile.

"Tia," I say.

"Do not cry for me, *mi sobrino*. I am going home."

I watch as my aunt and the Holy Mother, still holding hands, lean toward the open window. Holy Mother's robes and my Tia's flannel nightgown flutter as though heading into a strong wind. They drift through the open window, yet the curtains barely stir at their passing.

I gaze down at the bed. There my aunt's body lies, her eyes closed, a sweet, almost sly, smile on her lips. I kneel beside her bed and take my rosary out of the pocket of my grubby overalls. I rest my forehead on the edge of the bed and weep—long and hard and deep.

I have lost my second mother, my Tia Ana.

The screendoor slams. It startles me. Six appears in the doorway.

"I don't know why," he says. "I thought I should come back."

I stand and he enfolds me in his arms, a strapping embrace.

"We are both orphans now, Six," I say, sobbing into his shoulder.

"*Tonteria*. We're not orphans. I was wrong, Antonio. We've got a family: I am yours and you are mine—and we both belong to Nicky."

He makes me smile despite my heavy heart.

"Thank you, Six. You always make me feel better. I love you more than I know how to say, amigo."

I take his hand and we kneel beside Tia's bed. We say the rosary before I go back to our house and call for an ambulance. There is no hurry now.

* 5 *

We return home after another late Saturday at work. In the field at the other end of Calle Alegre I see a figure in black. The Federal Bureau of Investigation must not have documented enough of our very ordinary lives. Well, some of it is ordinary. If you leave out the parts about the Blessed Virgin Mary and Dr. Feynman and the Visitors from Alpha Carinae, the rest is pretty humdrum.

My Tia Ana left her house and possessions and two-acre property to Brother Asinus's order, the Benedictines. Neither Six nor I had any idea she planned to do this. My aunt further instructed that her house become a place for visitors and pilgrims to the Shrine of Our Lady of Roswell to rest. It is a beautiful legacy and it makes me cry with both sorrow and joy.

She has left the remaining $147 of her life's savings to Six and me. God bless, Tia. It has come in the nick of time. It will buy my amigo and me another two months of living on the knife-edge of ruin.

Six and I decide to watch the watcher in the field. We carry the telescope he got from Hypatia onto the rear porch. Six focuses the eyepiece. I grab his butt as he leans in closer to peer through the brass spyglass.

He stands up and looks at me. I thought he'd be smiling. Instead, he seems concerned. I look through the lens.

The man in black standing at the edge of Vigil's field wears a black hat and sunglasses like all the other FBI men. But beneath his suit jacket, the man in black wears a Roman collar. It is Father Consuelo.

"Looks like more trouble on the way," Six says to me.

"Maybe not,"I reply.

"*En serio*? You don't need to be a mind-reader to know that the archbishop will be privy to each detail of Father Consuelo's report. But we can't do a thing about it, amigo," he says. "We've done all we can. The rest of it is up to God."

"I kinda wonder whose prayers God will hear, Six: those of a pair of grubby gardeners or those from an archbishop in all his finery."

"I hope God listens to the wishes of His Mother, Antonio. She comes first."

I smile at him. He takes my hand and we go back into the house for our dinner, our midday meal. Then he will pick Nicky up from the babysitter Hermione's place.

I set the table while he slices the bread.

* * *

After our supper that night, after Six has put his son to bed, we sit beneath the rear *portál* and share a beer. If we are gabby tonight, we will probably have another. The sun is taking its sweet time, in no hurry to set. I love the long twilights of summer—the slow train through town from rose to red, then through to blue and purple and, finally, black, an imperfect black dotted with stars and planets and streaking meteors.

We watch a pair of zigzagging Fastwalkers perform their abrupt maneuvers before streaking off. If you're not looking up in the right place at exactly the right moment, you'll never see the strange meteors.

"Tomorrow will be a year since the Visitors arrived," Six remarks.

"It doesn't seem that long ago to me, but then I lost a coupla months in the infirmary. But I kinda wonder if the Visitors didn't get here a long time before that night, you know, huh?"

"Why do you say that?" Six asks.

"They spoke pretty good English for having just arrived. They knew Spanish, too."

"Maybe they listened to the radio," he suggests, grinning. "I mean it fans out in all directions, like ripples on a pond, right?"

"Hold that thought," I tell him. "I'm gonna get us another beer."

I look in on Nicky. By the time I return, Six has pulled off his workboots and socks, and is airing his toes along the porch railing. I pour more beer into our nearly empty glasses and sit down.

"So you're saying that Amos 'n' Andy were Earth's ambassadors long before Antonio 'n' Sixtus?" I ask, chuckling.

"Yeah, could be, Antonio. I dunno. Maybe we're not so special after all," he says.

"That would suit me just fine," I reply. "I'd rather not be anyone special."

"Too late for that, amigo," Six tells me. "You are *very* special to one *very* ordinary guy."

"Yeah? And who might that be?"

"Me," he says, leaning across and kissing me so hard it sets my rocker in motion.

"*It is your saying you are ordinary that makes you special,*" I tell him, quoting Kaptain Kosmos.

"Oh, God, Antonio. I love you so much," he says, smiling. "I think I can bear up under anything the world throws at me as long as you're next to me."

I pull him up from his rocker and hold him. I can't think of anything to say that conveys my feelings for my amigo as well as a bear-hug and a long, long kiss.

* 6 *

Six and I both need new overalls and work jackets and boots, but that has gotten moved far down on our list. All we seem to be doing is working more and having less to show for it. My amigo suggests we bring our sleeping bags to Mila-Grow and roll them out on a couple of the potting benches.

"We'd already be at work as soon as we woke up," he says. "Look at all the time we'd save."

"What about Nicky?" I ask.

"We'll put the little sprout in a window box," he says, laughing. "It will be his crib. When my little green man outgrows it, we'll transplant him."

It wouldn't surprise me if Six were serious about living at work. He is determined that we are going to pull out of our money mess and make a success of Mila-Grow. I'm not quite as confident.

We arrive at work at six-o'clock that Monday morning in August. It is the anniversary of the atomic bomb blast that flattened Nagasaki. It was three years ago.

There are notices pasted up on the shop and both greenhouses. There's another tacked to the fence railing surrounding the tree nursery. There is just enough light to read them. They are notices of an upcoming sheriff's auction for back taxes.

I'm not sure whose idea it was to wrap the other in his arms. I guess we thought of it around the same time.

"It's gotta be a mistake, Antonio, don't you think? Eduardo wouldn't do that to us."

I shrug. "I dunno. My Tio used to say that you didn't really know some-one's character until you had money dealings with him."

"So that's why you and me get along," he says. "We're both poor as church-mice."

I smile. Six looks at me, slowly alternating his blue and brown eyes. He does it to make me laugh. It always seems to do the trick.

"Ready to do battle?" he asks.

"You betcha," I say. "It's the two of us against the world, amigo."

"Well... with a little help from our friends," he adds, glancing skyward.

I wonder whether he means the Holy Mother or the Visitors—or maybe both.

"I'm gonna stay here and wait for Tomás and Diego and Alicia when they show up for work. Do you mind seeing what you can find out from Sheriff Pease?"

"No, I don't mind, Six. I think you've got the tougher job breaking the bad news to our workers."

"Yeah," he says. "It was so great of Alicia to pitch in at the shop until we find someone else. Now we've got to tell her she's out of a job."

"Just for a while, amigo," I tell him. "You'll see. We'll pull through this."

"We might need a winch," he says, smiling.

We are alone in the parking lot, so he kisses me. I climb up into the pickup and wink at him. If I can just believe my own optimistic forecast, then I ought to be able to convince anybody of anything.

* * *

Sheriff Warren Pease sits at his desk. He looks up and smiles.

"Care for some coffee, Sanchez?" he asks.

"Sure. Thanks, Sheriff," I reply.

He takes the coffee pot from the hotplate and fills a cup for me. It looks like used motor oil. I sit down across from him.

"Is there some kind of mistake, Sheriff?" I ask.

"Wish I could say there was, son. Looks like Eduardo forgot to pay last year's taxes, too. He owes about four-hundred bucks."

"Holy smoke. Four-hundred dollars?" I shout. "How we gonna make any money if we can't open our doors, Sheriff? We're just squeaking by, you know, huh?"

"The tax money should come off what you boys are paying Eduardo for the business, Antonio. Or else you might get lucky buying it at auction for only four-hundred bucks. Personally, I wouldn't chance it. The next guy only needs to bid one dollar more."

The sheriff stands up. He opens his billfold and takes out five dollars.

"I like you and your amigo. You're both hard-working fellas. I wanna see you boys make a go of Mila-Grow. A little strong, ain't it?" he says, looking down at my untouched cup of coffee.

He hands me the five dollars.

"Six's grandpa helped me out of a coupla scrapes. So did your Tio Nicolás. The kindness you do people doesn't always come back to you, Antonio, but it never goes to waste. It always gets handed down to someone who can use it."

I am choked up, unable to speak. I take the money he offers and nod to the sheriff.

"I wouldn't worry too much, son. I don't think Eduardo's trying to flim-flam you boys. He might be a scatter-brain, but he's no scoundrel. I'll be rooting for you."

"Thank you, Sheriff," I manage to say.

I shake his hand and leave his office feeling a little more upbeat than I did going in.

* * *

When I return to Mila-Grow, I find Six sitting on a pile of landscape timbers outside the nursery lot. He looks up. I climb down from the pickup.

"How did it go with the crew?" I ask him. "Will they ever want to work for us again?"

Six smiles. He takes out a handful of crumpled dollar bills from his pocket. He shows them to me. There are two quarters, too. A tear glistens in his eye.

"They took up a collection, Antonio—five-and-a-half bucks. *Interest-free*, Alicia told me."

I take the five-dollar bill from the sheriff out my Levi's and show it to him.

"From Sheriff Warren Pease," I tell Six. "He said it was only a down-payment on all the favors your Gramps did for him over the years."

"Oh, amigo," we say at the same time, taking hold of each other. I love holding him. Any excuse will do. My amigo feels so firm and solid to me, so sub-stantial—so *strapping*. We sob a little, but they are joyful tears, tears of gratitude for all the loving people around us.

We walk to the truck and get in. Six starts the engine and takes the wheel.

"So how close does our friends' generosity bring us to paying off the Chaves County taxes Eduardo left us stuck with?"

"Um..." I say, calculating. "Not quite four-hundred bucks to go."

"What?" he replies, stomping on the brakes. "Eduardo's lucky he's two thousand miles away. I'd like to take every nickel out of his hide."

"Easy, amigo," I tell him. "There's gotta be an explanation."

"There is. Eduardo's a damn liar and a cheat and a swindler."

"Sheriff Pease doesn't think so, Six. He thinks Eduardo just *forgot* to pay the tax bills."

"The result is the same whether it was on purpose or an honest mistake, isn't it?"

"Let's just hope it wasn't a dishonest mistake," I say. "That'd be twice as bad."

It makes my amigo laugh. I don't know what we'd do if we both looked on the gloomy side of things at the same time.

* 7 *

Each month brings a new setback and a deeper shortfall. Despite working harder and longer hours, we are not climbing out of debt. As in *Alice in Wonderland*, we are doing all our running just to stay in one place. We have not yet heard from Eduardo down in Florida. I'm guessing he's ashamed for not telling us about the taxes he owed.

We write a polite apology to Mr. Jeremiah Carson at Rocks & a Hard Place for being unable to pay him anything in September. We spend the last of Tia Ana's savings and the money set aside for the payroll at Mila-Grow in order to make a payment on the county tax bill. It will buy us another two months before the next installment is due.

We sit out back and share a beer while little Nicky naps on our bed. It is Saturday afternoon at home, our time for talk over a coupla beers, our time to speak what's on our minds.

"Oh, Six, I am so tired of this. Aren't you? How long can we keep this up?"

"Why? Have Peter and Paul had a falling-out?"

"No, I hope not," I say, chuckling. "But it reminds me of the uselessness of trying to shore up the walls of our foxholes in the pouring rain. We're not really getting anywhere, are we, Six?"

"We're staying afloat."

"But the sharks are circling, amigo," I tell him. I reach over and touch his arm. "I gave it a lot of thought, Six. I think we should take out a mortgage on the house."

"No, buddy. Your Tio Nicolás's grandfather built this house. Your family always owned this place free and clear, even if they couldn't afford new shoes. No. No mortgage."

"Then what're we gonna do, Six?"

"Keep praying," he says, taking hold of my hand.

"I hate to ask it, Six, but the Montoyas seem pretty well off, you know, huh? Do you think they might help us out? Señor Montoya sure spoke highly of you."

My amigo's face blanches. He sets his bottle of beer on the porch table. His hands shake.

"What's the matter?" I ask. "What happened?"

He stands up and leans back against the porch railing. I get up and face him.

"Once I realized I wasn't going to find my Gramps' will anytime soon—if ever—Señor Montoya was the first one I thought of, Antonio. He offered a couple of times to bankroll our purchase of Mila-Grow from Eduardo. But I figured I already had my Gramps' promise to help us out.

"I wrote Mr. Montoya down in Mexico to ask for his help—the address he gave me. I included one of our photos of Nicky. It came back *Address Unknown*. I tried again. Same thing. I sent a telegram. *Recipient could not be located*."

"How strange," I remark. "What's going on, Six?"

"It gets stranger," he says. "I wrote Hypatia at the astronomical observatory where she teaches. They never heard of her. There is no such teaching position at the observatory."

"What?"

"I was gonna tell you all this, Antonio, but what was I gonna tell you? A whole lotta nothin'? There was one more idea I had to reach the Montoyas."

I stand next to him at the railing and take his hand. He is trembling.

"A couple nights ago, when I went to get us more beer, I drove out to the Montoyas place to see if maybe one of their neighbors didn't have a different address for them in Mexico. I drove up and down their road three times before I realized their house was not there. I recognized the trees and a couple of the nearby houses, but their house was *gone*—not even the outline of a foundation."

"What's going on?" I ask again.

"Darned if I know," he replies. "I asked their neighbors. No one quite remembered them. It was as though Hypatia and her parents had been erased. Or were never there."

We hear his son holler from the bedroom. "Nap.. time... done..."

"Well, at least we know little Nicky is real," I say.

"Sometimes a little too real, you know, huh?"

We laugh. He goes to get the boy, who struggles to get down from the bed on his own, although he seems to do all right climbing up. I don't have to worry whether the child is being properly spoiled.

I hope Six and I will get another chance to talk about the strange goings on with Hypatia and her family. It makes me worry because it's both mysterious and frightening. I don't know what it means. Life makes less sense to me now than when I was a boy.

* 8 *

After supper, Six struggles with his son to get the boy to wear the Hallowe'en costume Hermione, the babysitter, made for him.

"Come on, Nick. Enough with the octopus imitation. Two arms and two legs is enough for any little boy."

"Octopoop," he says.

"Pretty close. Don't you want to see the treat-or-treaters?"

"No," he says, shaking his head until his woodland elf's cap falls off.

"Why not?"

"Me don't like gween."

"But you're my Little Green Man. Don't you remember the green pyjamas Tia Ana made for you?"

"No," he says.

I sense a storm brewing. I put Nicky's green acorn cap on *my* head, hoping to make him laugh.

The boy shakes his head. "No, Tio. You head's too *fat*."

Six laughs. There's a knock at the back door that startles all of us.

"Ready, Nick?"

I hand him his acorn cap. He stands up on his kitchen chair and slaps the cap back on his head. Six opens the door.

"Boo," comes the booming voice.

It is Sheriff Warren Pease. He takes off his official cap with the county emblem. Little Nicky jumps up and down in his chair, beside himself with glee. I close the door.

"Twick or tweat," Nicky says.

"How 'bout both, son?" the sheriff asks, reaching behind the boy's ear and pulling out a silver dollar.

Nicky's mouth grows nearly as wide as the old Morgan dollar. He takes it from the sheriff with both hands."

"Down, Papa," he says. "Me play."

"All right. But that's a real dollar, Nicky. It's special. Don't lose it."

The tyke runs into the parlor.

"All dollars are special," Sheriff Pease remarks. "Especially when you ain't got many of 'em. Good evenin', boys. Sorry to bother you on a Sunday."

"Can we get you a beer, Sheriff?" Six asks.

"Sure," he says. "I ain't on duty right now. This visit's unofficial. I just wore my uniform for the boy."

"I can tell you he was mighty impressed, Sheriff," Six tells him. "His eyes were big as... as big as silver dollars."

I bring three bottles of Dos Equis from our icebox. Six snaps the caps off and we clink them together. We sit at the kitchen table. Six angles his chair so he can keep an eye on Nicky in the parlor.

"Well, I'm not bringing good news, boys, I'm afraid."

"Except for bad luck, Sheriff, we wouldn't have any luck at all," Six tells him.

Sheriff Pease laughs.

"I'm trying to give you as much warning as I can."

"Warning about what?" I ask.

The sheriff takes a swallow of his beer and looks back and forth at my amigo and me.

"I got a property condemnation order handed down by a judge," he says.

"Condemning what?" Six asks.

I can tell my amigo is getting agitated. I don't think he realizes he's flashing his eyes. Luckily, the sheriff looks down at his hands and doesn't seem to notice.

"The condemnation order is for all of Calle Alegre."

"What?" Six says, jumping to his feet. "On what grounds, Sheriff?"

""The complaint says the *calle* wasn't designed for the heavy traffic the shrine is bringing. The road will have to widened. Both houses and the shrine are in the way. Didn't look like no shrine to me."

"We had more traffic when my Tia sold eggs," I tell him.

"We've already robbed Peter *and* Paul. Where we gonna get money to hire a lawyer?" Six asks.

"Look," Sheriff Pease says. "You got thirty days after I tack up the condemnation to file against the order. I been thinkin' of goin' fishin' one of these days—a week's vacation, maybe two," he says, smiling.

"My desk will be buried in mail and paperwork by the time I get back. Might take me a while to put my hands on that court order again. That'll buy you a little more time."

"Gracias, Sheriff," Six says.

The sheriff finishes his beer and gets up. He calls to Nicky. The boy comes running.

"What's that behind your other ear, son?" Pease asks.

Nicky flaps both his ears with his hands. "Nada," he says.

"I think you're mistaken, Nicky. Here. Look."

The sheriff extracts another Morgan dollar from behind the boy's left ear this time. Nicky makes a wide circle of astonishment with his mouth and runs to the parlor. He returns with his first silver dollar. Holding one in each hand, he says, "One. Two."

"That's right, Nicky," Six tells him, hoisting the boy up to his shoulders. "But I didn't hear a *Gracias*. Did I miss it?"

"Gwacias."

"You're welcome, son," the sheriff says.

Sheriff Pease puts on his cap and takes hold of the doorknob.

"Oh," he says, turning around. "How long you got before your grandpa's house goes to probate, Six?"

"With another continuance," my amigo replies, "we can maybe hold out until after Thanksgiving."

"Good luck to you boys. I'll ask my wife to say a prayer for you all."

"We can use all the help we can get," I tell him.

Six nods to him. "Thanks to you, Sheriff, Nicky is now richer than his uncle and me put together."

The sheriff chuckles. We watch him go down the steps and get into his well-dented pickup. It looks like a Chevy—1940 or '41. I close the kitchen door.

With Nicky still riding on his shoulders, Six wraps his arms around me and kisses me. The boy pats my head.

"Twick or tweat," he says.

"Where you gonna put it, kiddo?" Six asks, setting his son down.

The boy pulls on the leg of my overalls.

"Tio," he says, looking up at me. "Kwacker. Gwacias."

I close my eyes and reach into the box of animal crackers, fishing one out at random. Even I do not know what critter it is. I close my fingers around it and hold both hands behind my back.

"Watch this," I tell Six.

"Left," Nicky tells me. "A piggie."

I open both hands. There is a pig in my left hand.

"Lucky guess," Six says.

"Oh, yeah," I say. "He'll finish the whole box off with his *lucky guesses* if you let him."

Six turns his back and reaches into the box of animal crackers on the sideboard. He holds his closed hands out to his son.

"Horse. Wight," Nicky declares. "Bear. Left."

"We didn't try two at a time," I say.

"So what? We're trying it now," Six says.

He opens his palms to reveal a horse in his right hand and a bear in his left. Nicky takes them from his father's hands.

"One at a time, so you don't choke, my little green man."

Six takes another animal cracker from the circus wagon box. He looks at me and winks. He holds out his closed hands.

"Wight. Half a elephant," the boy says without hesitation.

Six hands him the half-an-elephant from his right hand.

"Me play now," Nicky says, running off.

My amigo and I look at one another. I see my astonished expression reflected in his wide-open eyes.

"Are we asleep, Antonio? Are we dreaming? What's going on? Things are getting stranger. Nothing makes sense these days."

"I don't know, Six. It kinda makes me smile. It doesn't have to make sense, does it? Maybe it's a gift *Santa Madre* gave Nicky when their fingers touched last Christmas. It's a small oasis in our desert of bad luck and sorrow, you know, huh?"

He smiles and puts his arms around me.

"Thanks, amigo. I'd be lost without you, you know that?" he says.

"Wait. That's my line," I reply. "Check the script."

"Then you know what comes next."

I nod my head, and kiss him with all my might.

* 9 *

It was going to be a pretty spare Thanksgiving this year except that there is still a chicken in Six's grandparents' freezer. His Gram also canned a lot of her garden, so we aren't going to starve. I pack up our crusts of bread to make stuffing.

We get ready to spend the holiday at his grandparents' house. We are slowly moving our things from our house, my Tio Nicolás's old place on Calle Alegre, to the Thorsons' house on Alameda Street. I wonder if it's not premature since Six has still not found his grandparents' will. I stuff some clothes for all of us into a duffel with a name tag that says *Thorson*.

Nicky is told he can bring only the toys he can carry. I hadn't realized I'd carved nearly all of Noah's ark for him. I'm still working on the ark itself. It'll be my Christmas present to the boy—and probably to his papa, too, who seems to be enjoying his childhood all over again through his son.

Nicky dumps the kindling out of the log carrier and fills it with his toys. He's unable to drag it even as far as the front door.

"Papa. Help."

"You know what I said. *You* have to carry them, kiddo."

"Tio. Help."

"You know what your papa said."

The boy stomps the floor with both feet. His lips curl into a fearsome pout.

"Oh, my. Are there *hormigas*, Nick? You got ants in your pants?"

The boy shakes his head.

"*Cucarachas*, then?"

"Nooo," Nicky says, dragging it out and laughing.

He runs to his father and looks up at him. Six wraps the boy up in his tiny jacket and scarf, and picks him up. Holding him in his arm, he takes up the log carrier laden with wooden toys. We go out to the truck. I hold Nicky while Six drives.

* * *

The Thorsons' house is chilly. Six turned their furnace down to save on oil. He lights a fire in the parlor while I light the gas oven. Nicky runs back and forth, offering to help both of us. I let him blow out the match. Six leaves him bundled up until the house gets warmer.

I slap the thawed chicken down on the sink drainboard. Nicky wants to sit in his old highchair so he can watch me. I wash the bird and start making the stuffing to put in the chicken.

"Horse," the boy says.

"No, Nick. It's a chicken," I tell him.

Six comes into the kitchen.

"You still playing that game?" he asks. "I gave up. The kid's never wrong."

I smile.

"Come on. Let me help you," Six says. "I got a good fire going in the fireplace. It'll be toasty in no time."

Six breaks the dried bread crusts up with his hands. I dice the onions and peppers and the last of the fresh celery for the year. I fry them in a skillet with some *chorizo*, a spicy pork sausage, and add a can of store-bought broth. I pour it over the breadcrumbs and Six mixes it with his hands. Then he stuffs it all into the rinsed bird. He sets the chicken in the roasting pan and I set the sliced potatoes and onions and carrots all round it. I open the oven door and Six puts the pan in.

"Horse," Nicky shouts.

Six chuckles. "Good thing we left his animal crackers at home, you know, huh?"

He lifts his son down from the highchair. I take two bottles of beer from the front porch where I left them to chill. I open them and we go into the parlor.

We sit near the fire and sip our beer. Six leans over and gives me a kiss.

"You know," he says, "despite our hard luck, there's a lot to be thankful for this year—starting with the little man here. Then comes you."

I smile.

"And you know what else I'm grateful for?" Six asks.

I shake my head.

"I'm really happy my Gram and Gramps never had to miss each other. God spared them the sorrow of a broken heart."

"And my aunt was spared a long disease like my poor Tio," I add.

Nicky races around the coffee table like a dog chasing its tail. "Horse. Horse," he shouts. On one of his passes around the room, Six catches him and sets him in his lap.

"Whoa, my little cowpoke. Simmer down. We heard you the first time. What d'ya say we head to the bunkhouse for a nap?"

"Nap," he repeats.

Six lifts him to his shoulders and trots down the hallway to his grandparents' bedroom. There is a store-bought crib for Nicky in their bedroom.

When Six returns, he asks how long before the chicken and vegetables have finished roasting.

"About an hour-and-a-half," I tell him. "That bird is stuffed full."

"Mind if I go looking around for the you-know-what some more?" Six asks.

"Come on, Six. It's a holiday. Tomorrow you can look for it to your heart's content."

"But if I find the will tonight, I won't have to look tomorrow, you know, huh?"

"You are impossible, amigo. OK. But I'd like to see some of you tonight. Is there anything you haven't checked here in the parlor?"

"I haven't flipped through all the books. I left off with the Rs. I fell asleep on the floor."

I stand up and walk to the tall bookshelves on either side of the hearth.

"Your Gram and Gramps sure had a lot of books."

"A lot of 'em are in Norwegian," he tells me. He takes the step-stool to reach the top shelf of books on the right side of the fireplace.

"Did you try this one?" I ask, pointing to the complete works of Shakespeare two shelves below where Six is looking.

"No, I'm still on R, Antonio. If I don't go about this systematically, I'll get lost."

"Let me help you then," I offer.

"What? Help me get lost? I can do that just fine on my own," Six tells me, smiling.

He goes back to flipping slowly through the pages of the books on the top shelf. I take out the Shakespeare volume. It's a heavy tome. I sit in the chair and hold it in my lap. There is something thick between the pages. I open *Will. Shakespeare - Compleat Works.* My hands shake and my heart races.

I wait until Six gets down from the step-ladder to tell him. I hold up "Last Will & Testament — Otto & Matilda Thorson."

Six's wide-open mouth and astonished expression tell me he never checked the Shakespeare even though it says *Will.* Shakespeare in large block letters on the leather binding.

"My God, Antonio. You're a genius," he says.

My amigo takes the heavy book from my lap and pulls me up from the chair. He wraps his arms around me and begins dancing with me. I step on his feet, following along like a heavy-footed rag doll.

We hoot and holler and spin each other around until we are out of breath and dizzy. Our joyful noise awakens Nicky who comes into the parlor rubbing his eyes.

The little one wastes no time joining in our celebration. Six picks him up and holds him between us as we twirl around the parlor, Nicky laughing as though he were on a carnival ride at the state fair.

At last we sit down again, winded. Nicky climbs up into his papa's lap.

"I'm a little jealous," Six tells me. "I been looking for the will for weeks, you know, huh? You come in here and the first place you look, you find it."

"It said *Will.* right on the binding, big as life. How could you miss it?"

"I wasn't looking for something that obvious, I guess."

Six hands little Nicky over to me, but the boy wants down so he can play with his carved animals.

My amigo picks up the open volume of Shakespeare and walks back to the bookshelf with it. He stops. He returns to show me the book, still turned to the page where his Gramps hid his will. Six points.

The play it is turned to is *Richard III.* The first lines of dialogue on the page are spoken by the Duke of Gloucester himself.

"*A horse,*" I read aloud, "*a horse! My kingdom for a horse!*"

Six looks at me, opening his mouth, but nothing comes out.

"Horse, horse," Nicky shouts, running up to us with the pair of equines I'd carved for Noah's ark. Nicky and the horses are the only ones who do not seem to be at a loss for words.

CHAPTER ELEVEN

SEMPER CRESCIS AUT DECRESCIS
Ever Waxing, Ever Waning

After the settlement of his grandparents' estate, my amigo and I thought maybe our tangle of troubles might begin to unknot. His grandparents left their house and property to both of us. We've decided to donate my Tio's old house on Calle Alegre to Brother Asinus's order, too, like my aunt did. It will become a visitor's center for the pilgrims who visit the Shrine of Our Lady of Roswell. We are still appealing the judge's condemnation order for all the property on the road in order to widen it.

We hope to finish moving into his Gram's and Gramps' house by Christmas. Little Nicky, soon to turn four years old, will have his papa's old bedroom on the second floor. It's a big room with windows on two sides, one looking out on a paddock and the other onto an apricot orchard. There is a small bathroom up there, too.

We celebrated the boy's name day on December sixth, the feast of *Santa Nicolás*. The boy, who usually provides all the entertainment, left it to his papa and me to amuse ourselves. Nicky was both listless and cranky, and Six put his son to bed early.

* * *

The boy has a fever this morning. Six decides to take him to Dr. Wiggins in town after he drops me off at Mila-Grow. He doesn't have to say anything. I know he's worried. Nicky has been "poopy" lately, not his usual high-spirited self.

We are busy just before Christmas so both Alicia and I are working in the greenhouse shop today.

I'm worried about Nicky, too. I find it difficult to concentrate. It takes me three attempts to make the right change.

"That's better," Mr. Olsen says. "I know you wasn't tryin' to cheat me or nothin', son. How's your partner? How's your nephew? How old is he gonna be now?"

I feel bombarded with questions. I don't know which one to answer first.

"Six is fine. Little Nicky's gonna be four in a couple weeks—just after Christmas."

"Time passes. I'm not gettin' any younger, either, you know, huh?"

"I guess not, Mr. Olsen."

"You're not s'posed to agree with me, Antonio."

"But the customer is always right," I remind him, grinning.

The old guy, about the same age as Six's Gramps lived to be, touches the brim of his cowboy hat and smiles. He turns and leaves the greenhouse with his pair of potted poinsettias, cradling one in each arm.

* * *

After the visit to Dr. Wiggins, Six is going to drop Nicky at the babysitter Hermione's place. I expect Six to certainly be back by noon, but the dinner-hour comes and goes.

The bell above the shop door jangles, like a pair of fancy spurs. It is Six.

My amigo's face is white. He rushes up to me, throws his arms around me, and puts his head on my shoulder. Six trembles, and stutters getting the words out.

"Doc W-w-wiggins wanted me to take Nicky to the hospital. Oh, Antonio. They kept him."

I stroke the back of Six's neck. Though it calms him, I'm a little bit em-barrassed getting so chummy with Six in front of anyone. Alicia comes in from another section of the greenhouse in case the bell was a customer. She goes around to Six's other side and puts her arm around him.

"The doc thinks he might have polio," Six says, fighting back his tears. Only one gets free, but there is a crack in the dam that holds them back.

"That's terrible, Six," Alicia says. "I feel so bad for you. I will pray to the Holy Mother for little Nicky."

Alicia separates from us when a pair of customers, an older man and a young woman, come in. Alicia waits on them. Six and I retreat to our office at the rear corner of the greenhouse. We sit next to each other on the edge of Eduardo's old roll-top desk. I put my arm around his waist; he places his on my shoulder.

"I can take all the shitty luck and bad breaks we've had this year, you know, huh?" Six says. "It was all just stuff, stuff that can be replaced, even my Gramps' house and the statue of the Blessed Virgin. They're all just things. But Nicky is my son. I love him more than anyone—yes, even you *mi amigo*."

I step between his legs and kiss him.

"Of course, Six. That's how it should be. Blood is thicker than water."

"I wanted to stay with him, Antonio, but they said I couldn't. I felt awful leaving him with the men in white coats. They want to do a bunch of tests on him to be sure it's polio. I hope they don't treat him like we were treated in the army hospital. The last thing I heard was him yelling, 'Papa. Papa,' echoing down the hallway."

He collapses against me, sobbing. I hold him. He breathes and sighs deeply.

"Why don't I take you home, amigo?"

"No, Antonio. I've gotta have something to do or I'm gonna crawl outta my skin. Show me what needs doing."

"You sure?" I ask.

He nods. "I know you've been stuck with more than your share of the workload lately, amigo. I'm sorry. I'll make it up to you: I'll work like *six* men."

"And all of you will have to love me for the rest of your lives," I tell him.

"We already do, amigo," he replies. "We already do."

* * *

Six visited Nicky during all hospital visiting hours: from eleven until noon, two to four in the afternoon, and seven to eight at night. I always went with him in the evening after work.

The boy held his own for the first couple of days but has been losing ground lately. His eyes are circled in shadow. His poor thin arms are bruised with needle pricks. It breaks my heart to see the child like this—and I am only his uncle. I don't know how my amigo bears up except by the grace of God. He broke down in church on Christmas Eve when he saw the baby Jesus in the manger. We had to leave.

Christmas was the grimmest affair I ever took part in. The hospital permitted visitors for a single hour in the late afternoon. Nicky seemed barely awake most of the time. Six knelt beside his son's bed and held his hand. I put my hand on Six's shoulder from time to time. It hardly seemed an hour had passed when the nurse announced it was time for visitors to leave.

I drove the truck home. Six didn't say a word. But I knew what was on his mind: he wondered whether this would be the last time we'd see little Nicky alive. I think, *The little one will be OK so long as we don't say it out loud.*

* 2 *

My amigo and I decide to go home from work early. The rush is over. It's four days after Christmas, Nicky's birthday. He is four years old.

It has been nearly a month since we moved the last of our clothes and personal belongings into his grandparents' house where we and the boy will live. We are leaving most of our old furniture behind for the use of visitors to the Shrine of Our Lady of Roswell.

Six takes off his work jacket and hangs it behind the kitchen door. He'll wear his newer jacket when we go to the hospital during the evening visitors' hour.

We get things set up for a late supper when we get back home: a pot of goat stew and rice. Six often heads straight for bed after visiting his son in the hospital. The visit seems to drain him. It's a struggle getting him to eat. It didn't used to be that way.

"Can you help me move Nicky's ark upstairs, Six. The varnish is dry."

"I thought it was Noah's ark."

"Previous owner," I reply.

The ark is not heavy, but it is awkward. We have to carry it sideways up to Nicky's bedroom where the carved animals are all waiting to climb aboard. I haven't varnished them yet because the little one used to put them in his mouth. But he doesn't chew on things any more.

We set the ark on the floor beside the boy's dresser. If he keeps collecting toys at the current rate, Nicky will be able to open his own toy store by the time he's ten years old. It is fun to watch him play with his toys and tell stories about what God's creatures are up to. That boy brings so much joy and laughter into our lives—and I'm only his uncle.

Six sits on the bed and I sit next to him. He turns to me and I touch his cheek. He looks so worn and grazed. I remember the first time my amigo and I made love in this room. Actually, it was out on the porch roof and we kept our boots and Levi's on because it was a cold night. It seems such a long time ago.

"Oh, Antonio..." he says, but he does not finish his thought. He takes my hand.

I gaze into his eyes, focusing first on his face and then deep into the bottomless black wells of his pupils, one circled by a blue iris, the other by a brown one. Even our blinking eyelids do not break our long fixed look at one another— our look *into* one another.

I have never seen my amigo in quite this way before. His hand is strong. I feel his firm grip and his pulse, rhyming with mine. But when I look into his face, I see a frightened boy, a boy whose heart is breaking. The boy wants to shed his tears in a torrent; the man wants to hold them back. I close my eyes and kiss him.

I imagine little Nicky, alone in his darkened room, longing for his father. I see the father wanting to be with his son, perhaps for the last time this side of heaven.

"Come on, Six," I say, pulling him up from the bed by his arm. "Nicky needs you."

We race down the stairs.

"They're not gonna let us see him, amigo," Six tells me. "They made me wait once when I got there five minutes early."

"Not tonight," I say.

He does not argue with me. He takes the knob and opens the kitchen door.

"No, put your jacket on, Six. How are you gonna help Nicky if you get sick?"

The telephone rings. We look at one another.

"Has the telephone ever brought us any good news, Antonio?"

"Not that I recall."

"Exactly," he replies.

We don't answer the phone. Six puts his hand on my shoulder. We go out, leaving the porch light on in case it's dark by the time we get back home. He walks to the driver's side of Tio's pickup.

"No, Six. You're upset. I'll drive."

"You're not upset?"

"Uncles do not get as upset as fathers, amigo."

"You could've fooled me," he says.

I push the starter several times but the engine refuses to turn over. Six climbs out and lifts the hood. Then he slams it down again. He stands with his hands on the hood, wagging his head. I get out.

"That damn squirrel that's been hanging around? He's made his lunch on the wires to the distributor cap. Chewed all the insulation off. Is this the last straw yet, Antonio? Or does 1948 have a little more bad luck in store for us?"

"Come on, Six," I say. "Let's see if we can borrow Mrs. Hinkle's car."

It's a bit of a hike to our nearest neighbor's place.

"Wait up," I holler.

He pauses in the road until I catch up with him.

"I promise you," he says, "that as soon as Nicky turns five, I'm taking him squirrel hunting like my Gramps did, even if it's only with a pop-gun."

"That's the spirit, amigo."

We turn down Mrs. Hinkle's driveway.

* * *

Maybe I should have let Six drive. I'm afraid I'll crumple a fender or have some other mishap with Mrs. Hinkle's spotless tan and burgundy 1947 Hudson Commodore convertible. Her husband bought it only a year ago, but he died before getting to drive it more than a few times, mostly up and down Main Street to show it off. Mrs. Hinkle keeps it in the garage under blankets. She seems less concerned with my driving it to the hospital than I am.

I berth the land-yacht in the hospital parking lot. I run to catch up with Six.

My amigo drums his fingers impatiently as the nurse receptionist at the front desk does her best to ignore us. She doesn't even look up at us.

"I saw you. I'll be with you in a minute," she says.

"Time's up," Six tells her, without even five seconds passing. I can tell he's at the end of his tether. "We're here to see Nicolás Thorson. Right now."

"Oh," she says. "I believe Dr. Nuñez tried to reach you on the phone. One minute please."

The nurse puts on a headset and makes a connection at her switchboard, mumbling into her mouthpiece. Then she goes back to ignoring us.

We step off to the side so we can talk privately.

"What if that was the telephone call we didn't answer, Antonio? What did the doctor want to tell me?"

His chest heaves. "Oh, God. Oh, no, amigo. It can't be. Tell me it isn't more bad news."

I fold my arms around Six and hug him. "I am here for you, Six," I say, though it sounds like an awfully weak remark. Over his shoulder, I see two doctors in their long white coats walk down the corridor. I release Six.

"Mr. Thorson?" one of them asks, unsure which of us to address. His expression does not look as downcast and mournful as I would expect for someone bearing awful news. Perhaps he has gotten used to it.

"Yes, Doctor," Six replies.

"Let's go into my office," Dr. Nuñez says, putting his hand on Six's shoulder.

My amigo looks at me.

"This is the boy's uncle. He's coming, too," Six tells the doctor, latching onto my elbow.

"Yes, of course," the doctor says.

We enter a small examination room. Dr. Nuñez sits behind his desk, his colleague, Dr. Miller, standing beside him. Six and I stand in front of the desk. My amigo touches my hand.

"We tried to call you at work, Mr. Thorson," Dr. Nuñez tells him. "They said you'd gone home for the day. I called you at home, but there was no answer. But I think it's better this way—a more personal way to deliver such astounding news."

Six squeezes my hand hard enough to hurt.

"I understand it is your son's fourth birthday today," Dr. Nuñez remarks, smiling. "This is probably the best birthday present little Nicolás could have received, Mr. Thorson. He's made a full recovery—in a matter of hours."

My amigo lets go of my hand and leans on the doctor's desk. "What?" he says. "Did I hear you right?"

"Yes," Dr. Miller tells him. "There is no comparable case in the literature that we are aware of. It's nothing short of miraculous, Mr. Thorson."

"Holy smoke," Six shouts. "Yahoo!" He flings the door wide and takes off down the hallway, calling, "Nicky. Nicky."

Dr. Nuñez stands up and comes from behind his desk.

"Naturally, we'd like to keep the boy under observation for a few days to monitor his condition," he tells me. "You might mention that to the father."

"Just this morning my colleague and I thought we'd have to be reporting a very different kind of news," Dr. Miller says. "Our concern is that a sudden reversal can just as easily go back the other way."

"But it's not going to, doctors," I tell them. "Quality miracles don't unravel."

I shake their hands and thank them, and leave the doctor's office.

Standing outside the door to Nicky's room, I wonder whether I've given Six enough time to be alone with his son. But I'd like to see the boy, too.

Before taking hold of the doorknob, I bow my head and thank the Holy Mother for her intercession on behalf of little Nicky. I thank Jesus for his miraculous birthday gift to an innocent child.

The scene that greets me when I enter Nicky's hospital room makes my jaw drop. My nephew wears a ridiculous green costume. He has a long green tail. I think he's supposed to be a lizard, maybe a gecko. He jumps wildly up and down on his bed. Six stands at the foot of the bed, ready to catch his son. My amigo turns when he hears me enter.

On either side, at the end of the bed next to Six, are Kaptain Kosmos and a second Visitor, younger, who wears a glowing headband with lights that chase around his cranium.

"Tio," Nicky shouts, holding his arms out to me. He hugs me and goes back to bouncing on his bed. "Happy Birfday to me!"

"The Blessed Mother asked us to look in on little Nicolás to see whether we might offer assistance," Kaptain Kosmos tells me.

"Allow me to introduce one of our medical experts, Antonio," the Kaptain says, bowing to the fellow with the glowing green headband. "This is Doktor Klas."

Little Nicky stops in mid-bounce—literally. He is suspended a foot-and-a-half above the bed, gleefully kicking his feet.

"Doktor Klas *fixed* me," Nicky announces.

"Stop it, Nick. Get down from there," Six tells him. "Nobody likes a show-off."

The boy drops down to the bed fast, landing on his kiester.

"See?" his father tells him.

Kaptain Kosmos says, "You can help us sing *Happy Birthday*, Antonio."

The Kaptain and Doktor Klas produce a pair of curlicue trumpets and two gongs. They manage to sing and blow on the horns at the same time. Nothing is in tune with anything else. Nicky clangs one of the gongs in a contrary rhythm. Six bangs the other.

It is the most bizarre rendition of *Happy Birthday* I ever heard. Even a dozen drunk soldiers could not compete. I wait for one of the hospital security guards to burst into the room. No one but me seems concerned about the great racket and uproar we're raising. The Visitors want to sing another verse. My ears ring.

There's a knock at the door. My heart jumps into my throat.

"Don't worry," Kaptain Kosmos tells me. "They cannot hear us. They were not invited."

I open the door and peer out. A nurse in her white uniform and shoes and cap stands holding a tray. There are five bowls of what looks like strawberry ice cream and five spoons. The nurse passes the tray to me and smiles.

"Don't let the boy eat too much ice cream," she says. "We don't want him to get sick or suffer a relapse."

"From strawberry ice cream?" I ask.

She laughs softly. "No, I suppose not."

I thank her and carry the tray into Nicky's room, closing the door with my foot. The two Visitors are jumping up and down as excitedly as the boy though without the benefit of the bounce provided by his bed. They nearly crash into the ceiling. Their antics make me dizzy.

"That's enough now," Six says, addressing his son. But they all stop their bouncing and acrobatics.

I set the tray on Nicky's bed and give the birthday boy the first bowl.

"Gracias, Tio," he says.

"Gracias, Tio," Kaptain Kosmos and Doktor Klas repeat as I hand them each a bowl.

"Ooo... Ooo... Ooo," they say, forming their lips into perfect circles. Their pursed lips extend into narrow tubes like a hummingbird's beak. They greedily suck in the strawberry ice cream as if it were nectar, leaving only the chunks of strawberry at the bottom of their bowls.

"The best part for last," Kaptain Kosmos declares, his mouth returning to its usual shape. He picks up each piece of berry between his thumb and finger and pops it into his mouth. His eyes narrow and lose focus as he murmurs in ecstasy. Doktor Klas follows his example.

"You can have my bowl," Six tells them. "We can get strawberry ice cream any old time."

I hand my bowl to the Visitors, too.

"This is most generous of you," the Kaptain tells us.

"It is worth the trip to your world for this alone," Doktor Klas says, licking his lips.

I have never heard such noisy eaters. They smack their lips. Their simple delight makes me smile. They do as good a job of cleaning their bowls as a Hoover vacuum. Hoover makes me think of his G-men and the FBI. And that makes me nervous. I wonder how the Visitors came into the hospital and if anyone saw them.

"I think we will be going now," Kaptain Kosmos announces. "We don't want anyone to worry."

Six laughs. "Why would anyone have to worry about you?"

"Most of our race considers humans ignorant, unprincipled savages, but I didn't want to tell you that for fear of making you feel bad. You are my friends."

"You smell bad, too," Doktor Klas adds, placing a finger over his tiny nostrils.

The Kaptain raises his glowing green palm.

"Farewell, Nicolás Antonio Montoya-Thorson. Happy birthday to you," he screeches.

"Happy birfday," Nicky sings.

This time, rather than vanishing in the blink of an eye, the Visitors, Kaptain Kosmos and Doktor Klas, do a slow fade—like fog in the first rays of sunlight. Nicky waves to them.

"Bye, bye," he says.

Six and I look at each other and smile. He picks Nicky up from the bed and holds him in his arms.

"What d'ya say we go home, sprout?"

"I didn't get a chance to tell you, Six. They want to keep Nicky for observation," I tell him.

"Not a chance," my amigo replies. "They can check him out some other time. Today is his birthday, and we're going home. Right, Nick?"

"Wight," the boy replies.

I raise the blinds and unlock the sash. It is already dark. After climbing through the window, I take little Nicky from his papa. Then Six climbs out, lowering the blinds and pulling the sash down. We crouch down behind the shrubs and make our way to the parking lot.

Taking the wheel of the Hudson, I leave the headlamps off until we leave the road from the county hospital.

"What d'ya say we stop at the grotto on the way home, Six? We have a lot of thanks to offer for little Nicky's recovery."

"Yeah, we sure do, amigo. That's a good idea. Wanna see Mama on your birthday, Nick?"

"Mama," the boy says, nodding his head. My amigo smiles.

"Oh, Antonio," Six tells me. "I'm so grateful to God and His Holy Mother that we don't have to take my son to the St. Giles' Home for Cripples in Albuquerque. He was awfully close."

He touches my arm. The little one, sitting on his lap, does the same.

It's a frosty night. There are no other visitors to the Shrine of Our Lady of Roswell, though there is a heap of bouquets added in just the last few days. There are many lighted *Santería* candles, too, flickering in the light breeze. I park our neighbor's car in the driveway of my Tia's old house on Calle Alegre.

"I'll get one of Mrs. Hinkle's blankets from the trunk and wrap Nicky up in it," Six tells me.

He returns with Nicky bundled up in a folded blanket. We cross the road and stand before my carving of the Blessed Virgin Mary. Six sets Nicky down, draping the blanket over the boy's shoulders. He holds his son's hand completely inside his own. We recite the *Hail, Mary.*

"Mother,"Nicky says, repeating his favorite word from the prayer.

"*Am I not here, I who am your Mother?*"

Nicky looks up and smiles.

"*Mis hijos,*" Holy Mother says.

"*Santa Madre,*" I say.

"*Madre,*" Nicky repeats.

Six kneels down on the frozen ground in front of the Blessed Virgin. The boy stands beside his papa, looking up at the Holy Mother.

Six bows deeply, hunching his shoulders far forward, nearly folding himself in half.

"*Santa Madre*, on behalf of all precious children, I thank you with all my heart for interceding to heal this precious child, my son."

"You are welcome, Sixtus. Please stand, my child. I am pleased that Doktor Klas was able to help. I have suggested that he share his discovery of a poliovirus vaccine with your medical experts. They have found a way to prevent children from ever getting this malady in the first place."

"Thank you, Holy Mother," I say.

"I wish to tell you that your Tia Ana's house, the wayside for those who come to my shrine, has seen a great many visitors, all by word of mouth. Their devotion warms my heart, even in the midst of winter."

Six picks Nicky up, bundling him in the blanket again.

"There have been several cures and improvements which Our Lord effected to honor me, my children. The pilgrims to my shrine have left behind many crutches and canes and braces."

"That is wonderful, Holy Mother," I say, smiling at her. "What would you like us to do?"

"The pilgrims have also left behind their testimonials and eyewitness accounts, their photographs and drawings, their letters and keepsakes. I would like you to put those items in Brother Asinus's chapel at the pueblo for safekeeping."

"We are under surveillance by government agents, Holy Mother," I tell her. "We do not want to alert them to what is hidden at the pueblo."

"I understand," the Virgin says. "I shall ask Kaptain Kosmos to send someone to whisk the mementoes away unseen."

Six jiggles Nicky in his arms.

"Archbishop Abelardo is determined to tear down the shrine, Holy Mother," he tells her.

She smiles. Her grin is a little bit mischievous, like the Mona Lisa's.

"He is welcome to try."

"But he is very powerful man," I say.

"He would not be so were he not given authority from above. Death comes for the archbishop, too."

Six passes Nicky over to me. The boy gets heavy very quickly.

"Tio," he says, patting my cheek. His little hand is warm.

"Your year of tribulation is nearly over, *mis hijos*," the Blessed Virgin says. "You have remained steadfast in your faith and devotions. You endured much without complaint. I am proud of you, and happy that the little one has so much love in his life.

"God bless you, my children."

"Bye, bye, Mama," Nicky says, waving to her.

The Virgin's smile warms the frosty air. Her glow melts the snow around the grotto. She fades slowly back into my wood carving. The moon rises.

We walk back across the *calle* to the borrowed Hudson.

"Wanna put the top down?" Six asks. "We may never get another chance."

"Are you crazy? It's cold out," I say. "What about Nicky?"

"I'll wrap him up in the other blanket, too. He'll be fine. Why don't you see if you can figure out how to get the lid off this can, amigo?"

I find the latch for the canvas top above the rearview mirror. It takes a bit of pushing to get the top all the way down. There are two more latches at the back to secure it. I get behind the wheel. Six and Nicky get in the car. Six turns the heater on full-blast. I wonder if I'm not a little crazy, too, for going along with him.

Our ride back home is not as freezing as I thought it would be. The windshield pushes most of the cold air up and over us. Nicky, standing up in his papa's lap, gazes up at the stars, oohing and aahing and pointing all the way home. I'm sure he gets his interest in the heavens from both his mother and his father.

Since it's a bit of a hike back home from Mrs. Hinkle's, I drop Six and Nicky off before returning the land yacht to our neighbor. Six tosses the blankets onto the back seat and hurries inside the house.

It takes me three attempts to line the wide car up with the narrow garage. Then I manage to wrinkle the rear fender and take the corner off the garage anyhow.

"What else?" I ask, reminding myself that there are only three days of 1948 left. I can't wait for 1949 to get here. To top it off, I pinch my fingers getting the canvas top back up. I cover it with the blankets. I ring our neighbor's back doorbell.

"Come in, dear," Mrs. Hinkle says. She ties her pure white hair up in a bun, held with hair combs. "How's the little one?" she asks.

"He's been released from the hospital, ma'am. We are so happy we could bust. It's little Nicky's birthday today."

"That is happy news indeed, Antonio. I've made tea."

I want to get home, but I want to be friendly. Mrs. Hinkle is lonely since her husband died. She goes into the kitchen and comes back with her tea-tray. I'm getting a lump in my throat thinking about confessing to the crumpled fender. I have to wait for the tea to cool.

"I had a little mishap with your car, Mrs. Hinkle. I'm very sorry. I dented the rear fender and clipped your garage."

"Oh, my," she says. "But I believe there are people who pound out dents and wrinkles and repaint them."

"Yes, there are, Mrs. Hinkle. I will pay for the damage."

"Not to worry, child. I just wish there were a place people could go to get our wrinkles smoothed out and given a fresh coat of paint."

I laugh and finish my tea.

"You boys should come by on New Year's Eve, Antonio. We'll have something a little stronger in our tea."

"Thank you, Mrs. Hinkle. And thank you for the use of your car. I'm sorry about the damage."

"Don't mention it, child. That's what neighbors are for—to help out."

I leave her parlor and go down the front porch steps. I race down Alameda Street, eager to get home. I think of all the people who have been so good to my amigo and me and the little one. We are so blessed. I am back home before I've thought of even half their names.

* 3 *

It is already the end of January 1949. While our luck may not have turned around, there have been no new setbacks or disasters. Nicky has returned to his former state of perfect health. Six and I are especially grateful for that. The boy nearly died of paralytic polio only one month ago.

My amigo and I pick his son up at Hermione's on the way home from Mila-Grow. We are still driving Mrs. Hinkle's slightly-dented Hudson Commodore convertible, even after the accident I had. She seems to have forgotten all about it, but we haven't. We didn't have the money to get the damage repaired at the body shop.

The nursery and greenhouse do not yet belong to Six and me, though we are inching closer. Eduardo has adjusted the price to reflect the county taxes he forgot to pay. We are on better terms with him again. He and the missus decided they like Florida and are going to reside in the Sunshine State.

I park the convertible in the driveway of our new house, Six's grandparents' old homestead on Alameda Street. We pushed my Tio's turquoise pickup into the barn once Six couldn't get it going again. It needs parts. We haven't had money for that, either.

Six holds his son. They go in the house and I go to check the mailbox. I always hope it will be empty. *No news is the only good news.*

The mailbox is chock-full. My pulse beats faster. "Oh, brother," I say aloud, taking out the letters. There are four of them: one from the Chaves County Highway Department, another from Mr. Jeremiah Carson's attorney, the third from the Archdiocese of Santa Fe, and the last from the Chaves County Treasurer. None of it suggests happy news.

There is another letter way at the back of the mailbox. There is no address and no postage, just our names, *Antonio & Six*, in Dr. Feynman's tiny scrawl. I'm sure that one was delivered by interplanetary postman, Kourier Kirkus. It's the only way we can communicate with the doctor without the FBI or the CIA reading our mail.

I wish I could spare Six any more bad news, but I can't very well hide the letters from him.

Six slices onions and peppers at the sink. Nicky plays with a small menagerie of animal crackers at the kitchen table. They both smile at me. Nicky has his papa's dimples.

"I see we're pretty popular today," Six tells me, glancing down at my handful of mail.

I put my arm around him, the letters still in my hand, and give him a kiss.

"Bribery's not going to work, amigo," he tells me. "Come on. Let's see the mail."

He wipes his hands and takes two beers out of the ice box. He snaps the caps off while I slice open the letters with a butter knife. We sit down at the table, Six next to his son.

We sort the mail according to the likelihood it contains good news, saving the best for last, the worst first.

"You're the Catholic. You get to open that one."

"Cat," Nicky says, showing us the animal cracker.

The boy makes me laugh, even with the letter from the archbishop shaking in my hands. It is fancy paper with an elaborate embossed letterhead as showy as the archbishop's flamboyant clerical attire. Six anxiously leans over my shoulder.

"It's not really bad news," I tell him. "The archdiocese has been asked to turn over the case of Our Lady of Roswell to the Vatican Office of Investigations. It's a long process to verify any apparition. It can take decades. See what you make of it, Six."

I watch his two-color eyes scan the page. "I take it as good news, Antonio. The Vatican probably has a smaller axe to grind than Archbishop Tubolardo, you know, huh?"

"Tubolardo," Nicky repeats.

We can't help smiling, but we try not encourage the boy with our laughter.

"Your turn," I tell Six, pointing to the stack of mail. He picks up the envelope from the highway department. It's dirty. It looks like someone chased it around the equipment yard and caught it with his boot before dropping it into the mailbox.

Nicky touches the envelope. "Bull," he says.

"I'm afraid that could apply to most of our mail, my little man."

I watch Six read, his face drooping lower.

"Oh, boy, Antonio," he says. "They begin work on the 'Calle Alegre Improvement Project' this Monday morning. I can't watch it, amigo. I can't be there. To begin the demolition, they're bringing in a bulldozer."

"Bull," Nicky says, holding up the cookie of a cow.

"Close, Mr. Smarty-Pants, but no cigar," he tells his son.

"Maybe they're just going to straighten the tight curves in the road first," I tell him.

"I hope so," Six says. "Maybe that'll give us time to file another protest."

"So we got one *thumbs-up* and one *thumbs-down*. It's a tie. I hate ties. They strangulate me."

He hands me the next envelope on the pile. It's from Jeremiah Carson's attorney.

"It better be a receipt that says, *Paid in Full,*" Six tells me. "Carson got the last nickel my Gramps had in the bank in order to pay him back."

The lawyer's letter is on two pages. The fancy letterhead of golden Scales of Justice and a forest of pillars looks like he's in competition with the archbishop. After I read the first page, I pass it to Six.

"Holy smokes," he remarks. "Now Carson wants to buy our meteorites back at twice their original price? This is unbelievable. Talk about a reversal of fortune."

"Here. Get a load of page two," I say, handing it to him.

"I go to my room to play," Nicky says.

"OK, Nick. We'll call you down for supper."

We watch the tyke climb the steep stairs, putting both feet on each step before ascending the next. Six's dimples deepen and his lips curve into a smile. Then he looks down and peruses the second page of the attorney's letter.

"*Mystery Meteorites from the Land of Enchantment,*" he reads. "The article quotes Dr. Feynman: T*he thing that doesn't fit is the thing that is most interesting.* The library oughta have a copy of *Science Digest,* don't you think, so we can read the whole article for ourselves?"

"Probably," I reply. "Mr. Carson's is a tempting offer. We could sure use the money. But I think we should keep them in Brother Asinus's crypt with the other meteorites."

"I agree with you a hundred percent, Antonio. So our mail score is two-to-one in favor of good news. Will this next one mean a stalemate of fortune or a winning streak?"

Six opens the last envelope before Dr. Feynman's letter. We will save the doctor's for after our supper. Like a dessert, his letters are always rich and filling.

"Here goes nothin'," Six says, opening the one from the county treasurer.

The smile returns to his lips. He shows me the letter from the county treasurer with *Paid in Full* stamped at the top. There is a check in the amount of $3.25 for an overpayment.

"Yahoo!" Six and I shout. Little Nicky stands at the top of the stairs.

"I'm hungry, Papa," he announces, cautiously descending the steps while hanging onto the bannister.

"Will you make supper for your Tio and me tonight, Nick? We're awfully tired."

"Sure, Papa."

Nicky joins us in the kitchen. He shines his big blue eyes up at us.

"What are we gonna have for supper tonight, Nick?"

"Stwawbewwy ice cweam," he says.

Rather than argue with his son, Six helps him scoop ice cream into three bowls. Not knowing when the Visitors might show up, strawberry is the only flavor we have on hand in the small freezer.

For dessert we have fajitas with beef and peppers, onions and mushrooms.

* * *

After tucking little Nicky into bed, Six joins me in front of the hearth. He has brought us each a bottle of Dos Equis. I wait to read him the interesting parts of Dr. Feynman's letter. Actually, it's all pretty interesting.

"I'm not sure I'll get used to having our Saturday night beers on Friday," Six tells me, clinking my bottle with his.

"Come on, Six. We deserve weekends off—especially in winter when it's slow."

"Oh, I'm not complaining, amigo," he says. "It just takes getting used to. So what does the doc have to say?"

"Here. Read it for yourself, Six."

"Why don't you read it to me? You're closer to the light."

I turn up the oil lamp on the deep mantle and stand next to it to read the letter. The doctor's tiny scrawl is so hard to read I almost need a magnifying glass.

"Dr. Feynman says, 'The photos of the Visitors are most interesting. Curious that they visited on Hallowe'en. I must accept that the photos of the Blessed Virgin are somehow genuine, too, since none of my *expert* colleagues can explain them except to say that the negatives haven't been altered in any way.'"

"We could've told him that," Six remarks, handing my bottle of beer up to me. "Did he say anything about the last meteorite samples we sent him—two of the ones we got back from Carson?"

"Um..." I say, scanning through the handwritten note. "Here. 'The best estimate is that your meteorites are fragments from the outer sphere of some sort of electro-magnetic generator—an engine, in other words.'"

"Holy smoke," my amigo says. "I wonder if it wasn't from one of the Visitors' other scout craft."

"Could be," I reply. "But that would mean they were buzzing around out there for at least three years before the night of the crash. I still think they got here a long time before that."

"You might be right, Antonio. Let's ask Kaptain Kosmos the next time he pops in for some ice cream."

I smile.

"You want me to put another log on the fire, Six?"

"Nah," he says. "Let's crawl into bed early and start our own fire, what d'ya say?"

He flashes his blue eye and his brown eye back and forth.

"Sure, amigo," I reply, chuckling. "There's just one more part of the letter I wanna read to you first."

"Shoot," he says, taking the last swallow of his beer.

"'Your Visitor's responses to my many questions convince me that your Visitor's knowledge of physics is light-years ahead of mine—perhaps *literally*.'"

"It's nice to be believed, you know, huh?" Six says.

"Dr. Feynman goes on to say, 'Fellow-scientist Katalyst Keen and I will be working on a joint project. I am far more comfortable knowing our messages cannot be intercepted by either Bragg's or Hoover's men. I will keep you boys posted on our progress. It is important work.'"

I hand the letter down to Six. He sets it on the table and holds his hand up to me. I hoist him up out of the chair. He wraps his arms around me and slips his hands down into the hip pockets of my Levi's. He likes doing that.

"I'd count the doctor's letter in the plus column, too," he says. "Three outta four in favor of good news. Things are looking up, amigo. We're on a roll—an uphill roll."

He kisses me and pulls me closer. Though the fire is going out, it's getting a lot warmer in the parlor.

* 4 *

Six and I decide we do not want to watch bulldozers tear down my aunt's and uncle's houses on Calle Alegre or demolish the grotto in honor of the Blessed Virgin Mary. Our hearts are heavy. Our hands shake and it's not just from the late January cold. After dropping Nicky at Hermione's house, we drive straight to work on Monday morning.

It is hard to concentrate on anything we do at work all day. By the time we lock up the greenhouse that evening, it is pitch black. We decide to drive to the shrine before picking little Nicky up from the babysitter's.

Maybe the demolition will not be so awful to look at when it's masked by darkness and shadows. I'm afraid it will be like Six's description of how the Montoyas' house was seemingly scraped off the face of the earth, leaving not a trace.

"Both *casitas* have a long history in my family, Six. I have only fond memories beneath both roofs. I don't know if I wanna look. But I can take anything with you beside me. God how I love you, amigo."

"Same here, Antonio. But we can't hide from it. I'm with you. We can cry together."

There are smudge-pot oil lanterns and painted sawhorses lining one side of the short road.

The rising crescent moon provides just enough light to show me that my Tia's and Tio's houses are still standing. So is the grotto and the statue of the Holy Mother. Six and I turn to each other and smile.

There is a bulldozer nearly blocking the first turn in the *calle*. Mrs. Hinkle's Hudson Commodore just manages to squeak by without tipping into the ditch. I'm glad Six is driving.

He parks in my Tia's driveway and we get out. There are pilgrims at the grotto. We're anxious to learn what happened, why the demolition didn't take place.

"Do you think our challenge to the judge's order had an effect, Six?"

"*En serio*? We didn't have a lawyer, amigo. We drew up the petition ourselves. What chance did we stand?"

"Yeah," I reply. "But we made sure to dot all the Ts and cross every I."

We don't seem to tire of repeating the Holy Mother's joke. I put my hand on Six's shoulder and we cross the road. There is another bulldozer parked at the opposite end of the *calle*.

There is a small crowd of pilgrims in front of the grotto. There are three men and three women of different ages and sizes. Each holds a lighted *Santeria* candle. They turn to us. I recognize Mrs. Cisneros from church. She smiles and takes my hand.

"God bless you, Antonio," she says. "And Sixtus, too. It's a miracle, my children."

"What is, Mrs. Cisneros?" Six asks.

"This," she replies, nodding left and right at the pair of stalled bulldozers. "They came to tear down *Santa Madre*'s statue, but their machines broke instead."

She laughs softly, pulling her serape tighter. Mr. Cisneros hands his candle to his wife. He takes my elbow and Six's, and leads us away from the praying pilgrims. He attends ceremonies on the pueblo, but they honor the Holy Mother, too.

Mr. Cisneros wears his hair in long gray braids like his missus. He offers my amigo and me one of his hand-rolled cigarettes, rolled with just his right hand

and the crook of his left elbow. His left arm is mostly paralyzed from the war, the First World War.

"They couldn't keep the first 'dozer running," he tells us, chuckling. "Each time they got her going, she'd stall again if she got too close the shrine. They sent for a mechanic."

His cigarette lights up the deep crags and wrinkles in his face as he draws on it.

"The mechanic couldn't figure it out. They sent for a second 'dozer. Same thing: stalled as soon as it got anywhere close. Wonder how many 'dozers the county's got, you know, huh?"

"Not nearly enough," Six tells him.

The three of us laugh. Mrs. Cisneros turns around, scowling at us for making noise while she and the others are praying.

We walk back to our car with Mr. Cisneros.

"Pretty fancy set of wheels," he remarks, looking at the Hudson convertible.

"It belongs to a neighbor of ours. My Tio's old Ford pickup finally gave up the ghost."

"Too bad about that. Nothin' lasts forever, you know, huh? There's a fella in my drumming-circle has got one to unload. Prob'bly just good for parts, though."

"Perfect," Six tells him. "That's all I'm looking for."

"I'll send you word through the missus when's a good time to go have a look at my buddy's truck. Might have to be towed, though."

We thank Cisneros who rejoins his wife among the praying pilgrims. Six and I, some distance off, bow our heads and say a *Hail, Mary* in thanksgiving to the Blessed Virgin for preserving her shrine—and for sparing the two houses on Calle Alegre for visitors—at least for now.

Six and I fold ourselves into the Hudson. I don't think there's any way we will ever own anything but a Ford pickup.

"I don't know what it is," Six tells me. "This car practically forces you to drive like an old lady. I don't like how low to the ground it sits, either. It feels like I'll be scraping my rear end on the next pothole."

"Yeah," I reply, "but it has one advantage."

"What's that?" he asks, negotiating the curve where the first bulldozer stalled.

"It runs," I say.

"Yeah, there is that," he says chuckling.

We turn onto the county road in the direction of home. I scoot closer to Six.

"Thanks for standing by me, amigo," I tell him. "It might've turned out different."

"Nah," he replies. "I know a dare when I hear one. Holy Mother practically dared them to tear down the grotto. So I knew it couldn't happen."

Once again, I wish I had half his faith. I turn to him and smile.

"It helps to have friends in high places," he remarks, pulling into the driveway of the babysitter's house.

"It sure does," I say, glancing up at the moon.

* 5 *

Today is my twenty-first birthday. Six had his last Tuesday, May twenty-fourth. It is *una gran cosa* for both of us.

"I wish my Gram and Gramps could be here," my amigo tells me.

"And my aunt and uncle, too," I add. "They all wondered if we were ever gonna grow up, you know, huh?"

"You mean we have? When did that happen? I must've been asleep."

I smile at him. Little Nicky comes in, slamming the screen door—just like his papa.

"Oh, Nick," Six tells his son. "No, you're not coming in the house like that. Do you have to find every mud puddle?"

"I falled down," the boy says.

"At least you didn't try to tell me the mud jumped on you again. Come on, my little brown man. Back outside."

As Six gets Nicky cleaned up on the back porch, I go over the list of food and drinks for our birthday party. I'm nervous. This will be the most people we've had at the Thorson house since we moved in last December. I'm sure I forgot something.

"Relax," Six hollers from the porch. "I can hear you worrying out here."

He knows me too well. I slip the pans of bread in the oven. It's awfully nice having a stove that runs on gas. It's nice having a hot-water heater, too, and a shower that's always ready. I feel like we finally entered the Twentieth Century.

Six returns with Nicky. The boy wears just his underpants. Father and son go upstairs to get the boy into clean clothes.

I hear the first car pull up out front. It's Alicia and her friend Martha from her book club. They're early. They come around back.

Martha is *mestizo*, Indian and Mexican, very dark and attractive. She wears her long black braids rolled up on the side of her head, fastened with combs. She's one of the best-looking girls I know. Her smile melts hearts—maybe even mine, at least a little.

Alicia gives me a kiss and Martha shakes my hand. We go into the kitchen. Six and Nicky come down the stairs, the boy wearing the tiniest pair of overalls I've ever seen.

"'Lithia," Nicky hollers, running to her. She picks him up and gives him a lipstick kiss. I probably got one, too. She sets the boy down again and hugs my amigo, planting another kiss-print on *him*.

"We came early to help out, Antonio," Alicia tells me. "Put us to work."

"You could help me set up the table on the back porch," I tell Alicia.

Nicky is already flirting with Alicia's friend Martha.

Six takes the trays of corn and tamales and peppers for roasting to his Gramps' iron grill in the back yard. I bring the platters of hamburgers and hot dogs and spicy sausage. Nicky helps his papa light the charcoals with a match put to newspaper.

The next vehicle in the back yard is Tomás's old Ford pickup. He and Diego, our other greenhouse worker, and the new kid, Ramon, climb out. It seems it's mostly a work party, but we also invited our old army pal Zeke Jackson. He said he hoped he could make it. We invited our former neighbor Vigil, his daughter Hermione—who watches Nicky—and our new neighbor, Mrs. Hinkle, too.

"This is a pretty nice place," Tomás says, looking around. "Lots better than your old house, you know, huh?"

"Well, it's about a hundred years newer," I tell him. "Why don't you bring some beer from our icebox, Tomás. See who wants what."

"They call them *refrigerators* now," he says, smirking.

"You can bring a beer for *me*," I say, "from the *icebox*."

Alicia and Martha and I go back to setting our table: boards across sawhorses with Six's Gram's fancy Norwegian tablecloth. They help me bring the bowls of salad from the icebox: tomato and green-onion, potato salad, roasted peppers, and *salsa*. I take the bread out of the oven. It's perfect every time now, not like our old wood stove. The aroma makes me hungry.

Six and our three male workers stand around the grill laughing and sipping their beer. Ramon is only fourteen. I hope Six watches how much the kid drinks.

I hear another car out front. Going back in the house, I look out the front window. It's Zeke Jackson in an old Ford sedan from the 1930s. Six would probably know the exact year. I go out back again. Alicia asks where the silverware is and I point her to the drawer in the kitchen sideboard.

"Six," I holler. "Zeke's out front."

He gets Tomás to keep an eye on the grill. Our new summer worker, Ramon, chases Nicky around the yard. Diego comes up on the porch for another beer from the stash of beer and Cokes on ice in the washtub.

Six and Zeke come up the driveway and enter the back yard. They have an arm around each other's shoulders. It's hard to tell who's got the bigger grin.

"This is our army buddy Ezekiel Jackson," Six says to our other guests.

"I go by Zeke," our friend says.

Going down the back steps, I hug Zeke and slap his back.

"I'm sure glad to see you, buddy," I say. "How was the drive down from Oklahoma?"

"Long and dusty," he says, "unless you wanna keep the windows rolled up. Took ten hours."

"Lemme get you a beer to wet your whistle, Zeke."

"Gracias," he says.

I return with a sweating-cold Dos Equis. He toasts me and Six.

Everyone welcomes Zeke, even little Nicky. But Ramon turns aside and keeps to himself. I excuse myself and go to have a talk with the teenager. I feel kind of strange. I'm only two years beyond being a teenager myself.

"Are you having a good time, Ramon?" I ask.

He nods. He's out of breath after chasing Nicky around. The little one won't run out of gas for another few hours—even without a nap.

"Six and I invited you because we like you, Ramon. We're sort of a family at Mila-Grow, you know, huh? My partner and I started working there when we were your age.

"Let me introduce you to our other guests, so you'll feel at home."

I put my hand on his shoulder and walk him over to where Zeke is chatting with Martha and Alicia. The girls return to the porch where they set out the plates and silverware and napkins.

"This is the newest member of our crew—Ramon," I tell our army buddy.

"Pleased to meet you, son," Zeke says, extending his hand.

The boy looks down at our friend's hand, but he remains motionless. I pinch his shoulder muscle hard enough to make his arm flinch.

"Sorry," he says, returning the Negro's handshake. "I'm a little sore from work."

"Wait'll you go in the army. The toughest job you've got now will seem like lolling in a hammock."

I release my grip on Ramon's shoulder.

"Listen, kiddo," Zeke says to him. "Would you do me a favor? I've got a basket of my grandma's fried chicken in the car. Special delivery. It's on the floor in back, under some blankets to keep it cool. Would you please get it for me?"

I happen to know Ramon is partial to fried chicken.

"Zeke counted the number of pieces, Ramon," I warn him.

The teenager looks at me, unsure how to take my remark. Then he grins.

"Nice kid," Zeke says.

"Most of the time," I reply.

"About like any of us at that age, I expect," my friend says.

"I guess I'd nearly forgotten what I was like. Want another beer?"

"I'll get it," he says. "I'm gonna go pester Six for a while."

The charcoal smoke and the aromas of the cooking food make me famished.

Our next guests to arrive are our former Calle Alegre neighbors Señor Vigil and his daughter, Hermione. I'm guessing Vigil is as old as all our ages added up.

Nicky runs to Hermione. She takes his hands and they dance around as though circling an unseen maypole. Our back yard is almost crowded with all the people who've come to help my amigo and me celebrate our twenty-first birthdays.

* * *

It is time to pick Mrs. Hinkle up in her own car and drive her to our party. I hold the door for her the way the chauffeur did for the archbishop.

"You are an old-fashioned gentleman like my husband, Antonio. You make a woman feel special."

I smile.

"It's just the good manners my papa and my Tio taught me, ma'am."

"Many are taught; few are learned. You learned well, young man."

The half-mile from her house to ours takes no time at all driving. I am mostly opening and closing car doors and holding out my hand for Mrs. Hinkle to take hold of. She tucks her arm in the crook of my elbow as we walk from the driveway to the back yard.

Nicky, helping his papa at the grill, is the first to see us. He holds his hand out. "*Abuela*," he says. I've no idea where he learned that word since we have no grandma's left in our family. The boy picks up words like a horseshoe magnet attracting nails.

Six introduces Mrs. Hinkle to our other guests. Zeke brings her a chair and sets it in the shade. She tells me she wouldn't mind a cold beer. Ramon brings it to her, an opportunity to get a second for himself. I warn him to go slow.

My amigo announces that the food on the grill is finished cooking. I clang the triangular bell on the back porch. Nicky comes running. He has to help me ring the dinner bell again. We take our places at the table. We're elbow-to-elbow.

Six asks Señor Vigil, as the oldest person at our party, to say our grace.

"Oh, my," he says. "I haven't prayed in a very long time, *mis hijos*."

"I help you," Nicky says, patting his arm. The oldest and the youngest sit next to each other.

"Thank you, baby Jesus. Gracias, *Santa Madre*," Nicky says. "Come and get it," he shouts, looking up at the sky.

Everyone laughs. "Thank you, Nicolás," Vigil tells him.

"You welcome."

Six mashes up half a tamale for the boy and puts a blob of potato salad on his plate.

"Gracias, Papa."

"You're welcome, kiddo."

The rest of us pass the bowls and platters and smatterings of conversations back and forth. We are a lively and friendly bunch. It makes me feel good to be among all our friends with my best friend. Mrs. Hinkle and Vigil seem engrossed in getting to know each other. They both have a sparkle in their eyes. Nicky has latched onto our army buddy.

"Are you a chocolate man?" he asks Zeke.

It is suddenly quiet. I think we're waiting to hear his answer. Zeke puts down his drumstick, wipes his mouth, and smiles at the boy.

"No, Nicky. I'm a person, just like you. My skin's a different color, that's all."

"Oh," the boy says. "I like chocolate."

Everyone smiles.

"I think we all like chocolate, young man," Mrs. Hinkle tells him.

"I should hope so," Nicky says, parroting a phrase he's heard some place. He uses his fingers to put a chunk of tamale onto his spoon.

* * *

After our birthday feast, no one is ready for dessert just yet. The guys from work open another beer. Alicia and Martha have Cokes. Nicky's babysitter brings out her *biscochitos*, "In case," as she put it, "you've got an empty corner in your tummies."

Nicky takes one from her, remembering his *Gracias* this time.

Six brings out the still unopened bottle of Presidente brandy he got for Hypatia's visit two Christmases ago. He is joined by Vigil, Tomás, Diego, and Zeke in downing a shot glass in a single gulp. I ask Six to fill mine just halfway. He pours another round.

Alicia brings out the three-layer chocolate cake she baked. There are twenty-one candles on top.

"You'll just have to share," she tells me and Six. "Any more candles and we'd melt the frosting."

"My birthday cake would burn the house down," Mrs. Hinkle says.

She's a very funny old lady. Six and I like her a lot. Our guests do, too.

Not to be outdone, Vigil says, "My cake would set fire to the whole neighborhood. I go back so far, I'm in front of me."

The rendition of *Happy Birthday* that our friends sing for us is pretty good. They are a nice mix of voices. They sound almost professional, quite different from the Visitors' screeching and discordant performance for Nicky's birthday at the hospital last December. My ears are still ringing.

My amigo and I lean down to blow out the candles. Nicky, of course, has to help us.

"Good job," Six tells his son, even though he provided most of the hot air.

We sit down to our birthday cake. Rather than insisting he use a spoon, Six lets the boy have at it with his hands. Nicky uses both of them. The whole table watches him, adding to our own delight.

"Careful, Nick. You'll get some in you mouth," his papa tells him.

We all laugh, including Nicky. He has more chocolate frosting on his face than he ever got past his lips.

Our buddy Zeke hands us an envelope that looks like a greeting card. He's not sure which of us to hand it to.

"We told everyone not to get us anything, Jackson," Six tells him. "The best gift any of you can give us is your continued friendship."

"It's not from me," Jackson says. "I didn't notice the envelope at first. Somebody must have left it on the front seat when I went inside the filling station to use the bathroom."

"I recognize the handwriting," I tell him. "It's from a friend of ours."

"How'd he know where I was gonna gas up? You've got some pretty strange friends, Sanchez."

"That's why we like *you* so much, Jackson," Six says, slapping his shoulder.

"You've gotta be strange to be their friends," Tomás chimes in. "A birthday toast," he proposes. "*Que vivas por el resto de tu vida.* May you live for the rest of your lives."

Zeke and Vigil join him in having another shot. The brandy bottle's nearly a third empty. I'm happy everybody is having a good time.

* * *

Little by little, our birthday guests drift home, like clouds dispersing at sunset. It is after eight o'clock and growing dark. Hermione has put Nicky to bed in his crib in our bedroom. He still fits in the crib I made for him, but not for much longer.

Zeke Jackson will be staying with us for a few days before he goes back home to Oklahoma. He'll be sleeping up in Nicky's room.

Our old neighbor, Vigil, drives our new neighbor, Mrs. Hinkle, home when the party breaks up. I think they have each made a new friend. I'm happy for them. Hermione sits between them like the chaperone.

The work crew, Tomás and Diego and Ramon, drive home in Tomás's pickup. Diego, who enjoyed just a single shot of brandy, takes the wheel. Last to leave are Alicia and Martha. Six and I walk them to Alicia's old sandblasted Buick, parked in front of the house on Alameda Street. Zeke runs to catch up with us.

"Your son has a gift, Six," Martha tells my amigo. "He asked me if missed Barkly, my dog. Barkly died two days ago. I hadn't told anyone yet."

"Yeah, we're pretty aware of Nicky's gift," Six replies. "But what it means or how he can best use it remains a mystery."

"There is a holy man at the Nubes de Tormenta Pueblo, Six. He is a Catholic friar. I think he could help you explore Nicky's talent."

"Do you mean Brother Asinus by any chance?" I ask.

"Yes. Do you boys know him?"

"We do indeed," Six says. "We've known the brother for a few years. He has been very good to Antonio and me."

"Then you are in the best hands," Martha tells him. "And so is the boy, with such a loving father and uncle."

My amigo and Zeke open the car doors for the girls and help them get in.

"The Brother's birthday will be coming up soon," Martha tells us. "Many of the old ones among my people believe he will be a hundred-thirty-eight years old this year."

"What?" we all say at once.

"He doesn't look a day over a hundred-twenty-five," Six adds.

We laugh. It is a wonderful way to close the evening. We are so blessed in our friends.

Zeke shakes Martha's hand. I see two smiles in the moonlight. It's one of the best birthdays I remember because everybody around me is happy—and we are all so fortunate to know one another.

CHAPTER TWELVE

SEMPER DECRESCIS AUT CRESCIS
Ever Losing, Ever Gaining

"Uncle Zeke. Aunt Martha," Nicky shouts, running to the back door.

We are celebrating Nicky's fifth birthday a few days late so we can also usher in 1951 with our friends. It is a year-and-a-half since Zeke met Martha at our twenty-first birthday party. They've been engaged for a year, around the same time Zeke began working at Mila-Grow Nursery & Greenhouse. My amigo and I now are the new owners.

Everyone has had supper at home. We will be enjoying Nicky's chocolate birthday cake, homemade by Martha. Six's grandparents' refrigerator is cold enough to keep ice cream, too—strawberry ice cream, of course.

Our old army pal sets two wrapped packages on the kitchen table: a thin squarish one and a squat oblong one.

"Is that for me?" Nicky asks, jumping up and down.

"Well, they were," Zeke tells him, "but since we missed your actual birthday this year, I'm afraid you'll have to wait until next year, kiddo. I'm sorry."

"No, Uncle Zeke," he protests. "Please. You can't do that."

Six takes Zeke's jacket and Martha's blanket coat and puts them on our bed. Nicky touches his presents with one finger. Six returns in time to catch him at it.

"That's cheating, Nicky," his father tells him.

"Forty-eight crayons, six times eight," he says. "Gee whiz. Thank you, Uncle Zeke. Thanks for the drawing paper, Aunt Martha. Can I open them now, Papa?"

"Better ask your aunt and uncle."

"Sure. Go ahead, Nicky," Zeke tells him.

The boy tears open the wrapping paper excitedly. He thanks Zeke and Martha all over again. My amigo and I present our joint gift to Nicky.

"Oh, boy," he says, "charcoals—like for sketches. Gracias, Papa. Thank you, Tio."

He opens the box of charcoals. Since Nicky expressed an interest in drawing, we discussed with our friends what to get the boy for his birthday.

Six and Zeke each have a beer. Martha and I share one. Nicky asks for apple juice. We go into the parlor. Six stirs the fireplace embers and adds two piñon logs.

Martha and Zeke share the couch. Six and I sit in the armchairs. We sip our beer. Nicky sits on the short stool beside the fireplace and puts the drawing tablet on his lap. He takes out a handful of crayons and the box of charcoals, and begins drawing lines and squiggles.

"So have you two decided where you're gonna set up house?" Six asks Zeke and Martha.

"No, not yet," our army buddy replies.

"Yes, we have," Martha says.

"Oh? When did we decide that?" Zeke asks.

"I guess it's unanimous then," Six jokes.

"I told you I don't mind living on the Nubes de Tormenta Pueblo, Martha."

"Yes, but I mind. I want a house with running water and electricity."

"But I really like your family, honey."

"Sure you do. They're crazy about you. You're their buffalo soldier. But I want a telephone."

I feel as though Six and I were listening in on another couple's argument on the party line.

"We'll discuss this later, honey," Zeke says.

"What's to discuss? My mind's made up. You can bury me on the pueblo, but I am not living there."

Nicky picks that moment to interrupt our conversation so he can show us his drawing. *Saved by the bell*, I think.

"My God, Nick. Where'd you learn to draw like that?" Six says.

Like the rest of us, he's clearly astounded by his son's color sketch of the four grown-ups in the parlor. The subjects of the boy's study have their arms and hands raised in conversation. There is nothing static about his depiction. You can almost hear our friends' brewing argument.

"You'd better sign it," Martha tells him.

"Can you help me, Auntie?" the boy asks.

"Sure. Bring it over here, Nicky. I think a red signature would look very nice."

"Yes," the boy says. "Red."

It strikes me as odd that Nicky has to be helped with his crooked block letters on a sketch that looks like he took drawing lessons. After signing his crayon-and-charcoal picture, Nicky presents it to his papa.

"Oh, thank you, Nick. It's beautiful. I'll have to get it framed, won't I?"

"Yes," the boy says, nodding his head.

"How about some birthday cake?" Martha asks.

"Yes, please," we all say at once. Like ducklings, we follow her into the kitchen.

Martha makes the tastiest pies and cakes and breads in her clay oven at home. I wonder if she'd do as well with a modern gas oven.

Six lifts his son onto a kitchen chair and ties a red bandana around the boy's neck. We sit down around the table.

Martha lights the five candles atop the cake and everyone, including the birthday boy, sings *Happy Birthday*. He stands up in his chair and leans forward to blow out the candles. We applaud.

Nicky holds his spoon in anticipation of a slice of chocolate birthday cake with a scoop of strawberry ice cream coming his way. He gets the first plate and dives in immediately. The boy manages to get most of it into his mouth this year.

The four grown-ups ask for a second slice of cake, polishing off half of it.

"It's almost nine o'clock, my little man," Six tells his son. "Time to say *Good night* to everyone."

Six lifts him out of the chair. He washes the boy's chocolatey hands and face with a wet washcloth.

"*Now you will feel no cold*," Nicky tells Zeke and Martha. They look surprised.

"Where'd you hear that one, Nick?" his father asks. "You're like a parrot. I better watch what I say around you."

Nicky gives Zeke and Martha a hug and a kiss. The boy puts his arms around his papa's neck and kisses him.

"It's your Tio's turn to tuck you in tonight. I love you, my little man."

I hold onto his hand as we climb the stairs to the boy's room. I pull back the covers on his bed. I remember my uncle's charcoal bed-warmer. This would be a good night for one.

After helping the boy get undressed and into his pajamas with feet, I pull the covers up to his chin. I sit in my storytelling chair next to the bed.

"Will you wake me up at midnight, Tio, so I can ring in the New Year."

I laugh. "Do you have a New Year's bell?"

"No, I don't. Can I use the dinner bell, Tio?"

"I don't know. It might make everybody hungry for the whole year, you know, huh?" I tell him.

"Really?"

"Why would I kid you, Nick?"

"To make me laugh."

"I don't need jokes for that," I say, reaching beneath the covers and tickling his ribs.

He giggles. I kiss his forehead and ruffle his hair.

"Good night, Tio."

"Good night, Nicky. May God's angels watch over you," I say, closing the door.

Though I know firsthand what a load of work children are, I can understand why people like having them around. Our lives would be so much poorer without little Nicky.

I go back downstairs to the parlor. Six has stoked the fire with a couple more logs. He has brought the bottles of tequila and brandy and set them on the coffee table with a tray of large and small glasses.

"Did you find out what Nicky was talking about?" Six asks me.

"I didn't ask him."

"*Now you will feel no cold*, is a line from an Apache wedding blessing," Zeke tells us. "The next line is, *For each of you will be warmth to the other*. Martha and I got married today—on the pueblo."

"Oh, my God," Six exclaims. "How did Nicky know that?"

"I think he's graduated from guessing animal crackers," Martha says. "I'm glad he didn't spoil our surprise."

"Congratulations," Six says, getting up from his chair. I stand, too.

"God bless you both," I tell them.

The newlyweds get up from the sofa. Six and I join them, the four of us with our arms around one another. Our eyes glint with merriment in the firelight.

I kiss Martha and slap Zeke's back. Six shakes his hand, and hugs and kisses Martha.

Mi mejor amigo and I have never kissed in front of anyone. My heart pounding, I lean across our circle of friends and kiss Six on the mouth. He does not flinch, as though he expected it. He looks right into my eyes and flashes his blue eye and brown eye back and forth at me.

Martha and Zeke smile at us. Six proposes a toast of tequila to the newlyweds. He knows to fill mine halfway. Zeke proposes another toast to "longtime best buddies—Six and Antonio." I down another half glass. It feels good going down, but it goes right back up to my head.

Six brings a round of beer for everyone. Again, Martha and I share one. The mantle clock chimes ten.

"Are you guys ever gonna level with me about what happened the night Six got shot?" Zeke asks. "I hope you trust me by now."

"We always trusted you, Zeke," Six tells him.

"The army doc got me pretty doped up," our pal says. "I knew it, but I couldn't do anything about it. After a while, it was easier to tell them what they wanted to hear, you know, huh?"

"Yeah, we know," I tell him. "We just didn't want you getting in trouble because of us."

Zeke continues. "The drug got everything jumbled up in my head. I didn't know what was real any more.

"I have kept a journal since I was fourteen. My grandma told me it's important to remember the past, our history as persons and as a people. The account of that night in my notebook did not jibe with the confession I put my signature on. I believe my journal."

"So what did your own eyes tell you happened, Zeke?" Six asks him.

"Let me apologize to Martha first," our buddy says.

"I am sorry I did not share everything with you, my love. But now that we are married, I want to share all of my life with you."

"Is this about the crashed spaceship?" Martha asks.

"How do you know about that?" I ask, astounded.

"It was in the *Roswell Register* a couple days later," Martha says. "The article said the airfield captured a 'flying saucer.'"

"Of course, a couple days after *that*, they said it was only a weather balloon after all."

"I saw a huge crashed disk," Zeke tells us. "It was silvery, a flying saucer. The army wanted me to say I saw a Russian spy plane—so that's what I finally reported: a plane whose wings broke off."

"A wise move," Six says. "Otherwise they might still be 'debriefing' you."

The clock on the mantle gongs eleven. Everyone looks up. Six pours some brandy in each of four small glasses shaped like tulip buds. We each take a sip. Martha makes a face.

"I know why my people called it *firewater*," she says, shuddering. "So then what really happened that night, guys?"

"A flying ship from another world, a world far away, crashed in a thunderstorm," I say. "It happened out by Foster's Ranch."

Zeke and Six nod their heads. Martha looks astonished.

"I told Bragg I saw you talking to a 'Russian of very short stature,'" Zeke admits to me. "I let him draw his own conclusion. Bragg was with some outfit called 'Majestic 12.' I never heard of it."

"I was talking to one of the Visitors," I tell Zeke. "He told me the army had recovered the body of one of his companions. He asked me to retrieve it from the army field hospital tent."

"Oh, my God," Zeke shouts. "So the rumors were true. Do you know where the Visitor's body is now?"

"The Visitor's body is on the pueblo," Six tells them. "It's in the care of Brother Asinus."

He looks at Zeke and his new bride.

"Are you serious?" Zeke asks. "*You* took the corpse that went missing that night?"

"No, Antonio did. He brought it to the chapel—where it still is."

It is Martha's turn to say, "Oh, my God."

Zeke takes her hand.

"The *ancianos* among my people say that the Sky People have been visiting humans since the Great Spirit put us on the Earth," she tells us "They are our brothers and sisters—our helpers. This is such a remarkable story. Why have you and Antonio been keeping it secret all this time?"

Six and I look at each other.

"The Visitors asked us to wait," Six tells our friends. "They were not ready to reveal their presence here when their ship crashed. We will wait until they say it's OK to tell the world."

"I don't know how you can keep such a thing quiet," Martha says excitedly. "I'd be blabbing the news to anybody who'd listen."

"That's why the Sky People came to Six and Antonio, dear, and not you."

Martha puts on a pouting face, but she winds up laughing. She gives her new groom a playful punch on the arm—and then a kiss.

We hear the half-hour chime. It is 11:30.

Martha opens a sack of pretzels and one of potato chips. She spills them into bowls she brings to the coffee table. She has made guacamole, too, that she serves with homemade tortilla chips. Six and Zeke have a little more brandy. Martha took only one sip of her brandy. She joins me in sharing one more beer.

"Should we call Nicky down for midnight?" I ask Six.

My amigo looks over at our friends.

"Yes, of course," Martha replies. "He's such a sweet child," she says, looking over at Six.

"All right," my amigo remarks. "I can tell I've already been outvoted."

As Six goes upstairs to collect his son, Martha brings out the other paper sack she brought. It contains silvery, glittery party hats, noisemakers, streamers and confetti, small horns, and paper leis.

From Nicky's sleepy-eyed expression, it looks like he might have sooner stayed in bed. He looks cranky. Six sets him down. The boy rubs his eyes and yawns.

"Only ten minutes to midnight," Zeke announces.

"Thanks for the warning," Six says. "Will you get the glasses, Antonio? I'm gonna get the champagne. I left it to chill on the back porch."

"Champagne?" Martha asks. "I've never tasted champagne."

"From California," I reply, getting the special glasses that Six's Gramps had for champagne. It will be my first taste, too.

Martha passes out the hats and leis and noisemakers. She helps Nicky put on his hat and stretches the elastic beneath his chin. The boy watches his father untwist the wire cage from around the champagne cork.

"Go get your popgun, cowpoke," Six tells his son.

I turn on the radio. "Five minutes to midnight," our local announcer says.

We stand around the coffee table trying not to look as ridiculous as we actually are in our silly party favors. Nicky looks up at us.

"Two minutes to 1951."

We smile at one another.

"Get ready, Nick," Six tells him.

The five-year-old sticks the cork, tethered to its string, into the muzzle of his toy rifle. He pumps it furiously. Six takes the cage off the champagne cork and loosens the cork with his thumbs.

"One minute," the announcer says, ticking off the seconds to midnight.

"Why's he counting backwards?" Nicky asks.

"Because after the count of *One* it will be midnight," I tell him, "a brand New Year."

Oh," he says, aiming the toy gun at the ceiling as he's been told to do in the house.

"*Four-three-two-one...* Pop! Happy New Year! Pop!"

Six pours the champagne without letting it overflow. I bring a cup of apple juice for Nicky. We sing *Auld Lang Syne* along with the radio and toast to our health and friendship. The champagne bubbles tickle my nose and kind of take my breath away, but it's refreshing.

My amigo shakes Zeke's hand, and kisses me and Martha and Nicky. Hugs and kisses and handshakes pass around and back and forth until I am dizzy. Nicky reloads his popgun.

"Take that you squirrely varmint," he says. We laugh.

"Six is taking him squirrel hunting tomorrow," I explain.

"Time to get back to bed, cowpoke," Six tells his son. "You need to be bright-eyed in the morning."

"Yes, Papa. Will you sing me good-night?"

"What? It's not enough your uncle and me tell you stories. You gotta have songs, too?"

"I'll sing you to sleep, little one," Martha tells him. "Say *Good night* to everyone."

Nicky hugs and kisses everyone *Good night*, throwing in *Happy New Year*, too. He takes Martha's hand and they go up the stairs.

"Care for a little more bubbly?" Six asks.

"Sure," Zeke replies.

"Half," I say. The champagne has gone to my head faster than the brandy. I gobble more guacamole and chips.

Martha's beautiful voice drifts down from Nicky's room like mist creeping gently down the mountainside. It is a simple melody, but haunting. It seems familiar, too, from a place at the back of my mind. I try to remember.

"Is that Dineh she's singing?" I ask Zeke and Six.

"You mean Navajo?" Six replies. "Can't be. My Gram used to sing that lullaby to me."

"My grandma, too," Zeke tells us. "She told me it was from an old Negro spiritual."

"What's going on?" I ask. "I remember my mother singing that song to me—in Spanish."

We put down our empty champagne glasses.

"It starts out with something about three strangers, three wanderers," Zeke tells us.

"Right," Six says. "They traveled in three ships."

"I heard they rode three horses," I remark.

"Me, too," Zeke says. "And they bear three treasure chests."

"Remember Dr. Feynman's visit, Six, when he had a little too much of your Gramps' *glögg*? He started singing the Jewish lullaby his mother sang to *him*. It's the same tune."

"Yeah, but I thought Dr. Feynman said it was Swedish," my amigo replies.

Martha rejoins us after tucking Nicky in. She jumps right into our conversation.

"The lullaby is common to many people, Six. It is very old—as old as mothers and children and the coming of night. The verses tell about the Sky People. They bring three gifts to humankind: compassion, forgiveness, and laughter."

"That has my vote," Six says. "And now I actually *get* to vote."

Though we've all heard Six's remark before, we laugh until we are out of breath. I guess the champagne has made us bubbly, too. We put our arms around one another. It is a wonderful way to welcome the New Year.

After we've made and finished off a pot of strong coffee in his Gram's electric percolator, we decide Zeke is in good enough shape to drive home. I'm glad Six and I do not have to travel any further than our bedroom. It's one in the morning.

We wave to our friends from the back porch. It's a cold night, but the fresh air feels good. We put our hands in our overalls. There's enough moonlight to see our breath. We lean toward one another and give each other a steamy kiss.

2

Six helps Nicky set up the brass telescope he got from the boy's mother, Hypatia, on the rear porch. I go pick up Nicky's school friend Bjorn. Nicky's chum is also part Norwegian, but Six doesn't know the family.

"So do you also have an interest in astronomy, Bjorn?" I ask him on the way back to the house.

"You can call me *Bear*, Mr. Sanchez. Everyone does. That's what my name means."

He looks nothing like a bear—not even a cub. He's light-haired and skinny. Nicky's half-a-head taller even though they're both ten years old.

"So do you like looking at the sky, Bear?"

"Sure. I even got my own constellation: the Great Bear, you know, huh?"

"*Ursa Major* is a she-bear, son," I tell him.

"You sure, Mr. Sanchez?"

"Pretty sure. You can ask Nicky's father. He's the astronomer in the family."

I park our new old pickup, a 1950 dark blue Ford, in the back yard. We still have my Tio's 1934 hand-painted turquoise pickup stored at the back of the barn. Six thinks he can get it going again with parts from the second pickup he bought from a fellow on the pueblo.

Bjorn takes his sleeping bag from the front seat and rushes up the back steps to join Six and Nicky at the telescope. I take my birthday present for Nicky from beneath the seat. It's one place I figured it might be safe from the boy's second-sighted snooping. I wrapped it at work in brown paper. I tuck it beneath my dirty work jacket. I got him "The Boy Scientist," a book by *Popular Mechanics* about experiments using everyday things. Dr. Feynman recommended it.

It looks like I will have to wait in line to get a glimpse through the brass spyglass. Instead I slip into the house and hide the book for Nicky on the very top of the sideboard—completely out of sight and out of reach for the ten-year-old.

I fill a saucepan with apple cider from the gallon jug and drop in a few cloves and a stick of cinnamon. Cooking with gas, the cider boils in no time. I fill three mugs for the back-porch astronomers and carry them out on a tray.

"Thanks, amigo," Six says, cradling the steaming mug in his cupped hands.

"Gracias, Tio," Nicky says. His chum thanks me, too.

"I'm gonna leave you boys to it," Six tells them. "The Pleiades will be rising soon—right about over there," he says, pointing.

We go into the warm, steamy kitchen.

"This feels nice," Six says. "Astronomers have been freezing their *patoots* off since the beginning of time, you know, huh?"

"For a greater good," I tell him.

We hang our jackets on the pegs and sit down at the table for more apple cider.

Bjorn comes into the kitchen from the porch. He stands at the sink, then goes over to the stove, and finally the sideboard where he inspects our dishes.

"Are you looking for something, Bjorn?" I ask him.

"Me? Nah. I just came in to get warm," he says, standing at the table. "Mr. Sanchez told me Ursa Major is a she-bear. Is that true, Mr. Thorson?"

"Yes, son," Six tells him. "And Ursa Minor is a she-cub."

"Oh, darn," the boy says. "The Great Bear was *my* constellation. My name means *bear*."

"Why can't you admire a she-bear, Bjorn? There's no creature more fierce than a bear protecting her cubs. You should value the best traits of both boys and girls, don't you think?"

"Well, maybe," Nicky's friend replies.

"Would you like some more hot cider?" Six asks him.

"Sure, Mr. Thorson. I'll go get my mug."

The boy returns with his empty mug. Nicky follows him, carrying his own.

"Are you finished stargazing for the night, Nick?" Six asks his son. "Did you cover the telescope?"

"No, I forgot, Papa. I'll go do it now."

While Nicky goes out to the porch, the rest of us prepare our surprise.

The boy returns to a darkened kitchen illuminated by the glow from ten birthday candles. We break into a rendition of *Happy Birthday* unaccompanied by curlicue trumpets and head-rattling gongs. Nicky blows out the candles. I turn on the lights.

Six refills our mugs with apple cider and slices the chocolate cake I baked. I reach atop the sideboard to retrieve Nicky' present. It's the wrong one— a different one. This one is wrapped in birthday paper. I find mine, too, in brown paper. They are the same size.

Bjorn takes his package from his jacket pocket and hands it to his chum. "It's a ten-power magnifying glass," Nicky's friend says, "before you get a chance to tell me what I bought."

"Thanks," Nicky tells his pal, looking at him with one huge eye. They laugh.

"Like *Rootie Kazootie, Boy Detective*," Bjorn remarks.

"Have you been using your gift in front of other people, Nick? I thought we had an agreement. You promised Brother Asinus, too."

"I'm sorry, Papa. I can't help it sometimes. I try not to listen, but some people are loudmouths, you know, huh?"

He nudges his pal.

"I think it's kinda cool, Mr. Thorson. It spooks the other kids, but I think it's cool. It sure comes in handy when I've lost something or left it behind."

"I wish you'd be more careful, Nick," his father tells him. "Now we'll have to cut that memory out of Bjorn's brain to make him forget."

Father and son trade glances.

"He doesn't have much brain to spare, Papa. You better be careful. You remember what happened to my other friend."

We all laugh, but I know Nicky is in store for a stern lecture once his birthday has passed.

Nicky opens the present from his father next. It's also a book—but not the same one I got him. *Phew!*

"What is this?" Nicky asks, flipping through the pages. "All the words are erased."

"It's a blank journal, Nick. It's empty until you write or sketch something in it. You'll thank me some day. Ask your Tio or your Uncle Zeke what to write in it. They'll help you."

"Gracias, Papa."

Nicky tears the brown paper off my present to him.

"Gee willikers. Thank you, Tio. I read a couple chapters at the library, but it was always out."

He shows the cover of "The Boy Scientist" to his school chum.

"You sure are one lucky kid," Bjorn tells him.

"Now you're telling *me* something I already know," Nicky says, smiling. "Can we go upstairs to play, Papa?" he asks his father.

"No seconds on the cake?" Six asks them.

"No, thanks," Nicky and Bjorn say at the same time.

"All right, you boys are excused. No shooting off fireworks in your room."

"Fireworks?" Bjorn asks, stopping in his tracks. Nicky nudges his friend.

"He's kidding," he says. "You'll get used to it."

The boys run up the stairs, sounding like a herd of stampeding hooves. The bedroom door slams. Then Bjorn thunders down again.

"Forgot my sleeping bag," he says sheepishly, before clattering back up the stairs. The door closes softly this time.

"I'm gonna get some fresh air before turning in," Six says. "Wanna join me?"

"Sure," I reply. "Lemme get my jacket."

He opens the kitchen door.

"Oh, no. Six," I shout. "The barn's caught fire."

I fly down the back steps with no more than my bare hands to carry water. I unlatch the barn door, forgetting that air feeds a fire. I turn to look for Six.

"Hah. I'm glad you got fooled for a change," he tells me.

I look back at the barn expecting to see it engulfed in flames. The Holy Mother stands just inside the wide doorway, framed by an open barndoor on either side and the old hayloft above. It makes me think of an advent calendar. I fall to my knees on the frozen ground. Six kneels beside me. We bow low before her beauty.

"Arise, my children," she says.

"Nicky is upstairs," Six tells the Blessed Virgin. "Shall I call him down?"

"No, Sixtus. My message is for just the two of you this time. Nicolás

290 • BRIAN ALLAN SKINNER

probably does not remember our last visit. He was only four years old. I do not wish to worry the boy."

"Worry him, Holy Mother?" Six asks.

"Yes, my children. I shall be going away for a time. Nicolás has already lost one mother from his life. It might be best if he doesn't remember me until I return. I do not want the boy to feel that he has been abandoned."

"Going away?" I ask.

"Yes. There are more of God's children elsewhere in the Universe who need our instruction and succor, Antonio. I shall be traveling with the Visitors aboard their ship."

"Do you mean our friends from Alpha Carinae will be leaving as well?" Six asks her.

"Not all of them, Sixtus. A few of their Katalysts will remain behind to work with Dr. Feynman. But their entire fleet of intergalactic craft will be journeying to another world."

Six puts his arm around me.

"The sky will be empty," he tells the Blessed Virgin. "We shall be all alone again."

Her smile lights up the air around her.

"You have each other and little Nicolás and all those who love you. God and His Angels watch over you. Please. You must get on with your lives and not wait for us to come back. I shall not be long, *mis hijos*."

"But... But..." Six and I sputter.

"You have both proved your strength and fortitude in adversity. Like the Prophet Job, you bore up and remained faithful to the Lord. I have every confidence that all will be well until our return."

The Holy Mother holds her hands out to us. She drifts forward from the barn.

"The Lord be with you," she says.

"And with thy spirit," we reply.

Santa Madre ascends from the ground, lighting up the chilly air around her. Up and up she rises until she reaches the treetops and then floats higher still. She becomes a glowing point of light lost among the ocean of stars washing across the sky.

My amigo and I, our arms still wrapped around one another, stare up at the winter sky, Orion the Hunter tracking over the horizon. My neck aches.

"I'm not sure I care for being left on our own, Six. It's frightening to think there's no one we can call on for help."

"I didn't hear that God was taking a vacation, did you?"

I chuckle. "No, I guess not."

Six and I shiver. We rushed out to the barn before putting our jackets on.

"Come on," he says. "Time to warm each other up."

We turn to go back to the house. We notice Nicky's light is still on. A pair of hand shadow-puppets scamper across the window shade. I turn to Six.

"Remember?" we say at the same time.

I smile. He puts one of his shadow-puppets in the back pocket of my Levi's. He's a frisky little fellow.

* 3 *

"How do you know when you love somebody, Pop?" Nicky asks his father at supper.

My amigo and I glance at each other.

"When you no longer have to ask that question," Six replies.

"Oh," Nicky says.

"Is this about Margaret?" Six asks his son.

"How do you know about Margaret?"

"All I had to do was open my eyes, Nick. When I picked you two up from the basketball game in Las Cruces, I could almost hear the butterflies in your stomach. And Margaret looked at you in that way that is reserved for a sweetheart—whether or not the *sweetheart* notices."

"Don't I get to have any secrets, Pop?"

"Oh. Now the shoe's on the other foot, huh, Nick? It was funny when you eavesdropped on other people's thoughts, wasn't it?"

"I told you, Pop. Most of the time I can't help overhearing. Most people think way too much and way too loud."

The doorbell rings. We finished our supper just in time. Nicky answers the door while Six and I clear the table.

It is Nicky's pal Bjorn and another kid I haven't met. Nicky introduces us.

"This is my Tio Antonio. You already know my father. This is Malcolm—from my American history class."

"Pleased to meet you, sir," the boy says, extending his hand.

They are all good-looking kids, handsome in their own way. I think the boys and girls in our class at Roswell High were less attractive. Or maybe we all just felt that way.

"Until what time do you want your Tio and me to stay lost, kiddo?" Six asks his son.

"My friends all told their parents to pick them up at midnight."

"You got it, Nick. Remember. No fireworks in the house."

"Fireworks in the house?" Malcolm asks, incredulous.

"He's joking," Nicky tells his friend. "We only shoot clay pigeons indoors."

Like son, like father, I think.

My amigo and I grab our winter work jackets and head out. On the way to the pickup we meet Margaret and her father, and another girl. Margaret is quite

292 • BRIAN ALLAN SKINNER

a stunner.

* * *

Though Six and I don't go to the tavern very often—preferring to drink at home—when we do, The Ornery Burro on Main Street is our favorite bar.

"Guess the wind was blowin' right today, fellas. Good to see you boys," Lloyd the bartender says. "What can I get youse?"

"A coupla Dos Equis," I say.

He opens the icebox beneath the bar and snaps the caps off our beers.

"Well lookee here," a guy a few stools over says. "Slap my britches if it ain't Romeo and Julio."

It is Jorge Carbón—the bully from our graduating class. He's a little thicker around the middle and a little shinier on top. I was never so unhappy to see anyone in my life.

"Here we go again," I remark.

Jorge and the bruiser next to him get up from their stools.

"Why does Jorge have to show up now?" I whisper to Six.

"You got a better time in mind?" he asks, nonchalantly taking a sip of his beer. "Holler if you need help, amigo."

Jorge and the other guy approach, clenching their fists. *Two against one. That's fair*, I think. They face me, narrowing their eyes and frowning.

I smile at them, placing a hand on each of their shoulders, as friendly as I know how to be. I lean in towards them, whispering. They have whiskey on their breath.

"There was something I never got a chance to tell you, Jorge."

"Oh, yeah? What's that, Sanchez?" he snarls.

"Forgive me, Jesus."

With my hands on both their jacket collars, I slam their heads together. Their foreheads ram into one another like bighorn sheep. They crumple to the floor where they stood, like sacks of seed. Not a single glass or bottle or ashtray has been overturned. I dust off my hands and climb back up on the stool next to Six.

"Thanks for being so neat about it, Antonio," the bartender says. "Those two looked like trouble to me as soon as they set foot in here, you know, huh?"

Lloyd comes from behind the bar. He takes hold of Jorge and his buddy one at a time by their jacket collars and drags them out to the curb. They both have bloody noses, and are still out cold. I feel kind of bad. It's cold outside.

Six touches my bottle of beer with his. "Salud, amigo."

"Weren't you worried you'd have to come to my rescue, Six?"

"Nah," he says, grinning his dimples. "You were a soldier in the United States Army. I figured you could handle yourself."

Two well-dressed couples around our age—early thirties, I'm guessing—enter the tavern. They take the booth nearest the jukebox. They are a jolly bunch.

The women are knockouts. Six and I nod to the group.

One couple orders their drinks and the other pair gets up and feeds a couple of nickels into the jukebox. The song they pick is the new kind of music called Rock 'n' Roll. Some of it's not too bad. We learn the tune is by a guy named Chubby Checker. The couple dances to "The Twist."

"It looks to me like they're tryin' to get themselves unstuck from the bog," Six remarks.

It makes me laugh, but the music is too loud for anyone else to hear.

"Aren't you worried about Nicky, Six, and all those teenagers alone in the house."

"Sure I am, amigo. I'm almost terrified. But he's fifteen. If Nicky doesn't know how to be *reasonably* responsible by now, he'll be an old man before he learns. I just have to trust him."

Lloyd sees we have finished our beers and brings us two more. "On the house," he says. We thank him. The next song on the jukebox is "Alley-Oop," a funny song about a caveman. At least it's a quieter tune. Six and I don't have to shout at each other.

"Nicky is a good kid," I tell my amigo. "He really is."

"I know. But good kids can be stupid, too. Look at you and me at their age."

"Speak for yourself," I tell him, beating him to his own punchline for a change. He laughs.

"I want to save him from mistakes, but I've got to cut him some slack, too. It's a tricky balance."

"Kinda like God giving us free will, and just hoping we're not gonna go kill ourselves with it," I remark.

"That's it exactly, amigo. That's it exactly. Come on. Drink up. We're going home."

We swallow the last of our beer and leave The Ornery Burro. "Good night, Lloyd," he says, waving to the bartender.

At least Jorge and the other troublemaker had the sense to take their hell-raising someplace else. We get into the blue pickup.

"It's nowhere near midnight yet, Six," I say pulling away from the curb.

"Yeah, I know, Antonio. We'll park across the road and keep the lights off."

I turn and smile at him. "Kinda like leaning over the edge of a cloud—just to keep an eye on things, huh?"

"Exactly," he says.

It is only eleven o'clock when we get home.

"It's gonna get cold in a hurry with the engine off, Six."

"What do you suggest?" he asks. I see his dimples in the faint moonlight. They tell me he has mischief in mind.

My amigo scoots across the seat and grabs hold of my crotch. He leans over and, lacing his fingers through my hair, he pulls my head back and kisses me with all his might. He massages me slowly through my Levi's until I come in my longjohns. It was kind of quick, but the chance of getting caught made it more intense for me, even though it's pitch-black out and no one could see us anyhow.

We both breath hard. I fumble with the buttons of his overalls and push my hand inside. His hard-on is waiting for me inside his longjohns and it does not take long to bring him to climax. Six flashes his eyes at me and grins.

"That's one way to pass the time," he remarks.

I don't notice the cold any longer. The truck windows are steamed up. The moon is circled by a foggy rainbow halo. We smile at one another.

I start the engine, turn on the lights, and pull into our driveway. Someone's parents drive in just behind us.

"Teenagers think they have all the fun, amigo," Six tells me, punching my shoulder. "But they have been seriously misinformed, you know, huh?"

* * *

The next morning, while Six is having a long, steamy shower, Nicky comes downstairs in his underwear and moccasins. He stands beside my chair at the kitchen table while I drink my coffee. He usually gets dressed before he comes down. I look up at him. He seems on the verge of tears. After his birthday party, he went to bed on top of the world last night.

I get up from my chair, careful not to step on his foot in my workboots. He puts his arms around me and sobs.

"What is it, Nicky? What happened?"

"Oh, Tio. I'm so sorry."

"About what? Tell me."

"I don't want to say anything in front of Pop. I had a dream last night, Tio. I dreamt your mama died—in the hospital, I think."

"She was in a state mental hospital, Nicky. They never allowed me to visit her. Do you think the dream was real?"

He nods and forces a smile. "Please don't tell my Pop, Tio. I'm not sure how he feels about dreams, you know, huh?"

"Don't worry, Nick. I'll say I got a telephone call from the hospital. Thank you for telling me this, *mi amado sobrino*."

I haven't heard that term since my aunt and uncle called me their beloved nephew. It sounds peculiar coming out of my own mouth. It's time I dusted the expression off.

"I was an orphan whose mother was still alive, just like you, Nicky," I tell him, getting choked up myself. "I am happy my mother has gone to her rest."

We hear Six coming out of the bathroom down the hallway. My beloved nephew tiptoes back upstairs and softly shuts his door.

* 4 *

Today is Nicky's twentieth birthday. He flies through the kitchen door. Slamming it behind him, he leans against it as though to barricade himself inside. He is out of breath. Six and I look up. We are having a beer at the kitchen table.

"The devil chasing you again, Nick?" his father asks him.

"I don't know, Pop."

Despite his exertion and the cold weather, Nicky's face is pale. He looks scared to death.

Six gets up and makes his son sit down.

"Did someone drop you off tonight, Nick? You're early."

"No, Pop. I ran. I cut across the p-p-paddock and through the orchard."

"This would be a good time for the president to visit," Six tells me.

I bring the bottle of Presidente brandy to the table along with three glasses.

Six pours some brandy into each of them. My amigo and I raise our glasses to Nicky in a birthday toast. Six sits back down and makes his son drink. Nicky coughs. His father slaps his back.

"OK. Feel better, Nick?"

The young man nods.

"What's the matter? What happened?"

"I took Sycamore home after Tomás closed up—like I usually do. I had this creepy feeling someone was following me. I turned around, but no one was there.

"Then I noticed this car with its lights off going down the street real slow. The driver kept looking over at me and smiling. He pulled over just as I was about to turn onto Alameda. He rolled his window down.

"*Hey. You're a good-looking kid, you know that?* the guy said. *I bet the girls are all over you. Don't see many Mexican fellows with blue eyes like yours.* It was real creepy, like he knew me from someplace. It felt like he was stalking me."

"Can you describe him?" Six asks his son.

"Not really, Pop. He flashed his badge in my face. That's all I noticed."

"Badge?" Six and I say at the same time.

"It said he was FBI, but he still seemed like a pervert to me. He had a weird name, too."

"Can you remember it?" Six asks.

"Maybe if I close my eyes."

I take out my notebook and pencil so we don't forget the name.

"M-X-Y-Z-P-T-L-K," he says, spelling out the FBI agent's name.

"Mxyzptlk," Six and I say.

"You know this guy?" Nicky asks.

"I had an unpleasant encounter with him a while back. You were just a

296 • BRIAN ALLAN SKINNER

baby," I tell him.

"*En serio*? 'My Uncle Is a Fugitive from the FBI.' Sounds like a bad movie."

"It was. And it spooked me just like it spooked you, Nicky," I tell him. "But most of their questions are very routine—boring, almost. They just gotta make things official by getting your answers for the record."

"Don't worry about your encounter with Agent Mxyzptlk, kiddo," Six tells his son "He's probably just interested in closing out the case from all those years ago. Next time, just tell him where we live, all right? We've got nothing to hide."

"I hope there isn't a next time, Pop. That guy gave me the creeps."

"You know, your Tio and I didn't get a chance to wish you a Happy Birthday this morning, Nick. Twenty years—two whole decades. That's *una gran cosa*. When did you leave?"

"At five-thirty. I wanted to hike to work."

Nicky glances up at the black-cat kitchen clock happily twitching its tail and shifting its googly eyes.

"Gotta run, Pop, Tio. I still have to change. Belinda is picking me up and bringing me home. So you don't gotta worry if I have a little too much to drink, you know, huh?"

"Doesn't mean you have to get plastered, Nick," his father warns him. "Take it from me. It's much better to remember all the fun you had."

"Yeah, yeah," Nicky replies, rushing up the stairs to his room. Belinda is his girlfriend of the past three months—a record.

"*Nothing to hide?*" I say to Six. "Brother Asinus's crypt is crammed full with things we're not hiding, Six."

He smiles his dimpled smile, but it falls quickly from his face.

"We've gotta send Nicky away from here as soon as we can, amigo," he says. "We can't let them use my son to get to us. Help me think of something."

I reach across the table and take his hand. It shakes.

We hear Nicky thunder down the stairs. I get up from the table to clear away the brandy and glasses, and get two beers for Six and me.

Nicky wears a white shirt and tie, brand new black Levi's, and his leather motorcycle jacket. He smells of too much English Leather aftershave.

"I thought you said Belinda was your ride tonight, Nick."

"She is."

"Then you don't especially need to wear that beat-up jacket, do you? Why don't you dress nice for your friends?"

"Because they take me as I come."

Six gets up and stops his son before he barrels out the kitchen door. He hugs him, now eye to eye with the "boy."

"I like you as you are, too, Nick—mostly. I just wish someone would steal that damn jacket of yours."

"Thanks, Pop," Nicky tells him, kissing his father on the cheek. "I'll ask around in case anyone's got itchy fingers for it."

A car horn blares in the back yard and my nephew flies out the back door, slamming it behind him like someone else I know.

"What're we gonna do, amigo?" Six asks me. "I'm worried enough that he's drawn a 1-A draft classification. We can't let the secret government—whoever they are—get to him."

We take our beers to the parlor, intending to finish them before we make supper.

"Let nature run her course, Six. Nicky won't need much encouragement from you to strike out on his own. He wants to, but he was afraid it would hurt you."

"Thanks for telling me this, Antonio. I'll have a talk with him."

My amigo smiles, but it seems forced. He looks dispirited.

"It's gonna break my heart to send Nicky away," Six tells me. "But we have to do it—for *his* sake."

"You're not gonna tell him the real reason for encouraging his wanderlust, are you?"

"No, of course not," he says, taking a sip of his beer. "The less he knows, the better. He probably wouldn't believe most of it anyhow."

Six leans over and rests his hand on my knee. He looks into my eyes.

"There's something I've thought about a lot lately," he says. "Though I have no idea why, I think Hypatia wanted to get pregnant by me. She'd be first to admit she wasn't good mother material. But it never made sense to me that Hypatia would just disappear from Nicky's life completely, and that her whole family would abandon the boy."

The back door slams. Nicky sticks his head in the parlor doorway.

"Belinda asked if I had another jacket. Can I borrow your navy blue sport jacket, Tio?"

"Sure," I tell him. "You know where it is."

Six and I grin at one another. The kitchen door slams again.

"You were saying," I remark, sipping my beer.

"I kinda wonder if Hypatia didn't vanish in order to protect Nicky, that maybe she was afraid the government would use him to get to *her*."

"What did they have on her, Six? It doesn't quite make sense to me."

"Yeah, I don't know, either," he replies. "No matter how I lay it out, there's either a piece missing or one that doesn't fit."

"You make it sound like the Montoyas are hiding from the Mafia or something, like in a witness protection program," I remark.

"I really don't know, Antonio. What's clear to me is that we can't let the FBI or the CIA or MJ-12 or anybody else get near my son. Let 'em try. I'm not

298 • BRIAN ALLAN SKINNER

kidding. They'll have to come through me first."

"And me after that," I tell him.

He smiles at me.

"Oh, God, Antonio. More and more," he says, taking hold of both my hands in his. "I love you more and more all the time. I just never seem to run out of it."

"*Mi mejor amigo*," I reply, kissing him.

"You and me," he says. "*Dos contra el mundo*."

AESTAS DE AMORE
The Summer of Love

"Wow, Nick," Six says into the telephone. "That's quite a supply of excuses you've got. Think you could give me a couple? On the other hand, if you keep screwing up the way you have, you might run out and not have enough."

"Dr. Feynman's here," I mouth at my amigo.

"Gotta run, Nick. Let us know when you're finally on your way home. If you're broke, call collect. I love you, my little green man. God be with you."

Six hangs up the receiver.

"Nicky hates it when you call him that."

"Why do you think I do it, Antonio? I do it to bug him," he says, grinning.

We go out onto the rear porch to greet the doctor. He is driving a cherry red 1967 Ford Mustang convertible. The top is down. Six's mouth hangs open as though the car were a tasty treat to eat. The doctor's hair looks like he it combed with an eggbeater.

"Hello, men," he says, his smile beaming. He extends his hand to each of us. "I trust you are none the worse for wear."

"We're pretty good," I tell him. "How was your trip, Doctor?"

"Not too bad—about twelve hours. I made it a two-day trip from Cal Tech. I want to thank you boys for putting me up for a couple of days. I'm on my way to visit an old colleague up at the lab in Los Alamos. Let me get my bag."

He opens the trunk of the Mustang. It's pretty small. I hope, with the way Six is lusting after the red convertible, that he realizes a small trunk isn't very practical for trips.

"I see you've still got your uncle's old pickup," the doctor remarks, nodding towards the open barn door.

"Yeah, my son is supposed to help me swap out some parts," Six says.

"But Nicky's been traveling a lot. His car broke down. He's not gonna make it today."

We go up the back porch steps and enter the kitchen. The doctor lets the screendoor slam. I must be the only person in the world it annoys.

"Do you realize I haven't seen Nicky since he was a year old?" Dr. Feynman says.

"He's grown some since then," Six replies. "He's gonna be twenty-four this December. You've got Nicky's old room upstairs, Doctor."

I bring three Dos Equis from the refrigerator. The doctor takes a thick notebook binder from his bag and sets it on the sideboard.

"I brought you boys my latest book," he says, winking at us.

"You'll have to autograph it for us, Dr. Feynman," I tell him.

In preparation for his visit, there are three pads of paper and several pencils on the table.

WIRETAPPED? the doctor writes.

PROBABLY, Six replies in writing.

"This is a nice house," Dr. Feynman says. "It was your grandparents' place, correct?"

"Yes," Six says. "We left our old house to a religious order."

"So what is Nicky up to these days?" the doc asks.

At the same time he writes, SOME PLACE TO TALK FREELY?

I nod. LATER, I print. AT THE LAKE.

"Nick says he's finding himself, Doc, but I didn't know he was lost."

The doctor chuckles.

"He was at that music festival in New York—Woodstock," my amigo tells him.

"I know Upstate New York, Six. The festival was almost fifty miles from Woodstock. But Bethel probably sounds too Jewish."

"Beth-El was where Jacob had his dream of angels going up and down a ladder from heaven," I say.

"Jacob's ladder," Dr. Feynman says.

"Building a Jacob's ladder was one of the experiments in *The Boy Scientist* that I helped Nicky with," Six tells us. "He was around ten. You recommended the book, Doc."

"You got a couple of good electrical shocks from it," I remind my amigo.

"A hazard of the profession," Dr. Feynman remarks, grinning.

"Have you had lunch?" I ask the doctor.

"Yeah, if a bag of potato chips counts."

"No, it doesn't," Six tells him. "We picked up pastrami and dark rye bread and cream cheese. We got some nice, crunchy dill pickles, too."

"I'm suddenly famished," the doctor says. "When do we eat?"

"Right now, if you like," Six replies. "I thought you'd never ask."

* * *

While Dr. Feynman naps after lunch up in Nicky's room, Six and I flip through the big report folder the doctor brought us. It concerns the project he worked on with the Visitors' *Katalysts*, their scientists. It will go into our "archive" at Brother Asinus's chapel.

We will have to ask our friends Zeke and Martha to smuggle it into the chapel "crypt" for us. They visit the brother every Sunday and it would not seem suspicious. But they will have to wait until winter when the thick binder can be concealed beneath a heavy coat.

WHAT DO YOU MAKE OF IT? I write on the tablet.

GUIDED MISSILES MAYBE? Six responds. **AND PART TWO?**

THE VISITORS' BIZARRE WRITING. NO IDEA WHAT THE SYMBOLS MEAN. WE'LL ASK THE DOCTOR.

ASK ME WHAT? Dr. Feynman prints on the third pad. He startles us. Six and I were so engrossed in going through his binder that we didn't hear him come down the stairs.

"Have a good nap, Doctor?" I ask.

"Yes, I did. It's about nine hundred miles from Cal Tech. I used to do that much in a day—easy. Now, I get tired. It takes me two days."

"Yeah, but that's a swell way to get around, you know, huh?" Six says. "Come on, Doc. We'll show you the lake."

I take my papa's old Navy binoculars from the sideboard. They get a lot more use than the awkward telescope from Nicky's mother Hypatia. Six takes his canteen from the peg and fills it.

"My wheels or yours?" Dr. Feynman asks.

"Are you serious?" Six remarks, grinning his dimples. "When are Antonio and I gonna get another chance to turn everybody's heads when we go through town?"

On the way down the back steps, the doctor hands Six the keys to the Mustang convertible.

I caught his son levitating a couple times back when he was younger, but this is the first time I've seen my amigo walk on air.

* * *

Six parks the car in the shade of the piñon at the crest of the embankment overlooking Bottomless Lake. The pine trees are much taller than they were more than twenty years ago when we brought Dr. Feynman out here the first time. But the view of the crystal-blue lake reflecting the crystal-blue sky has not changed.

This is the spot where the Blessed Virgin Mary first appeared to us and where Six tumbled over the edge down into the lake. It's also where we found the meteorites that Dr. Feynman's earlier report said were probably fragments of a spaceship engine.

"I'm glad they at least paved this road with gravel," Dr. Feynman says. "I got a deal renting the Mustang. This model's two years old already."

"Do you mean this is a rental car?" Six asks.

"I didn't want to chance my own car being *wired for sound*, if you catch my drift. We're safe out here. Your back yard is probably safe, too, but we'd better be careful what we say in your house."

Six pulls off to the side and we get out. My hair and face are coated with dust blown into the back from the road. Six notices and laughs. I shake my head and ruffle my hair in the breeze.

Up the road is a picnic table and fire-pit. We sit on the edge of the table, in the shade of a clump of piñon, and put our feet on the seat. Dr. Feynman lights a cigarette.

"We had a look at the new report you brought, Doc," I tell him.

"Did anything look familiar?" he asks.

"Some of the symbols in Part Two decorated the hems of the Visitors' ceremonial robes," I tell him, "but I have no idea what they mean or how to pronounce them."

"Well, that second half of the report is a translation of the first part of the report in English—sort of like a Rosetta Stone. Any idea what it's about?" he asks, taking a long drag of his cigarette.

"Six thought it might have something to do with guided missiles—with ICBMs."

"That's a good guess," the doctor says. "It's exactly right."

"Why would you and the Visitors be working on rockets together," I ask, "when they've already come from three hundred light years away?"

"I wish more of my students had your ability to reason, Antonio. It'd make my job a lot easier."

The doctor finishes his cigarette and crushes it in the dirt, putting the stub in his trouser pocket. He smiles.

"Do you know what Katalyst Keen, one of their scientists, told me? *Your solid-propellant rockets are like exploding a bomb beneath a bucket.*"

We laugh. Dr. Feynman paces back and forth with his hands in his pockets.

"Wanna go for a little hike?" Six asks.

"Sure," the doctor says, though his shoes are hardly good for hiking. The trail is wide enough for the three of us to walk next to each other, the doc in the middle.

"So what did the Visitors want to learn from *us*?" Six asks, chuckling.

Dr. Feynman stops in his tracks. He looks intently at my amigo and me. He lights another cigarette.

"I want to back up a little," he says.

"On the trail?" Six asks. "Or in your story?"

"In my story," he says, taking a drag.

"We worked for the United States Army at Los Alamos because we were told Hitler was working on an atomic bomb. Even when Nazi Germany was defeated, a swift end to the war with Japan was not assured. Up to a million lives on both sides hung in the balance if the war continued.

"I thought a powerful demonstration or two of the new weapon would be all that was required. I had no idea it would be used against civilians with no forewarning. The Virgin warned me in her letter. I wish I had believed her.

"If we start tossing those things back and forth on top of intercontinental ballistic missiles, we don't stand a chance. The cockroaches will inherit the earth."

It is a somber notion, one that has bothered my thoughts since I saw the first photos of the destruction of Nagasaki in the newspaper.

"Some might call my sharing of classified information treasonous," Dr. Feynman says, drawing long on his cigarette.

"Oh, my God, Doctor. You mean you gave our nuclear secrets to the Visitors?" Six asks.

"Not just ours, Six. I shared everybody's: the Soviets, Britain, France, and China, too."

"For what purpose?" I ask.

"You don't know how much I have wanted to tell another human being, Antonio, Six. Please don't judge me until I've had a chance to explain."

"Why don't we head back?" Six suggests. "It's getting pretty warm and there's not much shade out here."

He passes the canteen to the doctor and me. We stand in the shade of an ancient juniper tree. Some of them are between five hundred and a thousand years old—as old as Kaptain Kosmos.

"The Visitors are not here to take sides," Dr. Feynman says. "They have better things to do than referee squabbles. They don't care who started it."

Six and I turn to him and smile. We reach the wooden picnic table. It is still in the shade. We sit down on the seat and pass the canteen of water.

"With the information I provided, the Visitor scientists made sure that once an ICBM with a nuclear warhead is launched—it doesn't matter by whom—it will never re-enter the atmosphere to reach its target. The missile will just keep right on going, attaining an orbit beyond Earth that will take it on a slow spiral into the sun."

"Thank God for that," Six says.

"And thanks to you and Kaptain Kosmos, too," I tell him.

"I never got to meet the Kaptain," the doctor says. "I worked only with the Katalysts, their scientists. But I have a letter from the Kaptain I was asked to deliver to you in person. I've been carrying it around for fifteen years—never out of my sight for long. Good thing it's made of something sturdier than paper."

The doctor hands me the origami-folder letter in the shape of a humming-bird. It flutters in my hand before opening up.

"All their communications came to me like that," the doctor remarks, smiling. "They open only for the recipient. Who says extreme intelligence can't be touched with whimsy?"

I read the letter aloud to them.

My Dear Friends,

We do not intend to interfere in your culture or your civilization. But we could not stand by and allow you to carelessly cast aside the marvelous Gift of Life that God has given your race. Your entire planet is alive. You do not realize how rare and wonderful a Gift it is or you would regard it more highly than you do.

*We regret that our intervention was required regarding your atomic weapons. Dr. Feynman was an invaluable ally in keeping your planet safe. However, unless some madman is first to push his **LAUNCH** button, no one will know how useless those missiles now are. Some day, you will thank us.*

We shall not be returning to Earth again for some time. You are free from danger until then. We want to wait until those others who saw our crashed ship have forgotten. We wish to appear to fresh eyes, to those who are prepared to witness the truth.

Best wishes until next we meet,
Kaptain Kosmos & Krew

I hand the opened letter to Dr. Feynman to read. It closes up again before he has a chance to even glance at it. I tuck the mysterious letter into the pocket of my overalls.

"So that's the project you and the Visitors worked on?" Six asks.

The doctor nods. "And it all started with the letter from the Blessed Virgin you brought to me in Los Alamos. It seems ages ago now.

"I imagine the Joint Chiefs would not support my actions, but millions of Americans might—and billions more around the world."

"For what my opinion may be worth, Dr. Feynman," Six tells him, "I don't see how saving the lives of innocent Americans can be called *treason*."

"If you've a mind to twist one thing into the shape of another, the Laws of Physics won't prevent you. All we can do is what our lights tell us is the right thing," Dr. Feynman says. "It's not up to us to write our own histories."

I stand on the top of the picnic table and take my papa's binoculars out of their beat-up case. I am able to see the spot where the Visitor's scout ship crashed on Foster's ranch. I point it out to Dr. Feynman.

"There's not much to see now, is there?" he says.

"Just that gash in the hillside. It's filled up with sagebrush already," I tell him.

"I'm getting hungry," Six says. "It'll take me a while to get the grill going, too. What d'ya say we head back?"

"I want to take you boys out to dinner tonight. You pick the place. One of you drive, OK? I'd like to enjoy a cocktail—or two."

My amigo hands *me* the keys to the Mustang. I remember the first time I rode Nicky's Honda motorcycle. Like then, I am both excited and scared enough to have an accident before I even get on the road. Six takes the back seat. Dr. Feynman turns on the radio, but with the wind in my ears, all I hear is thunder.

I pull over on the shady side of Main Street so we can decide where to eat. We get out of the car and look up and down the street.

"Wanna try that new French place Alicia recommended?" Six asks.

"No, thank you," I say. "Any place called *The Two Maggots* puts me off my lunch before I'm even seated."

Dr. Feynman laughs. "*Les Deux Magots*, by any chance?" he asks.

"Yes," I reply. "Who'd wanna name their restaurant *that*?"

"A *magot* is a china doll, Antonio, not a larval fly."

"Oh," I say, feeling a little bit foolish. "But maybe some other time."

"How about Tia Maria's Cocina?" Six asks. "Never had a bad meal there."

"Have you ever had a meal you didn't like *anywhere*, Six?" I ask.

"Come to think of it, no, I haven't. I'm grateful for whatever is set before me."

We walk down the street to Tia Maria's.

"Except maybe maggots," he adds, smiling his dimples.

* 2 *

I hear a car pull into the back yard. It's a big old black Cadillac—a 1959, I think, one of the years with the rocketship tailfins. It looks pretty hard-traveled.

"Any idea who it is?" Six asks.

I shake my head. "Let's go find out," I say.

We stand on the top porch step waiting to see who it is. Nicky unfolds himself from the Cadillac and rushes to his father. Six leaps down the two remaining steps.

Father and son wrap each other in a bear hug and spin each other around.

Nicky's clothes are wrinkled and dirty. He hasn't had a haircut in months, his black mane hiding his ears. He hasn't shaved in a while either.

"Jeeze, you stink, Nick."

"I'm happy to see you, too, Pop."

"Well, you smell. Should I lie? I'm not sure why I love you—but I do."

"Tio," Nicky says, hugging me and kissing my cheek.

He turns back to his father. "We busted our butts to get here before Dr. Feynman leaves. Where is he? Is he gone already?"

"He went to the movies with your Uncle Zeke and Aunt Martha—something they all wanted to see," I tell my nephew.

"Did I hear you say *we*?" Six asks his son.

A young woman with a pair of thick auburn braids, gets out of the old Caddy on the passenger side. She wears a long patchwork skirt and a rumpled white Mexican wedding blouse. She stretches her arms and yawns. She is barefoot.

Nicky puts his arm around her waist. "This is my Pop," he tells her. "Pop, this is Jennifer Juniper."

The young woman extends her hand. Six turns away and bursts into laughter.

"Do you expect me to believe that's her real name? It's the title of a song. I listen to the radio, too, you know, huh?"

Jennifer unhooks from Nicky. She walks back and reaches through the open window of the Cadillac. She takes out a crocheted shoulder bag.

"Pop. Why are you being so rude?" Nicky whispers.

"She's a Jezebel. Are you blind, Nick?"

Jennifer returns with her bag and takes out her wallet. She shows it to Six. He bends lower and squints.

"Anybody can get a fake ID. It doesn't mean you are you," he tells her.

I scowl at Six, but he doesn't notice. I attempt to break the tension by suggesting a cold beer and then lunch. I lead everyone up to the porch. I bring four bottles of beer, afraid Six would only bring three. I don't know what's got him irked. He doesn't even know Nicky's friend.

"Maybe you'd like to shower first, Nick," Six suggests. "Or else we can all sit out here in the fresh air."

"What's with you, Pop? You've been a crab since we got here. You haven't given me a chance to tell you Jennifer and I got married. She's the newest member of the Thorson family."

We go into the kitchen and sit down. I've never seen Six look so cross—as though he were about to spit. I can only guess he suspects Jennifer Juniper somehow tricked his son—like *he* was tricked by Nicky's mother, Hypatia. Though Nicky is almost twenty-four, old enough to do as he pleases, it would have been a good idea to have at least consulted his father before taking the plunge into marriage.

My amigo gets up and unbuttons his denim workshirt. Then he strips off his T-shirt. Nicky and I know what comes next. Poor Jennifer does not. I touch her hand and wink at her. Six slams the screendoor hard enough that it probably opens inward now.

"When did you two get married?" I ask the newlyweds.

Nicky looks up at the black cat clock. "Twenty-two hours and fifteen minutes ago."

"Whack," comes the sound of the first chop from the barn.

"Well, congratulations then," I say, standing up from the table.

Nicky and Jennifer get up, too. I shake my nephew's hand and hug him. Then I hug his new bride and kiss her.

"Thank God that at least one of Nicky's kin doesn't snarl," she says, smiling at me.

"Whack."

"It might take my dad a while to get used to the idea of our being married, Jenn. But he'll come around. Don't worry. I can tell he likes you."

She looks askance at him. We touch our bottles of Dos Equis together and laugh.

"Whack."

"What's he doing out there?" Jennifer asks.

"Chopping wood," Nicky and I say together.

"For how long?"

I chuckle.

"Until he can no longer lift the axe or he runs out of logs to split, whichever comes last," Nicky replies.

"Where did you kids tie the knot?" I ask them.

They both smile.

"Back up the road where the Caddy broke down. It turns out the mechanic was a justice of the peace," Nicky says. "He had to send for the fan-belt a couple towns over. So while we were waiting, we figured, *Why not, you know, huh?*"

"It involved a little more discussion than that, Tio," Jennifer says.

"Yeah, like *Do you...?* and then *I do...?*" I ask.

They chuckle. We finish our beer. Nicky and his wife get up from the kitchen table.

"We'd like to shower, Tio. Can we borrow some clothes to put on afterwards. All our stuff got stolen."

"Bummer," I say.

They both look at me and laugh.

"I listen to the radio, too," I say, grinning. "We're fresh out of clean skirts, Jennifer," I tell her. "But I'll find something for you until you can do wash."

"Thanks, Tio Antonio," she says. "You are living up to all that Nick told me about you."

Her smile is big and radiant.

I'm sure I'm blushing, but blushing is one of those things which, the more you try to hide it, the brighter it glows.

I loan Nicky a pair of my Levi's and a workshirt, and Jennifer a pair of my longjohns, my last clean workshirt, and my moccasins. They will all be too big for the petite brunette, but she can make adjustments.

Jennifer and Nicky go upstairs to use the shower, tossing their dirty clothes over the bannister. I put them in the washing machine all together. Neither of them was wearing underwear.

Then I take the sweaty bottle of beer from the kitchen table to my sweaty amigo out in the barn, hoping to placate him with his beer and a couple of well-placed kisses.

* * *

The newlyweds glow. It's not merely the removal of their grime and dust. A good scrubbing with the old-fashioned lye soap Six and I still use makes anybody glow. But the bride and groom glow from the inside, too, the glow from enjoying intimacy beneath a stream of hot water. The shower, I will admit, is one of our favorite places for Six and me to make love, too. The water makes it intensely sensual, almost sacramental.

Nicky sits shirtless in a chair on the rear porch with a towel over his shoulders. Jennifer, a comb and barber's scissors in her hands, stands poised to clip his damp, shaggy hair.

"How short, Nick?" she asks.

"Just get it off my ears, Jenn. It bugs me, you know, huh? About like my Tio, I guess."

"That short?" she asks.

"Yeah," he says. "If I don't like it, you can paste some back on."

She ruffles his hair. Nicky cranes his neck up, Jennifer leans down, and they kiss smack dab in the middle. Even blindfolded I'd be able to see they're in love.

Six comes from the barn, soaked with sweat down to the thighs of his overalls.

"Care for another beer, amigo?" I ask.

"Lemme guzzle a little water first," he says. I can tell he's overdone it. He plunks down in one of the porch rockers while I bring him a tall glass of cool water. His hand shakes. Half of the water spills down his chest.

"Thanks," he tells me.

Jennifer stops clipping Nicky's hair. They both look over at Six.

"Good thing we're upwind of you, Pop, you know, huh?"

"Wise-ass," Six tells his son. I see faint traces of dimples on both their faces.

"That's a good haircut," my amigo comments.

He gets up from the rocker, still glistening with sweat. He bows to Jennifer and takes her hand.

"I apologize for my rude welcome, Jennifer"

"Oh, my God, Mr. Thorson. I didn't notice before. You've got *heterochromia*. Nick never mentioned it. Do you know how rare a trait that is. That is so groovy."

"Where'd you learn a two-bit word like *heterochromia*?"

"I read a lot, Mr. Thorson. Just because I'm head-over-heels in love with your son doesn't mean I'm stupid."

My amigo laughs long and hard. I am happy he has chosen the path of peace.

"Welcome to the family, Jennifer Juniper-Thorson. May God have mercy on you."

Nicky and Jennifer wrap their arms around Six, squeezing him from both sides. He motions to me to join them. We hug. Six's sweaty smell *turns me on*, as the kids say, but I'm sure I'm the only one it has that effect on.

Dr. Feynman's flashy Mustang pulls into the back yard. Martha is driving it. Her smile takes up most of her face.

The four of us on the porch unlatch from one another and look out at our friends. Our unplanned gathering is shaping up to be a good time.

* * *

Dinner and the Play

(*Zeke, Martha, and Dr. Feynman walk up onto the porch.*)

ZEKE: That was a cozy little scene. Glad to see everybody's getting along. Good to see you, Nick.

NICK: Hello, Uncle Zeke, Aunt Martha. (*He kisses her cheek.*)

MARTHA: That's a nice haircut, Nick. We figured, coming direct from the *Summer of Love*, you'd be as shaggy as my old dog Barkly.

NICK: The *Summer of Love* was two years ago, Auntie, in San Francisco. This was Woodstock, up in the Catskills.

ZEKE: I thought every summer was a *Summer of Love*. (*He nudges Martha.*)

MARTHA: (*She puts her hands on her hips.*) Do men ever have anything else on their minds?

THE MEN: (*in unison*) No.

(*Everyone laughs.*)

NICK: My wife Jennifer gave me the haircut. I sure needed a good pruning.

ZEKE, MARTHA: Your *wife*?

NICK: Yes. (*He smiles.*) Meet Jennifer Juniper-Thorson. (*To Jenn.*) This is my Uncle Zeke and my Aunt Martha.

(*The two couples exchange handshakes, kisses, backslaps, and good wishes.*)

FEYNMAN: (To Jenn.) Your name's like in the song, right? That's all they played on the radio driving down from Cal Tech.

JENN: Yeah, but I was on the scene before Donovan came up with it. If you ask me, the song's kinda sappy.

NICK: What movie did you guys see?

MARTHA: *The Learning Tree.* It's about a Negro teenager growing up in Kansas in the 1920s. There wasn't a dry eye in the entire theater.

ZEKE: I recommend it to all of you.

FEYNMAN: I triple that.

NICK: Who wants a beer to help us celebrate our one-day anniversary?

(*All hands go up.*)

SIX (*still shirtless*): Put your shirt on, Nick.

NICK: Will you give me a hand, Uncle Zeke?

ZEKE: Sure, kiddo. It's good to see you again. Long drive, huh?

(*They go into the kitchen.*)

ANTONIO: Six, would you please bring the sawhorses from the barn? Thanks. Here's your shirt.

(*He hands his denim workshirt to his amigo who slips his arms into it but leaves it unbuttoned.*)

MARTHA: Come on, Jenn. You can help me bring the boards for our "table." Maybe you can explain to me why you'd marry into such a kooky family.

JENN: Because I love him.

MARTHA: That's a pretty good reason.

(*They go out to the barn for the boards. Six returns with the sawhorses. Zeke and Nicky return with seven opened bottles of Dos Equis. They hand them out.*)

(*Jenn and Martha return with the boards. Six and Zeke set up the "table" and bring chairs from the house. Antonio brings the old Norwegian tablecloth. There's quite a commotion.*)

FEYNMAN: (*to Nicky*): You probably don't remember the last time we met, Nick. You weren't even a year old.

NICK: (*smiling*): Sure I remember. Here's your beer, Ritty.

FEYNMAN: *Ritty?* No one's called me that in more than thirty years—not since high school.

NICK: I must've heard it somewhere, Dr. Feynman.

JENN: Does everybody in the family read minds?

ANTONIO: No, just Nicky.

FEYNMAN: Read minds? I guess that wouldn't surprise me after all the other weird stuff that's gone on.

(*Martha and Antonio spread the tablecloth. Jenn brings plates and napkins, then goes back for bowls and silverware.*)

SIX: Zeke, can you help me at the grill?

ZEKE: Sure. I'm gettin' kinda hungry.

(*Martha brings out a platter of small steaks, chorizo, corn, and mushrooms and peppers for roasting. She hands it to Six.*)

SIX: Would you bring some newspaper, Zeke? And matches.

(*Six and Zeke go out to the old cast-iron grill.*)

MARTHA: Did you also meet the Visitors, Dr. Feynman?

FEYNMAN: Does everybody know about the Visitors?

ANTONIO: (*looking around*): Just the people here, Doctor. I'm not sure about Jenn. She's new in the family.

NICK: I told her—though I'm not sure how much of it I believe myself.

JENN: (*entering with a bowl of tomato and green onion salad*): What did you tell me, love?

NICK: About my Pop's and my Tio's overactive imaginations. Or maybe they just dropped acid before it became fashionable, you know, huh?

FEYNMAN: Skepticism is a good trait, Nick. But, generally, hallucinations don't leave physical artifacts behind.

(*Smoke from the grilling food drifts onto the porch. Antonio brings more bottles of beer and Coke.*)

NICK: So, have you ever seen the Visitors, Dr. Feynman?

FEYNMAN: No, unfortunately not. But I'm convinced of their existence, Nick. There are many ways of confirming something beyond visual observations. I learned the Visitors can see nearly the entire spectrum from infrared to ultraviolet.

JENN: Have you ever heard them speak, Doctor?

FEYNMAN: No, our communications were always written. Their responses convinced me they're definitely not from around here.

ANTONIO (*leaving*): Excuse me. I gotta get the bread out of the oven.

FEYNMAN (*to Nicky*): Your father and your uncle told me you met the Visitors when their Katalyst, Doktor Klas, cured you of polio.

NICK: I remember very little from that time, Dr. Feynman. I saw these dwarves—circus clowns—in my room. It was my birthday.

They made me laugh. I just assumed my Pop and my Tio hired them. (*Antonio returns with two loaves of bread on a cutting board.*)

ANTONIO: Could you slice the bread, Jenn, once it cools? I'll get you a knife.

JENN: Sure, Tio. Did you ever hear the Visitors speak?

ANTONIO: Many times. Six, too. Their speech was kinda sing-song. Their own language was all buzzing and clicking—like insects. Excuse me.

(*Antonio brings a beer to Six and Zeke at the grill.*)

JENN: What do scientists make of the Visitors from another world, Dr. Feynman? This is so fascinating to me. I couldn't believe it when Nick told me his father and his uncle were visited by aliens.

FEYNMAN: No one else knows more than a piece or two of the story, Jenn. The Visitors asked us to keep a lid on it until they return.

JENN: Nick, would you please get me another beer. Since I'm in Roswell, I'll try it with a slice of lime this time.

NICK (*going out*): Sure thing, hon. Ritty?

FEYNMAN: As long as you're at it, Nick. Sure. Thanks. No lime.

JENN: When do you think the alien Visitors will be back, Doctor?

FEYNMAN: No idea, dear. I hope it will be after I check out. I'm not sure I could withstand the ridicule from the scientific community after I report receiving origami telegrams from Little Green Men.

(*He chuckles.*)

NICK: (*handing his bride and the doctor their beers*) My Pop always called me his Little Green Man.

(*Six and Zeke return to the porch with the platters of roasted meat and corn and peppers. They set them on the table.*)

JENN: *Believe those who are seeking the truth, and doubt those who claim to have found it.*

FEYNMAN: That's good, Jenn. Who said it, do you know?

JENN: It was the French writer André Gide. I majored in French before I met Nicky.

FEYNMAN: And what do major in now, my dear?

JENN: In Nicky. He's learning French.

(*Nicky rings the triangular dinner bell. The hubbub of conversations hushes. Everyone takes a seat. The table is laden with food and three bottles of wine.*)

SIX: It looks like you're the eldest at our table, Dr. Feynman. You know what that means.

FEYNMAN: It means an atheist is going to say your grace.

(*All laugh, then bow their heads.*)

FEYNMAN: As we partake of this food in each other's company, let us first remember how it came to us and be thankful to those who made it possible. We are particularly grateful for those who have advanced our understanding of medicine and science, and who do their best to explain the workings of the Universe.

(*Martha and Antonio cross themselves.*)

(*Six at one end of the table and Dr. Feynman at the other, pour wine into the glasses. It is quiet while the bowls and platters are passed.*)

(*Antonio stands, raising his glass of wine.*)

ANTONIO: *God bless us, every one!* Here we are, at one table: Norwegian and Negro, Indian and Mexican; Christian and Jew, atheist and animist, men and women, young and... um... *older*. I love you all. God bless America—a home for all of us.

* 3 *

"Come on, Pop. Don't be such a crab," Jenn tells her father-in-law. "Nick wants to get going."

"I'm retired—well, semi-retired—and I don't gotta be in a hurry to do anything."

She looks over at me for sympathy.

"I tell you these aren't my Levi's," Six says, holding them up to his nose. "Antonio and I don't use detergent—only Fels-Naptha. You got 'em mixed up. These must belong to Nick."

Nick sticks his head in the doorway of the bedroom and offers his two-cents.

"We're just a coupla years away from a new millennium, Pop. You might wanna get ready for it."

I hand my amigo another pair of overalls from the laundry pile in the corner. He sniffs them.

"That's better," he says, slipping his legs into them. He stands up and buttons them, then pulls on his boots. We file out of our bedroom.

"If you wanna know," Six says, "I'm miffed because the twins aren't coming."

"They wanted to, Pop," Jenn says.

"If they wanted to, then they'd be coming, wouldn't they? Zeke's and Martha's kids are coming. What's wrong with Zack and Zoey?"

"They'd rather be with their friends, Pop," Jenn says. "You know how it is."

"No, I don't. I don't get it," Six remarks. "I liked old people when I was growing up. So did Antonio. Why do you only wanna hang around people your own age? What're you gonna learn from them, you know, huh? They're as dumb as you are."

"Should we force them, Pop?" Nick asks.

"Yeah. Try it. Maybe you'll even get away with it."

Everyone laughs, promising a sunnier forecast for our outing. Six and I take our lined denim jackets from their hooks. The forecast is for mid-forties tonight—about right for early September out in the boondocks of Socorro County.

The four of us climb into Jenn's and Nick's new Jeep Grand Cherokee. It's about the size a tank was back when my amigo and I were in the army. I put the three empty bushel baskets in the back. Six and I get in.

Nick and Jenn listen to the radio. It's turned way too loud. Six and I carry on our own conversation in the back. I put my hand on his knee. He turns to me and smiles.

"Did you ever think this day would arrive, Six?"

"Sure. Most things are pretty hardy. Johnny Appleseed just poked a hole in the ground with his stick and dropped in an apple core. He left a trail of apple trees."

"I'm not talking about just the apple tree, Six. I meant us—you and me, too. It's been fifty years since we planted that tree."

"I guess we're pretty hardy, too, amigo," he says, turning to me and kissing me. Nicky catches us in the rearview mirror and smiles at us.

"Eyes on the road, Nick," Six tells his son.

"Think there'll be enough apples for everybody?" I ask Six.

"If not, there are plenty of farm-stands this time of year. We won't go home with empty baskets, that's for sure."

It's about a hundred-twenty miles to the Rio Grande where Six and I planted an apple core a half-century ago. We have no idea whether it even took root.

My hand creeps up Six's thigh. Though we both turned sixty-six this past May, his muscles are still hard. Somehow, I don't feel as old as I thought being this old would feel. The sight of my amigo still gets me *horny*, as the kids like to say.

"I still think they're making too big a deal of this, Antonio. We're not married or anything, you know, huh?"

"Oh, let 'em, Six. They're happy for us. Fifty years is *una gran cosa*. Let's be happy for ourselves."

I lean towards *mi mejor amigo* and kiss him just as Nick checks his rearview mirror again. He smiles and says something.

"We can't hear you back here with the music so loud," Six tells his son.

Nicky turns the volume down. "I asked if you wanted me to pull over, Pop, so you two can have a romp in the field."

"Sure," Six replies. "That looks like a pleasant spot up ahead—by the cottonwoods."

I don't think even Six and Nicky know when they are joshing one another.

"You missed it, Nick," Six says.

"Then you'll just have to behave until we get there," Nicky says, turning the radio up again.

"Is that The Beatles?" I ask. "I don't think I ever heard that tune."

Jenn turns in her seat to face us.

"No," she says, "but a lot of people thought it was The Beatles. It's Klaatu."

"*Klaatu?*" Six and I say, looking at one another with startled expressions.

"Yeah," Jenn replies. "The song is *Calling Occupants of Interplanetary Craft*. It's from about twenty years ago, I think."

"Thanks, Jenn," Six tells her. She turns to face the front again.

My amigo and I trade more bewildered expressions.

"Guess we were too busy answering their call to have heard of the song," Six tells me, laughing.

"I think I agree with you, Antonio, that we're probably not the only ones the Visitors dropped in on. I also think the Queen of Heaven and the Visitors have been appearing to humans for centuries—maybe for thousands of years, you know, huh?"

"I believe my papa and my Tio saw them, too," I tell my amigo.

"We'll be coming up on the Rio Grande soon," Nick shouts from the front. "I'll slow down. Keep you eyes peeled for the spot."

"Look for Farm Market Road," Six tells his son.

"Wait," I say. "That was the river."

"Slow down, Nick. The road's just off the western riverbank. There."

Nicky's abrupt turn nearly sends me into Six's lap.

"Not too far now," I say. "It was an open meadow."

Nicky stops the air-conditioned white juggernaut. It is a Jeep in name only.

"That's it, Six. That's gotta be the tree we planted. There are no others around."

A large apple tree stands at the entrance to the grassy field. Its branches are so laden with fruit, they bend nearly to the ground. I jump out of the back and run to the tree. Six is right behind me.

My amigo reaches for my hand as we stand looking up at the crown of the tree. We fold our arms around one another and kiss. Six takes an apple from the tree and hands it to me.

"You can have the first bite," he says.

"You're name's not *Yves* by any chance, is it?" I ask.

"No," he says, laughing. "But the apple might be from the Wicked Witch in *Snow White*, you know huh? Have a taste, my dear. One bite is all it takes."

I chomp down on the apple. It is crisp and sweet, and cool from hanging on the morning side of the tree. Six studies my face.

"It's absolutely delicious, amigo," I tell him, handing the apple to him. I watch *his* face.

"My God, Antonio. It's as sweet as a candied apple," he says, taking another bite and passing it to me. "You'd think we watered and fertilized, pruned and dusted that tree for the past fifty years."

"We didn't have to take care of the tree, Six. God tended it."

Nicky and Jennifer bring the empty bushel baskets from the car.

"I see you two got a head-start. How are they?" Jenn asks.

Six picks one and gives it to her. We watch the smile of pleasure emerge on her face.

"Wow," she says. "They're really good—just about at peak flavor now. They'll get even better in the cellar."

She and Nicky begin plucking apples from the tree, placing them in the bushel baskets as carefully as if they were ornaments of glass. Six and I each take another apple and walk back up the road a short way to the bank of the Rio Grande. Six takes my hand.

We stand at the water's edge. The current of the Rio is slow this time of year, and shallow. But it is always cold.

"Wanna go for a swim?" Six suggests.

"No," I say, shaking my head. "We're too old to swim in our undershorts, amigo. I'm not walking around in wet Levi's for the rest of the day, either."

"So. You didn't mind it last time. We survived."

"We were sixteen years old, Six—practically indestructible."

"Yeah, or so we thought. Come on. It's warm out. We're gonna have a campfire later."

"I don't care."

"Aw, c'mon."

"No. You jump in if you want."

"Maybe I will," he says, unbuttoning his workshirt.

A car slows down and pulls into the clearing where Nick's and Jenn's white Jeep is parked. It looks like Zeke's and Martha's blue Ford minivan. I walk towards them.

Six changes his mind about a swim and rushes to catch up with me, his shirt flapping behind him.

"Where are Catherine and Mark?" I ask.

"They'll be coming later," Zeke says. "Catherine is staining their deck this afternoon. Mark went over to help them."

"It's not going to be so easy finding this place after dark, you know, huh?" Six remarks.

"Aren't we going to have a little bonfire?" Martha asks.

"If we can find enough deadfall," I tell her.

"Oh, my goodness, Antonio," Martha remarks. "Is this the tree you and Six planted? It's gorgeous—so perfectly formed. And so full of apples. I don't think we brought enough baskets."

"You don't have to pick 'em all," Six says. "You can leave a few for the other critters and the birds."

As if he'd been cued, a raven lands on a cottonwood branch near Six. My amigo takes another apple from the tree. The raven hops onto Six's shoulder. Six takes a bite out of the apple and holds it between his teeth. He turns to the bird who takes the chunk of fruit from him and flies up into the cottonwood. He pecks at the piece of apple and caws.

"You are quite welcome, Edgar," Six says to the bird.

"I get it," Martha says, smiling. "*The Raven*, Poe's poem"

Zeke chuckles. He and Martha fetch their bushel baskets and join Jenn and Nicky gathering apples.

"Antonio and I are gonna go find some firewood," Six tells his kids and our friends.

We start in the grove of cottonwoods looking for deadfall. Six and I take off our workshirts and knot the sleeves together, making a perfect log-carrier. We amass quite a pile in short order, but then we have to fan out further afield for ever-smaller chunks. We work up a bit of a sweat.

Nicky, Jenn, Martha, and Zeke stand around their seven bushel baskets overtopped with apples.

"It's almost like Our Lord's miracle of loaves and fishes," Martha tells us. "No matter how many we picked, there were just as many still on the tree."

We smile at her.

"We're gonna get one last load of wood," Six says. "The four of you can set up your tents over there," he says, pointing. "We're fine sleeping outside."

"Speak for yourself," I tell my amigo, nudging him.

We hike to the last clump of trees way at the edge of the meadow. They are hickory trees. Two camping vans squeeze between the unwired fenceposts and park. An old Buick joins the two vans.

"Oh, crap," Six says. "I was just gonna suggest a romp in the hay. There are people everywhere these days, you know, huh?"

"I wonder who they are," I say. "It's kinda strange to see other people out here in such a remote area."

We set our bundles of wood down and watch the other people in their vans. They begin unloading things from the back—ice-chests, tents, and a cooking stove.

"Looks like they'll be spending the night," I say.

"We're far enough away not to be bothered," Six replies, "unless they make a lot of noise."

We turn around to look at them one more time before we get back to our camping spot. From our campsite, the cottonwoods hide the other campers at the far end of the meadow.

Our two tents are staked-out. Zeke and Nicky fumble with the poles under the direction of Martha and Jennifer. They stop for minute when they see us return with two more bundles of wood.

"That's enough, Pop," Nicky says. "It's not gonna snow tonight."

"Are you sure?" he asks his son, smiling. "You can set up the campfire on that bare spot over there. Dig up some more dirt all around it, too."

"Sure thing, Pop."

"Your Tio and I wanna go look at something in the field, Nick."

"I'm going to get my papa's binoculars from the Jeep," I tell Six. He comes with me.

"You've had those field-glasses about twenty-five times longer than your papa did, Antonio."

"That's how I see things, Six. Each time I touch or use something that once belonged to someone else, I remember that person. The truck your grandson drives around in is still Tio Nicolás's 1934 Ford pickup to me."

"I wasn't making fun, amigo. It reminds me that we entered the world empty-handed and that's how we'll leave. Nothing lasts forever."

"Are you sure, Six? What about love and friendship?"

"That's different," he says. "You can't wear either of 'em out. Like a pair of Levi's they just get better."

I smile at him. He hugs me and slips both his hands into the back pockets of my overalls. He kisses me and I kiss him back, despite the fact that we are in view of his kids and our friends.

We put our shirts back on and trudge through the meadow to some place we can observe the other cars in the field without being seen.

"My God, Six," I say. "Look. There must be twenty cars out there now."

He squints and says, "Don't exaggerate. There are only seventeen."

I want to laugh, but I am concerned.

"What do you think is going on, Six?"

"Hand me the binoculars."

I take them out of their leather case and pass them to him.

"I make out five telescopes on tripods, amigo. I'm guessing they're an amateur astronomy club."

I see two more vehicles approach from the other direction and join the first ones, now assembling in at tight arc at the farthest edge of the meadow.

"I don't feel like we're trespassing so much now, Six. Maybe this is public land after all."

"Could be," he replies. "Let's see what Nick and the others make of it. We ought to get supper set up, too, before it gets dark."

We take our time returning to camp. I rest my hand on his shoulder, he puts his hand in my back pocket. If *mi mejor amigo* and I were alone, we'd be re-enacting the loss of our virginity, when we first gave all of ourselves to each other. Our love-making has only gotten better since then. *Practice makes perfect*, as Six likes to say.

After we join the others, Six returns to our vantage overlooking the convocation in the meadow with and Zeke and Nicky. Six takes my papa's binoculars. I stay behind to help Jenn and Martha prepare our supper for the campfire.

"What's going on out there?" Martha asks me, turning aside from the strong onions she slices on one of the camp tables. "What do they want to look at, Antonio?"

"There are a bunch of cars gathered at the other end of the meadow," I reply. "Six thinks they're amateur astronomers."

"We should go introduce ourselves after supper," Jenn suggests.

I go to the Jeep and take out one of the ice-chests. I notice several cars go by on Farm Market Road. They drive slow, like they are looking for something. One of them stops and rolls his window down. He looks like a leftover hippie.

"Hey, buddy," he says. "Is this where the landing is gonna be?"

"Landing? What landing?" I ask. I set the cooler on the ground.

"You know, the spaceship. Care for a joint? It's gonna be awesome, dude."

"No, thank you. It's up the road a piece," I reply.

"Muchas gracias," he says, and rolls up his window. The air wafting from his old beater could get you high three miles downwind.

I walk out to the road and look towards the east. Cars line both sides of the county road all the way to the vanishing point. More cars and vans and pickups go past.

I head back to the campsite with the heavy cooler. By the time I get there, I am breathless, anxious about what is going on in the meadow. The exertion of carrying the laden ice-chest does not help. I feel faint, lightheaded.

"Tio," Jenn says. "Why didn't you ask for help? Here. Sit down," she orders, unfolding one of the canvas camp chairs.

Jenn holds a bottle of water in front of me. Martha makes me drink. I take a few sips, then a long gulp. I feel better.

The other three men return.

"What a bunch of weirdos," Nicky remarks. "I'm sure there was a run on tinfoil hats today."

"What are you talking about?" Martha asks.

"The Sky People," Zeke tells her. "They're all waiting for the Sky People to return." He and Nicky go over to the ice-chest for a beer.

"Who is waiting for the Sky People?" Martha inquires.

"They're mostly just garden-variety kooks and loonies and misfits—

people like us, in other words," Six says.

"Speak for yourself," we tell him simultaneously.

We laugh, but it is worrisome to all of us who know about the true Visitors.

"Wouldn't the Visitors have sent word to Six and Antonio first?" Martha asks. "We should go find out who told all those people."

My amigo and I shrug.

"The Visitors never mentioned an exact date for their return," I say.

"Besides, no one said we were under exclusive contract," Six remarks.

"We ought to get our supper going first," Zeke says. "It'll be getting dark soon. We don't know when the kids will show up, either."

"You two can get lost for a while," Jenn tells Six and me. "We've got everything under control. Enjoy yourselves," she says, winking.

I put my hand on Six's shoulder and we walk away from the campsite.

"If you still wanna go for a swim, amigo, I'll go with you," I tell him.

"Thanks, Antonio," he says, smiling. "We can go swimming any old time we've a mind to. Let's go see what's going on out in the field. It bothers me if all these people were flim-flammed. I hate to think of everyone being disappointed, you know, huh?"

"I don't think anyone was deceived, Six. Something tells me they'll manage to have a good time anyway."

We walk along the bank of the Rio Grande until we come to the clearing by the meadow.

"My God, Six," I say, stopping in my tracks. "There must be two hundred people out there now."

"A lot more than that," he replies. "Probably closer to three hundred."

We watch clusters of colorfully-dressed people carry things from their cars. Some bring telescopes. Others carry guitars or folding chairs. Farm Market Road is a long, straight parking lot all the way to the horizon.

"Welcome, friends," a booming voice behind us says, startling us out of our skin. "Don't forget your free programs."

Six and I each take one of the fliers he offers. He's dressed in a sort of silvery jumpsuit like astronauts wear. He wears a football helmet painted silver.

"The free programs are a dollar each," he tells us. "Two for fifty cents."

My amigo and I both pat the pockets of our overalls.

"I was kinda hoping we'd go for a swim before," Six tells me, showing his dimples. "My wallet's back in the Jeep."

"Mine, too," I say.

"Sorry," the vendor says, snatching the programs from our hands. "Gotta make a living."

Six and I wade into the crowd walking single-file, taking turns leading and following, trying to keep each other in sight. Neither of us left a trail of breadcrumbs to find our way back. I don't want to lose him. I feel like I'm dreaming, but it's not my dream.

I hear the persistent rhythm of conga drums and bongos, a rhythm that pulses in my blood. People in bizarre get-ups meander past us, shaking maracas or slapping tambourines. Others, nearly naked, trill on flutes and pennywhistles. Abraham Lincoln is pretty good on the saxophone.

An Indian in full ceremonial headdress thumps on his tom-tom, chanting in strange ways that do not seem to be altogether human in tone. Others in the crowd dance behind him, drawing inward in tighter and tighter spirals.

"I think they must have all dropped acid, Six."

"Either that or we did," he says. "I'm not sure which."

As sunset approaches, little campfires blaze around the periphery of the gathering. Lanterns and candles are illuminated. People in black tights twirl sparklers and juggle torches. I don't notice anyone watching anyone else: everyone is a participant.

I hear harmonicas, banjos, and guitars in profusion, but also violins, accordions, and a cello played by a young woman with red dreadlocks.

Every now and again, I hear snatches of a tune borne on the wind, often played competently, sometimes coarsely, on a variety of instruments from a Jew's harp to a glockenspiel. The melody is the lullaby of the three strangers on three ships bearing three gifts. I no sooner think I hear it picked up again by a single voice than the breeze and the night bear it off in another direction.

It is dark, but there are enough lights and fires and smiling faces to keep night on the edges of our gathering. With sundown, it's getting cool out, too. A pair of acrobats tumbles between my amigo and me. I lose sight of Six.

It appears that the face-painters have been putting in overtime. No one's face looks entirely human—as though I were watching the world saunter past in a funhouse mirror. I hope I find Six soon. We should be getting back. Nick's twins and Zeke's kids have probably showed up by now. Zack and Zooey plan to surprise their Gramps. I kept their secret.

The serious telescopes are set up at the edges of our gathering, away from the lights and human hubbub. I figure that will be the best place to look for Six. I'm getting hungry, too. I'm sure Six is even hungrier.

Someone from behind puts his arms around me. But it does not feel or smell like my amigo. It is a woman—but not Jenn or Martha, either.

"Guess who?" comes the feminine voice. She releases me. I turn around.

"M-m-my God. Hypatia?"

She does not look more than two hours older than the last time I saw her more than forty-five years ago.

"Wha-wha-what..."

"I'm looking for Six. Is he with you, Antonio?"

"W-we got separated."

"I'm sorry to hear that. I hoped you two would still be together—for little

Nicky's sake."

"No, that's not what I mean, Hypatia."

"Is Nicky with Six? I can't wait to see him again," she says, smiling in the flickering torchlight. "The boy must be in his early teens by now."

"In his teens, Hypatia? Nicky's going to turn fifty this year. Where have you been?"

"I went back home for a little visit. Your astronomers haven't discovered it yet. But when they do, they'll call it *Kepler-1649c*. It's only about a hundred parsecs from here. Maybe you and Six and Nicky will visit one day."

"P-p-parsec..."

"Just a little over three hundred light years—not far at all, really."

CHAPTER FOURTEEN

DE HORA NEMO SCIT
Of That Hour No One Knows

"Hypatia!" comes Six's startled voice from behind me. "Where on earth have you been?"

"I wasn't, Six. I went back home."

I turn around. Six has been face-painted to look like a raven. Though the design on his skin is abstract, I had no trouble telling what animal he was.

"Edgar," I say, hugging him. "It's been a while."

"Edgar?" Hypatia says.

"An inside joke," I tell her. "*The Raven* by Edgar Allan Poe."

"Oh," she says. "I hated English literature."

"I always figured I'd be too angry to speak if you showed up again after all this time," Six tells her. "But I'm not. I'm glad to see you."

He takes her hands and kisses her cheek.

"Your eyes are different, Six."

"Heterochromia," he replies. "How it happened is a long, out-of -this-world story. I never thought I'd lay eyes on *you* again. What's the occasion, Hypatia? You look really good."

"So do you, Six—for the most part. How old are you now?"

"Antonio and I turned sixty-six this year—a year younger than you, but without the benefit of plastic surgery," he says, grinning.

"Oh, dear," she remarks. "I only went back home for a little visit. I guess I lost track of time."

"I'll say. But you could have kept in touch by mail. Mexico has a fairly good postal system, you know, huh?"

"I wasn't in Mexico, Six. I already told Antonio," she says, smiling. "My real home is on *Kepler-1649c*."

"What?" Six shouts. "Come on. But you look human. Don't tell me you're a Visitor, too?"

"No, Six. We are not the same race as the other Visitors, the Alpha Carinaeans you met. We Keplerians are from about as far out as they are but on the other side of the Milky Way Galaxy."

"My God, Hypatia. I can't wrap my head around this. So Nick gets his mind-reading abilities from you, not from the Holy Mother?"

"It's one of our everyday senses back on Kepler-1649c."

"So you seduced me just to have a child with an Earthling?"

"I'm sorry. I did it on a dare, Six. I heard Earth boys were easy and wanted to see for myself. I wasn't counting on a child, believe me. Breeding with Earthlings is discouraged, but alcohol weakened my will."

"It has that effect on a lot of people, Hypatia. So why did you run away?"

"I disappeared from Nicky's life to protect the boy, Six. Agent Mxyzptlk from the FBI and Sergeant Onan Bragg of Majestic 12 were getting too close. The Russians were not far behind them.

"It would have been a huge prize for any of them to capture an alien, and a bonus to net one of their Earth sponsoring families—the Montoyas. We all disappeared to prevent them from using Nicky to get their hands on us. It had to be that way, I'm afraid. I am most sorry for my son's sake."

A harlequin who is dressed all in white on one side and black on the other, carries a basket full of ripe apples. The patchwork clown is male on one side and female on the other.

"Pleased to meet you," he says. "My name's Leon Noel—same forwards and backwards—coming and going. Get it?"

We smile at him/her, but I've had enough apples today. I take Hypatia's elbow and Six's and lead them away from the densest part of the crowd so we don't have to shout to be heard.

"Is little Nicky somewhere nearby, Six? I really came to see him."

"I ran into him and Jenn not that long ago—just over there," my amigo says, pointing. His face paint is so good I expect him to caw.

"Jenn?" Hypatia asks.

"Jennifer," Six says. "His wife."

"His wife?" she asks, startled. "At thirteen?"

"I'm telling you, Hypatia. Here on Earth, Nick is gonna be fifty years old."

"I guess I'm all mixed up," Nicky's mother says. "Did the boy mind very much being raised by his father and his... um... *uncle* instead of having a normal Earth family?" she asks.

"Whatever that is," Six remarks. "Nicky was raised by *two* loving families, Hypatia—the Sanchezes and the Thorsons. And it is a fact that Nicky received more love from his Tio than he ever did from his mother.

"Please. I am not angry with you, Hypatia. I know you did the best you could and that you tried to protect Nicky. But I can't let you insult *mi mejor amigo*."

"I'm sorry, Antonio," she tells me, kissing my cheek. Her touch is slightly cold.

"I would like to see Nicky again, Six, but I cannot stay here on Earth."

Six puts his arm around Hypatia. He looks at her and smiles.

"I can't tell you that you shouldn't see your son, Hypatia. But it might be better for him if you did not just pop into his life and then pop out again. It might be more loving if you allow him to keep his memory of a mother warm and radiant who sang a lullaby to him and made him laugh."

"I don't understand what you mean," Hypatia says, pulling back from Six and looking into his face. Her expression is puzzled.

"The Blessed Virgin Mary appeared to Nicky on his fourth birthday. That is the only memory he has of his Mother."

"Then I do not wish to take that from Nicky."

"Thank you, Hypatia."

"I apologize for using you so carelessly and callously, Six. Will you take a message to Nicky for me?"

"Yes, of course, Hypatia," he replies, holding out his hand.

Instead, Hypatia touches Six's forehead with her middle three fingers. There is a blue flash. My amigo steps back. He appears stunned. It takes him a while to form his wavering lips into coherent words.

"I am sorry, too, Hypatia," he tells her. "I never considered how much you gave up to protect Nicky."

"Separation is a condition of all life, Six, but it is hardest for parents and children."

The breeze brings a few strains of the mysterious lullaby. It is played on a harmonica and a violin.

"I wonder who taught them that Keplerian lullaby," Hypatia says. "I haven't heard the melody since I was a child—many, many years ago now. It makes me homesick."

It is the same lullaby we all know by different names. I have not heard it in a long while, either—not since Jenn sang it to their twins Zack and Zooey.

Hypatia kisses us both on the cheek. "I must be going. God bless you, Six and Antonio."

She turns and leaves, disappearing among the crowd of strangers. I put my arm around Six and look into his crow-face. There is a clear spot in the face-paint on his forehead where it is smudged and smeared from the zap by Hypatia's fingers.

"This must have been very hard for her, Antonio. But it convinces me of her love for Nicky. She is a good mother. She protects her child."

He smiles at me, but there is sadness in his eyes.

"I hope I did the right thing, Antonio, in asking Hypatia not to barge into Nicky's life again. Maybe that was a mistake."

"You were doing what good fathers do, too, Six: watching out for your son."

"Thank you, amigo," he says. "Maybe we should head back."

"Did you find out where all these people heard about this *be-in* or whatever it is, Six? Who are they? They are going to be so disappointed if nothing happens tonight."

"I think they are all enjoying themselves anyhow, Antonio. I met tipsy revelers, sidewalk preachers, astronomy professors, leftover hippies and brand new ones. There are NASA groupies, clergy of several faiths, including a Buddhist monk and nun, and UFO buffs of all stripes and degrees of coherence.

"They heard about the news of an alien visit in everything from parish bulletins to scientific journals to kooky Ufology fanzines.

"Nobody knows where the rumor started. I met a reporter for the *Roswell Register*, too, but we got separated by a troupe of little green men."

He laughs.

"Come on, Antonio. We better get back before the others worry."

He puts his hand on my shoulder and we turn back towards the milling throng.

"I'm pretty hungry, too," he adds.

"*Man does not live by bread alone*," comes a familiar voice from behind us.

"Brother Asinus," Six and I shout.

"How did you get here, *mi Hermano*?" I say. "How did *you* learn about this gathering?"

The friar takes us by the elbows and leads along at the edges of the crowd.

"One of the young men from the pueblo drove me in his wagon. I've known about this evening for many years, *mis hijos*. I have done all God has asked of me. I have turned one hundred years old and I am at last going to my rest. I am finally going home."

"Will you be leaving with the Blessed Virgin, Brother Asinus, or aboard the Visitors' ship?" Six asks him.

"As God wills it," he says. The light shining on his face emanates from within. He takes a cardboard tube from his sleeve into which sheets of coarse paper are rolled up.

"From Nicky," Brother Asinus says. "You will be happy to know he has been keeping up with his drawing—an astounding amount of beautiful work. He wanted me to give this to you tonight. He said it is for both of you."

"Thank you, *mi Hermano*," I say. "We haven't seen any of Nicky's work for quite some time. I'm happy he has not abandoned his art."

The brother puts a hand on each of our shoulders.

"God is with you, my sons. His angels watch over you. The Holy Mother consoles you, and the Visitors offer their fellowship. You are many times blessed."

"Thank you, Brother Asinus," I tell him. "Thank you for keeping our secrets safe."

"The day is fast approaching when the evidence in the crypt will be made known to the whole world. Until that day, my sons, the Lord be with you."

"And with thy spirit," Six and I say.

The brother lifts his right hand in blessing and farewell and turns away, vanishing into the folds of his own cape like a figure blending into the night around a dark corner.

My amigo and I stand there a while, letting the people flow around us like a stream parting around stones. I put my arm around his waist. He holds the sketches from Nicky in his other hand.

A volley of bottle-rockets goes off. Someone with a portable boombox plays the Klaatu song "Calling Occupants of Interplanetary Craft." It makes Six and me laugh. We walk along, keeping one another in sight.

"Mr. Sixtus Thorson?" a voice behind us asks. "Antonio Sanchez?"

I don't know whether we should turn around or ran as fast as we can in the opposite direction.

"I'm a reporter from the *Roswell Register*. Your names came up on the article I just put to bed for tomorrow's edition. Your son and daughter-in-law told me where I might find you."

The fellow, probably in his late twenties, if that old, somehow looks like a reporter—for the high school paper. He is nerdy and wears thick glasses with heavy black frames. His tie, loose around his neck, is stained and crumpled.

"I'm afraid I forgot your name," Six tells him "What was your article about, Mr... uh...?"

"Jim Bennett," he says. "My story was about this here oddball gathering of crackpots. They're waiting for the Holy Mother or for Visitors from Mars or for Lord Krishna or the tooth-fairy. Take your pick."

"If you've already written your article, Mr. Bennett, what's your interest in my amigo and me?" Six asks.

"I just wanted to meet you—to see if you were green and had one eye in the middle," he says, chuckling.

"Well?" Six says, alternating his blue eye and his brown eye. "How's this?"

"Wow," Bennett says. "How do you do that? Nobody can do that. It's impossible."

"Are you so sure, young man?" Six remarks. "So what did you write about our screwball assembly?" he asks the reporter.

"Our editor just gives us the headlines, Mr. Thorson. That's our *slant*. The rest is up to us reporters. He honestly doesn't seem to mind if we make things up. He never checks anything.

"The frontpage headline my editor assigned for my story was KOSMIK KOOKS KONVO, so that's what I wrote about. I had fun writing it. Here."

Jim Bennett hands us a folded frontpage mock-up of tomorrow's morning edition of the *Roswell Register*.

"But you wrote it before you saw any who, what, when, where, or why?" I ask.

"Sure, that's pretty much how everybody does it. As my editor likes to say, 'Journalism is about covering the day's big stories... with six feet of earth and no headstone.' Ha. Ha. Ha. Nice meeting you."

Mr. Bennett melts into the crowd, leaving me and my amigo standing once again in the middle of the human stream flowing around us. We are speechless at Bennett's revelation that no one in the press is interested in what is really happening tonight.

I take the handkerchief from the pocket of my overalls and wipe off the rest of Six's face-paint.

"Do you think someone got to Bennett and his editor at the *Register*, Six?"

"I'll give you two guesses, amigo."

"Bragg? He can't still be around."

"If not him, then somebody in the secret government—the government nobody elects. Someone wanted this story killed before anything even takes place."

"But if something does happen tonight, Six, they won't be able deny what all these people witness."

"Why not?" Six says, chuckling. "All you gotta do is paint us as fools—as Kosmik Kooks, amigo. Then you don't gotta listen to anything we say—even if it's the God's-honest truth.

"But nothing's airtight. It's gonna leak out someplace, Antonio. *You can count on it*," he says, quoting one of Sergeant Bragg's trademark remarks.

I laugh and give him a kiss and a strapping hug.

"Don't worry," he tells me. "A hundred years from now, no one will remember that the *Roswell Register* called us *kooks*."

I laugh. "I don't care," I tell him. "I'm canceling my subscription anyway."

We put our arms around each other and laugh. I'd love to kiss *mi mejor amigo* right now, but not in front of all these people.

"There you are!"

It is Martha, with Zeke in tow.

"We've all eaten already," Zeke tells us. "We didn't know where you two were."

"Neither did we," Six remarks, "but I guess we found our way back. Have the twins or your kids gotten here yet?"

"No," Martha replies. "I left a note on the windshield of Nick's Jeep. I don't know how they'll find us among all these people."

"Where are Nick and Jenn?" Six asks.

"They weren't far behind us," Zeke says, "but unless you're tied together like mountain-climbers, you're gonna get separated. I've never seen this many people in one place in my life."

"We certainly have," Jenn remarks, emerging from the crowd, Nicky holding her hand.

"There were four hundred thousand people at Woodstock," he says. "I don't think there's more than a few hundred here."

"That's still a lot of people," Martha remarks. "It makes me feel kinda closed-in."

"Were you two trying to evade the federal agents," Jenn asks my amigo and me.

"Federal agents?" we say together.

"Yeah, Pop," Jenn says. "You don't have to be a fugitive to spot G-men, you know, huh."

"At Woodstock, they were the hippies with crisp creases pressed into their bellbottoms," Nicky says.

Everyone laughs, but the mere mention of federal agents gives me the willies, even if they're not after my amigo and me in particular.

"Should we head back?" Martha asks. "The kids must be there by now."

A bald and wrinkled old fellow—even older than my amigo and I are—doodles around on a harmonica. He is joined by a younger guy playing an acoustic guitar. They stand before the six of us. They don't seem to know what they ought to play for us.

"A waltz," Martha suggests. "A schmaltzy waltz."

The little fellow searches up and down the row of holes on his harmonica for the notes he wants to play. The guitarist plucks a couple of strings in response. They do a quick run-through of the melody and nod to each other. "Waltz No. 2 by Shostakovich," the taller fellow remarks.

Martha and Nicky push Six and me together. Jenn and Zeke applaud. The musicians begin again.

Six puts his arm around my waist and raises my right arm with his left.

"No, Six. I can't."

"Why not? You do fine dancing on the porch."

"That's because no one's watching. I can't. Not in front of all these people."

"We'll ask them to close their eyes."

The crowd around us draws back, forming a circle. Zeke pushes us into the center. The guitarist and harmonica player are joined by a violinist. They practice together for a couple of measures and then launch into the Shostakovich waltz.

It's clear that Six intends for me to waltz with him or be pulled along behind him in the dust. I lift one foot. Six pulls me off balance, forcing me to land on my other foot. And so we begin to dance. I'm more worried about embarrassing Six than I am about making a fool of myself.

Despite the hodge-podge of instruments, the sound they make together, while quite peculiar, is very tuneful. I get into the slow rhythm. Then we turn and reel the other way, skirting the perimeter of people.

The growing crowd makes me nervous. I don't think Six even notices. He looks into my face and flashes the colors of his eyes back and forth in the rhythm of the music. When I forget myself, I have fun. The musicians pick up the pace. The crowd begins cheering. The melody changes.

Taking larger strides to match Six's, I realize I am getting winded. If we don't turn around and spin the other way, I'm going to get dizzy, too. The brief slower movements give me a chance to catch my breath.

"I never thought this would happen in a thousand years, Six."

"I guess the millennium got here a couple years early." He smiles, grinning his dimples.

At last the waltz is over. I'm glad no one shouted for an encore. *Mi mejor amigo* and I collapse against each other.

"How you holding up?" he asks.

"I'm not," I say. "You're holding me up."

"Kiss. Kiss," the crowd chants. Our friends and Six's kids egg them on. I have to remind myself that times are different—but I am not.

"I can't, Six. Please. No. Not in public."

"OK. That's all right, then," he tells me. "Just stand there. I'll take care of it."

He gives me a kiss that is neither too long nor too quick—but just right. The crowd of revelers and onlookers applaud my amigo and me. My heart pounding, we bow.

No one seems to give our routine a second thought, as though seeing two men dancing in the meadow in the moonlight were the most ordinary sight in the world. We rejoin our kids and our friends.

The musicians play the waltz again. This time the crowd closes their circle. A dozen couples, some accomplished partners, others perfectly mismatched, dance around each other. In their colorful and bizarre outfits, they look like a costume ball held at a circus carnival.

I take Six's hand. He takes Jenn's who takes Nicky's who takes Martha's who latches onto Zeke. Our conga line snakes its way in the general direction of our campsite. Every face I pass is smiling, whether painted or not.

Martha's and Zeke's kids, Catherine and Mark, and my amigo's grandkids, Zack and Zooey, occupy the camp chairs in an arc around their small camp-fire. Zooey twirls a sparkler in figure-eights. They all stand when they see us and offer their chairs.

"We're gonna go have a look at the fireworks, Gramps," Zack tells Six.

"They got fireworks tonight, too? Jeeze," Six remarks. "The only thing missing is the main event, you know, huh?"

"Don't wander too far," Nicky tells his son Zack. "Stay together. We're not sure what's gonna happen tonight."

"Everyone says a spaceship is gonna land tonight," Zooey tells her father, zipping up her hoodie sweatshirt.

The four "kids," all in their mid-twenties, skirt the grove of cottonwoods and head for the meadow. Zeke's and Martha's pair, a lot darker than Zack and Zooey, are also good-looking young people. It thrills us that they are all good friends, too.

Jenn and Martha sit in the other two camp chairs. They offer Six and me the charred and dried-out hamburgers from the grill, putting each on a rock-hard bun topped with a squishy slice of tomato. Six and I are hungry enough not to complain. I could not eat one more apple if they were free.

Zeke and Nicky stand facing my amigo and me.

"What did you think of my sketches, Pop?" Nicky asks his father.

"I'm sorry, kiddo. I didn't have a chance to look at them yet. Your Tio and I were busy *tripping the light fantastic*."

"*Tripping* has different meaning now, Pop, you know, huh?"

"Maybe we were doing that kind, too," Six says, grinning his dimples.

My amigo takes the rolled-up sketches out of their tube. He unfurls them in our laps.

The first drawing is a realistic rendition of my amigo and me wrestling in the Rio Grande fifty years ago. We are just emerging from the icy water, the light glistening on our wet skin and soaked Levi's. The scene gives me a chill, but I am very happy to remember it.

"Nick. Oh, my God, Nick. I still don't know how you do it," Six says. "You hadn't even been conceived yet when that scene took place."

"If anyone around me sees something or thinks of something, then I see it too, Pop. It doesn't matter when it happened so long as it is remembered by someone."

"It's as though you snapped a photo of me and your Tio from the river bank, Nick. We'll have to get it framed, won't we. Thank you."

"Muchas gracias, Nicky," I tell my nephew. "When are you gonna have your own show, *mi amado sobrino*?"

"He was waiting until tonight to tell you both," Jenn says. "Nicolás Antonio Montoya-Thorson's first solo art exhibit takes place in Albuquerque on September thirtieth."

"What time?" Six asks. "There might be something else going on then."

We are mostly used to Six's bizarre sense of humor by now, but it still makes us do a double-take.

"Seven o'clock," Jenn replies.

"I think I'm free."

I set Nicky's first drawing behind the second and unfurl the next sketch. It is the scene from an hour ago when my amigo and I danced before the crowd to the waltz for guitar and harmonica. It is as abstractly realistic as the first drawing. It conveys our sweeping movements and the rhythmically-clapping onlookers and the smiling musicians.

"When did you draw this one, Nick? Brother Asinus gave it to us at least an hour before you and Jenn persuaded us to dance in public."

"I did both of them a couple months ago, Pop."

"Amazing," I remark, shaking my head.

"Why did you give them to Brother Asinus, Nick?"

"The brother told me something wonderful was going to happen tonight, Pop. I wanted you to have them. But the brother never told me *what* was going to happen."

"You don't feel anything coming?" Six asks his son.

"No," Nicky says. "I was really just counting on a quiet night of camping with a few hundred other people, you know, huh?"

We laugh.

"There's that melody again," Martha says. "The lullaby. Do you hear it?"

We stand still and listen, but there is too much noise and talking and music to hear anything else. We shake our heads.

I unfurl the third sketch. It is a beautiful portrait of Hypatia.

"I met my mother tonight, Papa."

Six lets go of the drawings and they curl up in my lap. He jumps to his feet and stands in front of his son, searching his face. Then he wraps his arms around him. Nicky returns the embrace.

"My mother tried to sneak away, but we recognized each other at once. She gave me her message herself," he says, touching his forehead with three fingers. "I know why she had to leave, Papa. She did it to protect me."

Father and son lean their heads on each other's shoulder and sob. Their chests heave. Jenn massages Nicky's shoulders. I get up and rub the back of Six's neck.

"Even though I understand why she had to leave, it still hurts, Pop."

"Of course it does, son. I had no idea myself why she left until tonight. Your mother truly loves you, Nick."

"I have been sketching her face for years, Papa, but I had no idea who she was. At least now, when I miss her, I will know who I am missing."

My amigo and my nephew give each other another strapping hug. Zeke brings a bottle of tequila and some plastic cups. He pours some for each of us—except Martha. I welcome a few warming sips of firewater.

"Tell me you can't hear that," Martha says.

"A woman singing," I reply.

"Yes," Martha tells us. "It's the lullaby we all know."

The others lean their heads into the faint breeze on which the melody floats like a feather.

"*Byssan Lull*," Six says. "Hah. Now I remember the name. That's what my Gram called it—not that I know what it means."

After the verse sung softly by the unseen woman, a violin picks up the tune, joined shortly by a guitar and then a banjo.

"My mother called it *La Cocina de Riquezas*," I tell the others.

"*The Galley of Riches*," Jenn says, translating into English.

"What's a galley?" Zeke asks.

"I guess you wouldn't have many galleys back in Oklahoma, Unc," Nicky tells him. "A galley is a ship's kitchen."

Each verse of the lullaby grows louder with more instruments and voices joining in. Someone with an amplified electric guitar does a raucous but competent rendition. A gypsy troupe with an accordion and two violins goes past playing it. Martha welcomes a band of Native American singers and dancers, thumping their tom-toms and shaking their rattles and ankle-bells.

The next verse of the lullaby, after beginning softly, is pounded out on congas and drums of every variety. It is the most rambunctious rendition of all. It strikes me as an African tribal dance, joyful and passionate. They are joined by a horn and a trumpet but not the Visitors' curlicue kind.

Then it grows eerily quiet. Even the crickets fall silent.

Catherine and Mark, Zack and Zooey return from the fireworks display in the neighboring field. Each munches an apple.

"Something's coming," Zack tells us. "I can feel it."

It is the first I have heard that Nicky's son has a gift like his father for knowing things before they happen. The talent probably comes down to him from Hypatia, his grandmother. I wonder if Zooey, Zack's twin sister, has the gift, too.

In a gradual swell, the lullaby is picked up again and hummed by a hundred voices.

Martha turns to us.

"Our mothers are singing to us so we will not be frightened by what we are about to see," she tells us.

We face the meadow, the four youngsters in front, the six adults in back. We look up at the crescent moon. The sky is ablaze with stars and planets and the occasional meteor—as though putting on a celestial fireworks display. Six and I draw closer and put our arms around each other. He slips his hand into my back pocket and smiles his dimples.

"I'm happy this day has at last arrived, amigo," he tells me. "I feel bad that Dr. Feynman is not alive to see it. He certainly did his part to keep our world safe. I miss him."

"Me, too, Six. The world is better for his having lived among us."

"There," someone in the field shouts, pointing up at the sky. Everyone looks up, but I don't see anything. Another arm, raised above the crowd, points in another direction.

I unhook from Six and go back to the Jeep to get my papa's field glasses.

The kids and our friends continue looking skyward. With so many eyes on the heavens, nothing is going to sneak past us tonight. I tilt my papa's binoculars up and survey a section of the sky. Then I hand the field glasses to Six.

Everyone sees it at once: three bluish pinpoints of light that grow large very quickly as they accelerate towards us. They brake abruptly. Then the lights take off in different directions, turning and banking in ways that no human pilot would be able to survive.

"Fastwalkers," Six remarks.

"How do you know that term?" Martha asks. "That's what my people on the pueblo call them."

"Dr. Feynman told us," I reply.

The Fastwalkers do their aerial acrobatics to the delight of the crowd, especially the children and grown-ups and old folks. There are hoots and hollers and whistles as though they were celebrating a holiday that calls for a marching band and fireworks. Then the Fastwalkers twist around one another in complicated geometric patterns before darting off as quickly as they'd appeared. The crowd applauds, continuing to look skyward in anticipation of the next breathtaking display.

"The stars are going out," Zooey shouts. "Look, Papa," she says, turning around.

"She's right," someone else in the crowd says. "Oh, my God."

"Oh, no."

"Dear Lord, deliver us."

"It's the end of the world, I tell you."

"*Hail, Mary, full of grace...*"

"No. Please. You're wrong," Six hollers. I feel his chest expand. "Something's blocking out the stars, that's all. Something huge."

"He's right. Look."

"It's getting closer."

"Watch out. It's going to crash."

The last remark gets everyone running for the exits—towards the outskirts of the meadow. They are not quite in a panic, but they're not out for a Sunday stroll either. My amigo and I, and our family and friends, stay put. I did not stop to wonder if we were safe.

As the disk-shaped craft descends, it blocks out more and more of the sky. If not for our man-made lights, we would be lost in the pitch blackness above us.

It is not until the spacecraft gets down to way above tree-height that it's smooth, silvery surface reflects our campfires and lanterns, our headlights and candles, our glowing headbands and bioluminescent necklaces. It is as though we are looking at our own image photographed by an enormous fisheye lens. Perhaps it is the view God encompasses when He looks down on what he has made.

The spaceship begins to glow so gradually it is hard to say when I noticed that it reflects more light than it receives. It hums—more like a low-pitched voice than the whir of a machine.

"*That* must be the Holy Mothership," Six says. "I can't imagine how it gets airborne, can you, amigo?"

I am speechless. I hear laughter and weeping, music and praying all around me. My amigo and I hold each other tighter.

A circular area in the belly of the spacecraft glows twice as bright. It starts to rotate, going fast enough to blur what is happening inside the craft.

"Look. It's the Holy Mother," Martha shouts. "Coming down on a cloud." She crosses herself.

"The Holy Mother?" Zeke says. "You're seeing things, honey. It's some wrinkly old guy on a beam of light or something. What do you see, Antonio?"

"Same as Martha," I reply. "I see the Blessed Virgin Mary in a glowing light."

"What about you, Nick?"

"I see the same old guy in flowing robes that you do, Uncle Zeke. I've seen him before, too, but I don't remember where."

"In your hospital room," Six tells his son. "Kaptain Kosmos arranged for your cure and recovery from polio."

"Really? Far out, Pop. Far out. I always thought what I remembered was some carnival clown you and Tio hired to cheer me up."

"I think I'll tell the Kaptain what you said, Nick. It would make him very happy."

"I see a beautiful woman, a glowing woman," Jenn says. "It must be *Santa Madre*. Her beauty exceeds every depiction I've ever seen—except maybe Tio's statue at the shrine to Our Lady of Roswell."

She reaches over and squeezes my hand. I smile at her.

The humming of the big ship becomes music I hear in my head as well as through my ears. The melody comes from the Holy Mothership and from the crowd of people—all singing in tune. It is haunting, eerie—beautiful. It is the Lullaby of the Stars, the gift of mothers and fathers—and sometimes uncles—to children everywhere to calm their fears.

"We never heard from you, Six," I say. "What do you see, amigo?"

"With one eye, I see angels going up and down a ladder to heaven; with the other, I watch aliens ascend and descend on beams of light. The Holy Mother comes down to Earth on a glowing cloud. At the same time, with my other eye, I watch Kaptain Kosmos float down from the Mothership on a flying sled."

"They are both true," Martha says. "They are *all* Sky People. I think each of us sees what we expect to see."

Six and I smile at her, each of us kissing one of her cheeks.

"I am sorry only for those who see nothing," she tells us, "for whom the sky is empty and dark, for whom there are neither wonders or glories, neither mysteries or questions."

Those around us drift toward the center of the meadow beneath the sky-spanning Mothership. They raise their arms and voices in welcome to the angels and the aliens, to the Holy Virgin and to the Visitors, to the saints and to the Katalysts and Kaptain Kosmos.

The strains of the lullaby, coming from the Holy Mothership and from the crowd of people, are carried on the wind. There is cheering and gleeful shouting as the Queen of Heaven and the Kaptain of the Karinaeans float down into the midst of the welcoming multitudes.

Our friends and family drift to the center of the meadow, too, leaving *mi mejor amigo* and I alone beneath the still-laden apple tree. Six and I watch the Holy Mother float down to where Nicky and Jenn and Martha stand. Kaptain Kosmos converses with Zeke.

"One day, not too far off, *everyone* will know about tonight's Visits," Six says, "even if you and me don't live to see that day."

"We did our part, Six. So did a lot of other people. When word about tonight gets out, everything hidden will come to light. And everyone will know there is something far, far greater than ourselves out there."

Six turns to me and kisses me. I watch the myriad lights glinting in his blue eye and his brown eye as he flashes them back and forth at me. He squeezes me tighter.

"I am grateful to God for these past fifty years of loving you a little bit more each day, amigo," he tells me.

I smile. "We have certainly been blessed," I say, "many times over."

I shiver. It is cold out. I'm glad to be cozy with my best friend next to me for warmth.

"Do you know what I could really go for right now?" he asks.

"Please, Six. Not another apple," I reply.

He grins his dimples.

"Nope," he says. "I've got a real hankering for some strawberry ice cream. How about you, Antonio?"

www.ingramcontent.com/pod-product-compliance
Lightning Source LLC
Chambersburg PA
CBHW080731250626
47170CB00011B/2896